Strongheart

Also by Jim Fergus

The Memory of Love

The Wild Girl

The Sporting Road

A Hunter's Road

One Thousand White Women

The Vengeance of Mothers

Strongheart

{ *The Lost Journals of May Dodd and Molly McGill* }

Edited and annotated
by Molly Standing Bear

Jim Fergus

ST. MARTIN'S GRIFFIN
NEW YORK

This is a work of fiction. All of the characters, organizations, and events portrayed in this novel are either products of the author's imagination or are used fictitiously.

First published in the United States by St. Martin's Griffin, an imprint of St. Martin's Publishing Group

STRONGHEART. Copyright © 2021 by Jim Fergus. All rights reserved. Printed in the United States of America. For information, address St. Martin's Publishing Group, 120 Broadway, New York, NY 10271.

www.stmartins.com

Designed by Donna Sinisgalli Noetzel

Library of Congress Cataloging-in-Publication Data

Names: Fergus, Jim, author. | Standing Bear, Molly (Fictitious character), editor.
Title: Strongheart : the lost journals of May Dodd and Molly McGill / Jim Fergus ; edited and annotated by Molly Standing Bear.
Description: First edition. | New York : St. Martin's Griffin, 2021. | Series: One thousand white women series ; 3
Identifiers: LCCN 2020045319 | ISBN 9781250303677 (trade paperback) | ISBN 9781250800671 (hardcover) | ISBN 9781250200990 (ebook)
Subjects: LCSH: Little Bighorn, Battle of the, Mont., 1876—Fiction. | GSAFD: Historical fiction. | Western fiction.
Classification: LCC PS3556.E66 S77 2021 | DDC 813/.54—dc23
LC record available at https://lccn.loc.gov/2020045319

Our books may be purchased in bulk for promotional, educational, or business use. Please contact your local bookseller or the Macmillan Corporate and Premium Sales Department at 1-800-221-7945, extension 5442, or by email at MacmillanSpecialMarkets@macmillan.com.

First Edition: 2021

10 9 8 7 6 5 4 3

For Larry Yoder

In olden times, the earth thundered with the pounding of horses' hooves. In that long ago age, women would saddle their horses, grab their lances, and ride forth with their men folk to meet the enemy in battle on the steppes. The women of that time could cut out an enemy's heart with their swift, sharp swords. Yet they also comforted their men and harbored great love in their hearts . . .

—Caucasus tradition, Nart Saga 26

Archaic Greeks had heard about people ranging over the Black Sea-steppes region, a warrior society that exhibited a remarkable degree of sexual equality. Their non-Greek name, sounding something like "amazon," was adapted to the epic form of ethnonyms, thus *Amazones*. The descriptive epithet *antianeirai* was added to call out the most notable feature of this group: gender equality. The epithet was feminine to emphasize the extraordinary status of women among this particular people, relative to the status of women in Greek culture. Unlike most other ethnic groups familiar to the Greeks, in which men were the most significant members, among *Amazones* it was the women who stood out.

—THE AMAZONS:
Lives and Legends of Warrior
Women across the Ancient World
by Adrienne Mayor

Everything that can be imagined is real.

—Pablo Picasso

{ PROLOGUE }

by JW Dodd, III

Editor in Chief, *Chitown* Magazine

June 2019

For the benefit of new readers of this magazine, a short explanation is in order here. This is the third and final installment of the One Thousand White Women series. The first installment was published more than twenty years ago by my late father, J. Will Dodd, the founding publisher and editor-in-chief of *Chitown* magazine, under the title *The Journals of May Dodd,* written by our ancestor of that name in 1875–76. Upon my dad's sudden death, I, JW Dodd, took over his dual positions on the masthead.

Shortly after I began my tenure as editor-in-chief, a young Cheyenne Indian woman by the name of Molly Standing Bear came to my office bearing a second bundle of journals, one that I myself edited and published here in serial form under the title *The Journals of Margaret Kelly and Molly McGill.* Those readers familiar with the magazine and that second installment may remember that the final journal entry ended rather abruptly, and without any particular resolution. This was not an editorial decision for the purpose of leaving readers hanging on the cliff (although that, ironically, is precisely where they were left, as I was reminded in numerous irritated letters to the editor), but simply because Molly Standing Bear, for justifiable reasons, did not entirely trust me and had withheld the remaining journals in her possession.

Although I had only been running the magazine for this short time, after a long and harrowing night of reading the journals, I decided on impulse to take a kind of unofficial leave of absence. To this end, from a storage barn on our family farm in Libertyville, Illinois, I resurrected my father's beat-up old 1972 Airstream trailer and the 1979 GMC Suburban with which he pulled it on our summer trips to Indian country when I was a boy. After roughly ten days of cleaning and trips to my mechanic doing our best to make both of these decrepit vehicles at least minimally functional and roadworthy again, I set out from Chicago for the Tongue River Indian Reservation in southeastern Montana. My ostensible reason for this flight west was to try to convince Molly Standing Bear to allow me to publish the rest of the story. But as I drove, entering the Great Plains under a vast sky and distant horizons, offering liberation from the constraints of the city, I realized that in a sense I was also paying homage to my father, and to my own childhood. We had lost my mother to cancer when I was seven years old and those summer excursions began shortly thereafter, and were to become the happiest times of my life with Dad. He was a western history buff, specializing in the study of the Plains Indian tribes, and so our trips west always had a professional purpose, which made me feel importantly grown-up, for I was his assistant.

Finally, as readers both new and old will discover in the following pages, in order to secure the rights to Molly Standing Bear's story, I was required to make certain concessions, chief among them to allow this mysterious young woman to serve as editor and annotator of the final installment of her tale without any editorial interference—hardly an easy decision for me, as it went against all my training and instincts. In addition, I must confess that certain revelations herein regarding my personal and professional behavior are frankly embarrassing. Still, I made a deal with Molly Standing Bear and in this spirit, I turn this series over to her.

The following journals are here reprinted with the exclusive permission of *Chitown* magazine.

Introduction

by Molly Standing Bear

I've decided I'm not giving the rest of this story to the white-man editor JW Dodd, after all. It belongs to me, to my family, to the People, and especially to the Stronghearts, and no one can tell it better than I. You see, first they invaded our country, sent their army to massacre us, stole our land, our way of life, our culture. To facilitate that process, they destroyed our livelihood by killing off our brothers, the buffalo, over thirty million of whom once populated these vast plains of grass. By the time the white man's extermination was complete, their numbers had been reduced to a few hundred left in Yellowstone Park, and those few of us who had survived the wars had been confined on reservations, which we were not allowed to leave.

They stole our children, and with them our language, sent them to schools run by priests, cut their hair short, beat them if they spoke their own tongue, and abused them in ways unknown and unimaginable to the People. And then, as if that wasn't enough, they stole our history and our stories, twisted and perverted them to hide the shame of their own behavior, to absolve them of guilt for their insatiable greed, their insatiable need to acquire. Does this sound like the America you know? No? Well, I didn't think so. But it is the one we know.

It's not that I have anything against JW Dodd. Quite the contrary, I like the man, and I remember having a little yearning for him way back when I was a kid on the res. We Indian girls didn't meet many white boys in those days, and if we did it wasn't the kind of encounter you'd want to have . . . in fact, JW was the first white boy I ever liked, and he liked me, too. He used to come out in the summertime with his dad, who went by the name of Will Dodd, a direct descendant of May Dodd. As white men go, Will Dodd was well liked and respected on the reservation, for the simple reason that he was a gentleman and honest, and he treated us with respect and consideration.

A few years back, I took another piece of the story to JW at his office in Chicago. Upon the sudden death of his father he was now running the magazine. I delivered it in my persona as a Strongheart warrior woman—beaded buckskin shift, leather leggings and moccasins, my hair in braids wrapped in rawhide straps with beads and small bones tied into them, knife and scalp belt around my waist, from which dangled real human scalps . . . white-man scalps. You see, I am a shape-shifter, I have the ability to assume different forms, which I inherited from one side of my family. Now let me state right here that I really couldn't care less if you believe this or not, and I'm not going to waste our time here trying to convince you one way or the other. I am just telling my story, our story, and maybe you will come to believe it . . . or not . . . that I leave entirely up to you.

On that day in Chicago, I was met at the front desk of the magazine by an insipid little white-girl receptionist named Chloe . . . I think . . . or another of those currently popular white-girl names. I have to say that I am a fierce-looking woman, especially in my Strongheart incarnation, and the receptionist looked me up and down with an expression that shifted between nervousness, disdain, and a kind of superior amusement. I was carrying a pair of old leather saddlebags over my shoulder that had belonged to one of the 7th cavalry soldiers killed on June 25, 1876, at the Battle of Greasy Grass, or, as the white men call it, the Battle of the Little Bighorn, or Custer's Last Stand. The saddlebags had been taken off the dead horse of the dead soldier, a boy named Miller, by one of my ancestors, the white woman Molly McGill Hawk, who had married into our tribe, and they had been passed down by the generations of women until finally arriving in my possession.

"May I help you?" asked the receptionist, Chloe.

"I'd like to see your publisher, JW Dodd."

"And whom may I tell Mr. Dodd is asking to see him?"

"None of your business," I answered. "Just tell him we know each other, and that I have something that will interest him."

This took her aback for a moment, and I could tell she was more than a little afraid of me now. "Would you mind taking a seat?" she asked, "and I'll ask Mr. Dodd to come out."

"Yes, I would mind. I'll wait right here."

"Since you got through security downstairs," she said, looking again at my attire, "may I assume you aren't carrying anything dangerous in those bags?"

"You may assume that," I answered, "but I suppose that depends on what your definition of 'dangerous' is."

Now she pecked something out on her cell phone, which shortly thereafter sounded a tone. This exchange of pecking and tones went on three or four more times.

When JW Dodd finally came out it was obvious he didn't recognize me. He regarded me with an expression of surprise and curiosity, but without judgment . . . I'll give him that. He led me to his office past a series of glass cubicles in which other workers appeared to be pecking things out on their various devices. They all looked up to watch me pass. I looked back at each of them with my best Strongheart, don't-fuck-with-me gaze, and when I did they were forced to cast their eyes away from its ferocity.

JW indicated that I sit in the chair in front of his desk, and took his own behind it. "My receptionist tells me that you mentioned we know each other," he said. "I'm sorry, but I'm afraid I don't recognize you."

"We met some years ago on the Tongue River Indian Reservation," I answered. "I didn't expect you to remember me. We were just kids. You invited me to go to the movies at the res community center."

He laughed, suddenly remembering. "Of course, how could I forget? I had just turned thirteen years old, and you were the first girl I ever asked out on a date. I was walking from my dad's trailer, where we parked on the res, to pick you up at your house, when a group of Cheyenne boys waylaid me and beat the crap out of me. You're Molly Standing Bear, all grown up."

"That's right," I said. "For a white boy to ask an Indian girl to the movies was overstepping tribal boundaries."

"Yeah, I got that part."

I remember that young JW came to my house anyway that day, all beat up and bleeding, his new jeans and the fresh white, white-boy button-down shirt he put on for the movies dirty, torn, and stained with his blood. I kind of admired him for coming like that. It showed a certain strength of character and tenacity on his part. But my mother wouldn't let me go to the door, and I watched from the window as she sent him away. That was the last time I saw him.

Because we had trusted his father, I left those saddlebags with JW Dodd that day in his office. They contained the journals of Meggie Kelly and Molly McGill, which as his father had done with May Dodd's journals, and after I gave him permission, he would later publish in serial form in *Chitown* magazine.

I could tell that day that JW still liked me; I knew he had been well educated by his dad in the history of the Plains Indians, at least the white man's version of our history. I have to give some credit to his father, Will, for he put in the time to get to know some of the elders, who still had the old oral stories in their heads. And just maybe it was my outfit that attracted JW, too, being authentic, my savage look maybe triggering a white boy's fantasy of seducing the Indian girl. He asked me if I still wanted to have that movie date, or maybe dinner, now that we were grown-ups, but I shut him down. I let him know this was a business call, not personal.

A few weeks later, JW showed up on the res, driving his dad's beat-up old Suburban, and pulling the vintage Airstream trailer they always stayed in when they came out here. Both the truck and the trailer looked like they had been parked and forgotten somewhere for a couple of decades. He didn't know it, but I was watching as he pulled up in front of tribal headquarters and stepped out of the vehicle.

It was a Saturday and only one woman was in the office, a Southern Cheyenne girl who had just recently come up from the res in Oklahoma. She was working on the weekend in order to familiarize herself with her new job. We didn't know each other yet, but I found out later that JW asked her where he could find me, and when she tried to look me up on their website, she found that I was not enrolled as a tribal member. The only records of me she was able to find in the digital archives were a twenty-year-old police report about domestic abuse, and my obituary.

After his inquiry at headquarters, JW drove his rig to a pull-off along the river outside town, the same place he and his dad used to camp, but these days a favorite spot for alcohol and drug users to party at night, especially on a Saturday. Of course, I knew of all his movements almost before he did because the res is small and not exactly a popular vacation destination for whites, who rarely spend the night there unless stranded by weather or car trouble. Word travels fast and it is ingrained in the tribal DNA to be suspicious of any white man who comes to town asking questions, looking for someone, and pitching camp for the night.

Just after dark, I walked down the river bottom from town to see JW. Before I approached his trailer, I hung back in the shadows for a moment and watched as he was being harassed outside his door by three Indians I knew to be meth heads. Hanging out by a pickup truck nearby in which they must have arrived were four more men and five women. I had to laugh because two of those at JW's door had been among the boys who beat him up when they were kids. They were threatening now to kick his ass unless he gave them his money and whatever alcohol he had in the trailer. I liked that he didn't seem afraid of them. He said he'd give them what he had, and he turned to go into his trailer to get it, when they called him a chickenshit. He stopped and turned back to them. "You know, I count seven of you altogether," he said, looking over at the others who were watching and snickering at the white man interloper, "and just one of me . . . so yeah, I guess maybe I am a chickenshit, or else maybe I'm just not stupid and don't want to get my ass kicked tonight."

I walked up then out of the darkness. "What about if it were only seven against two, white boy?" I said. "Would you be a little stupid then, and risk getting your ass kicked?"

I spoke sharply then to the men in Cheyenne, but they were already scattering like a covey of flushed prairie grouse at my arrival. They loaded their beer back into the vehicle, and the whole group piled into the pickup and sped off, their tires spinning in the sandy dirt.

"Yeah, if you were the second one on my side, Molly Standing Bear," said JW, as he watched them go. "I could get real stupid. But just out of curiosity, why are they so afraid of you?"

"I scare the shit out of the brave warriors here because when I appear like this they think I'm a spirit being."

"I don't believe in spirit beings," he said, "but I read a police report and your obituary today at tribal headquarters. It said you were the victim of domestic abuse, and that you died from injuries sustained. That was in January of 1997, a few months after my dad and I were here. There was a photo of you in the reservation newspaper. You were twelve years old."

"Are you going to be polite and invite me into your tipi, or not?"

"Of course," he said, opening the door, standing aside, and holding his arm out for me to enter. "But that's not an answer."

"You didn't ask a question." I stepped into the trailer.

"OK, so what is that all about? You look as alive to me now as you did in Chicago, so being the canny investigative journalist I am, I assume some kind of mistake was made in the newspaper."

"That is something I can't talk about, so please don't ask me again."

After we were settled on the narrow fold-out couch in the trailer, which also served as a bed, I asked him why he had come here.

"To return the journals you left with me," he answered. "I have to tell you, Molly, I made copies of them, which I haven't let anyone else at the magazine read yet. I wanted to ask you first for your permission to publish these in serial form. If so, you'll have to sign a release. I assume that's why you brought them to me. If not, I promise I'll shred the copies."

"I don't sign releases," I said, "we do business the old way, with our word. But then again, everyone knows that the white man's word is shit. Why else did you come here?"

"I don't know . . . I'm not exactly sure myself . . . maybe I came looking for the ghost of my father. I thought I might find it here. He left me so unexpectedly, and I have things I need to talk to him about. This seemed to be the right place to do that. I have wonderful memories of our summers out here."

"I thought you didn't believe in ghosts?"

"I'm speaking metaphorically."

"Why else did you come?"

"I see where the pages are torn out of the last ledger book you left with me. It ends suddenly. I'd like to know the rest of the story, and publish it in its entirety."

"I don't know if that's possible yet, JW."

"Why not?"

"Because the rest of the journals hold sacred tribal secrets, and, in case you haven't noticed, you're a white man. Everything your people have touched that once belonged to us, you have stolen or destroyed, and what little is left, we have to protect."

"You have white blood yourself, don't you, Molly? You're descended from one of the authors of these journals. Which, by the way, were also written by white people."

"Yes, but they are white women who became Cheyenne, and

some of them lived with us for the rest of their lives . . . and afterward, as well. They had our babies and were accepted as tribal members."

"What does that mean, afterward?"

"It's a metaphor, JW," I said.

"*Haha.* But, as you know, Molly, I, too, am related to one of the journals' authors, which is why your people let my father have them in the first place. It seems to me that you and I should share a certain ownership. Who knows, we might even be related somewhere down the line. We should run that by one of the genealogy websites."

"Your father proved his good intentions toward us," I said. "You have not yet done so, JW. You haven't even been back here in over twenty years."

"And what would that involve for me to prove myself?"

"Do you like my scent?" I asked.

"What?

"Do you like my scent?"

"I have no idea," he said. "What does that have to do with anything?"

"I know white people find such a thing strange, but in the old days we lived much closer to the animal world than you. All of our senses were more keenly developed, because you lived outside of nature, tried to suppress and control it, rather than living within it. You know, we always hated the way white people smelled. When we went on raids against the wagon trains that were moving through our country during the California gold rush, we used to tie the shirts and dresses we stole to poles and ride with them for a couple of days, letting them blow in the wind. It was a kind of primitive dry cleaning to air out the stink. You must have noticed in reading Molly McGill's journals that she was very attracted to the way Hawk smelled . . . remember? She said it was because he had a kind of wild scent. That excited her, and it was one of the reasons she fell in love with him."

"Yes, and as you well know, Hawk's mother was a white woman, so he, too, was half white by blood. How is it that he smelled so wild?"

"Because, as you yourself know from reading the journals, his mother, Heóvá'é'ke, Yellow Hair Woman, had been taken by the tribe as a little girl, and she, too, soon became all Cheyenne, and that washed the stink off her."

Now I stood and moved in front of JW. I leaned down and put my hand on the back of his head, and pulled his face against my neck. "There. Take a good deep breath of me."

I released him. "So, do you like my scent?"

He was clearly flustered, his face flushed, and he babbled on for a moment, admitting that, yes, he did like my scent, in fact, he liked it a great deal.

I leaned down again and put my nose against his neck, nuzzling it while taking a good whiff myself.

"If I'd known you were going to do that, I would have taken a shower," said JW, after he had recovered.

"And put deodorant on, right? That would only have disguised your natural scent."

"Well, did I pass?"

"Not so bad . . . for a white man. I could possibly get used to it."

"High praise, indeed," he said.

"I am Molly and Hawk's great-great-great-great-great grand-daughter," I said. "At least I think that's the correct number of generations. Most of my white blood has been well diluted by now, but perhaps I inherited some women's version of Hawk's scent, or of Molly's, or a combination of the two; these attributes I believe are passed down like eye and hair color. By all accounts they had wonderful chemistry together. I wanted to find out if there might be anything like that between us."

"Really? Don't tell me you're thinking about breeding with a white man."

"In your dreams, white boy. Tell me, JW, why have you never married, or had children?" I asked. "Are you gay?"

He shook his head.

"Impotent or sterile?"

"I was married, Molly, but my wife and I had no children," he answered. "She died very young of cancer. Speaking of scents, and chemistry, the last year or so of her life she no longer smelled like herself, but of the chemo drugs that had pervaded her body. After her death, I had to throw out all the clothes she wore during that time in order not to be reminded more than I already was. She was a fine woman."

"I'm sorry. I'm sure she was. Forgive me."

"And you?" he asked. "As long as we're getting personal. Did you marry and have children?"

"No."

"Why not? I'm sure you've had many suitors."

"I had other business to attend to."

"Such as?"

"You remember the Strongheart women's warrior society you read about in Meggie's and Molly's journals?"

"Don't tell me that's still in existence."

"Of course, it is. At least a modern version of it. Though now we simply call ourselves Konahe'hesta, the Stronghearts."

"And who do you war against in this twenty-first century?"

"I am not allowed to speak about that to nonmembers of our society. Suffice it to say that we war against crime and injustice committed by both individuals and organizations, but particularly against women and children, and there we find plenty of enemies. I will tell you this much: after the Custer battle at the Little Bighorn, a band splintered off from Little Wolf and Dull Knife and went their own way, with their own mission. This included a number of the white women about whom you read in the journals, as well as a number of Cheyenne and Arapaho, men and women. Eventually this band became a small tribe of their own, and lived in a world of their own. They never surrendered to the U.S. government."

"What do you mean, 'a world of their own'? Where did they go?

Where did they live? How did they survive? What happened to them? And why during all my dad's and my research have I never heard of them before?"

"I can't answer any of those questions for you, at least not now. If I choose someday to show you the rest of the journals, you will be able to read about it."

"And the descendants of the original Strongheart society still live in this world you speak of?"

"Yes, some of them do. I live there . . . part of the time. It's one reason I'm not enrolled as a tribal member on the res."

"One reason? You mean, in addition to the fact that you're listed as having died in 1997?"

"Well, sure, there is that, too, which makes for a convenient misapprehension."

"I'm confused . . . is this some kind of mythic world you've created in your imagination, Molly? Or maybe it's a virtual world, like a video game? Is that what you're trying to tell me? Maybe that's what you do for a living?"

"You ask a lot of questions, JW."

"It's my job."

"No, it is a very real world," I said. "I come and go between here and there."

JW looked at me then with an expression of concern and confusion. "Since you won't answer my questions, or give me any details," he said, "I don't know what you're talking about, Molly. But something about the way you just said that made the hair on the back of my neck stand up. Who are you, really? The last time you came to me, you spoke of being a shape-shifter, and now you talk of different worlds? What do you want from me? Why are we here together, right now?"

"Ah, yet more questions, JW. You came looking for me, remember? You still want to take me to the movies. You wanted to return the journals, but what you really want is to know how the story ends. That is a typically linear white-man point of view, a straight line from beginning to end. Our culture sees the world as being circular, elliptical . . . at least it did traditionally . . . a place where stories, like life and death, have no end, but rather intersect and bleed into other stories, other lives and deaths, in that way continuing indefinitely, and often ambiguously. If you've ever listened to a real Cheyenne storyteller, or an ancient storyteller of the Caucasian steppes, from whose people we are descended, you would know this. To most whites his or her stories might make little sense, and/or have multiple interpretations. Perhaps they have no real beginning or ending, but our people understand them perfectly."

"So you're a scholar as well as a shape-shifter, Molly," said JW, "or perhaps an anthropologist? And possibly even a time traveler if you've heard stories told by an ancient storyteller of Caucasia."

I stood now. "You know, JW, we Stronghearts, like our forebears, the Scythian Amazones, take our sexual pleasure when and with whom we wish. And we are very selective in our choices. To be frank, I was thinking possibly of spending the night with you. I like you, and have ever since we were kids . . . even though you're a white boy. And I know you like me, too. That's why I wanted to see how we reacted to each other's scents. But I'm going to leave you now, and take these saddlebags with me." I lifted the bags off the hook where they were hanging by the door of the trailer. "You can do what you want with the copies you made, publish them in your little magazine if you want. But I'm going to tell our story my way, and it's not the rest of the story, either, which implies an ending. It's simply a continuation of the story, another bend in the long trail. I'll be in touch. I'll find you when the time is right. Don't you worry about that."

ADDENDUM TO THE INTRODUCTION

Roughly three weeks after our first encounter on the res, the second serial installment of what JW Dodd had titled *The Journals of Meggie Kelly and Molly McGill* began to run weekly in *Chitown* magazine. Even though he stayed true to his stated intention in the prologue of using a light editorial hand on the journals, he allowed himself a good deal of fictional license in the epilogue, and especially the prologue. His most egregious falsity was the implication that I had spent the night with him in his trailer on my first visit there. He was clearly engaging in a sort of white man literary fantasy—seducing the Indian warrior woman—yet another form of subjugation and dominance. To set the record straight, in the preceding pages, I have recorded exactly what transpired between JW and me, which is an ever-evolving story.

In addition to quoting other historical source material, here and there, I have also taken the liberty of adding contemporary commentary of my own between some of the actual journal excerpts. As an Indian woman, I have, of course, full license to do so, whereas this would be forbidden to JW Dodd, due to obvious prohibitions against cultural appropriation.

We begin in the following pages with those that JW referenced as having been torn out of the last journal I left with him in Chicago . . . the beginning of the rest of the story.

–MSB

{ LEDGER BOOK XIII }

{begun by Margaret Kelly,
continued by Lady Ann Hall,
continued by Molly McGill}

The undated letter below appeared on the last page of Lady Ann Hall's journal entries.

Molly dear,

I do not know what precisely has occurred here today. I have considered the matter over and over again, from all possible angles, and the only firm conclusion at which I have been able to arrive, and surely the most important, is that in my last brief glimpse of you, you were quite alive, riding behind Phemie on her magnificent white stallion, with Pretty Nose upon her paint, galloping along beside you. You were smiling at me as you passed by on the ridge, and you cried out: "I told you, Ann, in my dream, I always fly!"

Just prior to this moment I witnessed you on the ridge, arms spread and letting yourself fall, if not precisely jump, into the abyss, when somehow Phemie and Pretty Nose seemed to appear out of nowhere, and Phemie swept you up off the ridge and onto the back of her horse as if you were a rag doll. The problem here, of course, is that neither the soldiers, nor Gertie, nor the others in our group, with the possible exception of Martha (who refused to discuss the matter with me) . . . none of them saw you rescued. They all saw you fall from the cliff, and were beside themselves with horror and grief, and, in the case of the soldiers, astonishment that you had actually gone through with it.

The question is, how does one reconcile these two quite

unreconcilable versions of events? I have always prided
myself on being a logical woman, Molly, for whom all
occurrences on earth have a reasonable explanation, even
if science has not quite gotten round to sussing out all
the details of the how and why. My late, dear companion,
Helen Flight, viewed the world quite differently than I,
due perhaps to her flighty artistic nature. For instance,
I believe I told you that she and I spent a good deal of
time on safari in Africa, where we intermingled with our
splendid native guides of the Masai tribe. These people,
like our Indian friends, are a superstitious lot, who believe
that among their people are certain seers, prophets,
soothsayers, mystics, shape-shifters, clairvoyants—call
them what you will—who possess various supernatural
powers. They believe, as well, in a remarkable array of
strange deities, ghosts, and sorcerers, some good, some
bad, who come and go among the living from time to time,
either wreaking havoc or performing miracles, depending
on their persuasion. In short, they believe in magic as
surely as they believe in their own noses. To be sure,
the Masai tales of such matters, told around the evening
campfire, were enormously entertaining—that I do not for
a moment dispute. And Helen seemed far more receptive
to the notion that there might be some basis of truth in
what the natives recounted. Indeed, I have been told by a
number of the Cheyenne that, based on the testimony of
certain warriors, she actually came to believe, as, of course,
did they, that the artwork she painted upon their bodies
and upon their war ponies really did serve to protect them
from harm in battle. Let us be perfectly frank, Molly, for
you, too, strike me as a logical woman, all of this nonsense
is just that—utter poppycock. Paint does not stop bullets.
Which, of course, does not explain your . . . I know of no
other word to describe it . . . miraculous . . . escape, which I

must say challenges my own logical nature to its core. Yes, on that score, I remain completely flummoxed, and I begin to doubt my own eyes and sanity.

You will presumably have already learned before you read this that having satisfied the initial purpose of my trip here, i.e., to discover what became of my Helen, I have decided that my time in these troubled plains is over. Thus, I am taking advantage of the escort offered by the soldiers who were charged with delivering you to Medicine Bow station, in order to catch the train there myself, as the first stage of a long trip back to England. Although she expressed her desire to return to her Cheyenne husband, I have insisted that little Hannah accompany me. I arrived here in the company of my maidservant, and I intend to leave in that manner as well. I refuse to abandon her to what I think you will agree is an extremely uncertain future, nor is she constitutionally equipped, in either body or spirit, to endure the impending dangers you surely face.

I leave this ledger book with Martha to deliver to you. Despite my initial irritation at not having been chosen as our merry band's "fearless leader," please know, Molly, of the extremely high esteem in which I hold you. You are a strong, brave woman, who has endured more hardship, heartbreak, and trials than any one person deserves. Not only couldn't I blame you for having leapt from the cliff, as horrified and devastated as I was, when . . . at first . . . I thought you had . . . I also admired your courage, and completely understood your decision. That you have apparently, at least from my eyes, been rescued by . . . let us just say . . . the fates, whatever those may be, brings me great joy, and even hope that perhaps you can help to lead the others to some safe haven. If any can do that, I believe it is the triumvirate formed by you, Phemie, and Pretty Nose (and don't you dare tell those Irish scamps that I said so!), three of the strongest, most courageous, and capable women it has ever been my honor to know. Perhaps to serve in that role, is, after all, why you were spared.

Good luck to you, Molly.

I sign this letter with love in my heart for you and all of our dear friends, and please do pass that sentiment on to the others.

I am, yours, respectfully,
Lady Ann Hall of Sunderland

The Glory of War

The images come to me both day and night, both waking and asleep. One minute I am riding in the air on the back of a giant raptor, my arms holding on to its broad neck, my naked body stretched across its back, my face buried in its soft, warm, pungent feathers that hold a scent exactly like the skin of the man, Hawk . . . and I am aroused. The next moment, I am simply riding across these plains on my mare, Spring, surrounded by my friends. Truly, I fear that I am going mad.

—*from the lost journals of Molly McGill*

(undated entry)
at the battlefield of the Little Bighorn

I do not know what day it is or how I got here. The last thing I remember clearly is hearing Ann Hall scream, *No, please, Molly, don't!* and the liberating sensation of falling. As I fall, I set my wings and soar like a raptor on the wind, free from this earth at last. It is the recurring dream I have had for most of my life. Now I wake up in this tipi, with Martha hovering over me, plucked thus abruptly from my dream. "Ah dear, Molly," she says, "welcome back to us. How soundly you have slept and for nearly twenty-four hours. I have been looking after you, as you once looked after me."

"Martha? Where are we?"

"In a grand encampment of a thousand tipis—Lakota, Cheyenne, and Arapaho—on the banks of the Little Bighorn river. There has been a great battle here but we did not arrive until it was over. The tribes have prevailed, they've beaten the soldiers. The Cheyenne's great nemesis, Lieutenant Colonel George Armstrong Custer, and his entire detachment of the Seventh Cavalry have been wiped out. There has been much dancing and celebrating of our victory, all night they danced. But now we are all busy packing our lodges, for the scouts report that more columns of soldiers are on the way."

"And how did we come to be here?" I asked.

"Phemie and Pretty Nose rescued you, Molly. They brought you here. Don't you remember?"

"Phemie and Pretty Nose brought me here? They rescued me? From what? From whom?"

"Why, from the soldiers who were taking you to the train in Medicine Bow station. Don't you remember?"

"Ah, yes, that I do remember . . . I remember that I escaped the soldiers, Martha."

"If you mean leaping from a cliff to certain death below as escape," said Martha, "then yes, Molly, I suppose you *almost* escaped the soldiers in this way. However, your actual escape was effected by Phemie and Pretty Nose. They swept in and carried you off, just as you . . . *almost* leapt."

"Yes, I remember falling," I said. "But I thought that was in a dream I was having, just now before I awoke. Where is Ann Hall?"

"Lady Hall decided that she had had quite enough of this adventure," Martha said, "and she left with the soldiers to take the train at Medicine Bow, the train that was meant to take you away from us. Hannah begged to return here to her husband, but Lady Hall insisted that she leave with her. You know how imperious the woman could be. Poor little Hannah never could withstand her force of character. It appeared that she was to resume her role as Lady Hall's maidservant."

"Perhaps they will both be better off, Martha, resuming their former life across the sea, so far from this violent place. Certainly, the rest of the world has no idea what is happening here."

"Lady Hall gave me something for you, Molly," she said, "the journal she was writing in, the one that Meggie began. And the box of what is left of the colored pencils they used." Martha reached behind her, brought forth the ledger book, and handed it to me. "She said it would compromise her and Hannah if the soldiers took it, and that you would surely need it here more than she did in England. She wrote a letter to you at the end of her last entry. I hope you don't mind, but I'm afraid that I took the liberty of reading it. And perhaps you, too, should read it now, as well as the last page of her final journal entry. Together they might help you to remember what happened."

I opened the ledger and did as Martha suggested, closing the book when I finished. "But this all poses more questions than it answers, Martha. I still don't understand."

"I'm not sure that anyone involved fully understands."

"Is it true that witnesses to the event have different memories of it?"

"Yes, Lady Hall was quite correct in that assessment. You, for instance, appear to have no memory of it, while Lady Hall seems to have seen some part of both your fall and the rescue. The soldiers, Gertie, and the rest of our group clearly saw you leap from the cliff. As Lady Hall writes in her last entry, there was great wailing and consternation about that."

"And you, Martha?" I asked. "What did you see?"

"I saw quite vividly what Lady Hall described in her journal," she answered, "though I was considerably farther away than she. I saw Phemie and Pretty Nose ride in at just the right instant, just as you had begun to fall from the cliff. It's true that they seemed to have suddenly appeared there on the ridge. I feared that Phemie and her horse would themselves slip off the edge of the cliff, so close to it did they appear to be galloping. Phemie held out her arm, and as you began to fall you reached out and grabbed hold of it, and somehow, she managed to swing you onto her horse's back. The three of you rode off, following the ridgeline into the distance. I watched you go. But none of the others appeared to see that."

"Then Ann is quite right, Martha," I said, "it makes no sense. And where are the others now?"

"Christian, Astrid, and I all returned here together, Molly."

"And the rest of our group are also here?"

"Carolyn, Lulu, and Maria are here, as well. And, of course, Pretty Nose and Phemie."

"What about Susie and Meggie? Where are they? Are they alright?"

Even before she spoke, I knew from Martha's face that they were not alright.

"Those girls did a strange, but courageous thing, Molly," she said. "Before the attack upon the soldiers, they dressed in their full battle regalia, their faces painted fiercely, their red hair released and wild about their heads, as they always ride to war. Yet the one thing they were lacking when they led the Strongheart warriors in the charge was their weapons. They carried no pistols, no rifles, no bows and arrows, no knives, no lances, no clubs, not even their shields. They rode unarmed into battle against the soldiers, far in advance of the others, hollering the eerie song of the kingfisher, their animal protector.

"All who witnessed the charge thought they were very brave, and that they were making this display in order to count coup and gain honors. But that wasn't the reason, Molly. It was Carolyn who told me, for they came to her that morning to say good-bye. They told her they did not wish to kill any more soldiers, that the anger that had driven them since the loss of their babies had finally been exhausted. Without the cold spirit of vengeance that kept them going for so long, they felt they had nothing left to live for.

"Meggie said to Carolyn," Martha recounted, now assuming a voice so like the Kelly twins that it was chilling to hear: "'So we're just goin' to ride at those boys, and scare the shite out of them one last time.' And Susie, she said: 'Aye, Carolyn, it'll be the final charge of the fearsome Kelly twins, scourge of the Great Plains. And when they see us, those soldier boys'll drop their guns, piss their pants, and run to the hills cryin' like lost babies for their mamas.' And Meggie, she said: 'Right ya are, sister, and they'll write about us in the history books, the mad Irish banshees from Chicago who took on Custer's army single-handed, and with not a weapon between 'em.'

"Can't you just hear those girls, Molly?" Martha said of her uncanny performance, and I saw the tears flooding her eyes, as they were mine.

"Some of the soldiers," Martha continued after she had composed herself, "who must have heard the tales of the Kelly twins, did indeed drop their weapons and run, just like Susie said they would. But, of course, others held their ground and fired steadily upon them. Carolyn, who was watching the charge from a hillside above with some of the other women, heard Meggie and Susie laughing wildly as they rode in ahead of the others, bullets flying all around them, kicking up bursts of dust from the ground.

"They seemed to ride right through the bullets for a time, and Carolyn watched as they nearly reached Custer's men before both girls were almost simultaneously shot out of their saddles. They fell to the ground, Molly, crumpled and motionless. Their horses flared off and though both were wounded by bullets, they survived. Meggie's and Susie's bodies were recovered after the battle, while the old men and women went about the terrible business of scalping and mutilating the bodies of the soldiers, as is their way to ensure that our enemies go to Seano without certain body parts intact. The twins lie now atop a single burial scaffold, ending their life as they had begun it in the womb, and as they lived it after they were born, side by side forever."

"Strongheart women to the end, Martha," I said. "I believe it was a kind of Christlike gesture on their part, sacrificing themselves as an example to teach the rest of us a lesson. Will you take me to their scaffold to pay my respects, and also show me the battlefield where they died?"

"I will take you to the scaffold, Molly," she said, "but the battlefield is a ghastly scene. I will show you where it is, but I have not gone there myself, nor do I recommend that you do so. I am told that the old men and women outdid themselves in their rage against the soldiers, whose butchered remains still lie there, beginning now to fester and bloat in the sun."

"I'll go alone, Martha, I don't mind. I need to see it for myself."

"Meggie left something for you with Carolyn," Martha said, "and Carolyn gave it to me to pass on to you." She picked up what I recognized as Meggie's beaded medicine bag and handed it to me.

I rubbed the soft deerskin of the bag gently between my fingers. "That was sweet of her," I said. "I will look at it later, but right now, I need to stand, I need to move, and I desperately need to pee. I'm so weak, Martha, can you help me up?"

I rose unsteadily with her support. I felt like I'd been drugged and asleep for days, but as Martha led me to the Kelly girls' burial scaffold, I began to regain my strength. It was a clear, warm day, and in the sunshine, I had the strange sensation of being reborn . . . It all came back to me in that moment . . . The soldiers had removed my leg shackles so that I could urinate, and they sent Gertie to guard me, though I could hardly run away from them. As there were no bushes or trees behind which I might have some privacy, we walked a fair distance away. I asked Gertie to turn around and face the soldiers while I went about my business.

"You know, Molly, I seen plenty a' gals pee," Gertie said, "seen you do it, honey, lotsa times. But sure, I'll turn around if that's what you want, and you do what you need to do." I think she knew what it was that I needed to do, for she honored my request and after she turned I kept walking. Because of the wind blowing, she couldn't hear my footsteps, and I had reached the edge of the cliff before she turned around again.

"That really what you want, honey?" Gertie called against the wind, and I saw that the soldier in charge of my escort was walking briskly toward us.

"You tell him to go back, Gertie, or I'll jump right now. I mean it."

"You let me handle this, Sergeant," she called, holding up her hand. "I got it covered. She's just takin' a little air. I'll have her back at the wagon in no time. You get on back to your men now. If ya scare her, she's gonna jump. An' Cap'n Bourke ain't gonna be real happy if ya lose the prisoner that way."

"I know what yer thinkin', Molly," Gertie said. "But you don't have to do this. As long as yer alive, there's always a chance we can get ya outta this mess some other way."

"No there isn't, Gertie," I said. "There is no other way, you know that as well as I do. I'm not going back to Sing Sing, I'm not going to have my baby there and have it taken away from me right after birth, given to a wet nurse and strangers to raise, while I rot in silence for the rest of my life, wondering what became of her, or him. I already lost one child; if I have to lose another, it is coming with me."

That was when I saw Christian Goodman and the others ride in toward the soldiers, and shortly thereafter Ann Hall walked out toward us. She conferred for a moment with Gertie, then called to me, asking my permission to come closer. I told her she could approach within five paces, but I stopped her well before that, and told her that if she came any closer and tried to touch me, I would take her over the edge with me.

Like Gertie, Ann tried to convince me not to jump, but I had been waiting for this opportunity since we departed for Medicine Bow station, and I knew that another like it would not come. Now I stood on the edge of the cliff, preparing myself. This was my recurring dream, being in this exact place. In my dream it always takes me a while to get my courage up to fall, but each time when I finally let go of the earth, I find that I can fly like a bird. I knew that my dream had brought me to this place, and that in this moment I was dreaming again. I heard a hawk scream overhead and I looked up to see it soaring high above. Ah, yes, Hawk has come to me, as he always does, as I knew he would, to teach me to fly. I raised my arms and let my body fall toward the abyss. "Good-bye, Ann," I said.

Yes, all that I remembered so clearly now as I walked in the sunshine, born again and regaining my strength, moving back and forth between my dream world and this one. Martha led me toward Meggie and Susie's burial scaffold on a hillside. In the valley below, the entire encampment of Cheyenne, Lakota, and Arapaho stretched out at least a mile long and a half mile wide, a constant hum of noise rising as all were at work breaking down tipis, loading pack horses and travois, our own wounded upon some of them. High in the air, dozens of vultures circled, telling of the plenitude of carrion to feast upon in the hills around.

Martha and I stood for a long while looking up at the scaffold, silently buried in our own thoughts, our own memories of those cheeky girls who had played such a large role in both our times here. The hides covering their bodies billowed gently in the prairie wind as if Meggie and Susie moved beneath them and might at any moment cast them aside, sit up, and announce the joke they had played on us. That would be just like those girls. But it did not happen. How courageous they were, both in life and death. Clearly, their characters had been hardened and honed growing up on the streets of Chicago, two little orphan girls who had only each other to depend upon, protecting themselves by assuming an armor of bold swagger and self-confidence that they carried into adulthood. Yet no armor, as I know personally, withstands the loss of one's child; it falls away, leaving us naked, defenseless, and only our own death will release us finally from the agony. Although we had had our differences, I was grateful to have made peace with Meggie and Susie, to have become friends with them. Our shared experience as grieving mothers of murdered children became the foundation of a mutual respect and bond to one another. Now I could only hope that the twins, in their brave gesture, had finally found the peace they sought.

"We cannot tarry here long, Molly," Martha finally said. "The scouts have reported that the Army troops are advancing, and we must flee before their arrival. Believe me, you do not need to see the battlefield."

"But I must, Martha. I don't know why, but I must. You show me where it is and I will be quick about it and meet you back at the tipi."

Martha was right, I shouldn't have gone to the battlefield at all, for the horror of the scene, and my own actions there, will stay with me forever. I still don't know exactly what drove my need to witness it, but after she left me, I followed a long trail of scattered corpses up and down the hills. The Indians had removed their own dead, and those I came upon were white men, and a few Black men. They had all been stripped naked, some had been scalped, others had cut their own hair short, as if anticipating their fate, and thus avoiding a scalping. Some, though not all, had been mutilated, limbs and organs severed, eyes gouged out. The buzzards, emboldened, were descending and I surprised some that had already alighted upon their chosen meals. They looked up at me, raising their wings in a threatening gesture, issuing a low, guttural hissing sound to express their irritation at being interrupted. I was not afraid of the unholy creatures, and as I approached I waved my arms and hollered at them and they lifted off with heavy, *whooshing* wingbeats.

The trail of the dead led me finally to the top of a hill, where at least several dozen dead soldiers lay together, most within a circle of dead horses roughly thirty feet in diameter, placed symmetrically enough to suggest that they had been killed by the desperate soldiers to serve as breastworks. A gang of vultures had descended upon both men and horses, and they, too, flushed at my screams. From one of the dead horses, I pulled the saddlebags free . . . taking perhaps a perverse trophy of my own. The soldier's name was stenciled upon it: MILLER. No first name, no rank, and of course, I had no way of knowing which of the bodies, being feasted upon by the buzzards, belonged to this poor boy.

Of these corpses, was it not sufficient punishment to have died this way, without being horribly mutilated as well? Skulls crushed with stone clubs; arms, legs, and heads hacked off with knives; eyes gouged out; genitals cut off. I came across one boy whose severed penis had been stuffed in his mouth, all this the work of the women and old men of the tribe, who immediately after the battle entered the killing field with their clubs and knives to finish off the wounded soldiers and perform their gruesome surgeries. Here is the detritus of the glory of war. What is it about human nature that drives us to commit such atrocities? Is it not enough that we kill each other, must we also defile our enemies' bodies? God help us . . .

Shaken to my core by this scene of carnage, I walked to a hilltop upwind of the stench and opened the saddlebags that contained soldier Miller's worldly possessions. There was a pouch of tobacco, and a box of wooden matches, several pairs of socks and undergarments, a pocketknife, a lock of brown hair tied with a red ribbon, and a faded photograph of a young woman, presumably his sweetheart back home, to whom the hair must have belonged. In the other saddlebag, there was a rabbit's foot that boys carry for good luck . . . it had clearly failed him. There was also a leather-bound diary inside. I opened the cover and saw that there was an inscription inside written in a woman's hand.

My dearest son Josh,
I began to weep when the Army conscription agent drove his wagon into our farmyard yesterday, and told us that you had been called up, and were being sent to fight in the Indian wars. I fought back my tears for I did not wish you to see me weak. I knew that I would have ample time to cry in private after you left us.

I give you this diary so that you might make regular entries in it, and describe your experiences in the Great Plains. Most importantly, I want you to bring it back and read it out loud to your mama who loves you so.

Please take care of yourself, my darling little boy. Come home to me. Come home to me.

Your loving mother,
Lucille Miller

I thumbed through the few scant pages of diary that young Josh Miller had filled in with a boy's poor handwriting, the last page a short letter to his mother.

Dear Mama,
Today we meet the enemy for the first time. Lt. Colonel Custer tells us that our troops have set a trap. Major Reno's three companies will attack the Indian village from the

south. Our five companies will cross the river and attack from the north. I am trying to be a brave soldier. I want you to be proud of me when I come home. But I am so scared, Mama . . . I am so scared. Please help me, Mama. I miss you. I love you.

Josh

I realized then that I needed to take these saddlebags back to the scene of the massacre and leave them there. This diary belonged to his mother now. I knew that the Army must keep records of their soldiers, and that they would have his family's name and address, or at least the name of the nearest town to which they lived, and they would likely send them his last effects. But when I stood to walk from my hilltop, I saw a massive force of mounted soldiers pouring like a blue wave over a distant hill of yellow grass. I knew that I must flee, and take the saddlebags with me.

28 June 1876

My friend Carolyn Metcalf, surely the most fastidious of those of our group still among us, has kept a calendar of our time here. She tells me that she also did so in the lunatic asylum to which her husband, the pastor, had unjustly committed her, because the simple act of keeping track of the date helped her to hold some grip on sanity in that ghastly place. The irony of this statement was not lost upon me. Carolyn says she keeps her calendar here "in order to maintain some slight connection to civilization, in case we should ever have occasion to return there," although she admits that this prospect seems increasingly unlikely.

And so I resume these journals, counting upon the accuracy of her dates, as I, for one, especially since my last strange experience, have completely lost track of time except in the broadest sense of the seasons and the movement of the sun, which we farm girls come to learn instinctively.

We are under way again. Apparently, Little Wolf and much of

his band did not participate in the battle here. After the fight on the Rosebud, he led away those who wished to follow him, and no one seems to know exactly where. It is true that the Sweet Medicine Chief has always tried to maintain as much distance as possible from both the whites and other tribes, his primary responsibility being to keep his people safe from danger. Perhaps he has found again some sufficiently secluded place in which to hide from the Army. Where that might be, or if such a place even exists, we do not know.

After the Rosebud battle, some of the young warriors in Little Wolf's band, and their families, including our white women and their husbands, had continued on to the valley of the Little Bighorn. Having tasted victory, these young men did not wish to miss the massive gathering of tribes there, and what promised to be another rare opportunity to defeat the soldiers, and gain honors on the battlefield. And so, apparently, they have.

I have had wonderful news from Pretty Nose that my husband, Hawk, is not dead, as the wretched maniac Jules Seminole told me when I was in his captivity. It is true that he was gravely wounded at the battle on the Rosebud, but his grandmother, Náhkohenaa'é'e, Bear Doctor Woman, made a camp for them on a tributary of Rosebud Creek, where she cared for him, nursing him back to a fragile health. Pretty Nose had come upon them herself after she escaped from her captor in Seminole's camp, and was following the trail of the People to the Little Bighorn. She tells me that Hawk was still too weak to travel, and she feared that the Indian scouts of the Army might discover them. That is the only news I have of him, and old news it is. Yet I remain certain that he is still alive, and will come to me when he is able.

We ride now with our small band of Cheyenne and Arapaho, our own little reunited family group led by the distinguished warrior chief, Pretty Nose. This includes the chaplain Christian Goodman, our Mennonite spiritual advisor, and his wife, the Norwegian girl, Astrid Norstegard; Lulu LaRue, our lively

French songstress and actress; the Mexican Maria Galvez, her skin bronzed by these months in the sun and, due to her own Indian blood, nearly indistinguishable in feature from the Cheyenne; Carolyn Metcalf, former pastor's wife from Kansas; Martha Atwood Tangle Hair of Chicago, May Dodd's best friend; and Euphemia Washington, escaped slave, but an African warrior princess in our minds. With Meggie and Susie gone, Martha and Phemie are all that are left now of the original group of white women to be sent among the Indians, though more than were thought to have survived. The attrition rate is high on these plains.

With the departure of Ann Hall and Hannah Alford, we are but five left in our small band of brides. We are strangely heartened to know that those two, at least, are alive and going home, as if we somehow share vicariously in that journey, for home is a place that increasingly exists only in our imaginations. The absence of our missing friends both dead and alive is keenly felt by us all, yet as we ride once again into the unknown, homeless and reduced in number though we be, we are long past the point of self-pity. Indeed, whatever is to come, I think we all consider ourselves among the fortunate . . . perhaps, I, more than anyone.

Except for the addition of several Arapaho families who have joined us, we know most of those with whom we ride. At this point we have no idea where we are headed. The thousands of Indians from the three tribes who congregated in the river bottom of the Little Bighorn have similarly split up into smaller bands and family groups, dispersing in all different directions in order to confuse and evade the soldiers, giving them too many tangents to chase in any effective way. In addition, because they have camped here in such great numbers, the game in this area have been largely depleted, and, to be sure, it is easier to feed a small band than a larger one.

I was stunned and relieved to be presented by Phemie with my mare, Spring. I had last seen her corralled in General Crook's supply base camp on Goose Creek, before I was to be sent to the train at Medicine Bow station, intended final destination Sing Sing. She told me that, emboldened by their victory at the Rosebud, some of the young warriors had trailed the defeated Army troops there and executed a successful raid on their herd, among which Spring had been turned out.

"We took it as a sign that you were coming back to us, Molly," she said. "We felt that no matter how dire your situation, you were too resourceful not to find a way out of it. And so you did."

"I have only the most scattered, contradictory recollections of the events of that day, Phemie," I answered as Spring nuzzled me with her nose, "but I am told that I owe my rescue to you and Pretty Nose. I am sorry, but I do not remember. The only thing I know is that I stood on the edge of the cliff, preparing to fall. Indeed, I believe that I did fall. I am not sure that act qualifies as resourcefulness, so much as simply choosing the last available option."

"Sometimes those are the same things, Molly," Phemie said. "And that appears to have been the case, for here you are with us again."

"And how is that, Phemie? Can you tell me now exactly how it happened?"

"I think it is best that you let those memories return in their own time," she said. "And I believe they will. Neither I, Pretty Nose, Martha, Astrid, nor Christian have spoken to the others about what happened that day. Nor will we, we have since agreed, for each of us carries a different version of those events . . . or perhaps I should say, a different interpretation, and perhaps you, too, will come to your own conclusion in time, uninfluenced by our disparate memories. I have been among the Cheyenne long enough now to know that sometimes things happen in their world for which there is no single rational explanation. All you really need to do now is take comfort in being back with us, however exactly that came about."

I did not tell Phemie or anyone else about the strange, disorienting visions I have been having since my return . . . I can think of no other word to describe them, although they sound a good deal like the "poppycock" of which Ann Hall spoke. It appears to be a kind of madness in which dreams and reality overlap, and I am unable to differentiate one from the other. The images come to me both day and night, both waking and asleep. One minute I am riding in the air on the back of a giant raptor, my arms holding on to its broad neck, my naked body stretched across its back, my face buried in its soft, warm, pungent feathers that hold a scent exactly like the skin of the man, Hawk . . . and I am aroused. The next moment, I am simply riding across these plains on my mare, Spring, surrounded by my friends. Truly, I fear that I am going mad.

I waited until we were fully on the move, some distance away from the great encampment and battlefield, leaving Meggie and Susie behind on their scaffold, before I opened Meggie's medicine bag. In it I found several of her totems—a smooth red touchstone from the Powder River; a petrified shell, an ironic portent of a long life; a piece of braided sweetgrass that lent the bag an aromatic scent; and a wing of the twins' spirit animal, the kingfisher. I remembered that one of the young Cheyenne boys, using a kind of slingshot device, had killed the bird as it sat on a branch above the river, scouting for fish in the river below. He threw a stone and made a direct hit, and the bird tumbled into the water. The Kelly girls gave the boy hell for killing the kingfisher, both because it was their spirit protector and for the fact that, due to its fishy-tasting flesh, it was not even palatable as a food source, thus the senseless waste of a creature they held in such high esteem. They told him that his act would bring bad medicine upon them all. The boy, terrified, ran frantically downstream to retrieve the dead bird, bringing it back as a kind of offering to Meggie and Susie, who each kept one of the bird's wings in their medicine bags. The kingfisher is prized as a protector in battle by the People for the way in which the water closes up over it when it dives into the water after fish. It was believed that this property would be transferred to the warrior who bore an image or a skin, or a wing of the bird, and that if a bullet struck him or her, the holes would close up around the wound in the same way. How superstitious these people are, and so some of us have become in our time among them, embracing a belief in the ability of spirit animals to protect us, in good and bad medicine, in the ministrations and predictions of tribal visionaries, even in the antics of the bizarre "contraries" of the tribe, men and women who do everything backward as a means of counterbalancing the inexorable forward movement of time. And why not? I seem myself to be slipping into that world of make-believe. Perhaps the relentless reality of life here causes all to eventually seek refuge there.

Also enclosed in Meggie's medicine pouch were two tightly folded pieces of ledger book paper, one with my name written on the outside in Meggie's hand. When I unfolded the other, I recognized it as the page I had found in the cave to which Martha had led us, where May Dodd died, written in her hand and torn from her journal. With all that had happened so quickly since then, I had completely forgotten about this, nor had Meggie ever mentioned it again in my presence. I read Meggie's missive to me first.

Our dear Molly,
Susie and me are both writin' this letter to ya. We do not know what has become a ya, and we will die tomorrow without knowin'. But here is what we think. We know ya to be a survivor like us, Moll, a strong, brave lass who knows how to land on her feet when the goin' gets tough. Aye, we believe you'll find your way out of whatever mess you're in, just like we always done . . . until now at least . . . and that you'll find your way back to your friends and family, especially your husband Hawk, and your baby that is on the way according to Woman Who Moves against the Wind. So we write this letter to ya, believin' that you're goin' to read it one day. Aye, Susie and me is tired now of the fight, we're done in, knackered . . . the truth is we ain't been able to get the image of that poor paddy laddy we killed

on the Rosebud out of our heads. He was so scared, that boyo, Molly, he begged us . . . he begged us . . . please don't kill me he said, please don't kill me . . . but we did and we butchered him, too, we cut his nut sack off . . . I was goin' to make a tobacco pouch out of it. We thought maybe goin' back to war and killin' more lads would erase the memory, or maybe just make it easier once we'd done it a few more times and had more scalps hangin' from our belt, more nuts on our testicle necklace. But no, it don't work that way, Moll . . . not at all. See, we got to thinkin' . . . that boy had a mam, too, aye, an' she was waitin' for him to come home, worryin' about him, just like all mams do. But now on accounta us, he ain't comin home . . . ever . . . an' maybe his mam will never even know for sure what became of him. Sure maybe someone else wuda killed him that day if it hadn't been us, but they did not, it was me and Susie who did the deed. See there just ain't no answers, Molly, they kill us, we kill them, there ain't no end to it. An' if we don't fight and try to kill 'em, the way Christian Goodman and his people believe, there goin' to keep killin' us anyhow. There goin' to keep killin' our babies. Aye, we are all done in now Susie an' me, our hate has been such a heavy load to carry all this time, and has finally wore us out. We thought maybe takin' vengeance might lighten the weight, but it don't work that way . . . no, not at all. Nor did it bring back our girls. So here is what we are goin' to do, Moll. We are goin' to make one last charge, aye, the Kelly twins are goin' to ride one last time against the soldiers, just to scare 'em, that's all. We won't be carryin' guns, knives, clubs, or lances, we are just goin' to charge those boys, ride in on 'em like the Gaelic banshee she-devils we are, but this time our howls will be announcin' our own deaths, not theirs. We figger that is the only way we are goin' to find some peace at last, maybe we'll even find our wee little lassies again in

Seano, who knows? That is a grand place, the Cheyenne say, where folks live just like they did on earth, huntin' and feastin', dancin' and makin' love. They say the men even go to war there, only they can't kill each other, see, all they can do is count coup because they be already dead. Ain't that brilliant? Susie an' me has talked a lot about it an' we figger those wee babes of ours must be in Seano now, but we believe they won't ever be able to grow up proper until their mams are back with 'em to show 'em the way. Aye, death will be sweet there with our girls, Moll, we figgered you more than anyone would understand that . . .

We leave the other piece of paper in this medicine bag to ya too because we don't know what to make of it. It is written in May Dodd's hand that much we know for sure, but what it says don't make sense. Because May was the leader of our group and you bein' the leader of yours, we are leavin' it to you. After all, yer the one who found it, an' maybe ya can figger it out. Who knows maybe May really is still alive, but then we wonder if maybe she jest didn't go a little delirious in the head at the end. If yad ever had the chance to read May's journals, yad know that she was a lass who liked to tell a tale, she could hardly stop writin' in that damn book a hers. An' we think maybe she was just imaginin' a story about herself not dyin'. Because if she really had lived, she woulda found us, or we'ed 'ave heard something about her. Brother Anthony himself said he saw her dead after Martha led him back to the cave, said he took the pencil out of her frozen fingers, and gave her the last rites. Dead is dead, and we know Brother Anthony to be a man who would not invent such a tale. Then again we all remember how dark it was in that cave when we went there with you and Martha. Now that her mind's right again you must ask Martha about it, because we ain't had the time, and we got more important business of our own to take care of just now.

Well, that is about it from Susie an' Meggie Kelly, Moll. Not much left to say, except we leave you believin' in our hearts that you are alive and well . . . which is a trick in itself these days ain't it? . . . an' that you found your way home and that yer readin this letter. Sorry our spellin' ain't better. We done the best we could given our poor education . . . but we are done writin' now. Moll, just to let you know, sure, we may 'ave had our differences between us from time to time, but Susie and me we loved ya lass, an' we know that ya loved us back. Aye, an' what better way is there than that for us to be sayin' goodby. May good medicine keep ya well, Molly, and may the spring winds be always at your back.

Your dear friends,
Susie & Meggie Kelly

I had to take a deep breath after finishing Meggie and Susie's letter and try not to let the others see me cry. How we'll miss those girls.

THE LOST JOURNALS OF MAY DODD

Alive

As we are leaving the cave, Molly spots a piece of paper in the shadows of the corner. She picks it up, looks at it, and hands it to me. Straightaway I recognize it as a page torn out of May's notebook, written in her hand. But it is too dark to read here, and so I fold it and put it inside the small beaded leather pouch I carry at my waist.

—*from the journals of Margaret Kelly*

Preface

by Molly Standing Bear

We Indians are a secretive people. By the way, I will not refer to us in these pages as Native Americans. That is a relatively recent name bestowed upon us by well-meaning white people to recognize Indians as the original residents on the continent they took away from us. It makes the liberal whites feel good about themselves to recognize that we were here first, and to tacitly, if not directly, admit to that grand theft and genocide.

Historically, of course, all the different tribes had different names for themselves, and each other, names that tended to evolve and change over the centuries. We called ourselves Tsistsistas, which in our language means simply "people," as opposed to "bears," "buffalo," "birds," "fish," "horses," etc., etc. . . . It was a modest, unpretentious name that recognized the fact that we were simply part of the animal world, neither above nor better than the others, just different. Later we became Cheyenne, by which name we are still known and also call ourselves, although "Tsistsistas" is making a comeback with the renewed interest in our own language and culture.

The name "Cheyenne" was at first believed by white ethnographers to have been derived from the French word *chien*, which means "dog." Later research revealed that it was an interpretation of the Sioux term *Sha hi'ye na*, meaning in their language "red talker," and can be translated as "people of alien speech" or simply those whose speak a language different than their own, for the Sioux called themselves "white talkers." Of course, I can't presume to speak for all tribes, or even for my own, but in our own modern vernacular, we collectively call ourselves "Indians," not to be confused, of course, with the people in the country of India. White people don't need to feel guilty about calling us Indians because it's a step up from "savages" as we've been called for centuries, and still are by some.

As I was saying, we Indians are a secretive people, and no one guards their secrets better than we. We learned long ago to keep secrets from the whites, to tell them nothing personal, nothing of value, nothing that can be used against us. But we are also, by nature, secretive with each other. We often simply don't talk about certain things. Because everyone deserves a modicum of privacy, this quality of secrecy can be a good thing. But it can also be a bad thing, as well. For instance, in the old days, such crimes in the tribal family as child abuse, spousal abuse, and sexual abuse were unheard of. Today, as a result of the historical trauma we have suffered, the resulting lack of self-respect, and the introduction of an easy escape into oblivion offered by alcohol and drugs, and, frankly, from behavior we learned from white culture and even from their priests in church, these crimes and others are sadly common among our people. As one who has suffered from it, I know this to be true. But no one speaks of it. If someone hears a neighbor being beaten by her husband, they say nothing, that is not their business, they don't get involved. Even if they see that neighbor the next day, bruised and bloodied, they greet her politely, but they ask no questions, and offer no comfort. It is not their business.

Certainly there were people down through the generations who must have known about the existence of the following journals, but for various reasons, both good and bad, they were kept secret all this time. As described previously, the first page, torn out of a ledger book, was found by my ancestor Molly McGill in a cave where May Dodd was said to have died. At the time, without reading it, she gave it to Meggie Kelly, who, before her death, gave it back to Molly. The original page was nearly illegible and clearly written under great duress. It was found tucked into the front of a ledger book written in Molly's hand, but I have placed it where it belongs, in sequence to the following journal written by May. I will explain later how her lost journals came into my possession. Right now, I think perhaps the reader wants to read it.

undated entry on page torn from ledger book, discovered by Molly Standing Bear in May's cave—ED.

I am May Dodd. I am wounded, I am dying. My friend Martha has gone to find John Bourke. I sent Quiet One, Pretty Walker, and Feather on Head to join Little Wolf, and to take my baby, Little Bird, with them, and my journal, too, leaving me this one page I tore out to say a final adieu to my short life on earth, which has known both misery and joy, serendipity and tragedy . . .

But I am not dead yet, for my husband Little Wolf has sent the prophet Woman Who Moves against the Wind to care for me. I leave this page here, in this dark cave . . . a message in a bottle . . . and in the unlikely event that someone finds it, you may also find my bones, picked clean perhaps by the scavengers. But if there remains no trace of me, then you must believe . . . I am alive.

(The following undated entry began another ledger book.—ED.)

I must have fallen asleep, and when I awoke Woman Who Moves against the Wind was squatting before me. She covered me with a buffalo robe. As she did so, I heard Martha and Brother Anthony speaking at the entrance to the cave. "I think this is the place," Martha said, weeping hysterically, "but I'm not certain, Brother, I can't say for sure. Oh, God . . . what have I done, I've lost May . . ."

"It's alright, Martha," said Brother Anthony, "calm yourself. I'll go in and see, you wait here for me." Then, as he was crawling in through the narrow opening, I heard Brother Anthony call my name.

The medicine woman gripped my arm. "Do not move, Mesoke,"

she whispered, "do not speak, do not let them take you away from here, if you do you will die, you must believe me, close your eyes and sleep now." And then she was gone, and Brother Anthony was crouched before me. I could not have moved if I wanted to. I was paralyzed, frozen in place. I believed that I was hallucinating. Perhaps I was already dead. With his forefinger, Anthony traced the sign of the cross on my forehead. His finger seemed so warm. "Through this holy anointing, may the Lord in his love and mercy help you with the grace of the Holy Spirit. May the Lord, who frees you from sin, save you and raise you up . . . Safe journey, my dear friend, May Dodd," he said, and I slept, comforted by the knowledge . . . relieved that the end had come . . . happy even . . . that surely, I was on my way to heaven.

I was awakened again by a sharp stabbing sensation in my back where I had been shot. A fire burned in the center of the cave. I was lying on my stomach with my deerskin shift pulled up over my shoulders. I cocked my head, and out of the corner of my eye I saw Woman Who Moves against the Wind kneeling at my side. "You're hurting me," I said. "Leave me alone, what are you doing?"

"Do not move, May," she answered, and she whispered some kind of incantation in a voice so low I could not make out the words. Then I felt a searing, burning pain and I screamed. I must have passed out. When I woke, I was propped up against the wall of the cave, wrapped in the buffalo robe. Woman Who Moves against the Wind handed me a wooden cup filled with some kind of broth. "Drink this," she said. "It will help with the pain, and replenish your lost blood."

"What did you do to me?" I asked.

Between her thumb and forefinger, she held up the piece of deformed lead. A dull flame reflected off it. "I took this out of your back, and I closed the wound with fire. You bled a lot, Mesoke. The bullet was lying against the bone of your back, but it did not go deep into the flesh. Your journal slowed its passage and saved you. Still, it needed to come out."

She turned to the fire and held a piece of meat impaled on a stick over the flames. The fat began to drip from it, sizzling in the coals . . . the smell of it . . . I could not remember the last time I had eaten . . . ah, the glorious smell of meat cooking, fat dripping . . . Well, alright, I was not in heaven, after all . . . I was alive and that did not seem so bad, either.

undated entry

I do not know how long we have been in this cave for I have spent much of my time here asleep. I have lost the feeling in my legs and cannot move them. Woman Who Moves against the Wind tells me that the soldier's bullet that came to rest against my backbone has done this.

"No, I ran a long distance after I was shot," I said. "My legs were fine. You must have done the damage yourself when you took the bullet out. You have made me a cripple. I'd rather be dead."

The medicine woman just looked at me then, neither denying nor confirming my accusation. "The feeling will return, Mesoke," she said, "and you will walk again. You will grow strong and be able to run again."

"How can you possibly know that?" I said angrily. "I suppose it is because you think you can see into the future, is that it? But you are not a real doctor, you're a charlatan. You should have let me die."

She did not answer.

I descended into a deep melancholia . . . and I slept. It was all I wished to do. She woke me to feed me and to massage my legs at least three times a day. All I wanted was to sleep. "Leave me alone," I kept telling her. "Let me sleep, let me die in peace."

She left the cave every day to collect firewood, and killed a deer with her knife to feed us. She obscured the narrow opening to the cave with rocks, so no one would come upon us . . . not that any-one would be looking. She said that more snow had fallen and obscured any tracks leading to us, and any distinguishing features of the landscape.

Who would be looking for us? Brother Anthony would have told the others that I was dead, and he would be attending to the living. Quiet One said that Little Wolf planned to lead the people across the mountains to seek sanctuary in Crazy Horse's village. Captain John Bourke's soldierly responsibilities would preclude him from coming to look for my corpse, and to what end? To give me a Christian burial?

"Leave me here, and let me die in peace," I said to her. "I do not wish to be found. What good am I to anyone now? How can I even care for my daughter when all I can do is crawl on the ground?"

"Your husband, Little Wolf, sent me here to look after you," she answered. "You will walk again, Mesoke."

I hated her.

It was a strange thing after believing I had been saved, to know again that this cave was to be my final resting place, after all. I was dead to all who knew me, and now to myself. Dead and embittered. I was no longer an escapee from a lunatic asylum, or the participant in a secret government program, nor was I the wife of a great Cheyenne chief, or the leader of a band of white women. I knew that my fellow wives Quiet One and Feather on Head, and Quiet One's daughter, Pretty Walker, were the most capable of women and would protect my daughter, Little Bird, with their own lives. And so, I was no longer even a mother. After all the ordeals of this past year, and especially that terrible dawn attack upon our camp, in this rare moment I had no responsibilities as wife, mother, friend. I was a cripple, and I was free to die. I slept, wondering if one can sleep oneself to death. I slept.

The medicine woman descended to our charred village and managed to scavenge certain articles and goods that had somehow been overlooked by the soldiers in their otherwise nearly thorough destruction of all we owned. She found a few intact blankets, buffalo robes, and hides, as well as an iron pot and a skillet obtained in trade that had survived the flames, and even, miraculously, a pair of unbroken china plates also secured in trade.

We had been rich as a band, and had enjoyed a successful hunting season to see us through the winter, and the medicine woman found, as well, two bundles of dried buffalo meat that the soldiers had neglected to throw upon the fires. She came upon several bows still intact, as well as four quivers full of arrows, and a bone-handled knife, charred by the fire but not destroyed. She also found a coiled lariat that was only partially burned.

These things she found while digging carefully through the rubble, but all else was gone, she said, burned, taken away by the soldiers and the scouts, or shattered beyond repair, in order to expedite the government's campaign to drive the last free tribes to extinction . . . as well as the white woman they had sent here to civilize the savages.

I had watched as Captain John Bourke killed a young boy, my little horse boy, who was guarding the horses on that freezing morning of the massacre. The brave child wrapped his blanket around himself and faced Bourke's drawn pistol with a stoicism beyond his years. The captain pulled the trigger. I hated him, and would never forgive him.

Woman Who Moves against the Wind brought the surviving items to our camp in the cave, making a number of trips back and forth to the village over a period of days. The last thing she returned with was, she announced, a gift for me: two unused ledger books, and a packet of colored pencils that had belonged to one of our tribal artists, a young man named Little Fingernail, who she said had died in the attack while fleeing the soldiers. She found the ledgers where he had stored them in an empty ammunition crate in his tipi that had been set afire like all the others, but had not burned completely. It is with this poor boy's implements that I make these entries.

"You know, some of the People call you Paper Medicine Woman, Mesoke, because you are always scribbling away in your journal. I thought these might give you something to do besides sleep all the time."

The cave seems rather full now with these few salvaged items.

It isn't much, and most of it at least partially damaged and needing repair, but when you have nothing, anything seems a lot. And so I have begun to write again, but I did not thank her for the gift. I can only assume that my other journals, besides that which I had carried strapped to my back and gave to Quiet One before the women left the cave with my Little Bird, were likewise consigned by the soldiers to the flames. It is of no matter to me now. I believed at the time that I was writing to my dear children in Chicago, who were torn from me by my parents in the first brutal act that led me first to the lunatic asylum, and then here to these inhospitable plains. I held then the notion that by some miracle, the journals might find their way to my babies, and they would not have to spend the rest of their lives believing that their mother, who loved them more than anything on earth, was insane.

Yet, since the Army's attack upon our village, and my injury, I have come to the inevitable conclusion that no one, and none of the scanty possessions that belong to this ancient race of native people, or even those of us who only speak of it in journals, nothing will survive the relentless invasion of the white race, with their ability to erase entire civilizations that happen to be in their way. And, certainly, my modest attempt to record the events of these times are of the very least importance. Now I just write for myself, with no further vain illusions that anyone else will read what I record, especially my beloved babies, Hortense and William . . . God bless you.

I remember that my dear friend, Helen Elizabeth Flight, who has always encouraged me in my writing, as I have encouraged her in her beautiful artwork, once told me of a line in a play written by an Englishman named Edward Bulwer-Lytton: "The pen is mightier than the sword." At the time, I found that to be such a lovely, uplifting sentiment, but now I realize that it flies in the face of human history, for no one kills people with pens.

I do not know how many of my friends survived the attack, and, if any did besides Martha, where they are now? When the Army charged, I did what all the mothers did that morning, I gathered up my baby and I ran. I fled with the others as the mounted soldiers stormed through the village, bearing down upon us with trumpet blowing and flag flying, these proud American boys firing their weapons, or wielding their swords in vicious arcs, mothers with their children, old men and women falling around me, cut down indiscriminately, while our own warriors tried valiantly to distract the soldiers and cover our retreat with return fire. I ran . . . I ran . . . only one goal in my mind amid the chaos and terror, the goal of us all, to protect our children.

In these last days, weeks in the cave . . . how many I do not know, I have relived that morning again and again both in dreams and awake. What has become of my friends? Now I will never know, I will never see them again, and I have lost a third child.

The days pass, one bleeds into the next—weeks perhaps go by, I don't know, I've lost all track of time, I don't care. I sleep, I wake, I write a few words, I sleep. Woman Who Moves against the Wind feeds me, massages my useless legs . . . she cleans my mess. Every morning, in all weather she goes down to the creek and breaks a hole in the ice if necessary, and hauls fresh water back in a pouch fashioned from the bladder of a moose. She cleans my legs and buttocks of the feces and urine that have spilled from my useless body in the night. I disgust myself.

And then one morning when I wake up, and Woman Who Moves against the Wind is massaging my legs, I suddenly realize that I can feel her strong hands upon them, I can feel the movement of her fingers pressing into what little remains of my muscles. I look up at her and she nods with the slightest smile on her face. My whole being floods with relief, and at the same time with an intense sense of shame at the recognition of how terribly I have treated this noble woman. I begin to weep, I begin to bawl like a child as the full depth of my endless, pathetic self-pity reveals itself to me. "I am so sorry,"

I blubber, "I am so sorry, can you ever forgive me? Please, please try to forgive me." But I do not deserve to be forgiven.

"You will not be able to walk yet," she says, "for your muscles are too weak, and if you try too soon, you may injure yourself again. You must be patient, Mesoke, we will know when you are ready to walk again."

I know well that Woman Who Moves against the Wind is Little Wolf's most trusted advisor, his seer into the future, and is also reputed to have sacred healing powers. I have always been a skeptic regarding such matters, yet in our time among the Cheyenne, it is true that we have all witnessed occurrences that seem to defy rational explanation. For instance, one day a young warrior had his leg broken when his horse stepped in a badger hole, fell, and rolled upon him. The horse, too, had broken its leg and they had to kill it. When his fellows extricated him and carried him back to the camp, we saw with our own eyes the shard of leg bone protruding through his skin. He was taken to the lodge of one of the medicine men, and a week later, he was walking about the camp with only a slight limp. We white women spoke often together of such inexplicable matters, and discussed them at length with Brother Anthony, who, of course, ascribed them to divine intervention, one of the luxury beliefs owned by the reverent.

"But they do not worship our God," I pointed out, "so how is it possible that he intervenes in the affairs of savages, when he has his own faithful flock to look after, and doesn't, frankly, even do such a good job at that?"

"The Lord works in mysterious ways, May," he said, one of those solemn aphorisms that has always annoyed me.

Finally, we all agreed that it was best not to question the strange occurrences in the savage world, rather just accept them, which is how we have adapted to life among these people from the very beginning. One thing that is certain, the medicine woman did, indeed, save my life, when I knew without a doubt that I was dying. I wonder how she even managed to find me here? Was that, too, accomplished by supernatural means, or simply a refined sense of direction and an exact description of the location of the narrow entrance to the cave, given her by Quiet One, Feather on Head, and Pretty Walker? They would, certainly, have been required to provide the medicine woman with this information when Little Wolf sent her back to care for me. But how could they possibly have done so given this rocky, largely featureless landscape?

At the same time, was it magic or simply sound doctoring skills . . . acquired God knows how . . . by which she had drawn the bullet from my back, sealed the wound, and finally brought life back to my legs? Perhaps it was some combination of all these things. When I asked her, for instance, how she had avoided being discovered that first day in the cave when Brother Anthony crawled in through the opening, she said: "I went into the shadows, Mesoke, and I became a rock." Was she speaking figuratively or literally, and, really, what does it matter? I have had, perhaps, far too much time to ponder such matters.

I realize that I still have a long way to go before I am able to walk. Wind, Háá'háese, as I have taken to calling her in the interest of brevity, continues to massage the muscles of my legs and flex my joints, and finally, one day she says: "Let us crawl out through the opening so that you may take some sunlight. After all this time in the dark, you will need to put a hand over your eyes at first."

As weak as they feel, I am heartened to be able to use my legs a bit to help push my body as I crawl, and when I see the beam of light shining through the opening, I have the odd sensation of being a newborn baby leaving her mother's womb, pushing out between her legs into this new world. Indeed, I need to cover my eyes for a moment in the face of the blinding sun. I pull myself up to a seated position in the dirt, and have a look around, as Wind follows me out the opening.

The landscape looks entirely different than I remembered it from that terrible morning when first we made our way here. I can see the tops of cottonwood trees down below in the river bottom;

the leaves just breaking their buds, the meadows and plains stretching away to the horizon already beginning to green up, the promise of spring carried on a soft breeze. How beautiful this world is.

"Good God," I whisper, "how long have I been in that cave?"

Woman Who Moves against the Wind raises both hands and begins opening and closing her fists, fingers flashing—ten, twenty, thirty, forty, and then she holds up her right hand with five fingers showing, and her left with three.

"Forty-eight days? So it must be sometime around mid-April."

She does not know what the month of April is, but she easily interprets my astonishment. "You slept for a long time," she says, nodding. And then with a sly smile, she adds, "You were very tired, Mesoke."

And we share a good laugh at my expense under the soft spring sunshine. And that feels good, too, to laugh. I have been forgiven my unforgivable behavior.

"You must help me to stand, Wind," I say. "I believe that I am ready to try."

Supporting me under my arms, she lifts me to my feet, and without letting go, helps me to take my first uncertain babylike steps. Every day we walk like this, a little longer and farther each time, and soon I am able to get to my feet, and, with the aid of a stick, walk on my own.

Prior to finding the bows and arrows, and the dried buffalo meat, Wind had only her knife to rely upon for procuring our food. With that implement alone, she had somehow managed to stalk and kill the occasional deer, as well as killing small game such as rabbits and grouse with rocks. She told me that in hunting the deer, she had to approach close enough to be able to leap onto its back and stab its heart, which in itself struck me as a magic trick.

"You have to become invisible," she explained of the stalk, "like a shadow cast by a passing cloud. And when the moment is right you leap like a cougar." But now armed with the bow and arrows, her hunts are both more productive and considerably easier.

At the medicine woman's urging, and after working hard to

regain my strength, I have begun to join her in the hunt, first just tagging along as a spectator and trying not to get in the way. "We have no men to provide us with food, Mesoke," she said, "or to protect us. And it will be some time, and a long way to travel, before we do. Now that you are stronger you, too, must learn to feed yourself and to defend against enemies in case we become separated, or something happens to me. You must become a hunter and a warrior."

I had never shot a bow and arrow before, for hunting is not the work of women in the tribe, though you would hardly know that from Wind's prowess. I, of course, was far less successful in my initial efforts, which were undertaken in the river bottom, where I aimed at and frequently entirely missed trees. But she is a patient instructor.

Wind has also given me the bone-handled knife she found in the village, that she cleaned and sharpened on a stone, and then set about teaching me how both to butcher an animal and to kill a man with it. "Unless they are wounded or feeble," she said, "you know the men will almost always be stronger than you. And so you must be quicker and smarter than they. I will teach you how to kick them where it most hurts a man, how to wrestle, how to slip from their grasp like a slippery snake, and how to slit their throats before they do yours. And I will teach you how to scalp them and cut out their hearts."

"If you don't mind, I think I might prefer to skip that last part of the training," I said. Yet Wind's words bring to my mind our treatment by the wretches who kidnapped us last year, how our brave little Sara, rather than submit to the brute who was trying to violate her, pulled the man's knife from the sheath at his waist and stabbed him in the neck. Still, he managed to kill her before he himself died atop her, and the rest of us were forced to submit to the unspeakable indignities of his compatriots.

I have spent my time among the People doing the endless work of women—digging roots, gathering firewood, hauling water, cooking, doing beadwork, looking after children, scraping and curing hides, stitching them together, breaking down and putting up tipis; I have been a dutiful wife, a mother-to-be, and, too briefly, a mother. But unless I am able to subsist on a diet of roots and wild legumes, I cannot feed myself, nor can I defend myself in physical combat. I need a man, or, in my present situation, Wind, to hunt for me, and to protect me. It occurs to me that this is the first time since I have been here in these plains that, but for my savior the medicine woman, I am alone and utterly defenseless.

"Yes, you are quite right, my friend," I said. "We are two women, surrounded by enemies. I must know how to feed and protect you, as you have done for me. I am ready to learn all that you have to teach me, both as a hunter and as a warrior, including how to cut a man's heart out with my knife, although I cannot imagine that will ever be a necessary act for me to perform."

"If ever you come upon Jules Seminole again," she said, "that is a skill you will wish to know, for it is the only manner in which he can be killed."

"What do you mean by that, Wind? He is just a man, and, like any other, can be killed with a bullet, an arrow, a club, or a knife."

"No, Mesoke, he cannot, for Jules Seminole is part man, part sorcerer; he moves between worlds spreading evil."

I confess to laughing at her superstition. "I believe that if Seminole ever bothers me again," I said, "Little Wolf will kill him. I am strong enough now. We must find our people."

"You should know, Mesoke, that Little Wolf has surrendered to the Army and turned his band in at the Red Cloud Agency at Camp Robinson."

"What?" I answered in astonishment. "But that is not possible. Little Wolf would never do such a thing."

"Crazy Horse did not welcome him and his band to his winter village," she explained. "As you know, the People left here after the attack with nothing, not even enough to cover ourselves from the cold. The chief sent me back to look after you, but the others traveled for over ten days to reach the Lakota. They had to kill and eat their few horses along the way, and they skinned them to use the raw hides to cover themselves. When finally they arrived, Crazy Horse shared very little with them. Those two great warriors have never been friendly, and Little Wolf was insulted by the Lakota's lack of generosity. That is why he left and turned his band in at the agency. He did it because the People were starving, and were promised food and shelter there."

"But how can you possibly know all this, Wind?" I asked. "For you have been here with me all this time, and never left my side except to hunt, and to scavenge in the village."

"Before he left for the agency," she answered, "Little Wolf sent a runner to tell me where he was going. He sent my sister because he knew she would be able to find us."

"And why did I not see her when she came?"

"You were asleep much of the time, and she looks as I do. Sometimes when you woke, it was she who was rubbing your legs, or cleaning you."

"Nonsense! How could she look so much like you that I would not know the difference?"

"She is my other half, my twin, you say, like your redheaded girls."

"I never knew you had a twin," I said. "I never saw her in our village. What is her name?"

"Woman Who Moves against the Wind."

I laughed. "You mean to say that you both have the same name?"

"You saw her in the village, you just thought she was me. We are not often seen together. Some of the people believe that we are one person who has the ability to be in two places at the same time. Others believe that each of us is half of one person, and both of those things are true. We live in separate bodies but we always know what the other is thinking. Little Wolf never asks which of us is which. He does not care. We advise him equally."

"I have heard some crazy things since I've been among the People, Wind," I said. "But that is one of the craziest yet."

"But it is true."

"Yet that makes you a charlatan, pretending to be something that you are not."

"We do not pretend," she said. "We do not control what other people believe. And all medicine works best when people believe in it."

"Yet I didn't believe in it," I pointed out, "and it worked for me, as well."

"You believed enough, Mesoke. You just didn't know it."

"Why didn't you tell me sooner that your sister had been here?"

"There was no reason to, and I did not believe you were strong enough to hear news that might upset you."

"And what news would that be?" I asked. "Your sister told you about my friends, didn't she, about the other white women?"

She nodded.

"And why do you keep this from me now? Tell me. Tell me everything."

"The redhead sisters, Hestȧhkhá'e, Twin Woman you remember we call them, for they, too, are thought to be two halves of one person. They both survived the attack and the journey to Crazy Horse's village, but they lost their babies to the cold on the way. Your holy man, Anthony, also reached the Lakota camp alive."

"And who else?" I asked, as the tears began to well up behind my eyes. "That can't be all."

She nodded. "I am sorry, Mesoke."

"Good God!" And I began to weep. "All the others, gone? . . . my friends Helen, Phemie, Daisy, Gretchen? And their babies? All dead? But this cannot be. It has helped to keep me alive in the darkest times, believing that we might one day be reunited."

"It is for this reason that I have not told you sooner, Mesoke. But now you are strong enough to bear this news."

"Do you know how my friends died?" I asked through my tears. "If you do, you must tell me."

"Mo'ohtaeve'ho'a'e, Black White Woman, and the artist, Medicine Bird Woman, Ve'kkesohma'heonevestsee, died defending the village when the soldiers attacked. They stayed to fight with the warriors to protect the women, children, and the old as we ran into the hills. They were both killed by the soldiers. Gretchen and her baby were shot as she fled with the others. The woman, Daisy, and her baby died of the cold on that first night."

"God help them," I said, weeping. "God help them . . ." It took me some time to collect myself again, and when I did, I asked Wind: "And where are Meggie, Susie, and Brother Anthony now? Thank God that at least they, and Martha and her daughter survived."

"Your holy man left with Little Wolf's band to go to Red Cloud Agency," she answered. "He wished to find your friend, Falls Down Woman and her child, whom he had left in the care of the Army captain after the attack. The two sisters stayed in Crazy Horse's village. They did not wish to surrender. They knew they would be sent back where they came from. They wished to go on the warpath against the soldiers to avenge the death of their babies. Now, as you say, you and I must leave here soon. We must find our people."

"But we cannot go into the agency, Wind, for the soldiers will detain me there, and send me back to the lunatic asylum."

"Yes, I know," she said, nodding.

"Then where do we go?"

"There were some among Little Wolf's band who refused to surrender," she said. "Some who had relatives in the Lakota camp stayed there. And then they, too, left, led by the young warrior Hawk, whose father was Lakota. Do you remember him?"

"Yes, I do, he of the fair hair," I answered, "whose mother is the white Cheyenne you call Heóvá'é'ke, Yellow Hair Woman. She, who has never been friendly with us, and refused even to speak English. Hawk is married to a pretty girl named Amé'ha'e, Flying Woman, and they have a young daughter, whom they call Mónevàta, Youngbird. Indeed, I remember them well because our friend Helen Flight was so charmed by their names. I can just hear her: '*Smashing, isn't it? An entire family of avians!*'" And I began to weep again as Helen's words spilled from my mouth.

"Yes, Mesoke. My sister told me that Hawk's mother, wife, and son were all killed in the attack on our village that morning. The soldiers fired low into their tipi, killing them before they had time to rise from their sleeping places. Hawk, too, wished to go back on the warpath, to avenge the death of his family. It is with Hawk and his band that the red-haired sisters are now traveling. And I must tell you one other thing, Mesoke, that I learned from my sister."

"If it is more bad news about my friends, Wind," I said, "I do not think I can bear to hear it just now."

"This is not such bad news, Mesoke, and it is not about your friends. When Little Wolf and our people arrived in the village of Crazy Horse, they learned that the Lakota warriors, led by our Hawk, had captured another group of white women off a train. They were sent by your government and were making their way to the People as more brides for our warriors."

"Oh for God's sake, you cannot be serious. Isn't that just what is needed in these times of carnage, more white women as cannon fodder for the soldiers. And where are they now, these women?"

"The twin red-haired girls were charged with looking after them, and they, too, are now traveling with Hawk."

"And you suggest we try to find them?"

"We must find them, Mesoke," she said, "or another band of the people to join. We are not safe traveling alone."

"But what about my daughter? How will I ever get back to Little Bird if she, too, has been taken into the agency?"

"You will have your Ve'keseheso back again, Mesoke," she assured me, "but not yet."

"How do you know that, Wind?"

"I have seen it."

Wolves for the Blue Soldiers

The commanding general (George Crook) assembled all his Indians (scouts) and laid down to them in a few well-chosen words, rules for their guidance during the campaign. He emphasized the fact that all these vast plains, all these mountains and valleys would soon be filled with an aggressive, hard-working population, the game would be exterminated, domestic cattle would take its place, and the Indian must make up his mind, and make it up now, to live like the white man and at peace with him, or be wiped off the face of the earth. They were going to get good pay as soldiers, as long as they behaved themselves . . . but they must not spend their pay foolishly. Save every cent and buy cows and mares. While the Indian was sleeping the calves and colts would be growing and someday he'd wake up and find himself a very rich man.

> —*from* Mackenzie's Last Fight
> with the Cheyennes:
> A Winter Campaign in
> Wyoming and Montana
> *by Captain John G. Bourke, U.S.A.*

3 July 1876

I did not unfold the page torn from May Dodd's journal until we had traveled for several days. But when I did, and read it, it took me back to the cold, dark cave where May was said to have died, and where Martha had led us that day in the rocky hills above their destroyed village. I was not surprised that Meggie and Susie thought perhaps May was hallucinating when she wrote this, dreaming perhaps of being saved by the medicine woman at the end of her life.

As to Brother Anthony, though our group did not have the chance to get to know him well, he seemed an earnest, devout man who, by all accounts of Meggie and Susie, cared well for his flock of white women . . . as well as he could, at least under impossible circumstances. It does seem nearly impossible that he would have been so careless as to mistake May for dead if she still lived.

I wonder, too, why the Kellys had withheld this information from the others. All I can imagine is that after Meggie folded the unread page and put it away in her medicine bag that day in the cave, in the face of ensuing events, she forgot all about it. I must admit that until I opened Meggie's medicine bag, I, who discovered the page in the first place, had forgotten its existence myself. We simply had too many immediate concerns of our own to face. I'm guessing now that Meggie and Susie didn't read it until shortly before they wrote their letter to me. If May really is still alive, it is impossible to guess in these fractured, desperate times where she might be, or what fate may have befallen her.

6 July 1876

We have been over a week now on the trail, and in that time our path has crossed that of other bands of Cheyenne, Arapaho, and Lakota. After the grand victory at Greasy Grass, there seems to be a palpable sense of trepidation and uncertainty in this dispersal. All report the presence of companies of soldiers in nearly every direction, as well as many sightings of the Indian scouts employed by the Army. It is they who offer the greatest threat to our safety, for, with the ever increasing number of bands surrendering at the agencies and Army forts, the number of scouts grows exponentially. We have already had bitter experiences at the hands of Crow, Shoshone, and Pawnee scouts, during the battle of Rosebud Creek, where Pretty Nose and I were captured and held captive by the cretin Jules Seminole and his band of degenerates. These tribes, longtime enemies of the Cheyenne and Arapaho, were the first to surrender to the government and accept the employ of the U.S. Army. More recently, they are being joined by Lakota, Arapaho, and even Cheyenne warriors, who have turned themselves in at one or another of the agencies, and are now willing to scout against their own people, in some cases, even their own families.

"Wolves for the blue soldiers," Pretty Nose calls the scouts, and she explains that they are especially dangerous because, unlike the soldiers, "the wolves know our ways, they know where we like to camp and make our winter villages. They know how we travel and how we fight."

I am riding between Phemie and Pretty Nose, Martha tagging along behind us on her spirited little donkey, Dapple, with Astrid, Maria, and Carolyn side by side just behind her. It is a warm summer day, but the recent heat wave has broken, and with the light breeze, the air is softer with a preview of fall, the sky a clear deep blue. We are riding through a rolling prairie in what the Indians call sweetgrass country, where Meggie must have secured her small sample for her medicine bag. There has been good rainfall so far this summer, the grass and wildflowers as high as the horses' bellies, undulating in the breeze like gentle swells on the sea. As we move through it, our noses fill with their sweet perfume. Some distance away a small herd of buffalo feed tranquilly upon this late summer bounty, the calves growing fat for the long, hard winter ahead. As we are already sufficiently well stocked with food, our hunters do not disturb them. It is on a day and in a place such as this that it is possible to forget for a moment our troubles, to imagine this country as a paradise, where men and women live in harmony with the earth and with each other. Isn't that, after all, what we seek?

We ride in silence for a time, as we often do, feeling, I believe, similar sentiments of this tenuous, if imaginary peace.

"But how is it then that the wolves agree to help the soldiers hunt down their own people?" I ask Pretty Nose, bringing us perhaps too abruptly back to reality.

"The men know that it is their last chance to be warriors," she explains. "They have been trained for that since the day they were born. There is nothing for them to do at the agency, no way to prove themselves, no way to count coup and gain honors on the battlefield. Most have even had their guns taken away from them, and on the land the government puts us on, there is hardly any game to hunt. The agents steal the government rations and sell them to white settlers, so there is never enough food to feed their families. The Army pays them money to join, gives them rifles and ammunition. It makes them feel like men again, warriors in the stronger army, the army that everyone knows is going to win this war."

"But they are traitors," I say. "If white men join the other side in a war, and get caught, they are shot or hanged for treason."

"Why would a white man wish to join our side?" she asks.

"That is an excellent question," I admit. "Except that we joined your side."

"Because you had to, you had no other choice, in the same way that the wolves have no other choice but to join your army."

"It is not our army any longer," I point out. "We have fought with you against it, and we, too, would be executed for our actions."

"Yes, because you, too, are traitors."

I laugh. "Of course, you are right. It is odd, because we have spent so much time while we've been here simply trying to survive, that I rather forgot we have become traitors to our own government, and would also be hanged if captured."

"Then again, Molly," says Phemie, "in my case, at least, I was never a citizen of America in the first place. Quite the contrary, my people were kidnapped and brought here against their will. They were property, not human beings with any rights. To attain my freedom, I was forced to escape to Canada. I cannot be called a traitor because I have never been considered as or treated like a real American."

"That's true, Phemie. And I can't say that I feel like a real American any longer, either. In Sing Sing, they even took our names away. They gave us numbers. That is how they addressed us, and called us out at morning roll call. I was 781645, a number imprinted forever in my memory."

"But you see," says Pretty Nose, "if this land is called America, which is not what we call it, then my people are the only true Americans. And since you, Molly, are now white Cheyenne, and you, Phemie, are Black white Cheyenne, you, too, can call yourselves real Americans, if you would like. Then you are not traitors. You are warriors fighting to protect your land against the foreign invaders."

Phemie and I laugh. "Yes, I like that," Phemie says, "and it's very clever and generous of you, Pretty Nose. However, I don't think it will prevent us from being hanged if we are captured by the soldiers."

Christian Goodman now rides back from the front of our little procession of seventeen souls, children and the aged included, to join us. He has been riding and conversing with the Arapaho families. Christian is one of those who absorbs new languages as sand absorbs water, and already speaks nearly fluent Cheyenne. He says that Arapaho is of the same language family, and though the tribes speak different dialects, they understand each other. I have no doubt that he will soon be fluent in that language as well.

Together we all speak in a strange combination of languages, depending on whom we're addressing, moving between English, Cheyenne, Arapaho, and French, and, when all else fails, with the sign talk of our hands. Phemie, too, speaks Arapaho, for it was to one of their villages that her husband, Black Man, took her after she was gravely wounded during the Army attack on Little Wolf's village. I am gradually learning both native tongues myself, and it helps me to listen to Pretty Nose and Phemie converse fluently in one or the other.

"The Lord has given us a magnificent day for traveling, hasn't he, ladies?" Christian says cheerfully. "One must believe that all is well in the world on a day such as this."

"Until it isn't," I suggest.

"Ah, Molly, always a bit of the cynic, aren't you?" he says. "While at the same time being a hopeful romantic at heart."

I laugh. "How do you know that, Christian?"

"Well, because I've seen you and your husband, Hawk, together, for one thing."

"I'm glad you said 'hopeful' instead of 'hopeless,'" I answer. "For my cynicism tells me that we may never see each other again, while my hopeful romanticism holds out at least for the slim possibility of a reunion."

"Exactly! As you can see, I am in a splendid mood today," says he. "However, while gabbing away as I have been with our fellow travelers, I seem to have lost my bearings. I'm just wondering, where we are headed? Do you know, Molly?"

"My understanding is that our ultimate destination is a safe haven with plentiful game, where we can make a long-term camp, unmolested."

"*Aha*," says Christian, "speaking of hopeful romanticism!"

"Exactly," I say. "And are you being the cynic now, Chaplain?"

"Not at all, my friend. You should know by now that my faith is unlimited."

"Apparently our destination will involve more days of travel."

"But of course. Doesn't it always?"

"Although no one seems to know how many."

"I follow blindly, Molly, secure in the knowledge that the Lord lights our path."

"You are a lucky man, Christian."

"There is a medicine woman traveling among us," says Pretty Nose. "Ma'heona'e is her name. It means Holy Woman. She is half Cheyenne, half Arapaho. She was at Sand Creek when Chivington's soldiers attacked and massacred the People. She escaped but as she fled she was blinded by the slash of a soldier's saber. The scars on her face across her blinded eyes are terrible to behold. Since that day she has been on a vision quest to save the People from the rage of the whites, to find a safe place for us to live. She is very wise and says that she knows now where that place is. It is Ma'heona'e who is guiding us."

"We are being guided by a blind woman?" I ask. "And you, Christian, are following blindly . . . as apparently are the rest of us. This does not seem promising news to me."

"Yet don't you find that it has the ring of a biblical story, Molly?" the chaplain asks.

"All I have seen of the Bible since we have been here, Chaplain, has been the violent parts."

"Is Ma'heona'e by chance a Christian?" he asks Pretty Walker.

"No," says Pretty Walker. "She knows nothing of your God. She worships the Great Spirit."

Christian is not discouraged by this news. "Well, it is quite possible that the Great Spirit is our God," he says, "and she just doesn't know it yet. One need not see with the eyes to be led by the spirit."

Phemie chuckles in her deep, richly amused way. "Always looking on the bright side, aren't you, Chaplain?" she says.

15 July 1876

Yesterday afternoon while traveling, we stopped to water our horses in a creek, when Lulu spotted a movement in the willows and heard whispers in what sounded to her like children's voices. Due to the circumstances, we are all in a state of heightened vigilance, and we quickly put together a small, armed contingent consisting of me, Pretty Nose, Maria and her husband Hó'hónáhk'e, Rock, Lulu and her husband No'ee'e, Squirrel, and Christian. I carried, as always, the knife at my waist and a Colt .45 I inherited from Meggie, and that Phemie had kept for me; Pretty Nose carried a knife and a hatchet; Maria, also a Colt .45, and Rock, a knife and a stone club. If there was to be any kind of confrontation in the heavy cover of the willows, it would presumably be at close quarters. The chaplain, of course, was unarmed, as was our guide, and nonwarrior, Lulu. Phemie stayed back with the others to guard our people.

We cautiously followed Lulu into the willows, and soon came upon a clearing in which we found two very rough shelters constructed of bent willow branches, the wilted green leaves still upon them. Pretty Nose called out first in Arapaho and then in Cheyenne, asking if there was anyone inside the huts and if so, to come out. In response, we heard only the frightened whimpers of children, but none appeared.

"It could be a trap," I suggested. "There may also be adults inside."

"Oh, for heaven's sake," said Christian, "I'm having a look." He strode purposely forward, and as he bent down to peer through the opening, he was met by the shrill war cry of a boy who threw a small rock that bounced off the middle of the chaplain's forehead, knocking him back on his butt. "*Oww!*" he hollered, rubbing his forehead as we three spectators couldn't help but burst out in spontaneous laughter. We take any opportunity for such a thing these days.

"I told you it might be a trap, Christian," I said, as we all approached. "That's why I didn't want to look in there first."

"From what little glimpse I got," he said, still rubbing his forehead, "I think that you are all overarmed to deal with the situation."

Now Pretty Nose knelt by the opening to the first shelter and made sign-talk gestures, in case they might be from some other tribe. Two young boys finally crawled out, followed by a small girl. From the second hut, three girls and another boy appeared. One of the girls, who did not appear to be much older than thirteen years, carried an infant swaddled in a piece of dirty calico. The rest seemed to be roughly between the ages of four and eleven years old. They were all filthy, their clothes ragged, their eyes hollow, and they looked hungry.

Two of the older boys glared at us defiantly, as did one of the older girls, already proud warriors despite their youth. The younger ones just looked scared. They reminded me of the immigrant children I had dealt with as a charity worker in New York . . . another lifetime ago . . . children without homes whose parents had turned them out because they could not afford to feed them, and who lived on the street or in abandoned buildings, fending for themselves as best they were able, and suspicious of all strangers. Using sign talk, I told these children that we would not hurt them, they were safe with us, and we were going to give them food, which I knew from experience were the things they most needed to hear.

They followed us back to our horses. I did not think any would try to flee, as it was clear that the older among them had assumed the care of the younger, which was how the immigrant children had protected their tribe. In any case, there was nowhere for them to go, and it was obvious that they had little, if anything, to eat. They knew they had no choice but to put their trust in us.

We gave them pieces of dried buffalo meat to chew while Pretty Nose questioned them. It was determined that they were from several different families in a mixed band like ours of Cheyenne and Arapaho. The oldest girl said her baby daughter was unwell and had stopped feeding. I asked her in sign talk to let me see the child, but she clutched it possessively to her breast.

"Please," I said in Cheyenne, "I may be able to help her."

At Pretty Nose's urging, but reluctantly, and regarding me with deep uncertainty, the girl finally handed her baby to me. Not until I held the tiny child in my arms and felt the stiffness of her body did

I realize that she was dead. I saw then the stain of dried blood and the bullet hole in the thin calico. With tears now running down her cheeks, the girl reached her arms out to me in a supplicating gesture. "Yes, sweetheart," I whispered, nodding, "I understand," and I handed her dead baby back to her.

The story we pieced together from the children's account was that since the confluence of tribes at the Little Bighorn, like us, their band had been traveling, trying to return to their traditional hunting grounds, or find new ones that were not overrun with Army troops. Three days ago, their people had spotted several mounted Shoshone warriors watching them on a ridge above the valley through which they were passing. The Shoshone disappeared quickly, and the leaders of the band, assuming that they were wolves, and fearing their return with soldiers, changed direction as an evasive tactic. Some of the band had horses and others, including all the children, were on foot. They moved as quickly as they could, the older children running alongside the horses, the youngest riding behind their parents. They traveled like this for several hours, until dusk came on.

Hoping that they had succeeded in evading the soldiers, they pitched camp for the night along this same creek, and they made no fires that might give them away. The adults and oldest children took turns standing watch beyond the cover of willows where the others slept. This allowed the night guards a clear line of sight to survey the hillsides, lit by a three-quarter moon that cast enough light to see the silhouette of horsemen on the horizon, or the approach of enemies.

The oldest boy admitted with downcast eyes that his was the last watch before dawn, and he had fallen asleep and did not see or hear the wolves and soldiers approaching on foot. Only the nervous nickering of their horses finally woke him, as it did the others in the camp. But by then it was too late.

All Indian children are taught from the youngest age that at the first sign of a possible attack upon their village, they are to run and hide wherever it is possible to conceal themselves, and not to move again or give any sign of their presence until it is safe. This they did, the older shepherding the younger, and all scattering. Six of them had escaped just before the soldiers and wolves stormed the camp, and from their hiding places, they listened to the shouts of the invaders, the gunfire, the yells of their older brothers, fathers, and grandfathers as they returned fire or engaged in hand-to-hand combat, the cries of their married sisters, mothers, and grand-mothers, and the bawling of the babies, whose mothers had gathered them in their arms but had not fled in time. The young girl with the dead infant was running from the camp just as the attack began, and without her being aware of it until later, a bullet struck her baby daughter and must have killed her instantly.

The chaotic noises from the attack went on for some time, until the guns finally fell silent, and the only voices heard calling to each other were those of the scouts and the soldiers speaking Shoshone and English, respectively. Dawn was coming on now and the children listened as the wolves rummaged through their camp for weapons and food, and anything else of value they could carry off. They took scalps, and they gathered the band's horses picketed nearby.

The children waited until well after the soldiers and wolves had finally departed before rising from their hiding places, regrouping, and walking back to the camp. There they found the bodies of their families. They keened and wept, and they wept again as they now told us about it.

The Shoshone had carried everything away, had even stripped the clothes from some of the dead. They left no blankets, no food, no weapons . . . nothing. The older children decided they could not stay in that place; there was nothing to keep them there and they were afraid of the unsettled spirits of the dead rising at night from the corpses that no longer resembled their family members.

Following the willow line, they kept to the river bottom and walked for two days, stopping last night and collapsing to sleep huddled together for warmth on the ground like a litter of puppies. The older boys had knives and when they arrived here earlier today, they constructed their poor stick huts, where they planned to spend the night. They had no food and when Lulu heard them in the bushes they were on their way to try to scoop fish up out of the creek with their hands.

It was decided that we would camp there for the night. "As the children were hoping for a fish dinner," Christian said, "then Astrid and I, with the help of the Lord, will provide one."

The two of them went down to the creek and in an hour caught enough trout to feed us all. Fires were made and the rudimentary lodges set up that we use when traveling for long periods of time. Of course, there was no question of not absorbing these orphan children into our band. Before the evening meal was prepared, I took the girl carrying her dead baby down to the creek, and I had her sit beside me on the bank. She, too, was Cheyenne, and I came to understand that her name was Sehoso, which I later learned from Christian, whose vocabulary is far more extensive than mine, means Little Snowbird.

I told her that we must first wash her baby in the creek, then find a tree where we could place her tiny body in the branches so that she might begin her journey to Seano. My own preference, of course, was to bury the child in the ground, in our own manner, thus protecting her body from scavengers, but I knew that this was not practiced by the Indians. I knew, too, that the vultures and crows would peck away at the corpse in the tree, until it fell to the ground, where they would alight upon it and continue their consumption. The birds would then perhaps be chased off later by a wolf or a coyote, who would carry the body away. What little remained when they were finished was left to the ants and worms; in this way, the baby would be returned to the earth with nothing left to mark her short passage here, not even alive long enough to be named.

Sehoso and I stood together in the middle of the creek. So

tiny and frail was her infant that I held the body in one hand as I washed her. It occurred to me then that in the relatively short time I have been here on the plains, I have seen and experienced such atrocities and heartbreak that I have begun to grow hardened to it . . . I think we all have . . . how else to survive in such a place? Yet now I felt my knees weakening in the cold water of the creek and I feared that they were going to buckle and I would collapse in grief. I thought of the worst day of my life when I found the body of my own little girl, beaten to death by her father, and now I was faced again with one of the greatest obscenities I have ever in my life witnessed . . . I held in my hand the tiny corpse of a newborn child with a bullet hole that passed through her head.

I washed, too, the piece of calico in which she had been swaddled; it dried quickly on a rock in the sun, and I wrapped her in it, tying knots at her head and feet. This small parcel I placed in the crook of the highest branch I could reach of a young wild apple tree that grew beside the bank.

"But my baby cannot go to Seano without a name," Sehoso said.

"Why don't we call her Màxeme?" I suggested, because I knew that was the Cheyenne word for apple.

"Yes, Mà'xeme," she said.

We stood by the tree and ate of the ripe, wild fruit, and we wept together for her daughter.

Three different fires burned for the trout dinner, with different family groups seated together in circles, some Arapaho, some Cheyenne, some mixed. Sehoso and I had brought back apples to give out and the children all sat with us. They ate with the intense concentration of the famished, until they could eat no more. We retired to our respective lodges, each of them shared by at least three or four others. Sehoso has attached herself to me, and curls up under my blanket. She whimpers in the night.

I woke up before dawn to the voices of a pack of wolves baying in the distance, alternately an ululating, howling, yelping, barking sound that chills the soul of us humans as if passed down in our blood from ancient times. As the sky lightened and the baying subsided, I slipped out of the hut without waking anyone and went down to the creek. As I expected, the baby's body was gone, and all that remained was the piece of shredded calico beneath the apple tree. I balled it up and threw it in the creek. Mà'xeme had made her journey to Seano.

23 July 1876

The children were the first of what we began to call "strays," some of whom, if they had no prospect of finding their own people, we have taken along with us over these last days of travel. These are the unfortunates who, due to skirmishes fought against the wolves and/or the soldiers, or simply the sudden appearance of Army troops, had become separated from their bands and were now wandering on their own. It is treacherous enough traveling with a band, but those families or parts of families, alone and on their own, of course are especially vulnerable. Besides the Army, there is an increasing number of miners, ranchers, homesteaders, and settlers of all stripe, either traveling through the country or trying to carve out a hardscrabble life in the small clapboard towns springing up. We have tried to avoid all contact with the newcomers, and give them a wide berth when our scouts come back with reports of their presence in the area, both because we know they do not have friendly intentions toward us, and because we fear that we will not be able to prevent the young warriors in our band from attacking them. We have since learned from having obtained a newspaper, by means which I will explain shortly, that the fears of these settlers have been whipped up by lurid accounts in the press of bloodthirsty savages terrorizing the whites, not all of which, I'm afraid, are untrue. Of course, such accounts have resulted in the settlers being "trigger happy," that is to say, exercising a natural penchant to shoot any

Indian on sight. Indeed, our newspaper contained an article about the Custer "massacre" that enthusiastically recommended the Indians' complete extermination.

Yesterday while traveling, we came upon a small train of four wagons bearing settlers. We spotted them before they did us, and managed to avoid detection. However, our friend Carolyn Metcalf, who has been from the beginning of our adventure the least well assimilated into tribal life, had the temerity to slip away without being noticed. She is the only one among us who has kept one of her white women dresses, which she wears and mends frequently, and was wearing today.

After roughly an hour, Astrid noticed Carolyn's absence. I knew perfectly well what had transpired, because of late, Carolyn has been expressing an increasing homesickness for the comforts of civilization. It was decided that Christian would go back to look for her, as Carolyn has a notoriously poor sense of direction, and if it was necessary to approach the wagon train, besides the fact that he is a white man, he is also, in his attire, the least Indian-looking among us. The fringed buckskin outfit he made for himself could be easily taken as that of a frontiersman rather than a native. Of course, if I was correct, and Carolyn had approached these people, we had no idea how she might have introduced herself, or how she explained her presence here. All we did know for certain was that she would say nothing to give us away.

We could not afford to halt the travel of our own band, and it was over two hours before Christian caught up again, with Carolyn safely in tow. Lulu, Astrid, and Maria, all disapproving of her visit among the whites, let her know this with a stony silence.

"I'm sorry, ladies, to have disappeared without telling you," Carolyn said. "However, I knew if I asked, you wouldn't let me go. I'm afraid that I felt an overwhelming desire to socialize with civilized folks."

At which remark, Lulu laughed. "*Ah, oui*, we are too *sauvage* for you now, *c'est ça*, is it not, Carolyn?"

"No, no, it is not any of you, of course. I speak of *here*, among these people," she said, with a vague wave of her arm. "They were a lovely group, four families of farmers and dairymen from Indiana who have thrown in together to brave the trip west and find fertile land to homestead. They stopped their wagons and the ladies made a cup of tea for me. It was heavenly."

"What did you tell them you were doing here?" I asked.

"I said that I was doing missionary work for the church, working at one of the Indian agencies. That proved to be a convenient lie when Chaplain Christian rode up in search of me, for he immediately assumed his role. They told us to be very careful, because there were still wild savages abroad in the area."

"Yes, us," said Maria. "We can attack them, Carolyn, if you want, kill them and steal their heavenly tea for you."

"Stop it!" Carolyn said, pulling a newspaper from her saddlebag. "Look what they gave me. When was the last time we saw a newspaper? On the train, it must have been. They said there are several stories here of Indian depredations in the Great Plains, including that about the massacre on the Little Bighorn. They said they are very well armed, and if they come upon any Indians, they are going to shoot them on sight before they give them a chance to take their scalps. That's what the newspaper advises all settlers to do. I'll let everyone read it after I've finished. They are such lovely people, and their children so beautiful and well-behaved. The mothers are schooling them as they travel, and, of course, they have a Bible. It made me so happy just to hold it in my hands. I confess that I did not wish to leave them."

I knew what was coming next, and later that afternoon, after we made camp for the night, Carolyn came to see me.

"Molly, you were my first, and have been my closest friend since we've been here," she began. "You saved my life when you had me take to the floor of the train during the attack. You've always been so brave. I don't know how I would have survived here without your strength."

"I'm not so brave, Carolyn. And you've survived because you, too, are strong."

"But not like you. When I heard that Lady Ann and Hannah had left us to return to England, I was so envious of them. I know that is an unchristian emotion, but I simply burned with envy. Of course, I can never go home, because like you, Molly, I have no home. My husband is an adulterer, a scoundrel, and a hypocrite, and I've lost my children forever. I can never go back there. But what, really, is my fate here? What is any of our fates?"

"What will you tell those people from Indiana if you go with them?" I asked. "And how do you know they'll take you?"

Embarrassed, she cast her eyes aside and answered in a low voice. "Because they've already said they would. I told them I have no money. They said that I could instruct their children in Bible studies in return for my passage with them. These are my people, Molly; I will never fit in here. You know that."

And I did. "You should go with them then, Carolyn. Do you know where they're headed?"

"Yes, to a small town called Bozeman, farther west in Montana Territory. They say it's beautiful country."

"And what will you do there?"

"I'll have to invent a story for myself. I've already told them my new last name."

"I hope you didn't say it was Vó'hó'k´áse."

"As a matter of fact, I did, Molly. The English translation, of course. I'm calling myself Carolyn Light. I think it's quite lovely, don't you? I'm thinking I could become a teacher, or find some kind of work in the church."

"It's a fine name, Carolyn. And it suits you perfectly. Christian will be able to pick up their trail and find them tomorrow. I'll come with you, but I'm not going to approach those people."

"Are you afraid you will be tempted to go with me?"

"Not at all. My only wish is to find my husband, Hawk. I'm going to have his child."

"Oh, Molly, you did not tell me. That's wonderful news."

"And you, Carolyn, you have not been shy about telling us how much you've enjoyed that part of your marriage. Are you certain you're not with child? It won't help you in starting your new life if you arrive in a family way and give birth to a brown baby."

"I have taken the most strenuous measures to avoid that possibility," she said, "and indeed, I have recently begun my monthly cycle."

"What will you tell your young husband, Mr. Light?"

"He is a fine, gentle boy, Molly," she said, "and I'm very fond of him. But he will get over me and take another wife . . . I must admit . . ." she added with a sly smile, "I have very much appreciated his attentions under the buffalo robes."

And we laughed.

Christian, Carolyn, and I rose early this morning. She said a tearful good-bye to our group, all of whom have forgiven her for her defection and could only wish her well. We set off in search of the wagon train of farmers from Indiana. The chaplain has become a fine tracker in his time among the Cheyenne, and he had no trouble picking up their trail. On horseback we moved faster than they, and caught up to them before noon.

We reined up on top of a hill and watched them traveling down below.

"I go no farther than this," I said. "I must say good-bye to you now, my friend."

We dismounted and embraced. "I shall miss you terribly, Molly," Carolyn said. "You will be in my thoughts and prayers every day for the rest of my life."

"And I shall miss you, Carolyn Light. Who is going to keep the calendar for me now?"

She laughed and reached into her saddlebag. "I'm so glad you mentioned that. I won't be needing this any longer," she said, handing me her calendar. "And by the way, if ever you should make your way to Bozeman . . ."

I laughed. "Yes, I will be sure to look you up. I'm sure your neighbors will be happy to see that you're entertaining a squaw."

"Thank you, Molly," she said, embracing me again, and beginning to cry. "Thank you for everything."

"You have no need to thank me, Carolyn," I said. "Travel safely. And remember that you're on the other side now, and this is still Indian country. Your newspaper tells of rogue bands who move through the territory, preying upon white travelers and settlers. Some of that is undoubtedly propaganda to inflame the citizenry and further encourage the extermination of the last free natives. But you know as well as I that some of those stories are true. It sounds as if your people are well armed, but you know, too, how stealthy the Indians are. Indeed, you have much to teach the farmers about the ways of the 'savages,' which you can pretend to have learned while working at the agencies."

"That is sound advice, Molly," she said, "and well taken. They seem a capable bunch, and I believe I will be safe in their hands."

"I wish you all good fortune in your new life, Carolyn. I'm sure it will be wonderful. You deserve as much."

I watched now as Carolyn and Christian rode down the slope toward the wagon train. She turned in her saddle several times to wave at me, and I waved back. I must confess to a small twinge of envy.

Warriors

Wind has made a pair of stone clubs for us, using rawhide straps from the hides of the deer we have killed to fix the smooth, oblong river rocks to the sturdy wood handles she carved. It is virtually impossible for me to imagine striking another human being's head with such a deadly instrument, but she says: "You will be surprised, Mesoke, at how easy it is, when that other human being is trying to kill you."

—from the lost journals of May Dodd

Mid-April . . .

Woman Who Moves against the Wind has put me to work rebuilding my largely atrophied muscles. She need not tell me that I can be neither an effective hunter nor certainly a warrior in my current weakened state. Therefore, she suggests that we build a sweat lodge. Having no access to hides or canvas for this structure, we must use the more than plentiful supply of rocks these hills provide us. This, she says, will give us the benefit of the pleasure of a good sweat at the end of our labors, in addition to a good deal of healthful exercise. We found a location for it closer to the river than our cave, and also well hidden from view so that anyone traveling down below would have no view of it.

We have been working for a number of days now, lifting, carrying, and stacking, lifting, carrying, and stacking, hard, tedious work but for the dubious art of fitting the rocks together like a kind of giant jigsaw puzzle. My entire body aches, but Wind seems utterly indefatigable. I find her strength and energy inspiring, as well as, inevitably, annoying, when I compare it to my own feebleness.

Though I am of average height and build, due to our many months of travail among the Cheyenne, I was, at least before I was shot, relatively strong for a woman, especially a white woman. I even reached the point, finally, when I believed that I was capable of working as long, hard, and fast as my native women tentmates, which goal I had set for myself, and from which, upon achieving it, I took no small pride. Then winter and the inactivity of being with child, and birthing our infants, weakened us all. Then, of course, the attack . . . and all attendant events . . .

Wind, is another species altogether. Having not yet provided here a physical description of the medicine woman, I think that might help to assuage somewhat my own sense of shame for my comparative frailty. I was often told as a child that I was overly competitive. First of all, the matter of her name . . . Previously, I knew her, and apparently her perfect replica sister, as well, only as a rather unapproachable advisor to Little Wolf, for she carries an unmistakable air of one not to be trifled with. She told me that she gained her name when she was a young girl. The People were traveling across a broad plain that offered no cover, when they were overtaken by a sudden tempest, with gales of wind of such unearthly force that people were blown off their feet. Even horses fell to their knees and flattened themselves on the ground. Travois carrying tent poles, hide coverings, sundry goods, and even small children were picked up by the maelstrom and flung into the air, sailing by overhead. The people could do nothing but cower on the ground, clutching their sons and daughters if they had succeeded in grabbing hold of them, and digging their fingers into the earth for purchase. That was when they saw two figures, a good distance downwind but walking against it back toward them. Both carried a young child under each arm, and in what seemed like an impossible feat, they moved steadily through wind, as effortlessly as knives through butter, reaching the main group finally, before taking to ground themselves, still clutching their charges. The two became known thereafter as Girl Who Moves against the Wind, a name that stuck, even after she, they, became women.

She is dark haired, very dark of skin, and has a broad, strong face, with high cheekbones and a prominent, slightly hooked nose, and the most piercing pair of eyes, the color of which I cannot well describe for they seem to change shade depending on her mood, the time of day, the weather, and the light—running the full gamut from a kind of deep yellow that brings to mind the color of the harvest moon, or perhaps the eyes of a wolf, to black as a billiard ball. She is of above-average height for a Cheyenne woman, and possesses a certain stature that makes her seem even taller. She has broad shoulders she carries proudly, strongly muscled arms that have clearly done more than their share of hard labor, and shapely, muscular legs that have just as obviously traveled many, many miles. It is impossible for me to guess her age. She is, of course, older than I, but not by any means an old woman . . . she could be anywhere from thirty to forty, perhaps even fifty years old. Her dignified bearing and calm, wise countenance perhaps makes her seem older than she really is, and lends her a certain air of permanence . . . All I do know is that she is an imposing figure, who, depending upon the situation, could either appear to offer a safe haven or be terrifying to encounter.

Let me see, for my own amusement, if I might be able to create a kind of allegorical means of describing this strong, resourceful woman . . . Imagine for a moment that you are a white man of the working class, in, say, my long-ago hometown of Chicago . . . and I think of my common-law husband, Harry Ames, as I concoct this scene . . .

You are walking down an alleyway, taking a shortcut home from the corner tavern on a dark night. You know better than to take the alleys at night, for dangers lurk there, but you stayed at the tavern for an extra few beers and are late returning to your family. You hear a noise behind you and you turn to see a pack of the city's ubiquitous feral dogs following you. Their eyes glow in the dark, they growl threateningly and bare shiny white teeth that are quite capable of tearing out your throat. Now you must consider an immediate escape route. You turn back, and suddenly this woman I describe, Woman Who Moves against the Wind, steps out of the shadows ahead of you. Now . . . your first reaction will undoubtedly be one of surprise . . . I should perhaps say fearful surprise. Is she friend or foe? Impossible to tell, but you have no time to ponder the matter, and she bears such a presence of implacable fortitude that your next reaction is one of relief. You know instinctively that this woman has the ability to save you from the pack of dogs, and so you hurry toward her. Just as you reach her, they charge, snarling and yipping viciously. You act the coward and slip behind her (yes, Harry, I am, indeed, thinking of you), but when the dogs see her they suddenly stop, casting their eyes away from the force of her gaze; they whine, tuck tails between their legs, and wheel in nervous circles until all disperse and run off. She has faced them down; she has saved you.

Yes, this is the woman to whom I unfavorably compare myself as we stack rocks upon our would-be sweat lodge, which is taking shape in a circular form, the construction of which she learned as a child on a trip to the Southwest with her mother's people, the Southern Cheyenne, who traded occasionally with the Pueblo tribes. Perhaps she is even older than I know, or find her to be, for she seems to own the strength and wisdom of the ages.

undated entry

Aha, we have completed the sweat lodge and take today our first sweat, at the beginning of which Wind blesses the structure and sprinkles a special medicine she has mixed for that express purpose upon the fire. She says it will protect us. I hurt all over, but it is true that these days of hard labor have benefited me; from my feet to my neck, I am all muscle and sinew, and stronger than ever. We sit naked inside with the plumes of steam swirling about us as Wind throws handfuls of water upon the fire-heated rocks, the sweat glistening on our skin. I can't help but admire my new physique . . . yes, I know, "vanity of vanities . . ." And I must admire and still envy hers, as well: her perfectly muscled body a rich, burnished bronze. Afterward we run down the trail to the creek and leap into the frigid water. It is magnificently invigorating.

undated entry

During the construction of the sweat lodge, Wind had continued my education in hunting and warrior tactics, but now that we have completed the task and I have gained strength, the real training begins. I am gradually becoming proficient in the use of the bow and arrow, and am sufficiently strong enough now that rather than having my arrows bounce harmlessly off the trees as they had in the beginning . . . that is, on the rare occasion that I actually hit the tree, now they stick regularly and firmly with a satisfying twang. And I have killed my first deer.

Having grown accustomed to skinning, dressing, and butchering the buffalo, deer, and elk the men killed in the hunt, I am not squeamish about blood and innards. Indeed, from my days working in a factory in Chicago that processed prairie chickens, I was already well prepared for this work. However, I must admit that the killing of a large mammal has a different effect upon me. I remember the mare I killed with my knife and whose stomach I split open in order to thrust Martha's baby son into its warm intestines during our flight from the attacking soldiers that terrible morning. But in that case, I was acting unconsciously out of life-and-death instinct, having been previously told of this method by my fellow wives.

I did not kill my first deer cleanly with the arrow, but struck him through the neck and had to track his blood trail for twenty minutes or so before he fell, still alive. I knelt beside his heaving flank, saw the terror in his wild eyes, and before I plunged the knife into his heart, I wept and told him, as I had the mare, that I was sorry. And I thanked him for his sacrifice, as I knew the People did with all the animals they killed and ate so gratefully.

We have been running to strengthen our lungs and legs, up and down the hills, in the rocks and in the river bottom. I can rarely keep up with Wind. It is one of the great talents of these people, who can run all day and night at a steady pace if they need to. When camp is made in one place for a long period of time, races are held, the warriors challenging each other, both in short and long distances. Our dear, departed Phemie, majestic in the field with her long legs and graceful stride, was the fastest runner in the tribe, undefeated by man or woman at any distance . . . Good God, how I miss my friends . . .

Wind has made a pair of stone clubs for us, using rawhide

straps cut from the hides of our game to fix the smooth, oblong river rocks to sturdy wood handles she carved. It is virtually impossible for me to imagine striking another human being's head with such a deadly instrument, but she says: "You will be surprised, Mesoke, how easy it is, when that person is trying to kill you."

Now we both have knives, bows and arrows, and clubs. "The next thing we must do is to find horses," she says. "That means we must leave here on foot, and try to find them as we travel."

"But where do we find horses, and if we do, how in the world do we catch them?" I ask.

"The catching is easy," she says. "It is the finding that is hard. If we come across a herd of wild horses, I have the lariat, with which I can catch a horse. If I catch one, I can catch a second. If we come upon a camp of our own people, or Arapaho or Lakota, and they have a good herd, it is possible that they would make us a gift of horses. We have nothing to offer in trade, except my medicine if they are in need of it. If we come upon a camp of enemies, Indian or white, we should be able to steal horses in the night. In our youth, my sister and I were among the best horse thieves in the tribe. We collected so many that we became rich. We neither of us married, but the men in the warrior societies traded hides, meats, the spoils of war, and anything else we needed to pick mounts from our string. And we gave many of the horses to those who were poor, or old, or unable to steal them for whatever reason. But there is always the risk of being caught, and then we will either be killed or taken captive.

"Now, Mesoke, we must begin to break camp. We take only what we can carry on our backs, and the rest we bury."

"Why don't we just leave what we can't carry in the cave?" I asked.

"Because someone may find it and steal what we leave. If we bury it, and ever need to come back here, we can dig it up again."

And this we have done. We have kept blankets, a supply of dried buffalo meat, the skillet, knives, clubs, and bows and arrows.

Having prepared for this day, Wind has fashioned two parfleches with straps from deer hides, so that we can carry our modest goods on our backs. In order to become accustomed to the load, we have run with these in place, as well.

I am oddly nostalgic, as well as apprehensive about leaving the safety of our cave—here, where, like a helpless infant, I was reborn, nurtured, and crawled out into the world to begin again my life, nourished and instructed by this fine Woman Who Moves against the Wind. I am ready, I feel strong. I have decided to leave in the cave, as a kind of offering, the sheet I tore out of my last ledger book before Quiet One, Feather on Head, and Pretty Walker took it away with them. Perhaps some weary traveler will seek refuge here one day, find it, and take some solace in the knowledge that another has been here before, and left this strange word for him or her to discover.

early May

We have been under way for six days, traveling on foot, keeping to the river bottoms when possible, where there is cover in case we need to hide. We try to find game trails to help ease our passage, avoiding, for obvious reasons, those that show too much sign of human traffic. Wind is an accomplished tracker and especially keeps an eye out for the prints of horse hooves, those shod belonging either to white travelers or soldiers, neither of which we are eager to run across. The horses of Indian scouts and wild horses, of course, are without shoes, though occasionally they will fit a horse with sore hooves with a kind of rawhide moccasin that leaves a different track. Sometimes we take game trails into the foothills, but we have not gone high into the Bighorns as they are still well covered with snow. The spring grass in the flatlands is just tall enough for the wild horses to graze, though we have yet to come across any.

It feels good to me to be part of the landscape again, and I am still sometimes amazed that having been city born and raised, I have adapted so thoroughly to life in the wilderness. Wind seems to have a firm idea in mind of where we are headed, and I do not question her, I simply follow. She knows this country in the intimate, instinctive way of nomads who have traveled it for too many generations to count, and whose sure sense of direction and recall for place seems bred into their blood. She is a fine traveling companion, by all appearance as liberated as I to be out of the cave, and moving again. At the same time, no matter how well prepared we may be, a sense of vulnerability haunts me, for we are, still, two women alone in this vast countryside, surrounded by enemies.

three days later

Good God, I recognize now, too late, that my last entry was a premonition . . . my sense of vulnerability has been confirmed . . . Wind and I were bathing in the creek just below our evening campsite, as we try to do first thing every morning before eating and resuming our travels. We heard horses approaching and men speaking in English. We realized that they had ridden directly into our camp. We quickly got out of the water, strapped our knives to our calves in the sheaths Wind had made for them, and I my ledger book to my back. We slipped into our leggings and moccasins and slid our hide shirts over our heads. Our parfleches and all the rest of our meager possessions—bows and arrows, clubs, lariat, blankets, iron skillet, tin cups and utensils, and my supply of ledger books, we had left in the camp. We had no way of knowing who these men were, and there was no question of going back to find out. All we could do now was to try to hide ourselves, or run. If they had a guide with them, he would easily track us no matter which we did. Using sign talk, Wind indicated that we should get back in the creek and walk or swim downstream, where we would leave no sign. We were just entering the water again when he spoke behind us.

"*Ah, mes filles, quelle belle surprise!* Hasn't Jules always said that he is the luckiest man on earth?" The voice alone chilled my heart, sent gooseflesh rippling across my skin. We turned around to face Jules Seminole standing on the bank with a rifle trained upon us.

"*Ah, oui,* not just one," he said, "but two . . . imagine . . . two of Jules' long-lost lovers returning to him together. *C'est incroyable,* it is unbelievable, no matter where Jules goes, no matter what Jules does, his women always manage to find their way back to him. For they are unable to forget the tender caress of his breath upon their breast." He pointed the rifle at me. "But you, *ma petite,* surely you must be a ghost, *non?*" He laughed. "Ah, yes, you see, even the dead come back to haunt Jules, so irresistible are his charms. They said you died of a gunshot wound in the rocks, and when Jules heard the news, he came looking for you, for Jules has always appreciated the affections of dead lovers. He searched and he searched, but Jules could not find you."

"What the hell's going on down there, Seminole?" a man's voice called. "Who you talking to?"

"Do not worry, *mon capitaine,*" Seminole called back. "I have found wonderful gifts for you and your men. I will return with them immediately. I believe you will wish to bestow a small supplementary bonus upon Jules for his excellent guiding services.

"Come out of there now, *ma petite.*" He waved the rifle barrel and spoke to Wind in Cheyenne: "And you, too, woman of the wind, for Jules must introduce you both to his distinguished colleagues. They are gentlemen, all, of that Jules can assure you, and how delighted they will be to enjoy the company of two such beautiful women."

Seminole herded us at gunpoint up to our campsite. Sitting their horses indolently were five of the most disreputable-looking white men I have ever laid eyes upon. "May Jules present to you, gentlemen," said Seminole with a flourish of his arm toward us, "*la belle* May Dodd, from Chicago, Illinois, and her *compatriote,* the personal medicine woman of the great chief Little Wolf—Woman Who Moves against the Wind.

"*Et mes filles,* please allow Jules to introduce you to the distinguished members of the Three Finger Jack gang, recently relocated to our territory from the Southwest, where they were being unfairly harassed by overly zealous officers of the law. This," he said, gesturing to the first mounted outlaw, "is the bold leader of our band, Three Finger Jack himself; to his left, Curly Bill Brody; behind him, Wild Man Charlie Beaman; to his right, Mad Dog Mac Jackman. *Et enfin,* and, finally, our holy spiritual advisor, known simply as the Deacon. You lovely ladies will come to know each of these fine gentlemen . . . *dans le sens plus intime,* in the most intimate way, that is to say, with the possible exception of the Deacon . . . due to the obvious religious prohibitions he observes."

"Seminole," said Three Finger, spitting a stream of tobacco juice to the ground, "shut the fuck up, would you please?" Slouching on the back of his horse, he appeared to be a tall, long-legged fellow. He was dressed like a ruined banker, wearing a dusty bowler hat, a filthy shirt that had once been white, buttoned high on his neck, and a dingy silk tie and vest under a ratty topcoat with small frayed lapels ringing his shirt collar. Now he touched the brim of his hat with thumb and forefinger and smiled. He clearly fancied himself as a gentleman bandit. "Howdy, ladies, so pleased to meet you both. Not often do we have the good fortune of running across a pair of charming women traveling alone, who clearly require the protection of gentlemen. And, of course, my associates and I will be grateful to enjoy the company of the fairer sex."

Gentlemen, indeed . . . now three of his associates dismounted, they, too, spitting tobacco juice through rotted teeth as they came over to us. The one called Mad Dog approached me. He was of stocky build, with short arms and legs, an enormous head, and his teeth set in an underbite, and tobacco juice dribbled from the corner of his mouth. Indeed, he looked like nothing so much as a drooling bulldog. He was no taller than I, and put his face up close to mine, spread his lips in a revolting grin, and said: "Why, you may be dressed like one, but you ain't a savage, are ya, honey? Damn, you pretty enough to eat." Then he stuck out his tongue, stained brown, and waggled it back and forth in front of my face, causing me to recoil in disgust. I thought I was going to vomit from the sight of it and the stench of his breath.

The bandit introduced as Wild Man approached Wind. He was perhaps the dirtiest of the lot, and one of the hairiest individuals I've ever laid eyes on, with a tangle of greasy hair over a low brow, thick black eyebrows, his beard crusted with tobacco juice and God knows what other filth. To say that he resembled an ape would be an insult to the simian. Standing now before Wind, he said: "This one looks like she'd bust your balls, you give her half a chance," and as if on cue, she kicked him a vicious blow between the legs. He fell to the ground, grasping his testicles and howling in agony. The others laughed as if it were the funniest thing they'd ever seen. "I guess you done gave her half a chance, Wild Man," said Three Finger.

"I'll kill you," cried Wild Man as he writhed on the ground, "I'll kill you, you *fuckin'* squaw bitch."

Seminole poked the barrel of his rifle under Wind's chin and lifted her head up with it. He spoke to her in Cheyenne, a rough translation of which would be: "Woman of the wind, Jules cannot protect you from these fine gentlemen, and neither can your medicine. But you know that if you wish to live, you must give yourself to them in every way they ask, the same way you once gave yourself to Jules . . . with love and tenderness. Yes, of course, *ma belle*, you do remember our magical time together . . . But as you can see here, I am only in their employ, and even after you submit to them, they may still kill you."

The one called Curly looked younger than the others and was dressed in cowboy attire, with chaps, high boots, and silver spurs. He had apparently been nicknamed with ironic intent, for when he took his hat off to wipe his brow with his shirt sleeve, his head was completely hairless and pink as a baby's. Now he picked up our parfleches, one after the other, opened them, and dumped the contents on the ground, toeing through them with the tip of his cowboy boot. He picked up my ledgers and tossed them in the fire. They smoldered a moment before catching flame. Then he threw in the bows and arrows, and the clubs, and kicked our little skillet, our tin cups and utensils into the dirt off the rock by the fire upon which they were perched. We had been so proud of our few modest possessions . . . they made us feel rich, and while losing them to the fire was the least of our problems, it sickened me nevertheless to watch them burn.

Curly gathered the blanket from my sleeping place and raised it to his nose. "Sweet," he said to me. "I can tell this one is yours, darlin' . . ." He looked at Wind . . . "'Cause I can smell the stench of a squaw a mile downwind." He stuffed the blanket in my parfleche and handed it to me. "I'll let you keep it," he said, as if this were an act of great generosity on his part, "and the lariat, too. That way we'll have a clean blanket tonight to snuggle up under together. And I'll have an extra rope, in case I need to tie you up."

"Don't get ahead of yourself, Curly," said Three Finger, spitting another stream of tobacco juice to the ground. "She ain't your property, son, you'll have to get in line."

"Sure, boss, I know that. And you, squaw lady," Curly said to Wind, "you can take your blanket, too. But I ain't gonna touch it." She picked the blanket up, folded it neatly, and put it in her parfleche, which she affixed to her back as I did mine.

The gang trailed a string of six additional horses, two in use as pack animals, well laden with goods, no doubt stolen. They tightened lariats around our necks and had each of us mount one of the horses. Wild Man had finally regained his feet and now swung gingerly into his saddle, groaning painfully as he tried to settle himself into a seated position. "Goddammit," he said, "I'll kill you, I'm gonna kill you sure, you goddamn fuckin' squaw bitch." He held the other end of Wind's lariat, while the one called Mad Dog was similarly charged with mine.

After all we had endured this past year, already kidnapped and violated once before by a band of rogue savages, our poor Sara murdered; the birthing of our infants; the nightmarish dawn attack on our camp, our friends and their babies killed; the running, the hiding, my wound, near death, and long recovery . . . after all this . . . I think I had never felt quite so helpless, so discouraged, so utterly bereft of hope, as I did now riding tethered at the neck behind a gang of outlaws, guided by Jules Seminole. I had no tears left to cry, could barely even summon the sense of terror I knew I should feel. All of that pain, struggle, loss, and heartbreak, only to come to this end. What was the point of it all . . . ?

We rode for several hours before stopping so that the bandits could have something to eat. They offered us nothing, planning apparently to starve us into submission. I didn't care, I had no appetite. I had already submitted, and was just waiting to be raped and beaten by one or all of them, and hopefully killed. I accepted the fact that this was to be our fate, and now I only wished to get it over with.

We rode on. I looked periodically at Wind. She held her head proudly, unbowed, and wore all day the same inscrutable expression upon her face that gave nothing away, even to me—no sense of fear, or discouragement, or even resistance. She simply looked as she always looked: calm, wise, imperturbable.

Later in the afternoon, they stopped, finally, to make their evening bivouac. They tethered our lariats to a tree while they went about the business of setting up camp. As we waited to learn what fate was to befall us, Wind whispered to me, blaming herself for our predicament. She said that when she mentioned Seminole in passing some time ago, she had conjured him up, alerting him to our presence and putting us directly in his path. I do not believe in such nonsense, or in sorcerers, and what difference did it make, in any case? The fact was, we were here, helpless captives of white men this time.

Three Finger announced that they would hold a poker game after dinner, and the winner would get to pick one of us as his private property for the first night, to do with as he wished, while the runner-up took the other. And this they would do every night, giving all a chance to share in the spoils.

"If I win the squaw," said Wild Man, "an' we get to do anything we want with 'em, like you say, Three Finger, well then I'm gonna *kill* the fuckin' bitch. My goddamn nuts are swoll up so bad, I couldn't get hard if I wanted to."

"That is one thing you can't do, Wild Man," said Three Finger. "You may whup on her some if you like, as long as you don't mark her too much. But you can't kill her or rough her up so bad you ruin her for the rest of us. You understand me?"

"Yessir . . ."

"If I win the squaw," said Curly, "I'll rent her out to one a' you boys. I cannot tolerate the stink of a savage."

"Hell, I'll take ya up on that, Curly," said Mad Dog. "She ain't so bad. Better than rough ole' five-finger Mary pulls your lil' baby weenie every night. I'll just stake her arms and legs to the ground first and put a damn gag in her mouth. That way she won't be able to touch me, kick me, or bite my balls off."

"Ah, *mais non mes amis,*" Seminole protested, "Jules can tell you from his own intimate experience that the medicine woman is a wonderful lover, sweet and tender as sweetgrass. *Bien sûr,* our brief affair of the heart occurred many years ago, when she was just a little girl. She has a twin sister, and we shared an erotic *ménage à trois,* the two of them gentle and soft as a pair of spring lambs cuddling up on either side of Jules. Jules looks forward to winning her in the poker game."

I looked now at Wind, and she revealed finally a different expression on her face, looking hard at Seminole with hatred and barely contained rage. I realized that he must have violated her and her sister when they were just children.

"Jules ain't playing poker tonight," said Three Finger, "or any other night. This game is for white men only. We ain't sharin' our valuable property with a half-breed."

"*Mais mon capitaine,*" Seminole protested, "it was Jules who found them and brought them to you. Surely he deserves to be rewarded for this gift."

"You heard the boss, Seminole," said Curly. "It's sure you've poked more lambs than you have women, and we ain't gonna risk you givin' everyone hoof and mouth disease." And they all laughed. Except for Jules Seminole.

"You would be very surprised, cowboy," he said, "*very* surprised at how many women of all ages have tasted the sweet nectar of Jules' love juices. And, you can be assured, they always return for another taste."

Now the Deacon knelt down before me. He was a tall, thin fellow, dressed in a black suit, as befits a preacher, with a hard, angular face and eyes as black and bereft of humanity as lumps of coal. "Well, well, well, missy," he said in a low, deep voice. "Aren't you just about the prettiest little thing? Our guide Seminole here tells us you were the wife of an Indian chief. That you bore his child. Is that true?"

I didn't answer, and he slapped me across the face. "What kind of disgusting harlot are you, consorting with savages, bearing their nigger half-breeds? You are a disgrace to your race, an insult to God. You will burn in hell for your sins. I would not touch you."

"Good, I am so glad to hear that."

And he slapped me again.

"You should probably wash your hand," I said, "because now you've touched me twice."

"*Whooeee,*" said Three Finger, "she's got spirit, this lady. I have to tell you boys, I am feelin' very lucky tonight. I have a strong hunch I'm going to win the honor of bedding this sweet pea. So you leave her be, Deacon. She does not belong to you, and like I said, I don't want the goods damaged. To tell you the truth, preacher man, we're all just about full up with your God talk, anyhow. You don't want her? Fine, we'll leave you out of the game."

"I never said I didn't want her," the Deacon protested. "I only said I didn't want to touch her, not in the way you godless boys are talkin' about, the way of filth and degradation of body and soul."

"You just want to beat on her, right?"

"She needs a good whuppin' to learn a lesson, to atone for her sins, and to beg forgiveness of the Lord."

"Whatever gets you off, Deacon," said Three Finger. "But we ain't dealing to the Lord in this game, so you keep your hands off her."

The men ate their dinner as the sun set, leaving us tethered to the tree, and still offering us nothing to eat. After they finished, they sat cross-legged in a circle in front of the fire, drinking whiskey sold to them by Seminole and playing hand after hand of poker, keeping track of their winnings using sticks as currency. When one of them lost all his sticks, he was out of the game and either staggered off to his bedroll or kept drinking by the fire until he passed out.

Although not invited to play, Seminole, nursing a grudge for having been excluded, was not prevented from drinking his whiskey. It recalled to me the night he had brought alcohol into our village, and got the warriors crazy drunk and they raped poor Daisy Lovelace. Little Wolf had banished him from the tribe then. Now, he staggered over to us, clutching a corked bottle, and fell to his knees before me.

"*Ah, ma chérie,*" he said, "Jules almost forgot to tell you my wonderful news. Your dear friends Martha and Jules were married in your absence. Had you not gone off like that, you would have been the maid of honor. *Ah, oui,* and such a loving couple we made."

"What are you talking about, Seminole?" I said, "Martha and her child were placed in the care of Captain Bourke."

"*Ah, non . . . non, non, non, non . . .* You see, she could not stay away from the embrace of her beloved. She was being sent back to Chicago, but she got off the train and came in search of Jules, and he found her. We were so happy together. Alas, she has been stolen away . . .*"

"You're insane. Leave me alone."

Dragging his bottle in one hand along the ground, Seminole crawled on all fours over to Wind: "Ah, *ma petite fille*," he said, "my darling little girl, such beautiful memories Jules has of you and your sister, my little kittens."

The rage had again descended upon Wind's face. The Cheyenne spoken language can be lovely in a certain intonation, but it can also be chillingly harsh. "One day," she hissed, "one day I promise you, Jules Seminole, I will cut your heart out and feed it to the camp dogs. I have seen it in a vision, and so will it be."

Seminole managed to stand again and began to stagger back to the fire. "Jules' wife was stolen from him, kidnapped," he mumbled. "But our love is too strong to keep us apart, *oui*, it will lead us back to each other. It always does." He collapsed again behind the poker players.

"Mesoke," Wind whispered to me. "You still have your knife strapped to your leg, do you not?"

Indeed, the outlaws had not yet discovered our knives beneath our deer hide leggings. "Yes, I do, Wind. I was thinking that while they're drunk and distracted, we could cut ourselves free and sneak away."

"No, the man Three Finger is not drunk like the others," she said. "We would be caught again if we tried to run. Listen to me, and do exactly what I tell you. We wait until the last two men have finished the game, and come to us. We let them untie our ropes and lead us to their sleeping places. They will take us outside the light of the fire ring, so that the others do not watch them with us. And you and I will be apart. Go quietly with yours. Do not fight, do not struggle against him. Tell him he can do what he wants with you. Tell him you want him."

"But I do not want him, Wind," I said, repulsed by the idea. "I do not want any of these wretches to touch me. I've had enough now of this life and I would rather die than be violated again."

"Listen to me, Mesoke," she commanded. "Three Finger is going to win you, and you must pretend that you like him. When he takes his pants off and lies beside you, you touch him there. Do you understand me?"

"Oh, good God . . . yes . . . I think I do."

"You touch him there the way a woman touches a man she loves. He will make noises of pleasure. Keep touching him until he spills his seed, and when he does, you kill him the way I showed you. Can you do this, Mesoke?"

"Yes . . . yes, I think I can. But what if he tries to mount me before he spills his seed? I will not let him enter me."

"You kill him in the same way."

"And then?"

"Do not move after you kill him, unless you must to free yourself. If any of the others wake, they will try to kill us, or worse. We wait until all is quiet and we are certain they are asleep. I will come to you. Watch for me. We will go to the horses. I will steady them so they do not give us away. Pick up your parfleche beside the log where they laid the bridles. Put it on your back. Then very carefully pick up a bridle, taking the bit in your hand so it does not rattle, and warm it. Go to the horse you rode today, he knows you. Put the bridle on him, and untie his lead rope from the picket line. Tie the end of the lead rope to the halter so it does not drag on the ground. Then begin to untie the leads of the other horses, as I will, and tie the ends to their halters. They will be getting restless now. We mount quickly, I will give the signal, and we ride. The other horses will bolt, most will follow us. Some of the men will wake but they will still be too drunk and too slow to rise to catch horses, and to catch us. Do you understand me, Mesoke?"

"Yes, I do, Wind. I understand you perfectly."

And so we waited for the end of the long poker game. It is cold still at night this time of year, and we were tied well beyond the warmth of the fire, nor had they given us our blankets. The last two men left in the game finally finished, and approached us. Wind was right, Three Finger knelt beside me and held his mutilated hand up to my face.

"My darling, I know they are not real pretty to look at," he said, wiggling the three remaining fingers, "but when these little piggies crawl into your secret places, they will give you all the pleasure you ever dreamed of." He untied my rope from the tree. "You look cold, sweetheart, but we will soon take care of that."

Wind was won by Mad Dog, the one who had said he would gag her and stake her to the ground. He yanked her roughly to her feet. "Do what I told you, Mesoke," she said in Cheyenne, as he began to lead her drunkenly back to his bedroll. He was a full head shorter than she, and she put her arm around him to support him. "No need to be rough with me, sir," she said in English. "I will take very good care of you under the buffalo robes, and you may do with me whatever you wish."

"*Thata* girl," he answered. "That's what we like to hear. Didn't I tell 'em you ain't so bad? Come on, my squaw lady, you may stink like a savage, but I'm so goddamn drunk I don't give a damn, you and me got a night a' love ahead of us."

I did as Wind had told me, and as Three Finger was leading me to his sleeping place, I told him that I had been hoping he would win the game, that I found him very attractive, and that I would not resist his advances. "I want to make you happy under the blankets, Jack," I said. "So that we can travel together as a couple."

"I was thinkin' just the same thing, May," he said. "Hell, this is my gang and I ain't gonna share you with those bums. I used to play cards for a livin', and I cheated them so I'd win you." At his place, Three Finger removed his topcoat, vest, and necktie, folded them fastidiously, and placed them on the ground. He then took off his bowler hat and set it gently upon the clothing. Finally, he sat down and pulled off his boots.

"It is too cold for us to undress here," I said. "Let's get under the blanket, and I'll take your shirt off there. I want to touch you, Jack, I want to get to know your body."

"Oh, yeah, darlin'," he said huskily as we covered ourselves. "Yeah, my darlin', this is just how I imagined it would be. Three Finger Jack don't need to take a girl by force."

"I know, Jack, you are far too much of a gentleman for that."

And so we lay beside each other under a thick Hudson Bay blanket. I unbuttoned his shirt as he fumbled clumsily beneath my buckskin shirt, trying to get at my breasts, which he finally managed to do, his fingers, indeed crawling across them. I unbuttoned his suspenders. "Pull your trousers down, Jack," I said, a little breathlessly, as though I were aroused. "I can't manage it alone, and I want to touch you there now, I want to make you happy."

"*Oh yeah*, my darling," he said. "*Yeah*, let me do that." Though not as drunk as the others, he had been drinking, and he struggled with his pants, finally managing to pull them down over his knees but not bothering to free his legs. As he did so, I drew my knife from the sheath and placed it on the ground beside me.

"Now you lie back, Jack," I whispered to him, "you lie back and let me take care of you. First I'll touch you, and then I'll take you in my mouth if you want."

"*Oh, yeah, darlin', yeah, darlin',*" he kept repeating. It happened much faster than I thought it would, for just as I had unbuttoned the fly of his long johns and fished his erect member out, he convulsed with a moan, spraying his revolting discharge, his hips bucking beneath the blanket. "*Oh yeah, darlin',*" he said, "*that's good, yeah, that's so goddamn good.*"

I picked up my knife and drew it across his throat in one motion and with all the pressure I could summon, just as Wind taught me to do. A gust of whiskey-scented air escaped his severed windpipe, and a faint gurgling noise issued from his mouth as the blood flooded from his throat, his eyes in the moonlight wide in terror. "It was good for me too, Jack," I whispered, as his eyes went dead.

I had never killed anyone before, and I always imagined that if ever I was forced to under any circumstances, I would feel terrible remorse and guilt. But I did not. I felt only a great sense of vindication, righteousness, liberty . . . and power. Only later did it occur to me how much the violence I have witnessed and experienced in my time here has changed me . . . and perhaps it was in this moment when I became a true savage.

I looked up then to see Wind, already standing in the shadows behind me. She motioned me to come to her. I wiped my hands and both sides of the knife blade on the blanket and slipped from beneath it. We made a wide berth outside the perimeter of the camp to reach the picket line of horses on the far side. This, I knew, was the most dangerous moment, for if one or more of them snorted or whinnied in alarm, everyone who lives on the plains, Indian and white alike, awake or asleep, is attuned to this disturbance that warns of potential intruders. But as she said she would, murmuring almost inaudibly in Cheyenne, Wind somehow steadied the horses, who simply raised their heads in curiosity. The bridles were all draped in a row over a fallen tree next to the picket line, our parfleches lying on the ground beside them. These we fixed upon our backs. Very carefully I picked up a bridle, grasping the bit in my hand. I went to my horse, slipped an arm around his neck, and with the other hand gently stroked his face. He blew just the slightest exhalation of content from his nostrils. I slid the bridle over his head, pressing the bit gently into his mouth. I untied his lead rope, then looped it and tied it to the top of the halter. Wind and I both quickly untied the lead ropes of the other horses from the picket line and tied them as I had mine. We mounted our horses and reined them in the direction of our escape. Now from a pocketlike pouch on the side of her deer hide shirt, Wind pulled a bloody object I could not identify. She looked at me, smiled, and nodded, raising the dripping object in the air, shaking it fiercely, and then issued the most savage, the most enraged, the most bloodcurdling, the most triumphant war cry I have ever in my life heard . . . and I have heard a few.

My horse and all the others bolted at her cry. I almost lost my seat but for the fact that I grew up in the rarefied milieu of monied Chicagoans, riding thoroughbred jumpers from the time I was a little girl, and have since vastly broadened my equestrian experience riding bareback the wild ponies of the plains. And so I managed to hang on. We broke free of the trees in the river bottom and crested a hill into the open country, listening to the hollering of our now awakened but still drunken captors fading into the distance. As we galloped across the plains, we watched the nine other horses, spread out under the light of a half moon, running with us, as if they, too, were escaping their captors.

As dawn was breaking, and after finally putting sufficient distance between us and the outlaw camp, we slowed to a walk to rest our horses and then stopped to let them drink at a water hole. It was then that the other nine reappeared, perhaps having smelled the water, nickering to our two in greeting as they arrived. While the horses were watering, I asked Wind what exactly it was that she had raised up to the sky. It was light enough now that I saw the dark bloodstains on the front of her shirt, and the blood of my deceased captor on my own and dried on my hands. We dismounted to rinse our faces, also bloodied, and our hands.

She pulled the object, I should say the organ, out of her pocket. "It is the heart of the man called Mad Dog," she answered. "He cannot go to Seano without it. I wished also to take the heart of Jules Seminole, but he was asleep by the fire in the middle of the camp and I was afraid I would wake the others."

sometime in May

During our escape from the nest of bandits guided by Jules Seminole, though Wind and I recovered our parfleches, all that was left in them was our blankets. Still, we are accustomed to this spartan existence, and not counting our knives and the two lariats we took from the bandits' saddles at the picket line, we do have one valuable asset: a herd of eleven horses.

It is the purview of medicine men and women to take credit for extraordinary occurrences, and though she never boasts of such things, I can safely say from our experience that Wind has big medicine in matters equine, among additional talents. For what other explanation can there be for the fact that all the horses, free from the picket line, followed us as we fled? I came to understand that somehow, as we were riding yesterday with the bandits, Wind had identified the dominant horse in the herd, and that was the one she expressly chose to ride for our escape, with the hope that at least some of the others would follow the leader. They had all fanned out in the plains as we galloped, and I was not confident we would ever see any of them again. Perhaps they might even return to the bandits' camp. For my part, I felt lucky just to have the two we rode. Now it is reassuring to know that our captors have not a single horse between them, and a long way to walk in all directions.

One thing is clear, we need somehow to resupply. Our requirements are modest, and we can cook meat by impaling it on sticks, and eat with our fingers, which all Indians and all of us white women are long accustomed to doing. Still, we need something with which to hunt besides our knives, at least a bow and arrow, though as we travel these past days, we have managed to kill a few prairie chickens and rabbits with rocks, and scoop fish from the streams with our hands, securing enough sustenance to at least keep us alive.

I have devised a bolder and more profitable plan for us, a rather entrepreneurial idea. Whereas we have previously given wide berth to settlements and homesteads, now we seek them out. We risk traveling along the foothills of the Bighorns, to within a dozen miles of Fort Fetterman, in northern Wyoming Territory, where a large garrison of soldiers is stationed and which serves as headquarters for General George Crook. My friend Gertie had warned us that it was from Fetterman that Crook's forces would launch the winter campaigns that destroyed our village, and which were designed to finally break the resistance of the last free bands. It occurs to me that Crook's aide-de-camp, my former paramour and the father of my daughter, Little Bird, Captain John G. Bourke, may well be in residence here.

To get the lay of the land, Wind and I have been moving through the area as surreptitiously as possible, as only Indians can. She has known this country since she was a girl, long before anything was here, but much has changed in recent years. There is now a small settlement of homesteaders and ranchers in proximity to the fort, whose needs are serviced by a fledgling town, still mostly a collection of tents, with a handful of new buildings, and others under construction.

The first homestead we come upon is a small ranch/farm operation, with a modest clapboard house, the hand-hewn lumber still fresh and unpainted. Across from the house is a lean-to shed beside a corral holding a horse and a dairy cow. Next to that is a pen with two pigs, and a litter of piglets. Behind the house is a fenced pasture with a small herd of cattle. We have been watching the place now from the hills above for a full day and a half, to get a sense of the owners and their movements. They are a young couple, without children, and the man carries a Winchester rifle wherever he goes, setting it down within reach while doing his chores. The woman works in the garden, tends the chickens and pigs and hauls water from a spring creek that runs through the property.

This afternoon, Wind stayed back at our vantage point, while I rode in, trailing another horse by its lead. As soon as he spotted me, the man picked up his rifle, cocked it, and held it across his chest.

"Stop right there," he called to me, holding up his hand in the universal sign.

I did so.

"Who are you and what do you want?" he asked.

"I'm a white woman," I called back, "even if I don't look like one. I'm unarmed and I just want to talk to you."

"Alright. Come in . . . real slow . . . and watch your hands."

I held up my empty hands. His wife now came out of the house and watched me from the porch. I rode up to him and dismounted.

He looked me up and down, with curiosity. "If you're a white woman, why are you dressed like a savage?"

I followed the man's eyes to look down at my own attire. My hide shift, leggings, and moccasins are stained and torn in places, though Wind has soaked most of the blood off them and mended them where possible. I could only imagine how I must appear to these people.

"I've been a captive," I said, "but I was released. Yours is the first house I've come upon. I want to trade you for this horse."

"What tribe took you?"

"Pawnee," I lied, giving him the name of one of our enemy tribes.

"The savages with the strange haircuts, right?"

"That's right."

"How long were you with them?"

"I've lost track of time . . . about two years, I think."

"Did they . . . ?" He cast his eyes away and scuffed the toe of his boot in the dirt. "Did they . . . ?"

"No, they didn't do anything like that. They treated me well, and they let me go."

"Why don't you go into Fort Fetterman," he said. "It ain't far from here, and I'm sure the Army can help you."

"I plan to do just that," I said. "But first I want to see if we can make a trade for this horse."

"We might be able to use him. Is he broke to saddle?"

"Broke to saddle and pack."

"He ever work cattle?"

"Not that I know of. But he's biddable, and he neck reins. I see no reason he couldn't learn to work cattle."

"What do you want for him?"

I looked now at the woman. "I want to take a bath, and I need a dress, undergarments, a pair of shoes and stockings, a hairbrush or a comb." I looked back at the man. "And one hundred dollars cash."

"That's awful high," he said.

"I don't know what the market is for horses these days," I answered, "but I do know that a few years back, a good saddle horse was worth $200. This one is sound, he's still young, he's gentle, and he's well shod. Go ahead and look him over." I looked again at the woman. "I'm not asking for your best dress or your finest pair of shoes. Anything will do—a pair of work clothes. I just want to be able to go into a town without getting jeered at, beaten, or killed for being a white squaw." I cut my eyes back to the man. "I'm asking a fair price."

Now his wife smiled. "Will you join us for supper, miss," she said, "after you've had your bath and are dressed in your new clothes?"

"Yes, thank you, that's very kind of you. I would be delighted."

Her name was Sarah, and she heated water on their cookstove and let me bathe in a tin tub with real soap. I unwound my braids and washed my hair. God, it was heavenly. She gave me a simple faded red-and-white-checked gingham dress, an undergarment, a pair of long cotton stockings that had been darned in a number of places but were soft and warm, and a well-worn pair of canvas shoes with thankfully short heels. Accustomed as I am to flat moccasins, the shoes were still a challenge, and I teetered clumsily when I took my first few steps.

Sarah was apologetic, even embarrassed about her offering, but I assured her that to me it was all quite elegant and luxurious. I brushed my hair, and she pinned it up. Then she held a mirror up in front of me. "Have a look, May," she said, "and see how lovely you are." Nearly all lodges in our village owned trade mirrors, but it had been a long time since I had looked in one. Now I felt like I was gazing at a perfect stranger. "Who is that woman?" I asked, under my breath. "I don't recognize her." Indeed, I realized in that moment that I am, and will always be, two different people, and that I need to reacquaint myself with this stranger staring back in the mirror, who did not appear to recognize me either.

It had been even longer since I had sat for dinner at an actual table . . . not since Fort Laramie, when I dined with Captain John Bourke . . . another lifetime ago . . . Good God, it seems an eternity gone by . . . How suddenly and profoundly our lives change . . .

nothing ever returning to the way it was, only going forward to the way it will be . . . and often, as hard as we try, we have little control over the destination.

I had to consciously watch my manners at table, avoid picking up the pieces of stew meat with my fingers and then licking them clean. It occurred to me that I am no longer really suitable company among civilized folk. The gentleman's name was Wendell Peterson, and he and his wife, Sarah, had traveled here to homestead from Missouri less than six months ago. They asked many questions about my time among the savages, and, as I had reflexively when he was trying to suss out a polite way to ask if I had been violated . . . a question, to be sure, which there is no polite way of asking . . . I found myself defending the comportment of our enemies the Pawnee. All savages are the same to the whites, who make little effort to differentiate between the tribes. The only good Injun, goes the old trope Gertie had told us, is a dead Injun. And, therefore, in order to avoid reinforcing my hosts' prejudices, I made my invented captors sound like perfect ladies and gentlemen within their own culture. I secretly sensed that Mr. Peterson was disappointed that my account was not more lurid, and I spared them the tale of my encounter with the white outlaws.

"Have you had any contact with Indians since your time here?" I asked.

"We see the hangs-around-the-fort Indians when we go into the mercantile in town," he answered. "A sorry lot of beggars and drunks they are, but not threatening. With the fort so close by, the dangerous renegades stay away from here." (To which I felt like saying, *That's what you think,* but, of course, I did not.) "The Army patrols the region regularly, and we have been assured that the savages have been largely subdued, and most of them confined to reservations. But they tell us to remain vigilant, and always armed. That's why I keep my rifle handy."

I recognized that these were fine people, just trying to survive, to make a life for themselves, as are we all. It did not concern them, or even really occur to them, that this land the government had parceled into 160-acre homesteads and was giving away to settlers like them, or selling cheap in larger tracts to more affluent ranchers, had, for a thousand years, been the home of these native peoples, the last of whom were now being hunted down, slaughtered, or confined to reservations, so that the colonizers could take over the earth.

The Petersons paid my asking price for the horse and offered me a place to sleep for the night, which I declined . . . a bit reluctantly even. I have to admit that my first foray back into the civilized world was seductive: a bath with warm water, clean hair, wearing a simple gingham dress freshly washed, and eating dinner at a farm table with people who spoke my native tongue . . . plus I now had $100 in my pocket.

I wrapped my hide clothing up and tied it around my neck. Mounting my horse thusly attired proved to be problematic, and riding sidesaddle without a saddle was equally improbable. I finally had to hike my dress up to my waist and swing onto my horse's back, which made Sarah giggle, and had already caused her husband, Wendell, to turn his back to me out of a sense of Christian decorum. I touched my heels to the horse's flanks and went from a walk to a brisk trot out of their ranch yard, heeled him again, and broke into a lope. Without turning to look back at them, I raised my arm in good-bye and gave out my best Indian war cry, a chilling sound even to my ears, just to remind them, and myself, that despite my new outfit and my pocketful of money, I was still not fully civilized.

Wind looked at me with some amusement when I returned. "I wondered if you were going to return, Mesoke," she said.

"You know that I would never leave you, Wind."

"You look just like a white woman."

I laughed. "Sometimes we forget that I *am* a white woman. But

I must get out of these clothes now. I'll save them for tomorrow when we go to town."

"When *you* go to town," Wind corrected me. "I must stay here with the horses. And besides, I am afraid to go there. I have bad dreams about being in the iron jail."

the next day sometime in late May

Early this morning, in addition to my mount, I leave our camp with three more horses, two of which I hope to use in trade, and the other to carry back whatever goods I might be able to secure. Wind and I have decided that the first thing I should try to find are good saddles, and then I hope to acquire a rifle, both for hunting and to defend ourselves, and to purchase more suitable white-woman riding attire.

It occurred to me that it would be awkward and arouse unwanted attention for me to ride into a white settlement bareback with my dress hiked up to my waist. Thus, as soon as I caught sight of the town, I dismounted and walked in leading the horses. I still hadn't shaken the sense that I was an outsider and no longer dressed in animal skins, and I had to keep reminding myself of my new role as a respectable white woman. I was relieved to see that there were enough people about that no one paid me much attention. Due to its proximity to the fort, a number of what appeared to be officers' wives were in town shopping, as well soldiers with wagons picking up supplies.

I went first to the stables, which were easy to find, and tied my horses to a hitching rail in front. A sign read: P. J. BARTLETT & SONS. There was a riding ring beside the stable, and a corral behind it. Inside the stable, two boys were mucking out stalls. I asked them if the stablemaster was available, and they directed me to the office in the middle of the hallway of stalls.

When I reached it, I saw that the office also doubled as a tack room. A man was working at the desk in front, and he stood when I appeared in the open doorway. He was a tall, stout, middle-aged fellow, balding and with an impressive handlebar mustache. "What can I do for you, young lady?" he asked.

"Are you Mr. Bartlett?"

"I am," he said, coming around the desk. "Please, come in. And to whom do I have the pleasure of speaking?"

"My name is Abigail Ames," I said, taking my ex-common-law-husband's family name as an alias. "I have two horses for sale. I wondered if you might be interested in buying, or know someone in town who would be. I'd also like to buy a pair of saddles, if you can direct me to a saddlery shop."

"Yes, ma'am, I can sure do that," he said. "I own the saddlery, and it's right around the corner. But we sell used tack here, too, in case that's of interest to you. Got a good selection of it, as you can see. As to the horses, I'd be happy to have a look at them. They outside?"

"Yes, sir, they're tied up to your hitching rail."

"Let's do that first."

We went outside and P. J. Bartlett looked over the horses, all three of them geldings, one a bay, the other a buckskin, the third a paint. "Buyer's pick of two out of the three," I said. "My horse with the bridle is not included. And the third that you don't take, I need to pack some goods with. You'll find that they are all sound."

He opened the horses' mouths to check teeth and gums, picked up hooves, ran his hand down their flanks. "Where did these horses come from, Mrs. Ames?" he asked.

"My husband and I bought them off a trader in Grand Island, Nebraska."

"And why are you selling them?"

"It's our business, that's what we do, we buy and sell horses. We have a good string right now, and it's time to divest ourselves of a few. All three of these are broke to saddle and pack, they have soft mouths, and they've been trained to neck rein. Of course, you're welcome to ride all of them, or your boys can."

"Why isn't your husband here to make the sale, if I may ask?"

"He broke his leg. He's laid up for a while. But I'm quite capable of making the deal myself, Mr. Bartlett."

He looked now at the horse I ride. "Where's your saddle?"

"Stolen, both our saddles. That's why I need to buy new ones."

"By Injuns, I'll wager . . . thievin' bastards . . . pardon my language . . . surprised they didn't get your horses."

"You'd lose that wager, sir," I said. "They were stolen at gunpoint by a gang of outlaws, not Indians. They took some of our horses, too. You ask a lot of questions, Mr. Bartlett. Are you interested in buying, or not?"

He looked at me with a wry smile. "Yes, ma'am, I can see that you are quite capable of making the deal."

He called the two boys out and introduced them as his sons— Clive, the elder, roughly fourteen years old; and Cooper, the younger, perhaps twelve. He told them to fetch three saddles and bridles. When all the horses were saddled, they mounted and rode around the ring, putting them through their paces, then switching so that each of them rode all three. I already knew what these horses could do, for Wind has been working with all of them, fine-tuning those that required it. While some are, by nature, wilder, more skittish, or less biddable than others, she is a master at smoothing out their faults and refining their skills.

Before dismounting, P. J. Bartlett and Sons gathered in the middle of the ring to compare impressions. The father kept a good poker face when he rode over to me at the railing and dismounted, giving nothing away. "We'll let the boys take care of the horses," he said. "Why don't you and I go back to the office, look at some tack, and see if we can't come to terms."

I sold the two horses to P. J. Bartlett, and he wanted to buy the third as well, but I repeated that I needed it to carry the supplies I hoped to purchase at the mercantile, and the tack I was buying from him. This included two used McClellan saddles of the same style used by the cavalry, both with saddle blankets, saddlebags, rifle scabbards, two additional lariats, and a pair of used canvas pack panniers in which to load my goods. I told him that we had lost our currycomb on the trail, and he gave me one at no charge. After a good deal of haggling, the price of all these items was deducted from the purchase price of the horses, and I still walked away with just over four hundred dollars in cash. I didn't mind a bit that the tack wasn't new, for it was all in good condition and well cared for, the used saddles broken in and more comfortable for both rider and horse than new ones, and the leather on the other items equally softened and pliable with a little age and saddle soap. In addition to costing a good deal more, I knew that had I purchased all new tack, Wind and I would look like greenhorns, or more likely be taken for thieves.

"You mentioned that you and your husband have a good string," Bartlett said, after we had closed our deal. "I might be interested in buying a few more horses from you. How many head do you have left?" He was being casual about it, careful not to be overly eager, but I could tell he was impressed with our horses.

"After this sale, we have four left to sell, not counting our two mounts and the two we pack, but I think we'll hang on to all of them for now."

"I can see why your husband lets you make the deals, Mrs. Ames. You drive a hard bargain, but you won't get a better price from anyone else around here. When people want to buy and sell horses, including the stock buyers at the fort, they come to P. J. Bartlett and Sons."

"It's not that my husband *lets* me make the deals, sir," I said. "We're full partners and he trusts me to do it. I don't have to ask permission." I have never been a shrinking violet and have often been accused of being headstrong, which quality, indeed, landed me in the lunatic asylum at the hands of my father. My time living with the Cheyenne, and fending now for myself with Wind in this treacherous country, has further emboldened me, and the bloody act of killing the outlaw Three Finger Jack made me even less tolerant of being treated like a girl. And so here I find myself defining and defending my relationship with my nonexistent husband.

P. J. Bartlett smiled wryly at me, again. "My apologies, Mrs. Ames," he said, nodding. "I didn't mean to imply anything. I can see that you are more than capable. Your husband is a lucky man to have you as a partner."

I liked P. J.; he was fair and honest, and not afraid to treat a woman as an equal. "We might be willing to sell you a few more of our string, Mr. Bartlett."

"Where are you quartered?" he asked. "With your husband laid up, I could come out and have a look at them myself."

"We have no fixed location right now. But we have a Cheyenne woman with us who is a gifted horse trainer. She and I might be able to bring the horses to you. However, she is afraid to come into a white-man town. And who can blame her? You would have to provide some assurance that she would be protected from harm."

Before I made any commitment, I needed to speak to Wind, and to consider the risk of making another trip to town. I left my purchased tack and the horses at the stables and walked the short distance to the mercantile to try to buy suitable riding attire. It goes without saying that they had no breeches or any other style of trousers for women, nor did I even bother asking. Indeed, in Chicago it has long been against the law for women to wear trousers in public. Instead I asked the owner if they sold riding pants for small men that might fit me, and he showed me a pair of blue denim trousers that he said ranchers wore, and which I bought in the smallest size he had in stock. I also purchased a pair of leather chaps that were not unlike our Cheyenne leggings, a pair of riding boots sized for boys that fit me well enough, a pair of socks, a boy's canvas shirt, a fringed leather frontiersman jacket, and a wide-brimmed felt hat of a style worn by cowboys on the prairie, with a stampede string— that is to say, a string that secures the hat under the chin so as not to be lost to the wind or at a gallop. I also purchased sewing needles and thread, so that I might be able to alter my clothing to fit, or patch them when necessary. I may be dressing like a white man in the days to come, but I am still vain enough to wish to appear with a modicum of feminine style. And in that same spirit, I purchased a mirror.

In the way of supplies for Wind and me, I bought a tin coffeepot and two cups, two tin plates, utensils, an iron skillet and a Dutch oven, a sack of sugar, one of flour, a bag of salt, and the all-important bag of coffee. Of course, the Cheyenne themselves had traded for such items for decades, but it felt strange to me stepping back into the world of white commerce, and having money in my pockets with which to pay for it. I also bought a small canvas tent to facilitate our evening bivouacs. Finally, I purchased two second-hand 1873 Winchester carbines with a box of cartridges for each. These rifles are light and short-barreled, making them easier for Wind and me to handle on horseback.

Now, from beneath the counter, the proprietor withdrew a wooden box, which he set before me, opening it and turning it around for me to view the contents. "As long as you're buying arms, madam," he said, "perhaps you might be interested in this for personal protection. It is the new Remington Model 1875 Single Action Army revolver. It just came out last year. The fort placed a large order with me, and I had a few left over. This is my last one." And that was my last purchase. I felt as though Wind and I would be well stocked for some time.

I paid for all the items and asked the owner of the mercantile if I could go into his back room to change my clothes, as I would be riding this afternoon. I told him that I would like to leave all my other purchases here, and return later with my horses and panniers to pick everything up. He was an agreeable fellow, grateful for my purchase, and said that he would see that everything was put aside and ready for me upon my return.

In the back room, I dressed in my new clothes, folded my dress, and carried it and my canvas shoes back into the store; I saw that two soldiers had entered and stood at the counter, speaking to the proprietor. They turned at my entrance. I had my hair pinned up and was wearing my broadbrimmed hat, beneath the rim of which

I looked directly into the dark, deep-set eyes of Captain John G. Bourke. I quickly averted my gaze and strode directly out the front door, uncertain as to whether he had recognized me. There was no reason he could expect me to still be alive, and dressed as I was, with only that short glance between us, he may not have made the connection.

I returned to the stables. My two horses were tied again to the hitching rail. The boys had saddled mine, fixed the panniers on the other, and loaded them with the rest of my tack. I went directly to the office.

"I have a small problem, Mr. Bartlett, and I wonder if you and the boys might be able to do me a small favor?"

"We are at your disposal, Mrs. Ames. What can we do for you?"

"I purchased a number of goods at the mercantile, and I told the proprietor that I would return shortly to pick them up. I've paid my bill in full. I'd like you to ask one of your boys to lead my pack horse over there, load the goods in the panniers, and return here with them. I would be happy to pay him for his time."

"That is easily enough arranged, Mrs. Ames," he said, "I'll send the boys together, and no further payment is necessary. Of course, they know the proprietor, Henry Bacon, quite well, and he will certainly release your goods to them. And while they are on this mission, perhaps you and I can conclude our conversation about your other horses."

"I was thinking similarly, sir," I said, "which is why I hoped the boys could run that errand for me."

Upon their return, I asked the boys, as casually as possible, if anyone else had been in the mercantile when they picked up my goods.

"No, ma'am," said Clive. "Only Mr. Bacon. He was real curious to know who you were."

"And how did you answer?"

"We said you were a horse trader, ma'am, and that's all we knew. Weren't we supposed to?"

"No, that's fine, of course, thank you, boys," I said, relieved. Had he recognized me, Bourke would have surely questioned Mr. Bacon and waited at the store for my return, or come looking for me. Although, as the captain was presumably there on Army business, perhaps he did not have the time to do either. Regardless, I was anxious to be on my way, and in short order I mounted and said my good-byes. Only after I had left Tent City behind and entered the foothills did I finally relax. And then, although it would have caused me nothing but trouble, I felt a sudden absurd pang of regret, even a faint, distant longing that Bourke had not recognized me . . . and come looking for me.

THE LOST JOURNALS OF MOLLY McGILL

Reunions

Today, as we traveled across the prairie, I heard the distinctive cry of a hawk overhead and looked up to see it circling high in the air. I know that cry, I know that pattern of flight. I scanned the horizon and saw a lone horseman in the distance, dragging a travois. Without another thought, or a word to my friends, I turned Spring, touched my heels to her flanks, and galloped toward him.

"Be careful, Molly!" Christian called after me. "You have no idea who that is!"

"Of course I do!" I called back.

—from the lost journals of Molly McGill

5 August 1876 .

Having filled with the tiniest handwriting I could muster all the remaining space left to me in Meggie and Lady Ann's ledger book, I confess to having put my pencils to work on the mostly empty pages of soldier Josh Miller's diary, the only source of paper available to me. What shame I still feel, and always will, for having essentially robbed the boy's corpse . . . or at least that of his horse, thereby denying his mother the chance to read her son's last words.

We continue to collect strays—several more families, and a few small bands of young warriors—mostly those who sneaked away from one or another of the agencies to participate in the grand coming-together of tribes on the Little Bighorn and have decided to enjoy their freedom a while longer, as well as the last chance to hunt the fast-diminishing herds of buffalo. Better that than becoming wolves for the blue soldiers, hunting down their own people. And so we welcome them to join us. This is the last trace of the only world they have known and been prepared for in their short lives, the only world a hundred generations before them has known. As winter comes on, they will return to their families at the agencies, where they will barely subsist through the cold season on the starvation rations of food and supplies the government provides them, after the agents in charge of distributing them have stolen their share. This is the new world the white man is making and which they must enter, for all feel the door to their own world closing behind them. As do we, who having already lost one world seem about to lose another. We continue to flee toward an unknown destination, blindly following a blind woman.

Today, as we traveled across the prairie, I heard the distinctive cry of a hawk overhead and looked up to see it circling high in the air. I know that cry, I know that pattern of flight. I scanned the horizon and saw a lone horseman in the distance, dragging a travois. Without another thought, or a word to my friends, I turned Spring, touched my heels to her flanks, and galloped toward him.

"Be careful, Molly!" Christian called after me. "You have no idea who that is!"

"Of course I do!" I called back.

I could not yet make out his face as I approached, but I could see that he wore a single feather in his headband, as is his way. Hawk has always eschewed the sartorial trappings of other warriors before they go off to battle—the elaborately beaded shirts, the painted faces and decorated braids, the bone chokers and sundry totems they attach to themselves and their horses, and the majestic headdresses whose feathers trail nearly to the ground. The warriors believe in looking both magnificent and fierce when they go to war, both to impress and to strike fear in the hearts of their enemies, as well as to protect themselves from harm . . . and, just in case their medicine fails them and they are killed in the fight, so that they will enter Seano in all their full splendor. Hawk, on the other hand, whether it be in war or in peace, always wears simple, unadorned deer-hide shirts, leggings, and moccasins, his hair unbraided and with a single red-tailed hawk feather in his headband, to honor his spirit animal.

As I drew closer, I saw that the travois Hawk's horse pulled bore his grandmother, Bear Doctor Woman. I reined up sharply before them, leapt from Spring's back, and ran to him as he, too, dismounted. We looked in each other's eyes, my entire body flooded with love, with joy, with passion. We embraced tightly, kissed deeply, and held on for a long time, as if afraid to let go for fear of losing each other again.

"I wondered if I would ever see you again," I whispered in his ear.

"And I you. Pretty Nose told me the soldiers had taken you away."

"They did, but I have come back. And now you are home."

I went to greet Bear Doctor Woman on the travois. Her eyes were closed and I leaned down and whispered to her. She opened them and looked up at me blankly for a moment, as if she didn't recognize me. But then she smiled, and whispered one of the names by which the Cheyenne call me, Heóvá'é'ke, Yellow Hair Woman, the same Indian name as Hawk's mother, the little white girl Bear Doctor Woman had raised from a young age after the child was kidnapped from her family.

"Heóvá'é'ke, it makes my heart glad to see that you have returned to us," she said in Cheyenne. "I am dying and Little Hawk needs you." I wondered if perhaps the old woman did not think I was his mother, her daughter, rather than his wife.

"As I need him," I said.

"I told him to leave me by the side of the trail and let me die in peace. But he is afraid to lose me, as he lost you."

We had already witnessed the way of the elderly Cheyenne, who, when they become sick or simply too weak from age to travel, go off by themselves to die so that they do not slow the tribe, or, if camped in a long-term village, become a burden to their family. It is a brutal life, but one lived to the rhythm and rules of nature.

"You must tell him to let me die, Heóvá'é'ke," Bear Doctor Woman said. "I am ready. And you must take care of Little Hawk now that you have returned."

Hawk and I decided that for the sake of privacy after our long separation, we would ride roughly parallel to the band, but separate from it, and that we would camp with some distance between us. My friends will not worry about me, for they will know that I am with him. As we rode on that afternoon, I brought up the matter of his grandmother, and I told him what she had said to me.

"Yes, I know well that she wishes for me to leave her to die," he answered. "But I cannot. She did not let me die."

"But you are a young man, too young to die, and she is an old woman, sick and tired, and ready to go to Seano. You must let her go, Hawk, if that is what she wishes."

"I give her food and water. She eats and drinks. I make her comfortable at night to sleep."

"I think you do that for her, and also for yourself, my husband."

"Yes, in these last months," Hawk admitted, "I have lost my grandfather, my mother, my wife, and my son. I do not wish to also lose my grandmother. She is the last person I have left in my family."

"No, Hawk, that is not so, you have me left, and the child we are going to have."

We try never to be far from running water when we travel, and we dropped down later that afternoon into a small creek bottom to make an early camp. When we stopped, Hawk and I hobbled the two horses to allow them to graze on the lush grass, and we unlashed the travois from his mount. Before we bore his grandmother to the place where we would camp by the river, Hawk bent down to tell her that we had arrived for the evening. It took us both only a moment to recognize that Bear Doctor Woman was dead. I know she had been waiting for me, or perhaps for his mother . . . it makes no difference . . . to return to look after her grandson, Little Hawk, so that she could die in peace and begin her journey to Seano.

Hawk cut some sapling trees and built a burial platform, upon which we placed the travois bearing the old woman. She seemed almost weightless as we lifted her up. Hawk also placed a few of her possessions and spirit totems on the travois, to aid her passage. Darkness has descended as I write. I have built and lit the fire. Hawk sits cross-legged beneath his grandmother's remains, and in a very low voice he begins to sing to her, or to the Great Spirit, or perhaps to both . . . I do not know and do not ask.

I sleep, and I wake in the night, and still he sings, and when I wake again at dawn, he sings still. Finally, he stands, raises his arms toward the heavens, and turns to bless each of the four directions. I stoke the fire and warm a little meat that had been meant to serve as our evening supper. We eat in silence, then prepare the horses for departure, pack up our own few belongings, and ride out as the sun breaks the crest of the eastern hills, and a new day arises.

22 August 1876

More days of wandering, though often where we find buffalo herds or other game animals plentiful, we stay in one place for a longer period of time. I still visit my friends regularly, riding back and forth from our respective camps and often spending the afternoon with them. Yet Hawk and I are still camping and traveling away from the others, for we cherish our time alone together. How I love this man, and he me, and how our love grows from day to day. We are happy talking together, or just riding in silence, setting up and breaking down our camps. I accompany him on his hunts, becoming rather accomplished, if I may say so, in the art of archery, and I help him to skin and butcher what we kill. Although no one else will ever read it . . . I blush writing this . . . we are incapable of getting enough of each other's bodies, we seem never fully sated, always wanting more. We make love when we wake in the morning, after the midday meal, before we go to sleep, and often in the middle of the night. I feel always wanton in his presence, hungry to give and receive pleasure; we are like animals in rutting season, and often all it takes is simply a glance between us to make us ride into a copse of trees, dismount, and throw ourselves at each other. I cry out lustily at my release when Hawk pleasures me, and frequently I begin weeping, a feeling I have never before experienced. This is where love grows, how hearts swell and bodies burst with joy. God . . . it is wonderful.

I have spoken at length to Hawk about Ma'heona'e, Holy Woman, the blind one who leads us. He says she is very wise, and when I ask him where she is taking us, he admits that he does not know. He explains that some believe in an ancient tribal creation story that tells of a real world behind this one, a world from which the first People came thousands of generations ago, a world where there is no war or famine, where the earth is fecund, the animals, birds, and game plentiful, the buffalo herds endless, the rivers and seas full of fish, a world where the mountains, plains, and oceans are so vast that much of it has never been traveled by human beings, and where people of all tribes and all colors live in peace and harmony, with endless space for all, the way this world was supposed to be.

"It is said that the People live there much in the same way as we do here," Hawk says, "they are born and they die, sometimes they have accidents on their horses, or are killed by bears or wolves, or trampled by buffalo, but they do not die of the sicknesses the whites have brought among us. The children do not starve to death, nor are they shot by arrows, killed with knives or lances or bullets, for people do not kill each other, and there are no guns. They dance, sing, feast, marry, make love, and give birth. They hunt, gather roots, plants, and fruits, and they plant small crops to feed themselves. They play games and have contests of athletic skill, physical strength, horsemanship, archery, and running. The women, too, compete in these contests, and often against the men. And sometimes all compete against other tribes, and though the competition is spirited and sometimes even fierce, it is all friendly and in good nature."

"How lovely. And this is the world to which the blind woman is leading us?" I ask.

"Yes, she says she knows how to find it," he answers. "She saw it in a vision."

"It sounds like the way the People describe heaven, except everyone is not dead. It sounds like a wonderful dream." I laugh, a bit sarcastically. "No wonder it's taking so long to get there. And you believe this?"

"I do not know what to believe."

"Which means you don't really believe. And yet we follow her."

"Yes."

"Why?"

"Out of respect. My grandmother said that Holy Woman has big medicine, and to follow her is the correct thing to do."

"How did your grandmother know it was Holy Woman who was leading us?" I ask.

"Because she knew her," he answers, "and because my grandmother was a fine tracker. She knew how Holy Woman travels and she recognized her horse's gait and the imprint of its hooves on the trail. We have been following you for some time."

"I feel that we've been traveling in ever widening circles."

"Yes, that is true."

"It makes no sense."

"No, it does not make sense," Hawk admits. "Yet we have found buffalo to hunt, and other game to feed us. We have not cut the trail of soldiers, and their scouts have not cut ours."

"Not yet, at least," I say. It is true that we have been well nourished in our travels so far, and have not encountered enemies. Except for the inescapable sense of trepidation and fragility, the sense of our own tenuousness, it has been a pleasant sojourn thus far. Especially for Hawk and me, since we have refound each other.

"But must we not soon be looking for a place to make our winter camp?" I ask. "Or find Little Wolf and his people? We cannot just wander forever."

"Yes, but it is in winter when we are settled that the soldiers attack us. And the larger the village, the easier it is for the wolves to find. As all have learned, we cannot defend ourselves against such attacks; we cannot protect our families."

"So we just keep moving, indefinitely?" I ask. "Following a blind woman in ever widening circles, hoping to find the entrance to a perfect, mythical world, a utopia that does not exist? That is madness. We cannot stop winter from coming on, and we must be settled before the snow falls."

"Ma'heona'e takes us in circles because in her vision that is how she found the real world behind this one, by traveling the sacred circle. She has been there, and seen it, and came back to tell the People, and to lead them there."

"Yes, she had a dream, and she found herself in that perfect world, and in her dream I'll bet she could see again. And now we're all traveling to find her dream. Except dreams only exist in one's dream world, not in the world in which everyone else lives. It is a beautiful notion, a beautiful dream, and it describes a place where I wish we could all live. I admire Holy Woman for all that she has suffered and endured, but it is madness to follow her in circles."

Hawks looks at me with that sly, almost imperceptible smile that has always melted my heart . . . and my body. I take his strong brown hand, so lean and perfectly formed, in mine, press my lips to it, slide them across his fingers, and take them in my mouth. I adore the way he tastes and smells. His other hand slips under my antelope hide shirt to find my breast . . . and then . . . and then . . . maybe we have already arrived in the perfect world to which Holy Woman is leading us, and we just don't know it yet.

5 September 1876

Early this cool, autumnal morning, as Hawk and I sat by our fire wrapped together in a trade blanket, we heard the first morning call of a meadowlark. I was surprised when Hawk answered with one of his hawk calls—not the screeching, high-pitched sound the raptors utter when flying, rather a kind of inquisitive single chirping tone, as if he and the meadowlark were engaging in conversation. We heard then at some distance a horse whinny, and snort, and several others respond to it and I thought there must be a whole group of riders approaching us. I was alarmed but Hawk did not seem to be.

Shortly thereafter, two women rode into our camp, each trailing a pack horse, well laden with goods, and a string of half a dozen additional horses, three attached to each of the pack animals. I recognized the first woman, the prophet Woman Who Moves against the Wind. She greeted Hawk in Cheyenne and slid agilely from her saddle. He stood and answered her warmly. I have always been a little intimidated by this woman, Little Wolf's most trusted advisor. She is tall, powerfully built, and has the unmistakable air of authority about her. She was dressed in traditional beaded leggings and moccasins and a deer hide shift, split up the middle for riding. She carried a quiver of arrows on her back, with a bow tied behind her saddle, and a Winchester rifle in a scabbard strapped to her horse's neck. She pointed in the direction from which we had heard the horses and spoke again to Hawk, something about a number of horses hobbled and grazing in the meadow behind our camp, a gift she said they had brought to us. He smiled, nodded, and thanked her.

The second rider was a white woman. She sat her horse for a moment, taking in the scene with an alert gaze that missed nothing, seeming to size us up before also dismounting. She wore a stylish, broad-brimmed hat of a sort we saw recently when we came upon a cattle drive headed north, the Texas cowboys wearing headwear such as this. Beneath the hat, light brown hair worn loose spilled over her shoulders. She had a fair complexion that, like my own, has been darkened a few shades by exposure to the sun. She cut a fine figure, dressed rather stylishly in a canvas shirt, denim trousers tucked into high leather boots, a pair of leather chaps, and a fringed frontiersman jacket, similar to the one our Christian Goodman sports. Beneath her jacket, I saw that she wore a holstered revolver on her hip.

Hawk clearly knew her, as well, and expressed both pleasure and great surprise to see her now. She seemed to speak like a native, answering him in what sounded to me like perfectly fluent Cheyenne, of which I was envious. In fact, I admit that on first sight I experienced a slight twinge of jealousy. It is not an unattractive language once one becomes accustomed to it, with a certain lilting cadence, and this was an undeniably pretty girl who had interrupted our honeymoon. I wondered for a moment if she had been captured as a child and grown up among the People, as had Hawk's mother, though if that were the case, she would clearly not be dressed in white-woman attire.

Hawk invited them to join us at our fire. Woman Who Moves against the Wind said that she had coffee to share and pulled a rawhide bag of it from her saddlebag, while the white woman fetched a tin coffeepot and two cups from a parfleche strapped to her pack horse. Some of our group have coffee and other items taken from the Army's pack animals captured at the Little Bighorn, as well as tobacco taken off dead soldiers. Hawk and I had run out of coffee some time ago, and have since been drinking a kind of bitter tea brewed from roots, mint, or whatever other edible herbs and berries we come across.

As is customary when one has visitors, from his saddlebag Hawk took his pipe and pouch of tobacco, which now included that of Josh Miller, to offer them a smoke. In order to make it last longer, we have mixed it with the native herbs the Cheyenne smoke when the real thing is not available. Now we sat around the fire, drinking coffee and passing the pipe. I tried to absorb as much of the conversation as I could, though I made no effort to try to participate in it. They appeared to be discussing the movements of the troops, the scouts, our own plans, a winter camp, the location of Little Wolf's village. The white woman had not yet addressed me, and finally, feeling a bit left out, as I passed the pipe to her I asked her in my rudimentary Cheyenne if she spoke English.

She laughed. "Rather well. Do you?"

I, too, laughed. "A great deal better than I speak Cheyenne." I held out my hand to her. "My name is Molly."

"And mine is May," she said, taking my hand.

I felt a small shiver run up my back.

I stood and fetched Josh's saddlebags, inside which I keep Meggie's, Ann's, and my ledger book, the young soldier's diary, and Carolyn's leather-bound calendar book. I came back to the fire, took out the ledger, and slipped the single loose sheet of paper from inside the cover.

"I believe I may have something of yours. That is, if you are who I think you might be."

"And who would that be?" she asked.

"May Dodd?" I suggested tentatively.

"Yes . . . it's true, I was May Dodd a long time ago, before I became May Dodd Ames, upon taking the name of my common-law husband, later reverting to my maiden name. Then I became May Dodd Little Wolf, known familiarly as Mesoke, Swallow, after

I married the great Cheyenne Sweet Medicine chief. More recently, since I have been interacting again in the world of the whites, I go by the alias Abigail Ames. Now I'm not really sure who I am any longer. And who might you be?"

"I am Molly McGill Hawk, known familiarly as Heóvá'é'ke, Yellow Hair Woman, or Mé'koomat a'xevà, Woman Who Kicks Men in Testicles. Take your pick . . . both names, I must say, are considerably less charming than Swallow." May laughed heartily, and with the formal introductions out of the way, we shook hands again, firmly and warmly, like two old friends reunited, though we had just met.

Now she took the piece of ledger paper from my hand, placing it on her crossed leg. She looked down at it and smoothed it lightly with her fingers, smiling ironically. "Good God, if it isn't the proverbial message in a bottle." She looked into my eyes with a searching gaze. "How in the world did you find this?"

"In your cave, where you left it."

"But how? When?"

"Some months ago, in the spring, late April or early May, I would guess."

May laughed with a slightly bitter edge. "You must be one of the new group of white women in the brides program, aren't you?" she asked. "I should have known. And you've kept a journal. I see that it did not take the government long to replace us. Surely you must know by now that the program was discontinued before your arrival, and that you have been abandoned in the wilderness by your government?"

"Yes, of course," I answered. "We know all about that. We are fugitives. You and I have a great deal to talk about, May."

"Indeed we do, Molly. But, please, tell me first, what in the world led you to the cave?"

"Your friend Martha took Meggie and Susie Kelly and me there. You see, Martha lost her mind for a time, and she was certain she would find you there. She hadn't accepted the fact that you were dead . . . and, indeed, you aren't. We went with her to humor her, to try to coax her back to reality. However, not finding you in the cave had exactly the opposite effect."

"Then you must have seen our burned village. What brought you there in the first place?"

I told May then about the capture of our group, and the time we had spent in Crazy Horse's village, and I explained that after we left the Lakota, Hawk took our little band to Little Wolf's burned winter village, to pray to the remains of his mother, wife, and son.

"But that's astonishing, Molly," May said, "because Martha almost did find me there. Perhaps in her madness she somehow sensed that. Wind and I stayed in that cave for forty-eight days while I was recovering from my wound. The medicine woman saved my life and nursed me back to health. We must have only recently left when you arrived. It is true that I had no calendar, but Wind had counted exactly how long we had been there, and I computed that it must be sometime in late April or early May. We couldn't have missed you by more than a few days. Had we only stayed a little longer, we could have joined you . . . and . . . believe me . . . saved ourselves a great deal of trouble."

"May, I'm very confused about something," I said. "Woman Who Moves against the Wind was with Little Wolf's band. How could she have been with you in the cave at the same time?"

May laughed. "Because there are two of them?"

"What in the world does that mean? Two women with the same name?"

"Like the Kelly girls, they are identical twins. I lived for ten months in Little Wolf's lodge and I never knew that myself, for they are rarely seen together. It was the two of them who built the burial scaffolds upon which the charred bones of our dead were placed, including those of Hawk's family."

"You must tell Hawk about this," I said.

"Wind has already done so."

We sat in silence for a long moment, perhaps both of us pondering the strange and desperate circumstances that had brought us together.

"In your time here, May," I asked, finally, "has it ever occurred to you that you're living among a different species of beings, in a world other than our own?"

May laughed again. In spite of it all, she seemed to have maintained a pointedly ironic sense of humor that fully appreciated the otherworldliness of our lives. "Well, of course it has, from the very first time we laid eyes upon our future husbands and our new lodging among their people. It occurs to me still. I believe it is why the Indian and white worlds have never successfully intermingled, have never come to terms with each other, and probably never will. It is why the whites exterminate the Indians, or lock them up on reservations, because they fear the sheer otherness of them; they're terrified of a people who aren't like them, and whom they are incapable of understanding . . . and they make pitifully little effort to do so."

"Yet there is much to be afraid of in both worlds, isn't there?" I said. "And from both peoples."

"Indeed, and as you must also know well by now, we are directly in the middle of them, aren't we? Speaking of that, it is true then that Seminole took Martha captive?"

"I'm afraid so. But how did you know?"

"Because we, too, encountered the lunatic in our travels here, more than once. Of that I will tell you later. Good God . . . my head is spinning . . . or maybe it's from the tobacco to which I am not accustomed. I must stand and walk a moment. I've been too long in the saddle, and I'm beginning to feel like a centaur. Please come walk with me, Molly."

We walked down to the creek and then along the bank, in silence for a long while. The sun had risen, taking fast the morning chill from the air. Insects were hatching in clouds over the water, bringing the trout up to feed on the surface, the pools pockmarked by their rises. Swallows worked the hatch, too, skimming the water, the tips of their wings leaving delicate wakes behind as they snatched up their prey. The prairie birds had taken up their full morning songs.

"Isn't it odd, too," May said, "how sometimes this country can seem like paradise on earth, and other times like hell? I can't stop thinking about Martha being captured by Jules Seminole."

"I had my own moment in his company," I said, "but I escaped more or less unscathed. Truly, he is a lunatic, and I'm afraid that poor Martha got the very worst of it."

"Of all our group, she was the least prepared for such an ordeal."

"That is exactly what Susie and Meggie said. But she's strong now. You will hardly recognize her."

"I'm so glad to know that those Irish scamps survived the attack. Are they here with you now?"

I had to tell May then about the fate of the Kelly twins. When I finished she fell silent and pensive again.

"You know, Molly," she said finally, "when first we came out here on the train, we all had to watch our purses and other personal effects, for those girls were incorrigibly light-fingered. Take your eyes off them for a minute, and suddenly you'd see that one of them was wearing your brooch. They always said they had no interest in being mothers, and had just signed up for the brides program to avoid prison. They intended to do their two years here, have their babies, leave them with the Cheyenne, and go right back to their life of crime in Chicago. But, of course, they loved those tiny infants as much as all mothers love theirs. I understand their rage against the soldiers . . . I share it. To hear you tell of their exploits, they became true warriors in their own right, avenging the murder of their children. And I can imagine how they must have terrorized the soldiers. Good for them. I would like to have done so, myself."

"I, too, got off to a rocky start with Susie and Meggie," I said, "but we became quite close after a time. They spoke often of you; they called you a fancy, educated girl. Yet you were a kind of model to them. They loved and respected you, and said you were the glue that held them all together . . . I probably shouldn't tell you this, May . . . but they also said you were a bit of a tart."

At this, a shadow of great sadness descended over May's face and I immediately regretted having spoken thus.

"I am so deeply sorry, May," I said. "I did not mean to hurt you. I assumed you knew this as the twins always said you teased each other about such matters.

"It's alright, Molly, it's not your fault," she answered. "I did know, and the girls were right, we never stopped teasing each other about who was the most promiscuous among us. It's just that more recently the fact of my being a bit of a tart has come back to haunt me. I'm sure they told you of my short . . . and deeply inappropriate tryst with Captain John Bourke, which they never let me forget. For my part, I took great pleasure in reminding them of their career in Chicago as ladies of the night."

"After everyone thought you were dead, the Kellys tried to assume your role as leaders," I said. "You were a tough act to follow, but they did their best, and were of great aid to us after we were captured by the Lakota. They made us laugh with their irreverent antics and Irish cheekiness. I think if we had only found you back at the cave that day, and you had been reunited with them, their story might have had a very different ending . . . they might still be here with us . . ."

"I've been thinking the same thing," May said, "and it breaks my heart . . . I miss them so . . . those damn foolish girls . . . and all the others . . ." May started crying now. "So many gone, Molly . . ."

I felt it might help May if we rode over to our main group so that she could see her old friend Martha, as well as meet the others in our group, and when I suggested it she was thrilled. Although she appears so outwardly strong and quick to laugh, at the same time it was impossible for me not to notice in her a deep weariness . . . a fragility. I thought that being reunited with at least two of her old friends would do her good. I did not tell her that Phemie was also among us, as I wanted to save that for a surprise.

Wind and Hawk seemed to have a great deal to discuss, and back at the fire they were still in deep conference. It was agreed that May and I would rejoin the main group, and the two of them would join us in a day or two with the pack horses, and those Wind and May had brought as gifts.

As I saddled Spring and gathered my few effects, I felt a great sense of wistfulness that the time spent alone on our first real honeymoon had come to an end. And I know Hawk did as well. It is true that the communal life of nomadic peoples allows far less privacy to the individual or couples, and clearly our overactive erotic life was going to be greatly curtailed. There would be no more crying out loud in the ecstasy of climax, perhaps only soft moans muffled by burying my face in the thick curly hair of the buffalo blanket. Hawk and I looked deep in each other's eyes before I mounted, and, without speaking, shared this mutual regret.

We rode out. The main band was camped across the broad valley, on the banks of another creek, which would only take us a bit over an hour or so to reach. May and I had in this short time already formed a comfortable bond between us. In her presence, I was more aware than ever of how much I missed Carolyn, Ann, Hannah, Meggie, and Susie, our closeness and daily banter, our sense that we were all in this together. And I well understood May's heartbreak for having lost so many of her friends, and all so violently.

"You seem to have adapted well to this life, Molly," she said.

"As you certainly know better than I, May, one adapts here or perishes. That became our group's motto. Of course, too frequently one adapts *and* perishes."

"I see how much in love you and Hawk are. I'm so glad you found each other. I know from Wind what happened to his family. That was such a horrifying day . . ."

"And I am so deeply sorry for you, and for all you have suffered. That short time we spent camped near your burned-out village was unsettling . . . to say the least. Especially at night and in the disturbing dreams we all shared, we had the sense that we were haunted by the presence of the unsettled spirits of the dead."

"Yes, believe me, I, too, felt those spirits, and had those same dreams in our cave, both sleeping and awake for forty-eight days and nights . . . and surely even more vividly than you for having lived through it."

"Yes, of course," I said. "I'm sorry, May, I seem to be so clumsy speaking to you about these things. I did not mean to suggest otherwise."

"Of course you didn't, Molly," she said. "Nor did I take offense. I'm sure Susie and Meggie told you of this, but after the battle, or, I should say, the massacre that morning was over, the soldiers built a giant funeral pyre of all our possessions and upon it placed the bodies of our dead. Where we huddled for warmth in the hills, the odor of burning flesh wafted in the air, sickening us, a stench I shall never be able to rid from my nostrils. I could never bring myself to go back down to the village. Even had I the strength to help Wind and her sister build the burial platforms of which you spoke, and collect the charred remains of our people to place upon them, I would not have had the courage."

We rode on now across the valley. The grass had been grazed by buffalo in places, but in others it was still up to our horses' bellies and just beginning to yellow with the approaching autumn. Meadowlarks squirted up out of the grass at our approach, and we flushed a covey of prairie chickens that fanned out ahead of us. It was a splendid autumn day. As we rode side by side, I thought about how far both May and I have come from our beginnings, how unlikely it was that two white girls, one from Chicago and the other from New York, would find ourselves here together on horseback, I dressed as an Indian, and May as a frontierswoman, two homeless fugitives crossing an empty prairie.

"By the way, May," I said, "you and Wind seem extraordinarily well stocked, and, I have to say, I'm envious of your attire, not to

mention your fine saddle and tack, your horses and packing panniers, your revolver, and rifles. I hope you don't mind my asking,
but how in the world did you come by all these goods?"

She laughed. "The same way we came by our horse herd, Molly. I
have become rather an accomplished stock rustler, and Wind taught
me everything I know on the subject. We got our start after being
taken captive by a band of outlaws, guided by Jules Seminole. I won't
go into detail other than to say that we managed to escape and in
the process we stole their string of horses. That was the beginning
of my career. We had nothing between us when we got away except
for two blankets, and the horses, which latter, as you undoubtedly
know, are an important commodity on the plains. We became en-
trepreneurs. The first items I purchased with the proceeds of our
initial sale of horses were my clothes, boots, and hat so that I could
appear as a white woman at the trading posts, stables, and mercan-
tiles in some of the settlements that are springing up. I am treated
with far more respect and can strike a better bargain than I could
as a white squaw . . . in which attire many wouldn't deal with me
at all. Not to mention the fact that most white men assume a white
woman who has gone savage must be of loose morals and deserves
to be beaten and violated. Whereas now I am received as a respectable businesswoman. I also purchased the Winchester rifles
and this Remington revolver. As for Wind, though she will accompany me into the agency trading posts, she does not enter the settlements, and if we happen to be stopped by someone on the trail,
which has only happened twice, I introduce her as my servant, a
deception of which I am not fond, but that protects her. And so
that is how we earn our living: we are professional horse thieves.
After we stole and sold our first small herd, we targeted wagon
trains, cattle drives, ranches, and even once, General George
Crook's Army base camp. We also captured wild prairie mustangs
to supplement our stock. Wind breaks and trains them. She has a
true gift. Indeed, we would have become quite prosperous as horse
traders had we not given most of our stock to Indian bands we

have encountered along the way, or to those other poor souls at the agencies."

"If horse thieves are apprehended, they are hanged, are they not?" I asked.

"Of course, strung up from the nearest tree," May answered. "But then, as my old muleskinner friend Dirty Gertie puts it: 'A gal's gotta make a livin' in this godforsaken country.'"

I laughed. "I met your friend Gertie in Crazy Horse's village. She is quite a character; we got on splendidly together."

"I'll just bet you did."

"She spoke fondly of you, and would be thrilled to learn that you've come back to us, if ever our paths cross again."

"Now, Molly, you clearly know a great deal more about me than I do about you. I don't want to pry, but do you mind telling me what brought you here? If you'd rather not say, I understand. Our group never pressured anyone to reveal anything they did not wish to."

"At this point, May," I answered, "I have very few secrets left to guard . . . or any reason to guard them, especially from you. I shall give you the short version, and then we do not need to speak further of it.

"I grew up on a farm in upstate New York, got pregnant by and married too young the wrong man, gave birth to my beautiful daughter, Clara, and moved to New York City with my husband. I taught school there and worked for a social agency whose mission was to find homes for abandoned immigrant children who were living on the street. My husband was a drunk, and when it became clear that he was not going to realize his absurd dream of becoming a prosperous banker, which was why we moved to New York in the first place, his drinking got worse. He was unable to hold a job, any job, even the most menial. He became violent. We kept moving to less expensive lodgings, as I tried to support the three of us. One day I came home after work, and I found that he had beaten our little girl to death in an alcoholic rage. I killed him with a butcher knife and was convicted of murder. I prayed to be sentenced to death, but instead they gave me life in Sing Sing prison . . . and that is how I got here . . ."

"Good God," May whispered.

It was then that we both noticed the cloud of dust in the distance across and up the valley from us, and moving our way. As it came into focus we saw that it was a small war party of half a dozen or so Indians. Two of the riders wore the headdresses of chiefs, and now we could hear their war cries.

"Crow," May said.

"Follow me," I answered. "We're not far now from our people. We can outrun them."

We kicked our horses into a gallop and bent low in the saddle. We heard rifle fire, but it sounded too distantly tinny for us to be in range. Our horses ran with an intensity that suggested they were aware we were being chased. We could see the smoke rising from our band's camp on the river, and I knew that by now our sentries would have spotted us.

As we approached closer to the camp, our mounted warriors began to ride out at a full gallop. From a running horse it is hard to identify individuals at a distance, but I was certain that at least some of our Strongheart women would be among them. I glanced over my shoulder and saw that our pursuers had stopped, their horses wheeling in circles. I hollered to May to rein up, and did so myself. The Crow must have been assessing the size of our own war party now bearing down upon them, and recognizing that they were outnumbered, they had a sudden change of heart. Turning in one motion like a flock of birds in the air, they headed back in the direction from which they had come, becoming now the pursued. We watched until both they and our war party disappeared over a distant hillside.

There was no point in wearing out our horses, and we walked them the rest of the way into camp. As we went, I told May about our women's warrior society and the training sessions under our leader, the Arapaho girl, Pretty Nose, who had the distinction of being a woman war chief. "Perhaps you knew her," I said, "for she has Cheyenne blood and moves back and forth between our tribes."

"Yes, I did know her," May said, "though not terribly well. She came to our lodge several times while visiting her Cheyenne relatives to consult with Little Wolf. She is younger than I, but my husband had great respect for her courage and skills as a warrior, and he spoke to her of military matters, a subject, as you must know by now, reserved for counsels between men."

I told May about some of our girls she was soon to meet, and others who had left us: the Mexican Indian, Maria; our Norwegian, Astrid, who was married to our Mennonite spiritual advisor, Christian Goodman; our French actress and dance instructor, known to us all by her stage name, Lulu LaRue. I told her about Carolyn, and Lady Ann Hall, who, with her maidservant, little Hannah Alford, had come in search of her lover, May's friend Helen Flight, and who had left us to return to England.

"Helen was a dear friend," May said. "She was a wonderful artist, courageous, and a great warrior in her own right. She spoke often of Lady Ann. How extraordinary and brave of her to travel all this distance to find her lover, and what a tragedy for her to make the journey only to learn of Helen's death. I don't blame her for going home. I wish I had one to go to. I have a little money in my pocket now from our first horse sale, and I could well afford a train ticket to Chicago. I've been dreaming of returning and reclaiming my children, taking my daughter, Little Bird, with me . . . Wren, I call her, who is with Little Wolf. I would make a new life for us somewhere under a new name. Do you ever dream of returning to New York, Molly?"

"There is nothing there for me now, May . . . except heartbreaking memories and Sing Sing. Come what may, I'm staying right here, and I am going to have Hawk's child. Even if I had a choice, I wouldn't do otherwise."

"That is wonderful news," May said. "I hope you will forgive me for saying so, but, given the experience of my group, that might be the best reason of all for you to leave, to save your child . . . having . . . I'm sorry to say this, dear . . . having already lost one as you have."

An extraordinary thing happened when May and I rode into camp. Two eager young horse boys ran out to greet us, in order to picket and curry our mounts. When she saw them May suddenly hollered, "Oh my God!" and nearly fell off her horse in her haste to dismount, dropping to her knees in front of one of the boys and grasping him in her arms. She began weeping, blubbering, and through her tears, speaking in a combination of Cheyenne and English to the boy, alternately pressing him to her breast and holding him out in front of her, as if to confirm his very existence. The boy himself was weeping now, and crying "Mesoke, Mesoke," as he threw his arms around her neck when she pulled him close. And she cried: "Mo'éhno'ha, Mo'éh-no'ha" as they embraced, "My little Horse Boy, I thought you were dead, I saw the soldier shoot you, I saw you fall down dead." And the boy answered: "They told me you were dead, Mesoke, they said the soldiers shot you." Now May held him away from her again, holding his upper arms tightly in her hands. "I saw you shot dead," she repeated, weeping and shaking him, as if she was angry, "I saw the bullet hole in your head." Then she desperately grasped him again to her breast.

"The soldier shot over my head, Mesoke, he did not kill me. The hole you saw was charcoal I put on my face before I went to the horses. The medicine woman said it would protect me. I am ashamed, for I was a coward. I was so scared I made pee in my pants when the soldier pointed the gun at me. And I fell down asleep on the ground."

"I love this little boy, Molly," May said, still weeping and holding him close. "He was my first friend among the Cheyenne. And all this time, I've believed that John Bourke killed him. I could have sworn I saw him shoot the boy, and I've hated him for it ever since. But he just fainted out of sheer terror. And who can blame him?"

May and I were on the far side of the camp, setting up our lodging for the night, when our war party returned, the sun just dropping behind the hills. Of course, she had wanted to go immediately in search of Martha, but I insisted that we do this first, for I was certain that Martha had ridden out with the warriors, which I did not wish to tell May, who would only have worried.

The People were gathering now at the edge of the camp to greet our victorious warriors as they rode in. The women and girls took up the joyous trilling sound, not joined this time by any keening, which told that all had returned alive, perhaps only a few with minor injuries. The two warriors in the lead wore the headdresses of their enemies, and others behind them led Crow ponies and carried extra rifles, shields, scalps, and other trophies of war. I glimpsed several members of our Strongheart society bringing up the rear of the procession. The men warriors have not yet accepted us as equals, and for now we are relegated to this position, but that is going to change as soon as we have a meeting to form our new tribal council. By the time May and I had succeeded in jostling our way to the front of the crowd, the warriors were dismounting, gathering their arms and whatever trophies they had won in battle. As they did so, the horse boys ran out to take charge of their assigned mounts and lead them back to the picket line where they would unsaddle, unbridle, check for wounds, wash and curry them, then hobble them and turn them out in the river bottom to drink water and graze. Just before dark, they would gather them and reattach them to the picket line, and teams of three boys would take shifts throughout the night to guard the precious stock. There would be no horse thievery here.

"But where is Martha, Molly?" May asked. "I've been looking for her as we came through the crowd, and have not caught sight of her."

"Martha is a member of the Strongheart warrior society, May," I said. "We must look for her among the incoming horsemen."

"Don't be ridiculous," she answered, "although I admit that is an amusing joke. Martha can barely walk without falling down, let alone ride with warriors."

"It is true that she still lacks certain athletic skills," I admitted, "but as I told you, Martha has changed a great deal since last you saw her. In addition to her donkey, she now has two war ponies of her own."

"Nonsense," said May. "Martha a warrior ... please ... truly, you have an evil sense of humor, Molly."

I laughed. "Well, let's go looking for her, why don't we?"

And so we moved through the horsemen, who were chattering among themselves, boasting of their exploits on the field of battle, no doubt exaggerated. All gave May, dressed in her white woman attire, wary regards.

"Don't worry," I assured them, "she is my captive," which made May laugh.

"I don't know what I was thinking," she said. "I should have changed into my hides before we came. I think I was just too eager to get here. I risk being scalped. By the way, Molly, your Cheyenne is not so bad. You're picking it up well."

Now we approached a rider who had her back to us and was loosening her horse's girth strap. "Hello, Martha," I said, "look what the cat dragged in."

"Ah, Molly!" Martha said, turning to us. She had blood on her shirt, her face, and her hands. Her smile of greeting faded as she saw May, her face registering a full gamut of emotions—confusion, doubt, disbelief, relief—and then it contorted into a half smile, half grimace, as she raised her hands to cover her eyes, her shoulders shuddering, her legs giving way beneath her as she collapsed to her knees.

May knelt before her. "Is that any way to greet an old friend?" she said, putting her hands on Martha's forearms. "Are you injured, Martha? Is that your blood?"

"It isn't really you, May," Martha managed to sputter through her tears, still covering her eyes with her hands as if afraid to look again. "You're dead, this is some kind of dream, or a trick, I'm going crazy again, aren't I? You're dead!"

May couldn't help letting a laugh escape. "I'm not dead, Martha. Nor am I a dream, or a trick, and no, you're not going crazy. Take your hands away from your eyes, look at me, and please tell me if you're injured."

Martha slowly lowered her hands, her tears subsiding, snot running from her nostrils. She wiped it away with the back of her bloody hand, streaking blood across her face. May helped her to her feet, and they embraced.

"Oh, May," said Martha, "my dearest friend. No, I am not injured, I killed an enemy, it is his blood I carry upon me." Then she cupped her left hand at her waist and displayed the scalp dangling from the braided rawhide belt she wore. "Look, I counted coup and I took my first scalp."

"Good God, Martha, you scalped a man?"

"I scalped an *enemy*, May. He tried to kill me, but I killed him first, and I took his scalp. Kills in the Morning Woman showed me how to do it." She looked hard again at May. "My God, you survived, how is it possible, and where have you been all this time?"

"All of that later, Martha. I see that you have much to tell me, as well. We will have plenty of time to catch up, my friend, because I'm not going anywhere . . . that is, if your band will permit me and my companion, Woman Who Moves against the Wind, to travel with you. We've been on our own all summer, and it would be nice to have some company for the winter."

Phemie had now come up behind us. "I believe that can be arranged, May," she said in her low, sonorous voice.

May did not turn for a long moment upon hearing Phemie's unmistakable voice. When she finally did, she stared at the negress, shaking her head in amazement. "Now it is my turn to say, 'I thought you were dead, Phemie.'" Then she leapt into Phemie's embrace, and when they separated they held each other by the forearms.

"And I you, May," said Phemie, with a rich chuckle. "Why, just look at you, girl, the cat with nine lives, and you don't appear much worse for the wear, either. As a matter of fact, you look fine, May, strong and healthy. And all dressed up like a white girl."

"You look pretty damn good yourself, Phemie, as majestically beautiful as ever."

"Where in the hell did you come by that outfit, girl? Don't tell me you've gone over to the other side?"

"Don't worry, Phemie," May said. "I'm just pretending to be a white girl. I'm still just as Cheyenne as you." And they both laughed.

A feast and dance has been announced by the camp crier this evening to celebrate the victorious war party's return, and for the warriors to dance an account of their individual triumphs in the battle against the Crow. All have cleaned up and dressed in their finest party attire . . . such as it is in these rather spartan times . . . It goes without saying that none of us have extensive wardrobes to share, but fortunately May had brought her own shift, leggings, and moccasins along in the pack behind her saddle. Given the suspicious, even slightly threatening looks cast her way by some of those in our band who do not know her, she was aware that it would be inappropriate, even insulting, to attend the dance wearing her white-woman attire. We did manage to put together some beaded necklaces, armbands, bracelets, and earrings to dress her up a bit, and we braided her hair, so that when she appeared in front of the others, she was fully transformed.

"Well now, *that* is much better, May," said Martha, who we all couldn't help noticing wore her first scalp on her belt to display at the dance. "Much better, indeed . . . You know, after I got over my initial shock and confusion when first I saw you, I feared that you had reverted to your old race, which, of course, would not do here."

"Martha, dear," May answered, with a laugh, "please don't tell me that you were thinking of adding my scalp to your belt?"

"No, no, of course not, my friend," said Martha. "It is simply that I have embraced this new life of ours so thoroughly that I have grown quite wary of the *ve'ho'e* . . . and given our treatment at their hands, even rather vindictive toward them. They clearly do not have our better interests at heart."

"Yes, that much is clear, Martha, and I do share your wariness. However, now and again, I believe it is useful to have a look in the mirror, and recognize that however well we may have adapted to Indian ways, we are still *ve'ho'à'e*—white women—ourselves. It is true that I have reentered that world over these past months, having dealt with traders and merchants, ranchers and settlers. And I must say, I did rather appreciate being treated far better by them than I would have been dressed as a squaw, and a white one at that. Nor can I deny having felt a certain nostalgia, even longing, for the old life we left behind." May laughed. "Well, except, of course, for my time in the asylum. But now you see . . ." She held out her arms. "I have put my feet back on Cheyenne earth, with no regrets. And I do so look forward to watching you dance, dear!"

It is the first opportunity we have had to hold a dance since we left the Little Bighorn. Fires have been laid and lit, the meat of various game animals—buffalo, deer, and elk—has been installed on spits, and the musicians, dancers, and spectators have begun to gather. Of course, the occasion also provides a timely opportunity to celebrate the return of May Dodd, Mesoke, who, before the evening is out, I suspect, will have a new name bestowed upon her in honor of her resurrection from the dead. Having heard so much about this woman from Meggie and Susie and the others, and now to see how she is received by those in the camp who know her, I more fully appreciate what an important figure she had become among the People.

Dog Woman, our tribal *he'emnan'e*, half man/half woman, is in her element, bustling about, organizing the preparations, giving orders, squawking at the miscreants, and scolding the children. She had elected to leave Little Wolf's band and join ours after the battle on the Little Bighorn, partly, I believe, because she has taken rather a shine to us white women, despite all the distress we caused her with the preposterous, yet amusing cancan performance we put on in the village. She seems to find us exotic, and, being such a social being herself, she carefully studies us and our strange ways, even those of which she disapproves. However, when the poor thing first laid eyes upon May before the celebrations began, she promptly burst into tears and ran off. We assumed at first that these were tears of joy, mixed perhaps with a bit of shock at finding Mesoke alive. However, May explained to us that Dog Woman, being a sensitive soul, believed that she was gazing upon a ghost. The misunderstanding was quickly straightened out, and the two embraced tenderly.

It was fully dark now, and May's little Horse Boy, Mo'éhno'ha, having gathered and picketed the herd with the other boys, joined us at the fire. So preoccupied have I been with my reunion with Hawk that I have neglected to write of my own little orphan girl, Mouse, Hóhkééhe, whose parents were killed in the Mackenzie attack, and whom Hawk and I had intended to adopt—a plan abruptly interrupted by his wounding and my capture at the battle of Rosebud Creek. The child had remained in the care of her grandparents, Bear and Good Feathers, who had taken her in after the deaths of her parents. I was reunited with my little Mouse at the Little Bighorn, and the old couple told me she had pined for Hawk and me almost as much as she had for her real parents upon their death. There is so much of that here . . . death follows us all, young and old, as inescapable as our own shadows . . .

Bear and Good Feathers elected to rejoin Little Wolf's band, as did virtually all of the elders, and left with the chief from the Bighorn battlefield, leaving the child with me. They told me they were tired and ready to begin the journey to Seano, and she would be better off in my care. When I galloped off so impulsively to rejoin

Hawk, I knew my friends would look after her in my absence. As May had suggested when speaking of our respective worlds, in this one we live tribally—our own small family, within the larger family of the band—and we take care of each other. I see how easily May has fitted herself back into that structure, especially after donning her native attire. It is quite true that all would have looked upon her differently had she come to the feast and dance in her white-woman outfit, as if she were an outsider, or had chosen to set herself apart from the tribe. It would have been disrespectful.

My little Mouse now sits in my lap before the fire, while Horse Boy, too old now to thus position himself upon May, huddles close beside her, his arm through hers, as if afraid of losing her again. In looking at us together, I am struck by the fact that although we come here via quite different paths, May and I share the unbreakable bond of an insatiable hunger for our lost children, and that we need these two little ones in our arms as much as they need us.

The others are taking their places cross-legged around us. We can smell the game cooking over the smaller open fires, the flames of the largest in the center of the dance circle, towering like giant burning arrows shooting into the sky.

It is then that we hear a commotion on the edge of the camp and warning cries from the sentries. Those of our warriors already seated stand quickly and take up their arms (we have all learned to keep them close at hand at all times); the children scatter as they are taught, to hide in the underbrush, the older collecting the younger. Horse Boy leaps from May's side to run to the picket line and help secure the stock. We women warriors, also armed, stand and begin to move toward the noise. But for the trillions of stars, the night sky is black and without a moon, the darkness beyond the fire ring complete.

Then, just as suddenly, the sentries issue the all-clear signal, the collective, relayed call of the Great Horned Owl, telling us that there is no danger after all. Hearts beating double time, we relax and move back toward the fire. Now in the shadows, we see two of the sentries, leading three people toward us, though we can't at first make out their features. "*Goddammit to hell*," one of them says in an unmistakably familiar voice, "I told these fellas: '*ole Gertie here snuck right past your outside guards, an' damn near got all the way into your camp, 'fore you caught me. Now what the hell kinda sentry duty is that, boys?*'" The three figures walk into the light and stop, as the sentries return to their positions. Gertie takes off her old sweat-stained, broad-brimmed cowboy hat and slaps it against her thigh, a puff of dust rising. "Hate to crash the party, ladies," she says, "but I never could resist a Cheyenne feast and a dance. Heard the drums and smelt the game cookin' in the air a mile back." She takes a little jump and clicks her heels together. "And I got my dancin' boots on."

Now for the first time Gertie appears to suddenly recognize May and then me, and she becomes very still. "*Holy . . . bejesus . . . Christ*," she says under her breath, "so you come back from the dead, did ya, May? And you, too, Molly?" And to her companions, she says: "I do believe we done wandered into a ghost camp, ladies. I been hearin' about such things on the plains for years, Injun camps on a moonless night, peopled by nothin' but the dead, all those killed in these long wars, men, women, and children, only they don't know they're dead yet, so they keep goin' on about their business just like they ain't. I think we best turn right around and ease our way back down the trail. I seem to have lost my hankerin' for a dance tonight."

"You know, I am growing awfully tired of being mistaken for a ghost," says May. "Come give me a big bear hug, Gertie . . . if I can stand the smell of you . . . and you'll see that I'm still made of warm flesh and blood."

As to the two other women who have stepped out of the shadows with Gertie, we're nearly as stunned to see them as she is to see May—Lady Ann Hall and Hannah Alford have returned to us.

by Molly Standing Bear

Amazons

"Achilles removed the brilliant helmet from the lifeless Amazon queen. Penthesilea had fought like a raging leopard in their duel at Troy. Her valor and beauty were undimmed by dust and blood. Achilles' heart lurched with remorse and desire . . . All the Greeks on the battlefield crowded around and marveled, wishing with all their hearts that their wives at home could be just like her."

—*Quintus of Smyrna,* The Fall of Troy
(*from* The Amazons: Lives and Legends
of Women Warriors Across the Ancient
World *by Adrienne Mayor*)

I hope the reader will forgive me this short intermission . . . although as the editor of these journals, it occurs to me that I am not really required to apologize . . . though maybe I should at least beg your indulgence. I didn't have much of an education, unless you count the kind learned while being abused by a Catholic priest in the dark basement of the Indian school to which we were all sent away. This hands-on experience kind of soured my interest in formal education, not to mention in the church.

I became an obsessive reader as a means of escape, and books became my teachers. I read everything and anything I could get my hands on, which, in a Catholic boarding school, is a limited selection. Of course, most readily available was the Bible, Old and New Testaments, both of which I read from cover to cover more than once. I learned a great deal about fratricide, matricide, patricide, infanticide, genocide, ethnic cleansing, slavery, sex slavery . . . pretty much everything one needs to know about the evil, violence, and debasement of human nature. But I read the good parts, too, and tried to take heart from them.

Because of my interest in the bible, I was considered to be an industrious student . . . a candidate to become a nun . . . or so the good "father" assured me while abusing me. It was a truly biblical relationship, my initiation as a sex slave of god and his earthly representative. And, by the way, it is not my lack of formal education that prevents me from capitalizing those names, rather my utter contempt and disgust. Finally, I ran away, which was to become a chronic pattern in my life. I ran away from the boarding school, from the church, from father so-and-so (whose last name I won't mention for fear of reprisals). I ran away from my family, from a sexually abusive uncle, from an alcoholic man I lived with briefly who beat me up and raped me when he got drunk, which was regularly. I stopped reading . . . that was my fatal mistake . . . well, one of many . . . I moved to Denver and became a prostitute on Colfax Avenue, and a drug addict, whatever I could get my hands on, heroin, cocaine, morphine, speedballs—a combination of heroin and one of the others. I fucked men to get money for drugs. I was lucky I didn't kill myself, though later I recognized that had been my goal. One morning I woke up robbed, bloody, and beaten in a filthy motel room that stank of paid sex, a place where the johns take whores for an hour or less. My shoes and clothes had been stolen. I walked out wrapped in a sheet. The police picked me up, took me first to jail, then to detox, and finally to a city-run treatment facility. I got clean, I got a job in a library, I started reading again, escaping into books, into the stories, the lives of others. It saved my life, and there I learned of my long dormant talents as a shape-shifter. I learned that I could enter those stories and lives, I could assume them, I could become those characters, or at least a kind of hologram version of them. I can't even really explain how, I just do . . . As a child I had heard stories from the tribal elders about my ancestor, the man they called Hawk. They said he could become a raptor, that he could fly. The elders who had bothered to guard them and pass them on, and had not become drunks themselves, told many such stories about impossible events in our history, individuals with impossible talents, about animals who could speak, and men and women who could understand them. I never doubted any of the stories, and never asked for proof of them. I still believe them. The women elders told tales about white women, and women of other races who came to live among us, and about female warriors who were great horsewomen, and fought alongside the men, who could pierce an enemy's heart with an arrow shot from a galloping horse. The old women passed these stories on secretly, for the tribal chiefs and the men elders did not like them because they portrayed our women as something other than docile wives and mothers who took care of the lodge and the needs of their husbands, and raised their children. I have never forgotten any of these stories, or any of the books I have read; they live on in me. The only black holes in my memory are during that period when I was a whore and a drug addict, which is just as well, for I remember enough to bring the bile up into my throat whenever I think of it.

After I became a reader again following my long, dark hiatus, I revisited and was newly intrigued by those tales of the warrior women. Via my own bitter experience, which I must here say I do not blame on anyone but myself, I came to the inevitable conclusion that the only way for an Indian woman to survive on the white man's earth is to stay sober, get strong, and fight back. We women have learned the hard way how far passivity has gotten us. I read the myths about the Amazon warrior women who, in these stories are, of course, always defeated in battle by the Greek men. In addition to being courageous, worthy opponents, the Amazons were also beautiful and sexually attractive to our mythic heroes. For instance, after Achilles slays the Amazon queen Penthesilea, who "had fought like a raging leopard," . . . even in death "her valor and beauty . . . undimmed by dust and blood. Achilles' heart lurched with remorse and desire. All the Greeks on the battlefield crowded around and marveled, wishing with all their hearts that their wives at home could be just like her."

I mean, really . . . could anyone other than a man be capable of writing such drivel? Achilles wishes that instead of having killed her, he could have fucked her, which, for starters, is sufficiently perverse, and then, of course, the other warriors "wish with all their hearts" that their dowdy housewives could be "just like her" . . . even though this was not permitted by the strict patriarchal structure of Greek society . . . not to mention the fact that if the wives actually were like the Amazon queen, their husbands would be terrified of them . . . though also sexually turned on . . . which I suppose is a trade-off some men might be willing to make.

These are the ancient myths and fantasies men have created

through the ages to keep women in a passive, submissive posture, because deep in their hearts they are afraid of our strength. I knew from the stories the elder women told me that our warrior women, like those of other societies, were quite as capable on the battlefield as men, and it is their example I follow.

One afternoon, and for a reason I didn't yet fully understand, I was compelled to go visit an ancient medicine woman named Buffalo Woman, Esévóná'e. I knew of her, as all did, and had met her as a child. She lives alone, and has for many years, in a tipi just on the edge of the res, on property owned by a Cheyenne rancher along Rosebud Creek. Her needs are met by his family, who bring her food and whatever else she requires, and by tribal members who come for her wise counsel and strong medicine. Because the women on the res no longer know how to make tipis, the old woman had made her own from buffalo hides donated by a rancher couple in South Dakota named O'Brien, who raise the native bovine in the most natural habitat possible, which also involves restoring the native prairie—honorable white people, doing sacred work. Buffalo Woman said she could not live in a tipi made from cowhide, that it would poison her in both body and spirit.

I scratched on her tipi flap, and she invited me in. A small fire burned in the center. It took a moment for my eyes to adjust to the dim light. They say she is well over a hundred years old, but no one, including her, seems to know exactly how old. She is tiny and nearly bald, her shrunken skull covered in translucent skin that looks as fragile as old parchment paper, with a network of thin red veins running through it. I don't know if she ever learned English, for she only speaks in her native tongue, or in Arapaho, in which she is also fluent. I speak both those languages myself, so that is no problem for me. I had been told that she liked to smoke, and when one goes to visit an elder or a medicine man or woman, it is essential to arrive with an offering. So I brought a bag of tobacco to give to her.

She looked at me with tiny bright eyes, like the eyes of a bird of prey, that seemed to own both prescience and omniscience. "I know who you are, child," she said to me. "I have been waiting for you for many, many years. I knew you would come. You are the little girl who was murdered."

"No, grandmother, that was my sister," I answered. "It was a mistake in the newspaper. I was not murdered, I ran away."

"No, it was you, child," she said, nodding with certainty. "I do not read the newspaper."

"However you wish, grandmother. But for what reason have you been waiting for me?"

"To give you something that belongs to you. Something my grandmother gave me to keep when I was a child. I asked her what I was supposed to do with it. She told me to keep it safe, and one day a woman would come, and I would recognize that it was to her I must give it."

"But how do you know that woman is me, grandmother?"

She did not answer that question, she just looked at me with those shiny, piercing eyes, which was sufficient answer.

"And what is it that she gave you?"

"That I do not know. It is all wrapped up. I have not opened it. I have never looked at it. It is not my business. My business was to keep it until you came. Let us smoke a pipe together, child, with this fine tobacco you have brought me, to honor this gift. And then I will give it to you and be on my way."

"On your way? Are you going somewhere, grandmother?"

"It is time for me to walk the hanging road in the sky to Seano, child. I have been waiting for you, so that I could do this last service for my grandmother before I left. When I see her, I wish to be able to say that it is done, that I have fulfilled my promise."

The old woman pulled her pipe from a beaded bag, and between her gnarled, skeletal thumb and three fingers took a generous pinch of tobacco from the pouch, expertly packing the bowl. Then she held a stick over the fire until the end took flame, and lit the pipe, sucking on it until the tobacco glowed. She held it up now to bless the sky, then lowered it to bless the earth, and finally turned it to bless the four cardinal directions, took a deep drag, and handed the pipe to me. I did the same and took a draw.

We smoked in silence, passing the pipe back and forth until the bowl was finished. Then Buffalo Woman tapped the ashes into the fire and slid the pipe back into its bag, which she handed to me. "You keep this, child," she said, "I do not need it any longer." She reached behind her and dragged a package from against the wall of the tipi. It was wrapped in an old hide and tied with a leather thong. She pushed it toward me. "Here you are, granddaughter. I have carried this around most of my life. I am happy you finally came for it. Thank you for accepting this gift from my grandmother. I must sleep now."

A buffalo blanket lay by the wall of the tipi beside her. She crawled over and curled up upon it, so shrunken with age that she looked like an ancient ten-year-old child. I moved to her side and placed my hand lightly on her forehead. "Thank you, grandmother. Sleep well." I sat with her like that for some time, until her breath grew increasingly shallow, and finally stopped altogether, her forehead cooling. It was the most peaceful of passings, and I imagined a younger version of her now walking the hanging road to Seano.

I untied the thong and unfolded the dried, cracked hide, beneath which I found a stack of old ledger books with faded covers. When I picked one up, it shed small fragments of time-yellowed paper. It was the first six of these books that I took to Chicago and left in the care of the magazine editor JW Dodd at his office, and which he reprinted in his city magazine, under the title *The Journals of Meggie Kelly and Molly McGill*. The others you are presently reading.

I mention all this backstory because more recently I went to see JW again where he had parked his trailer on the res several weeks ago. I was surprised that he was still here. I hadn't seen him since his first night when I had chased off the meth heads who were harassing him.

Again, it was nighttime, late, by my own design, and he had all the lights inside the trailer turned off, with just the outside porch light left on. He had pulled his awning down and set up a little folding table under it with a single chair. I assumed he had gone to bed. I tried the door and was surprised to find it unlocked. I opened it and went in. He was sound asleep in his bed, lying on his back, snoring lightly. I was in my incarnation as a nineteenth-century warrior woman, wearing my hide shift, moccasins, and leggings as he had always seen me, but dressed up a little tonight with a buffalo bone choker, my hair in braids wrapped with raw-hide straps, an eagle feather dangling from one of them, a beaded headband, and my knife in a beaded sheath at my waist. I will admit here that I wanted to look pretty for JW Dodd. At the same time, I wanted to scare the shit out of him.

It was a warm night, and he was covered by only a sheet, under which he appeared to be nude. I took off my leggings and moccasins, hiked my dress up, and climbed onto the bed, straddling and settling lightly upon him. I pulled my knife from the sheath and very gently laid the dull top edge of the blade against his throat. He opened his eyes but did not move. "If you're wondering what woke you up . . ." I whispered, putting slight pressure on the knife. His eyes took a moment to focus on me and consider this situation. "Little Molly Standing Bear," he finally said, "I must be having an erotic dream."

"Not yet you aren't, white boy . . ." And I admit to being disappointed that he wasn't afraid of me.

"Has anyone told you how nice you look tonight?"

"Just my mirror." I could feel him growing between my legs. "You always sleep nude?" I asked.

"You always go without panties?" he answered.

"We don't wear panties. Where do you think this outfit came from, Victoria's Secret? And how do you know that I'm not wearing them?"

"Because I feel a certain specific warmth emanating from you." Now he moved a little under me.

I slightly relaxed the pressure on the knife. "You see how easily I could kill you?"

"Yes, I've certainly considered that. But then I was thinking, why would you want to?"

"Because I'm an Amazon, and that's what we do. And because you lied about me in your magazine. You made me sound like a cheap slut who slept with you on our first encounter and wanted to have your baby. What was that all about?"

"I did lie, and I'm sorry. I believe that journalism is often more interesting when slightly fictionalized . . . which, of course, is not a popular position among my peers."

"If it's fictionalized, it isn't journalism," I pointed out.

"Quite true, Molly . . . but it always helps to titillate one's readers. Is that really what you do? You're an assassin?"

"Of sorts."

"Ah . . . would you mind taking that knife away from my throat now?" he asked.

I did and slipped it back in the sheath. "I just wanted to make our respective positions clear," I said, as I climbed higher upon him and settled myself gently on his face. "I told you that we Amazons take our sexual pleasure when, how, and with whom we wish."

"That you did," he said, his voice slightly muffled. "And you could hardly make your position any clearer."

"OK, stop talking now, white boy, and start paying your dues."

"You know, Molly," said JW Dodd as we lay in each other's arms in the bed of his trailer, "you come on as a Strongheart nineteenth-century warrior woman, but you have a gentleness, too, a softness. And if I may say so, a great reserve of untapped love to give. And by the way, that was a much better first date than going to the movies."

"Let's not get ahead of ourselves, JW, with talk of love, and I'm not sure I would call this a date, exactly. I simply wanted to be pleasured, and for you to know how I smell . . . and taste."

"Hmmm . . . OK, then," he said, "let's see if I can describe it . . . Like a . . . like a freestone trout stream in the early fall, when the tendrils of bright green algae wave in the clear current, and the sharp mineral taste of midsummer is enriched by the pungent falling leaves of autumn . . ."

"Wow, that's not bad, JW," I admitted. "No one's ever said anything like that to me before."

"No one's ever done anything like that to me before. It deserved a thoughtful description."

"Although I'm not so sure about the algae and pungent leaves part."

"You know, Molly, I have to tell you this," he said . . . "you are without doubt the strangest woman I have ever met. And the most mysterious. Yet I sense that you have a vulnerability lurking just beneath your tough façade. Even when we were kids, and the res boys were already scared of you, I sensed that about you. I'd like to know more about your life."

"Little by little, JW," I answered, "maybe . . . but slowly. Right now it's hard for me to trust people, especially men. I don't mind coming to you like this now and then, having these encounters, but let's not confuse it with making love. I'm not at all ready to confide in you or have what you would call a . . . 'relationship' . . . I wouldn't even know how to do that."

"OK, Molly, understood, but then just tell me one thing that might be revealing about you," JW proposed . . . "I mean anything at all. Tell me a story. And then I'll do the same."

I had to think about this for a long while.

"OK," I finally said, "so I'll just tell you this . . . knowing your fondness for metaphors. You may have noticed that there are a bunch of stray dogs who wander around the res . . . maybe you've even seen a few of them out here, although they tend to hang more around town. Some have been abused, abandoned, others just ignored, most of them starving, many of them sick. When I was a kid, I worked part time at the trading post in town during the summer, and over holidays. You remember, you used to come in and try to flirt with me? That's when the res kids decided to beat the white boy up.

"So anyway, one day I was taking out some trash behind the store, and I saw that there were three mutts, all males, skulking around, clearly interested in something behind some cardboard boxes. And from there I heard another dog growling. So I made a little circle around the males and came up behind the boxes to see what was up. I found a little dog there, who looked very young, and I soon learned was a bitch. It was Christmastime, and she had made a little nest for herself in a pile of old insulation someone had dumped there, a kind of dog bed for the homeless. She hardly paid any attention to me, because she was completely fixated upon those three males, staring at them intently, baring her teeth and growling. I mean, she was tiny in comparison, any one of them alone could easily have torn her to pieces, and the three of them together would have killed and eaten her in an instant. But they didn't. Every now and then, one of them would make a kind of feint, or two of them would come up on either side of her, like they were going to charge. But she stood her ground, her back up, showing her teeth, her growls deeper and more threatening. She was one tough bitch, who intended to defend her territory, and those three big male dogs didn't dare call her bluff. They were either afraid of her, or just respected her, because they finally slunk away, frustrated maybe by their own cowardice.

"I wanted to take that little dog home, but I knew my family wouldn't let me have her in the house, so I started bringing food to her whenever I could. And a little later, when I ran away from home again, I took her with me. I got all the way to Billings that time, and I went to the animal rescue shelter there. They gave her free shots, and the vet on duty told me she was only about a year old. Only one year old and she scared off those three big adult male dogs . . .

"That little dog taught me a lesson about the source of power, about acting tough and unfearful in the face of danger, even if you're not feeling tough and are terrified. She taught me a lesson about defending my territory, because no one else is going to do that for me. I learned not to let myself be a victim, even though I already was one, and would continue to be at the hands of a family member, who was bigger and stronger than me, and on whom my bluff and toughness were not adequate defense. And later, I just became a victim of my own weakness . . . but it was thinking about that dog that helped bring me out of my victimhood.

"Anyway, I knew it was only a matter of time before I was caught again and sent back to the res, so I left the bitch at the shelter, and one of the ladies who worked there promised me she was going to adopt her. I loved that little dog, and it has always given me great solace to imagine her spending her life in a nice home with a yard to run in, and maybe some kids to play with . . . I think I wanted that lady to adopt me, too . . . so I could run around in the yard with that little dog."

I started crying a little then, surprising myself with my own emotion. JW held me close against him so I could cry into his neck, and he whispered: "That's a good story, Molly." He didn't ask me any more questions or say anything more than that, which I appreciated, because there was nothing more to be said. It's funny the things we carry around all our lives, both the good and the bad, both the things that make us happy and those that make us sad.

THE LOST JOURNALS
OF MAY DODD

A Life of Crime

I did something strange then, and as much as I've thought about it since, I'm still not exactly certain why. I held both lead ropes in one hand, and the other hand I placed affectionately on the boy's cheek, and I kissed him directly on his lips, a real kiss like a lover. And he kissed me back. "Thank you," I whispered, in his mouth, "thank you so much." And then I led the two horses away, turning only once to see him staring after me with a look of utter astonishment on his face, as I disappeared into the darkness beyond.

—from the lost journals of May Dodd

12 June 1876

We sold the additional four horses to the stablemaster, P. J. Bartlett, in the foothills of the Bighorns, eleven miles from Fort Fetterman. Considering that Wind and I had stolen the mounts from the outlaw gang who captured us, we made rather a handsome profit for our efforts. Having lived in a barter society of hunters, gatherers, and hide traders, it is still a strange feeling to return to a cash economy, and to have all this money in our possession, not to mention for me to be dressed as a white frontierswoman, in which role I continue to feel like an impostor. I live with one foot in both worlds.

As well as our two favorite horses, Wind and I kept two more of the string as pack/riding animals to carry our new supplies, and to alternate with the others. I also purchased a calendar and several more ledger books at the mercantile, though I have written virtually nothing these past days.

For our second transaction, Mr. Bartlett and his two sons met us at a designated spot outside Tent City, so that we did not have to bring the horses into town and either risk another encounter with Captain John G. Bourke or expose Wind to the indignities and possible dangers facing an Indian woman in a town of whites. In any case, as I mentioned earlier, she had steadfastly refused to enter any village or homestead ... and who can blame her?

The Bartletts went through their routine of riding and inspecting our equines for handling and soundness and, after a bit of negotiation, a price suitable to both parties was amicably reached. I could see that they respected me in our dealings, while largely ignoring Wind, and I considered how different ... indeed, how impossible such a transaction would have been had I arrived dressed as a squaw. This is yet another rationale used by my race to exterminate or incarcerate the native population, simply because they are different than we are; they have darker skin, and Mongolian features, both strikingly handsome and foreign; they live in tipis instead of houses; they are nomads instead of permanent dwellers; they believe that human beings are simply a part of the natural world, and not lords over it. Yet they are also, it must be said, a culture of warriors, and this, perhaps, is what we have most in common . . . except that we whites are more numerous and have better weapons than they. It is, finally, the history of civilization against wilderness, a battle that wilderness doesn't stand a fair chance of winning.

"Mrs. Ames," said P. J. Bartlett upon conclusion of our business, "when and if you and your husband should acquire more stock for sale, I am always in need of sound horseflesh, and you seem to have a fine eye for it. Do keep us in mind. I think you can see that we run an honest business and are fair in our dealings."

"I can, indeed, sir, and I will keep that in mind. I should also like to give credit where credit is due, to our partner, who goes by the name of Wind," I said, indicating my friend, who all this time sat her mount, watching the proceedings with a wary eye. "It is she who has trained all of our string, and is also known in her tribe as one of their most accomplished horse breakers. If you have no objection to the native . . . or perhaps I should more accurately say, the wild descendants of Spanish equines, we might also be able to bring you some of these to inspect. They are hardy and well suited to this plains country, and once broken and trained, they are every bit equal and, in our opinion, superior to the average Army horse, having spent generations living in this landscape."

To his credit, P. J., looked over at Wind and touched the brim of his hat in a gesture of polite acknowledgment. "I would be happy to look over whatever you bring me, ma'am," he said. "Speaking of the Army, I must tell you that a certain Captain John Bourke came to see me the day after our first transaction." Bartlett looked at me inquiringly before proceeding, as if to ascertain if the name alone might elicit some expression of recognition on my part. "He asked many questions about you, Mrs. Ames."

Although my heart registered a quickening, I do not believe that my face gave it away. "Did he? I'm afraid I don't understand, Mr. Bartlett. What sort of questions, and for what purpose was the captain asking them?"

"Apparently, he saw you briefly in the mercantile that day, and he seemed to think he might know you. The questions he asked were to determine whether or not this was the case."

"I do not know a Captain Bourke, sir, nor does the name itself mean anything to me."

"In his questioning of me, Mrs. Ames, I mentioned that you had not wished to return to the mercantile to pick up your goods . . . although I did not know for what reason. I also told him your name, and that you and your husband were from Nebraska, and in the horse business. I hope I did not in any way violate your privacy, ma'am, but I do a good deal of business with the Army, and I must be forthcoming when interviewed by an officer. My reputation is at stake."

"Of course, Mr. Bartlett. And I can assure you that nothing you said to the captain could possibly compromise my privacy. Clearly, he must have mistaken me for someone he once knew. No harm is done."

"I must also tell you, ma'am," he continued, "that depending on your and your husband's plans, travel in the country north of here is likely to be treacherous due to a reported massing of hostile Indians over the border in Montana Territory. These are largely Sioux, Cheyenne, and Arapaho bands who refuse to go into the agencies as demanded by the government and are fixing for a fight. General Crook has left Fort Fetterman with a massive force of soldiers to intercept and defeat, once and for all, the last of these miscreants."

"I see . . . I thank you for that warning, sir. It appears that my husband will not be in any condition to travel for some time. However, our partner, Wind, and I, must continue to ply our trade. It seems as if such a gathering might provide business opportunities, for surely the commodity of horses will be much in demand. Of which side do you feel an Indian woman and a white woman traveling alone together have the most to fear, the natives or the soldiers?"

"Both, Mrs. Ames, and especially of the confrontation between them. I am surprised, if I may be so bold to say, that your husband would let you go off alone. Believe me, you do not want to get in the middle of those two armies, of that I can assure you." Little did Mr. Bartlett know how much in the middle of them we had already been.

"I highly recommend that you consider settling right here in our region," he continued. "It is a growing community with a great future, and a safe haven from the heathens due to the presence of the fort. Furthermore, as I suggested, P. J. Bartlett and Sons will purchase all the horses you bring us. You need not risk your lives by going afield to ply your trade."

"Well, sir, you have generously depleted us of our stock, so we must go a bit afield in any case."

"Confine your search to the east, west, or south, then, ma'am, I highly recommend."

And so we parted company. I told Wind that we must leave immediately and not return here.

"And where do we go, Mesoke?" she asked me.

It was a good question, and there were two quite different answers I had been pondering. We could continue our wanderings, or we could go back toward the Red Cloud Agency at Fort Robinson and possibly be reunited with Little Wolf's band, assuming they are still there . . . I could rejoin my daughter . . . my Little Bird, for it is her, if no one else, whom I must save from this place. It has taken me nearly all this time to feel truly alive again, as if my near death—all that precipitated it, and came after—killed some essential part of me, overwhelming even my maternal instincts, only now reawakening. I have lost three children, not to death, thank God for that, but lost only to me . . . and I long to recover at least one of them . . . my baby. But then once again, at the agency I would be reported to the Army and the government, and certainly sent back to Chicago, to resume my incarceration in the Lake Forest Lunatic Asylum. And I would lose my child again. Better to push on.

"We go north," I said, "where the tribes and the Army are gathering. The People will always need more horses, and on the way, we will find some for them."

23 June 1876

And thus have we been traveling, keeping largely to the foothills of the Bighorn Mountains, as we know that the Army, with its ungainly mule-drawn supply wagons, will follow the more easily traveled routes in the plains to the east. For the most obvious reasons, we wish to avoid contact with them . . . unless we decide to risk a raid on what must be their own enormous herd of horses.

This is lovely, rich country we are moving through in the early summer. The Bighorns are fragrantly green with forests of lodgepole pine trees, and stands of aspen in fresh new leaf, wild rosebushes, and mountain meadows with an impossible fecundity and variety of flowers in bloom, so beautiful that one does not wish to disturb the flora by riding a horse through them. Of wildlife, there is an equal bounty: mule deer and whitetail deer, elk, moose, antelope, bighorn sheep, hawks, eagles, falcons, owls of all sorts, grouse and wild turkey, bears, coyotes, and mountain lions.

There are creeks, and feeder streams, that enter into the larger rivers in the flatlands at the base of the mountains; the water still high and muddy with spring runoff, but clearing now in the foothills. We have no trouble catching trout in the smaller, more intimate creeks. Indeed, one of my purchases at the mercantile in Tent City was a bamboo fishing rod and a reel with braided horsehair line. According to the proprietor, these items are kept in stock because fishing has become a popular pastime among the soldiers at Fort Fetterman, and General George Crook himself is a particular aficionado of the sport . . . that is, during their leisure time when he and his soldiers are not busy hunting down and killing hostile Indians.

Yet it is easy this time of year, in this landscape, to imagine a false sense of security, as if the wars are very far away. Thus we dawdle somewhat in our travels, reveling in the mountain paradise, ignoring for these precious moments the true task at hand, to rejoin the fight.

Wind seems for once uncertain of herself, for she receives no messages from her twin sister, nor has she had a vision in which she has received news of where she and Little Wolf's band are.

1 July 1876

Three days ago, we ventured back down into lower country in search of horses, wild or otherwise. As if by providence, before we had descended completely from the foothills, we saw in the plains some distance to the east a great cloud of dust rising, stirred up, we soon learned, by a cattle drive moving north, on its way, we assumed, to Montana Territory, where, according to Mr. Bartlett, ranchers are staking out vast tracts of grazing land now that both the buffalo herds and the tribes have been so decimated. It brought to my mind a similar scene we had witnessed from our train when first our group was headed out west. Those scamps Meggie and Susie had put their bare fannies up to the train windows, which shocked a number of our women, but amused others of us, and clearly charmed the cowboys who were driving the herd. They took their hats off, whooping and waving them in the air to greet those naked Irish butts. How long ago that now seems . . . how innocent we all still were . . .

As Wind and I moved closer to the drive, we guessed that there must be at least two to three hundred head of longhorn cattle, although their numbers were impossible to accurately estimate, partly due to the dust cloud that obscured them. Several wranglers were also driving a remuda of extra horses. In order to get a sense of their daily routine, we followed them for two days, at a sufficient distance not to be discovered. At night, we made forays on foot closer to their evening fires to see how and where the horses were corralled. I was dressed again in my deer hide shift, leggings, and moccasins, and the two of us moved as silently as only Indians can, like ghosts. Wind said the horses would know that we were about, and it was good, for they would catch our scent and we would thus be familiar to them when we went in to steal them. Some of the mounts the cowboys rode were picketed together, while other hands kept theirs tethered next to their individual sleeping places. The remuda was held in a roughly circular picket line. This would be our primary target and as there were only two of us, we knew we could not be greedy and attempt to take too many. Wind said that unlike those we stole from the outlaws, these horses did not know us yet, only our vague scent, and when we first appeared among them they would likely be a little spooked.

"In the old days, when I was just a girl," she said, "and my talent with horses had become known to the tribe, I would go on raiding parties with our men. All knew that I brought good luck. The important warriors of our enemies kept their favorite warhorse, or two, tied beside their lodge, as do we. These are always the best and most prized horses to take, but also the hardest and most dangerous to steal, for the slightest noise will wake someone in the tipi. This task was usually given to me, for, as you know, Mesoke, I gentle them, I speak to them without words, they recognize me as a friend. It has always been this way with me and horses. You are a white woman, and these cowboy horses know how white people smell. I saw how the outlaw horses accepted you and so I believe will these. For our first raid, we will each take two, one to ride and one to lead. But we will go among them the night before we steal them, to make them familiar with us, to touch them, and to choose those we wish to take."

And this we did, coming into the night camp of the cowboys very late, while all slept. There was only a thin sliver of moon in the sky, but our night vision was keen from the fact that we spent so much time in the dark. We already knew where the single wrangler who watched the remuda at night would station himself, for every night on the trail their bivouac was set up the same. At this hour he always slept, and when he woke, he walked around the circle of the picket line and then slept again, using his saddle as a pillow.

It wasn't such an easy life these white men led. But during the several nights we had been following and watching them, we heard them singing after their supper. One of the men played a guitar, and another a harmonica, and the cowboy songs they sang were lively with a jaunty tempo, while others were sad, both the instruments and the words telling tales of failed love. I rather liked their music, though Wind did not, which made me recognize again that a part of me . . . the white part . . . missed my people.

That first night we each picked out the two horses we were going to take, and we introduced ourselves to them. I picked a small sorrel mare to ride, and a bay gelding who was tied near her and who I thought had a particularly well-formed head. Wind told me I had a good eye for horseflesh. I touched mine gently along their flanks and caressed their heads. She picked a palomino and a buckskin, both of them geldings.

We followed the drive again all the next day, and that night after the music died, we lay awake outside their camp. Having watched them for three days, I had begun to feel some attachment to these cowboys, and a certain sense of guilt about the prospect of stealing their horses. They were just young men, some of them mere boys, trying to make a living at what must be a very hard job, day after day in the saddle, weeks and months on the trail, breathing dust kicked up by a herd of bawling cattle. But I tried to put these sympathetic thoughts out of my mind for we, too, had a job to do, and we, too, had faced more than our share of hardship.

Once again we sneaked silently into the remuda. A few of the horses reacted nervously, as they had the night before, stepping sideways and turning their heads to look at us. We stopped then and stood motionless until they calmed again. It was not enough of a disturbance to cause worry or wake anyone up, just the normal night sounds and shifting of picketed horses, the more distant sounds of the cattle herd also providing cover noise. We separated, Wind going one way to gather her two, and I the other way. I quickly located my mare, stroked her and untied her lead rope, led her to the bay, and untied him. Our plan was simply to lead them away some distance before we mounted. But as I turned, my heart skipped a beat, for I was looking directly into the eyes of the young wrangler who should have been sleeping beside the remuda. Instinctively, I raised my index finger to my lips in the universal sign of silence, hoping he wouldn't call out to his compatriots. And he didn't, he simply regarded me with a puzzled expression. "What are you doing, ma'am?" he whispered, evidently respecting my raised finger. I had no answer to this but to tell the truth. "Taking these two horses. Please don't give me away. I beg you." Now he looked me up and down. "You're dressed like a savage, but you're a white woman." I did something strange then, and as much as I've thought about it since, I'm still not exactly certain why. I held both lead ropes in one hand, and the other hand I placed affectionately on the boy's cheek, and I kissed him directly on his lips, a real kiss like a lover. And he kissed me back. "Thank you," I whispered, in his mouth, "thank you so much." And then I led the two horses away, turning only once to see him staring after me with a look of utter astonishment on his face, as I disappeared into the darkness beyond.

I did not believe he would follow me, or alert the others, and maybe, after all, that was the instinctive reason I had kissed him. But perhaps, mixed up with that instinct, was a simple longing on my part to have physical contact with a man. He was a handsome boy, and I have to confess that I enjoyed the kiss myself . . . I felt a certain sense of intimacy, a long dormant stirring of . . . what? . . . lust? Susie and Meggie always used to tease me about being "a bit of a tart" as they put it, and maybe they were right. Or perhaps I am simply lonely . . .

Wind joined me, leading her two horses, and after we had walked them far enough away in silence I told her about the boy, and what I had done.

"That was a wise thing, Mesoke," she said, "for you gave him something else to think about. But it was also dangerous because young men can act recklessly when the blood rushes to their *vétoo'otse*. He may try to follow you for more than a kiss."

I laughed lightly. "The last I saw of him, he looked too stunned to move."

We had both wrapped lengths of rope around our waists, which we each now rigged on one of our horses' halters, to make of them rudimentary hackamores with two reins, a trick Wind had taught me. We mounted bareback somewhat gingerly, for one can never be certain if a horse can be controlled without a bit in its mouth, but my mare responded beautifully, as did Wind's palomino gelding. We rode, each leading our second horse.

It was a full hour or more before we reached our own camp in a secluded coulee where we had left our panniers and picketed our four other mounts. We didn't think that the cowboys, assuming by now that all had learned of the theft, would try to track us in the dark, but they might do so at first light, which was only a few hours away. And so we loaded everything and moved out in the dark, headed back toward the foothills in order to put as much distance between us and the cattle drive as possible. I wondered if the boy I kissed would even mention that four horses had disappeared on his night shift, for fear of being punished, in which case it would take the others some time to realize they were missing. Perhaps they would simply absorb the loss, and not even try to follow us, which would only slow down the drive. But that was not something we could count on.

We traveled through the dawn and then for a half day before making an early camp alongside a creek in a small, secluded valley Wind led us to, a place she said she remembered as a child that would be a safe place for us to rest for a day or two. We were tired, for we hadn't slept in over twenty-four hours and before that our late-night excursions to get the lay of the cowboy camp had cost us further sleep. I was learning that horse rustling is hard work.

We set up the canvas tent I had purchased, which seemed such a luxury, and hobbled the horses to let them graze on the new spring grass. Wind entered the tent and fell immediately asleep, while I went down to the creek, stripped off my clothes, and waded into a pool to wash off the dust and sweat of our efforts. The mountain water was icy but felt wonderful. I floated on my back for a moment to wet my hair, and rubbed my face and body as clean as I could. But my skin was already beginning to go numb, and I couldn't stay much longer in the pool. I roused myself and stepped back up on the bank. The sun was still high and bright, and I lay down in the warm grass. It was then that I heard a horse whinny down-valley from whence we had just come, and one of ours answered it. I sat up to watch a lone rider coming out of the trees at a brisk trot, breaking into a gentle lope. Good God, Wind was right, the foolish young cowboy I kissed had somehow managed to follow us.

Wind scurried agilely out of the tent, as alert and fully awake as are animals suddenly roused from sleep. She held her rifle in one hand, stood, shouldered it, and pointed it at the boy.

"Don't shoot him, Wind," I called to her. "At least not yet. Let us see what his intentions are."

"We already know what his intentions are, Mesoke," she answered. The natives tend to be a literal race, but when she said this I couldn't help thinking that I detected a rare hint of irony in her voice. I wondered if she had perhaps picked this up from me during our time together.

"Then let us hear him express them," I said.

I did not wish to put on my dirty hide shift over my still wet and relatively clean body, and was planning now to dress again in my white-woman outfit, having slept. And so I stood naked in the sun, making no effort to hide myself. I have largely abandoned conventional notions of modesty . . . and perhaps I wished, as well, to further titillate the boy.

He slowed his horse to a walk when he saw Wind aiming the rifle at him, raised both hands in the air, and called out: "I don't mean ya no harm, I come in peace, you can keep the horses, I don't even want 'em back. That ain't why I came."

Roughly halfway between me and Wind, he reined up and dismounted, his horse raising its head and whinnying again, answered by my mare, who was hobbled and grazing with the others. Clearly, they knew each other. The boy wore a wide-brimmed hat tilted back on his head, leather chaps and a vest, a cartridge belt and holstered pistol. He walked partway toward me, with his hands raised, his head comically tilted down and away from me, averting his eyes from my naked body.

"Awful sorry, ma'am, to interrupt your bath," he said. "Does your friend speak English? If she don't, will ya tell her she can lower that rifle? I come as a friend."

"She speaks English, but it's unlikely that she's going to do that," I said. "If you don't want your horses back, what are you doing here? How did you find us?"

"I been trackin' you the whole way, ma'am."

"You must be a good tracker then. I thought only Indians owned that skill."

"That I am, ma'am, I learnt to read sign as a boy from my grandpa. He was half Comanche."

"And why have you come?"

"To ask you why you kissed me like that, ma'am?"

I laughed. "You followed us all this way just to ask me that question?"

"Yes, ma'am . . . I guess I did."

"You can stop calling me ma'am. I'm not an old lady."

The boy allowed himself a small, wry smile. "Yes, ma'am, that I can surely see."

"I don't know how, if you won't look at me. Go ahead if you want." But he shook his head. I laughed. "Shy fellow, aren't you?"

"No, ma'am, just respectful of womenfolk, that's all . . . the way my mama taught me. Wouldn't be Christian of me to stare at ya after I rousted ya outta your bath."

"You really needn't concern yourself with being unchristian here, we're heathens."

"So why did ya?"

"Why did I what?"

"Kiss me like that?"

"To distract you, to keep you from calling out to the others." I could see from the shadow crossing his face that he did not find this answer entirely satisfactory. "What did you think? That I'd fallen instantly in love with you?"

"No, ma'am, I did not think that . . . but you sure kissed me like you had."

"Have you never been kissed by a woman before?"

"Not like that, ma'am. And you were right . . . it sure did distract me. Ya know that sorrel mare you took? See, she belonged to me, an' her name is Lucky. I was just lookin' in on her when I came upon you. And then when ya kissed me like that . . . well, darn't . . . I thought I must still be dreamin' . . . ya know how sometimes you have those dreams where you think you've woke up and gone about your business, but ya haven't really and you're still dreamin'?"

"Yes, I do."

"It was like that. That's why I didn't holler to the others. It was just like in a dream, where I try to holler, but nothin' comes out."

"I'll give the mare back to you."

"I don't want her back. I want ya to keep her. But ya gotta keep her name, so she stays lucky for ya."

"OK, so now that you know why I kissed you, you're going to turn around and go back to your drive, right?"

"No, ma'am, I was just gettin' round to that part . . . I want to ask you if I can throw in with you and your pardner?"

"What?"

"I think you heard me, ma'am."

"Why would you want to do that?"

He shrugged. "I left the drive a little after you did, and I didn't tell no one, neither. I just packed my kit, saddled up, and hit the trail. They're gonna think it was me who stole those horses. Ya know what they do with horse thieves in this country, don'tcha, ma'am? They hang 'em from the nearest tree. Anyhow, I was gettin' tired a' drovin' all day, suckin' dust, listenin' to cattle bawlin'. See, I got a little money saved up, because every time we passed near a town on the way here from Texas, the trail boss, he give us some of our pay. All the other boys took turns goin' into town, spendin' their money on whiskey at the saloon . . . and . . . and on the gals who work there . . . ya know . . ." I swear he blushed beet red when he referred to the working girls in the saloon. "But, see, I saved my pay, so I got a little nest egg. I been thinkin' on it all day. I wouldn't get in your way, and I could help protect you from outlaws, and Injuns, too . . . well, I guess ya are Injuns, aren't ya . . . sorta, anyhow."

"I would have to talk to my partner about that," I said, "for she, yes, is an Indian, as I think you could see. And even if we let you ride with us for a time, you'd have to understand that there would be no more kissing involved."

"Yes, ma'am, I understand that . . . I sure do . . . that was just in my dream."

"I told you to stop calling me ma'am. My name is May Dodd, what's yours?"

"Chance Hadley, ma'am. Tascosa, Texas. Real pleased to meet ya, May Dodd." He touched the brim of his hat as he said this, but still kept his head cocked to the side, his eyes averted.

"We're not really meeting unless we look at each other," I pointed out, "so if naked women embarrass you, Chance Hadley, you just look me in the eyes."

"Yes, ma'am . . . I mean, yes, May." Finally, he looked up at me, took off his cowboy hat, and blushed again. I'm not sure I've ever seen a man blush so much as that. I wondered if he had ever seen a naked girl before. I have to say that he did seem harmless enough, but also I suspected that he was competent. I rather liked the boy . . . I keep referring to him here that way, but in the daylight, up close, he didn't actually seem any younger than me, maybe even roughly the same age, or older. He was tall and slender as he stood straight, trying to look me directly in the eye, though he was hav-ing some difficulty in keeping his from straying, his own dark eyes crinkled in what looked something like amused wonder. His light brown hair was long, matted and unruly, and as the blush began to fade, his skin took on a leathery saddle-brown hue, weathered but taut on his face, his features more manly than boyish—a broad forehead, straight nose, well-formed chin, and strong cheekbones. He wore at least several days of light beard stubble that I remem-bered from our kiss. He was a handsome fellow, as I had even noted in the dark, and I wondered if perhaps that was also part of the reason I had kissed him so enthusiastically. And now I was think-ing that it might be a relief to have a man along with us. Wind and I have been alone for a long time, first in the cave, and now since traveling. I love her, and owe her my life, but she is hardly what one would refer to as loquacious, and we have long since exhausted our conversational topics that don't revolve around weather, food, horses, and hunting. In addition, ever since separation from the tribe, we have lived in a state of constant vulnerability. I rather hoped she would agree to letting the cowboy join us.

"OK, Chance, we're going to walk over now to my partner. Her full name is Woman Who Moves against the Wind, but I call her simply Wind. I will introduce you two. If she says you can ride with us, so be it. If she says no, then you'll have to leave. And if that happens, I'll give you back both the horses I stole. But in our world, her two belong to her, and those I can't give to you."

"That's fair enough, May. And I told ya, I don't want the horses. I want you to keep 'em. Specially Lucky. Keep her as a special gift. You chose well, she's a real good horse."

"That's good of you, Chance, thank you. And I won't change her name. It's nice to know she's a gift and no longer stolen property."

We walked over to Wind, who still stood at the entrance of our tent, holding her rifle, though she was no longer pointing it at the cowboy. While observing our conversation, she had clearly identified the fact that he was not threatening. I told her in Cheyenne that he hadn't come to take back the horses we had stolen, he just wanted to talk to me, and I explained about his grandfather being half Comanche, as I thought it might soften her a little to know that he had Indian blood himself. I felt she must already be impressed by the fact that he had been able to follow our trail, even starting out in the dark as he had. I said he seemed like a decent fellow, and she admitted that for a white man he was polite, and had behaved properly by not staring at me. However, when I told her about his request to ride with us, she scowled and shook her head. "No, Mesoke," she said. "I do not trust him."

"Why not?" I asked.

"Because he is a white man, and is moving his stinking cows into our country, to take the place of our buffalo brothers they are killing."

I tried to explain that they weren't actually his cows, he was just working for the people who owned them, but this distinction made no difference to her. "But doesn't it count," I asked, "that he has one-eighth Indian blood?"

She looked directly at Chance now, and she said something to him in a language I wasn't familiar with, but that I assumed was Comanche. I was not even aware that she spoke it. To my enormous surprise, he smiled and answered her back in the same language.

"You speak Comanche?" I asked him.

"I lived with my grandfather when I was a boy. He wanted me to learn his mother's tongue. He took me among his Comanche family. He knew it would be useful if ever their warriors attacked our ranch."

He said something to Wind that sounded like a question, and she answered.

"What did you just say?"

"I asked her how she learned Comanche."

"How did she answer?"

"She says that her mother was Southern Cheyenne, and she grew up in the south. The Comanche and Southern Cheyenne are allies. They speak different languages but they roam some of the same country and they trade together. She said that she, too, has distant Comanche relatives."

Wind spoke again to Chance, and he answered, and then she answered him back.

"Now what are you talking about?" It did not escape my attention that the cowboy was translating for me. And I was a little ashamed that after all this time together, I did not know these things about Wind's life. How odd to learn them now from a random stranger from whom I had stolen a horse.

"She asked me the name of my Comanche family, and when I told her, she said that she knows them. I think maybe she's going to let me ride with ya."

I couldn't help but laugh at Wind's sudden change of heart. "It is agreeable to you," I asked Wind in Cheyenne, "for the cowboy to join us?"

"I trust him only a little," she said. "He may ride with us for a time, but he is still by blood mostly a white man, and he lives as one, so we must keep close watch over him."

"She doesn't trust white men," I said to Chance, "so your invitation is provisional."

"I don't know what that word means, ma'am."

"It means you can come with us, but she'll be watching you, and you still have to prove yourself trustworthy."

"I can sure do that, ma'am."

"Right now Wind and I need to get some sleep, and I expect you do, too. Turn your horse out with ours, and pitch your camp a bit away from us."

"Yes, ma'am," he said, happily . . . "I mean . . . sorry . . . yes, May, thank you. And I will surely do that. You and your partner will have all the privacy ya want, and I promise not to get in your way. You just let me know if you need anything. I'm a pretty fair hand, and I know how to do plenty a' real useful things."

"I'll just bet you do, Chance."

27 July 1876

I have neglected my journal these past weeks, and have much to tell. We have encountered scattered bands of Cheyenne, Arapaho, and Sioux, and have learned of battles fought, victories won by the People and our allies. One on the Rosebud last month, in which the combined forces of Crazy Horse's Lakota warriors and Little Wolf's Cheyenne defeated General George Crook's army, a second several weeks ago on the Little Bighorn, where our archenemy George Armstrong Custer and his entire command were destroyed. Thus, now we have confirmation that Little Wolf has indeed left the agency, free again, although we do not know where he is. We are told that all the bands have split off in different directions, in order to evade the many soldiers who have converged here. With the Army, we have had encounters, as well . . . have raided their horses and given them to the Indians, all of which I must record before it is overwhelmed in the melee of events that have transpired and continue to unfold. Suffice it to say, for now, that we are in the middle of it all, over the border in Montana Territory, near the Tongue River again, our tribe's home country. For the moment and with the dispersal of the Indian bands and the soldiers, we seem to be experiencing a lull, a strange quiet in the tumult, as at the end of a violent storm, when the sky finally clears and the sun returns. Good God, the havoc the human species wreaks upon each other, upon the earth . . .

As it happens, both Wind and I are grateful to have the cowboy

Chance Hadley in our company, at least for a little while, each of us perhaps for certain similar, and other diverse reasons of our own. As he himself said at the end of my last entry, he is a "pretty fair hand" (a modest understatement on his part) and "knows how to do plenty a' real useful things." Which is to say, he is a competent fellow, as I suspected he would be. He hunts, he cooks, he tracks, he looks after the horses, and he is good company on the trail, both for Wind, with whom he frequently converses in Comanche, and for me. He is forthcoming when I ask him questions about his life growing up on his family's ranch in Texas, and so discreet about asking me about my own that I tend to open up to him in a way I have had neither the occasion nor the time to do with a man before. Despite my promiscuous reputation among some of my friends, I've only been with three men in my life: Harry Ames, my common-law husband; John Bourke, my first impetuous and very brief affair (and the improbable father of my daughter); and the great Chief Little Wolf, a marriage arranged under the auspices of the U.S. government. Three more radically different men it would be hard to imagine, and none of whom I could converse with so easily as I can with this young cowboy.

At the same time, Chance has such an aura of innocence about him that I must here confess I gave him a highly edited version of my past . . . no, actually, a largely false version. I told him that in Chicago I became involved with a missionary society, and joined a group of high-minded women parishioners (hah!) traveling west under the auspices of the U.S. government and the Episcopal Church to live among the Cheyenne, our mission to help convert and civilize the savages. This was partly true, and seemed to me a more palatable story than the more morally tainted details of the Brides for Indians program, and the truth of how I and the others came to join it.

I did tell him about the attack on our camp by the Army, which we later learned was due to misinformation received by the command leader, Colonel Ranald Mackenzie, from a disreputable Indian scout named Jules Seminole, who reported that ours was the winter village of the Oglala Lakota Crazy Horse, not that of the Cheyenne chief Little Wolf, where we white women were known to be in residence. I told him about my wounding and long convalescence, and that I was now seeking the remnants of our band, in order to be reunited with my fellow missionaries. I said that in our time among the Cheyenne, we had come to know that our government and the Army's treatment of the natives was deplorable, shameful, and unchristian, that we still wished to help them, and that we hid from the soldiers now for we knew that they would arrest us and have us prosecuted as traitors for having taken the side of the savages. All this, too, of course, was a slightly sanitized version of the truth, but accurate in spirit at least. I did not, needless to say, tell him that I would take up arms against the Army if I had to.

Despite Wind's affection for the cowboy, her one objection to him traveling with us was that he is a white man and his allegiance will lie with his government, nor would he take our side against the Army. And he clearly does not approve of our profession as horse thieves, nor plan to help us in that activity.

"You see, Mesoke," Wind said to me in private, "he may have a little Indian blood, but we are enemies, and the time will soon come when we must part company and return to our people, and he to his. The boy is in love with you, it is plain to see, and that is why he is here, and perhaps you begin to be a little in love with him?"

"I hardly know the boy. It is too soon to speak of love."

"But not to feel it between your legs. If you fall in love with him it will end badly."

Her words were sobering, nor could I dispute them. "All my loves end badly, Wind."

We spent those first several days in our hidden valley in the Bighorns—resting, hunting, and fishing. Since we have been travel-

ing in this region, we have been roughly shadowing from the
foothills, what, according to the cowboy, the whites call the Bozeman Trail in the flatlands below. This is the original overland
route that prospectors in the last decade followed from the Oregon
Trail to the gold fields of Montana, and it cuts directly through the
Cheyenne and Sioux homeland. Now it is much traveled by Army
troops, wagon trains of homesteaders, and ranchers staking out
large tracts of rangeland on which to pasture their cattle; this indeed is where and how we encountered the drive Chance was on.

After those idyllic few days, we left the valley regretfully. I wish
I could live in such a place, with the mixed forest of lodgepole pine
and aspen stands, the meadow of grass and wildflowers with the
creek running through it, and the abundant wildlife we encountered every day. It is dangerous to tarry too long in such a place,
even that short time, enough to become attached to it, to begin to
yearn for a place to call home again. How long it has been and how
tired I am of the constant travel. I think our race was not designed
to be nomadic.

I have resumed wearing my frontierswoman outfit. In antici-
pation as we move north that we were likely to run into as many
whites as we were Indians, it seemed convenient for Chance and
me to play the role of a young couple traveling with our "civilized"
native servant, as repugnant as that notion seemed to me—the servant part of it, I mean to say. On the other hand, I rather like the
idea of posing as a couple, the normalcy and comfort of it, even
though it be imaginary.

We were only four days down the trail before Wind, who was
scouting that day, returned to tell us she had spotted a train of sixteen oxen-drawn wagons moving north on the road to Montana.
They had roughly forty horses between them, some being ridden
by the settlers, others driven by boys and dogs as a remuda. We
moved lower into the foothills to be able to observe and follow
them for a couple of days, as is our way.

That evening around our fire, Chance, who had been unusually quiet that afternoon, said: "You ladies do understand that I ain't gonna help ya steal horses?"

"You've made that clear," I answered, "and we're not asking for your help."

"Why do ya want more? Ya already got more than we need."

"I've explained that to you, Chance. We're going to give them to whatever friendly bands we come across. Those who are still fighting and holding out against the Army need all the help they can get, and they can always use fresh mounts. Think of it as our small part in the war effort."

"And those folks traveling in the wagon train, good folks just lookin' for a better life for their families, ya think they deserve to have their stock stole?"

Now Wind spoke up in Comanche that Chance later translated for me: "They are stealing our land, and slaughtering our buffalo brothers, leaving them to rot in the plains. Do you think we deserve that? Why do we care whether they are good or bad people? We did not invite them here. We did not give them this land. We did not ask their army to attack our villages at dawn in the winter, kill us, and drive us from our lodges or make us live on agencies we are not allowed to leave, without enough food to feed our children and no game to hunt. Do you think we deserve that? You have Comanche blood. Why do you not listen to it?"

For this, Chance did not have an answer and did not try to give one. He just stared into the fire. But after we all sat in silence for a long while, he said: "Well, I suppose if ya only take a few of their horses, and you don't hurt no one, maybe I could help ya a little."

"We didn't ask for your help," I repeated.

"I know ya didn't, but now I'm offerin' it."

"OK, but if you're going to help us, you have to give us all the help we might need, not 'maybe,' and not just 'a little.' What the hell good is that?"

"You got a mouth on ya, ma'am," he said without rancor, in fact with a certain amusement.

"I cannot tolerate equivocation."

"I don't know what that word means."

"It means, you're either in with us one hundred percent or you're out. Wind is in charge of this raid. Stealing horses is her specialty. She's a master; we can do it with or without you."

"Ya know, this is real good for me. I didn't get much schoolin' back home, too busy workin' the ranch, and tryin' to keep the peace, but now I'm learnin' all kinds a' big new words. Awright, then, May, count me in. No more . . . e-quiv-o-ca-tion . . . Did I get that about right?"

I laughed. "You got it exactly right."

"Any chance I'll get kissed by a pretty girl on this raid?"

"In your dreams, cowboy."

This time, Wind devised a different, and, as it happened, a simpler plan. She sent Chance and me down from our bivouac in the foothills to visit with the wagon train one afternoon, in order to get the lay of their camp. We each led one of our pack horses, and we had devised our story. We were ranchers from Texas and had come up to explore rangeland in Montana Territory, which we had heard was opening up to white settlers, now that the Army was taking care of the "Indian problem" once and for all. We said we wanted to get in on it early. They asked us how it was that we dared travel here all alone and without a guide; hadn't we heard about the Indian unrest? In addition to that, they told us that gangs of bandits were said to work this trail, holding up and robbing vulnerable settlers. They suggested we ride with them, for there was safety in numbers, and detachments of soldiers frequently escorted them and patrolled the trail.

It was true what Chance had said; these were fine people, farm families from different parts of the country who had gotten together in Grand Island, Nebraska, lured there by promotions in the eastern newspapers and periodicals describing the West as the next frontier, where land was plentiful and free, and the earth rich. Professional outfitters had set up business in Grand Island, and when they had enough families gathered, they organized wagon trains to guide the settlers into this virgin paradise. They invited us to stay for dinner and to camp with them overnight, and we accepted the invitation. As we came to know some of them, heard their stories, and met their children, I began to feel uneasy about our charade, and to have grave misgivings about robbing these people, as I knew that Chance did, as well.

After dinner, the men shared whiskey and tobacco with Chance, and the women took me aside to discuss womanly matters. Other than my brief visit with the homesteader and his wife, when I procured my white-woman dress for the trade of a horse, this was the only time I had been among so-called civilized society since our arrival in the plains less than a year and a half ago. It is astonishing how profoundly life's events can change one in such a short time. I was struck by how similar was the relationship between men and women in both the native and white cultures, and I realized that I now occupied some strange middle ground, neither fully one nor the other, but a kind of shape-shifter moving between them. These women could not have been kinder or more attentive to me, but I knew that I no longer occupied the same world as they, and perhaps would never again be able to.

Chance and I set our bedrolls close together beneath the stars that night, just on the edge of the circle of wagons, our horses staked beside us.

"You seem troubled tonight, Chance," I whispered, after we had settled in.

He turned toward me, raised himself up on an elbow. "You got every right to call it equivocation, May," he said, "but I gotta tell ya, I can't do it, count me out. I just can't steal from these folks. They asked us to join 'em, they fed us, they're good people . . . I'm sorry, but I never stole before in my life and I ain't gonna start now, especially with them."

I turned toward him and raised myself similarly on an elbow, so that I could look in his face in the dark. "I know that, Chance, I just wanted to hear you say it. And you have nothing to apologize for. I can't do it either."

"I'm real glad to hear that. But we'll have to go back and tell Wind. She's gonna blame me for changin' your mind, that's for sure. Ya know, even though we talk together in Comanche, she don't really like me, I know that. And I don't hold it against her. Ya see, May, I seen all this happen in Texas, too, with the Comanche. The last of 'em have mostly gave up now, and are fixin' to go onto a reservation in Oklahoma where the government is sendin' 'em. They were great warriors and horsemen, folks called 'em 'the lords of the plains.' But, see, everything they had they got by stealin', they even stole people, white folks, and Mexicans, settlers and travelers movin' through their country, they killed the men and stole the women and children. Finally, the U.S. Army, the Texas Rangers, and the ranchers just wore 'em down, until there weren't enough of 'em left to fight. My grandpa's father was a white man, a rancher, who made friends with the Comanches and married into the tribe. He helped them when he could, gave 'em cattle when they needed it and horses, so they left him alone because he treated 'em good. And so my grandpa was accepted into the tribe because his mama was Comanche . . . that's the way it works. He came and went among them, but he was raised mostly by his father as a white man. They was fiercer than any other tribe on the plains, but I got a lotta respect for 'em, and because of Grandpa, they more or less left my folks alone, too . . . but not completely. That's a story, I'll maybe tell ya another time . . ."

"Why are you telling me all this now, then?" I asked.

"Just to let you know, from what you've told me about yourself, that I understand the position you're in, with one foot in both worlds. Thing is, May, when everything is said and done, you and me are still white folks."

"I saw how easily you talked to those people, Chance, easier than I did, and I started wondering if maybe you might not want to travel with them. I would understand that, because eventually Wind and I are going to find our people, and when that happens, you're not going to want to stay with us, and they won't want you to, either. This is not your fight. Wind knows that, that's why you think she doesn't like you. And I know it, too."

"So ya want me to leave ya, is that what yer tryin' to tell me, May?"

I leaned forward and put my other hand on his cheek again, as I had that night in the remuda when I was stealing his horse. "It's not that I want you to, Chance," I said. "It's just that I know you have to. If not now, later, and this might be your best opportunity to get out safely."

He smiled at me then, and moved his head closer to mine, or maybe I drew him closer, or both. He smelled faintly of whiskey and tobacco, man sweat and horse, not a disagreeable scent, quite the contrary. "Yeah, maybe so, May," he said, "but the thing is, I don't want to get out."

"Would it be alright if I kissed you?" I asked.

"You didn't ask me last time."

"I'm asking you now." He didn't answer, he just kissed me, and I kissed him back.

We did not sleep a great deal that night. We opened our bedrolls so that we could lie together, undressed fully, and held each other. His hands were callused and rough as one would expect of a cowboy, but gentle, and he touched me as if I were made of fine china and he might break me. I was certain this was his first time. He explored my body so lovingly, almost reverentially, that it brought tears to my eyes and a surge of longing. I don't know that I have ever wanted a man so much as I wanted this one. I caressed his muscled arms, kissed his biceps with an open mouth, ran my fingers over his hard buttocks, and took his manhood in hand.

In this way, the night passed, whispering to each other for a while afterward, in wonder of such things, sleeping briefly to wake and make love again, whispering, sleeping, waking, making love . . .

The next morning we thanked our generous hosts, and they tried once again to convince us to join them. But we rode out, I on his sorrel mare, Lucky, and he on the paint he had ridden into our camp. Chance looked over at me and smiled. "I'd say we played our role as a married couple real well, May," he said.

I laughed. "Ah yes, that's what happened last night, isn't it?" I said. "We were still playing our roles as a married couple when we got into our bedrolls. Except we were newlyweds on our honeymoon. Was it your first time?"

He laughed, embarrassed. "Was I that clumsy?"

"There is nothing clumsy about you, Chance. You're the most graceful man I've ever known . . . it just seemed like you were making new discoveries . . . and I've never felt so loved before."

When we entered our camp in the foothills, Wind was sitting in front of the fire. It took only a moment for Chance to point out that there were three unfamiliar horses tethered to our picket line that was stretched between two aspen trees. Both of us knew right away where they had come from, and that Wind had sent us down to the wagon train as a diversion, or perhaps just to get us out of her way. When I questioned her about it, she said: "I knew after you visited the whites that you would not wish to steal their horses because you are white people. It is best for me to steal my enemies' horses alone, because only I among us is Indian and move like a ghost. I only took three. I will not ask you again to join me on a raid." She smiled. "I see that you have other things to do together at night."

She is an enigmatic soul, and I could not tell if she was angry with us, perhaps jealous that Chance had come between us, for we have been alone together for so long. Had she seen us making love last night? Or was she just now witnessing, with her uncanny perception, that the cowboy's and my relationship had fundamentally changed in the past day?

On our ride back, Chance and I had discussed the question of whether or not I was going to camp with him after what had transpired between us. As we are hardly adolescents living under our parents' roof . . . to put it figuratively . . . it seems absurd that we should try to maintain a pretense of not being lovers . . . sneaking around at night to see each other. Wind knew I had informed Little Wolf before the attack on our camp that after we turned ourselves in at the agency, he would have to give up his two additional wives—Feather on Head and me—and she also understood that I considered the great chief more of a father figure than a husband. Still, compared to many tribes the Cheyenne culture is quite conservative in matters of a woman's sexuality, and one who is perceived as being "loose" is generally regarded in a negative light and sometimes ridiculed. There was, for instance, one woman in our band whose name, *Eehe'e,* translates to Camps All Over Woman, a subtle way of suggesting promiscuity . . . and a name I'm just hoping Wind is not going to start calling me. Although, frankly, as I explained to Chance, I am long past worrying about my reputation . . . and rather enjoy being considered a "bit of a tart."

Yet I knew that I needed to make peace with Wind, and did not want her to feel abandoned in the wake of my fledgling love affair. Despite my reservations about stealing horses from the settlers, I wanted her to know that my primary allegiance was still to her and to the People. Chance went off to unsaddle and curry our horses and turn them out to graze, and so I sat with her by the fire. I told her that during our dinner with the settlers we had learned that General Crook's supply camp was only several hours' ride north and east of where we had camped with them last night.

"You say you don't want me to raid with you any longer," I said, "but you have taught me well and you know that I, too, can move like a ghost. It is true that I could not think of those people as my enemy, but the Army is my enemy. Do you believe that I have forgotten what they have done to us, to the People, to me, to my friends and their babies? I have not. The soldiers will have many horses in their camp, and I wish to go there with you and steal as many as we can. Of course, the cowboy will not come with us, but he will stay here and look after our remuda while we are gone."

"How do you know he will do that, Mesoke?" she asked.

"Because I will tell him to."

At this she smiled slyly and nodded. "Yes, I can see that he is like a puppy," she said, "and he is going to follow you wherever you go."

I laughed. "Not everywhere, he isn't. I tried to leave him with the wagon train, among his own people, for I know that he cannot stay with us. But he refused."

"He is a fine boy, Mesoke, I like him. I admire his loyalty to his people, and to you. But he cannot have both."

"I know that, my friend. We will leave for the soldiers' camp tomorrow at dawn."

I will not dwell on our raid on Crook's supply camp. It was in some ways the easiest of all, and by far the most productive. The bivouac was set in a small valley, surrounded by hills. Most of the soldiers were clearly out in the field chasing Indians, with only a small detachment left behind to guard the stock and care for the wounded. Those left to this duty could not have expected that the enemy would return to their stronghold to steal horses. Indeed, in the two days we watched them before acting, the remuda, numbering well over one hundred head, was frequently left unattended, grazing in the hills while the soldiers went fishing, clearly a favorite pastime given that they seem to have few other distractions from their dull daily routines. As a result, Wind decided that rather than a night raid, we would take as many horses as we could safely gather in broad daylight while their keepers were thus occupied.

Between the hilly pasturage ran a series of coulees, providing ample places to conceal ourselves. We rode up one long draw, each carrying two halters and lead ropes. Wind chose the two horses we were each to take. The others, grazing placidly in the bottoms, were obviously accustomed to being moved about, and her notion was that many would simply follow the four we were leading, in the herd mentality. And so they did. We made off with twenty-seven head altogether, neither accosted nor chased.

Altogether we had been gone from our camp along the Tongue River for six days, and upon our arrival, Chance, though disapproving of our mission, was suitably impressed by its results. Before we had left, I told him that if we were away longer than twelve days, he should assume that we had been caught or killed, and so he was also relieved to see us back. On the return ride, Wind and I had discussed our future plan. This would be the last raid; now it was a question of finding our people and/or bands of allies and distributing our wealth of equines. We decided we would rest here for a few days and then move on, but now was the time to tell Chance that he must leave us. We would be heading back into Indian country . . . as bifurcated as that has become . . . and they would not be receptive to a white man in our midst. "It is time to let him go, Mesoke," Wind said.

That evening we ate our dinner by the fire—an antelope Chance had killed and roasted over a spit he constructed. He was a man who knew how to cook, among his other talents. Wind and I described our raid and the lay of the Army supply base, and then she retired to her tent and Chance and I to our "lodge" that he had also built in our absence. It consisted of bent willow branches with a canvas covering, and, inside, a sleeping place of pine boughs covered with blankets and our bedrolls. It was cozy and felt oddly domestic, as if he had made us a little inverted nest, our first house.

I did not want to spoil the mood and our reunion by telling him of Wind's and my decision, but I sensed he already knew and that the subject would inevitably arise tonight. We undressed and lay together. There was already no awkwardness between us in this regard.

"Ya know that all them Army horses are branded, don'tcha, May?" he asked.

"Of course."

"We're real exposed here, and if soldiers should happen by, they'll recognize their stock. You'll be arrested."

"I know."

"So we should move out soon."

"Yes, Wind and I have already discussed it."

"What's your plan?"

"I think you know, Chance. We are going to find our people and try to give away some of these horses."

"Wind's people, May."

"No, mine, too. There is nowhere else for me to go."

"Yes, there is, you go with me. This is big country, we'll get married, you'll have my name, official then. From all you've told me, everyone thinks May Dodd is dead anyhow. You and me can have a new life together."

"I have friends out here who survived the attack, Chance. I can't abandon them. I am not dead, and I don't want them to go on believing I am. Besides, even if things were different, this has all happened so fast between us, and we don't really even know each other yet."

"I know I never felt this way about a woman before."

I laughed. "That might be just because she took your virginity, Chance. Somewhere down the road you might look at me and wonder what the hell you've gotten yourself into."

"Damn, May," he said, "I already wonder what the hell I got myself into." And we both laughed.

We held each other then, our naked bodies moving together. I pressed my breasts to his chest, caressed his arms and back with my hands, as he did mine, felt him hardening against my sex. Of course, it was too early to say that I was in love with this man . . . but not too early to say that I wished we had more time together than we did.

Afterward, we lay together in silence for a long time, deep in our own thoughts.

"Where will you go, Chance?" I asked at last.

"That's a darn good question, May. Been thinkin' on it a long time myself. I can't go back to the drive. They gotta be near their destination by now, and even if I could convince 'em I didn't steal them horses, they'd want to know where the hell I've been all this time."

"Couldn't you go home to your family's ranch in Texas?"

"I could do that, but the trail boss, Zeke Pardue, is a real nasty piece of work. He'll know where to find me when he gets home, and he'll come lookin', that's for sure. After that, no tellin' what could happen . . . I'm in a bit of a pickle, May, but I'll sort things out."

"It's all my fault. I'm so sorry, Chance."

"I don't blame ya a bit, May. Ya know, I figger if ya'd picked any other horse than my mare outta the remuda, ya mighta slipped away without me ever knowin' ya. I'm real grateful that didn't happen. I've always thought I was a real lucky fella that you rustled Lucky . . . and I got that kiss."

"I wish now that I had stolen another horse, Chance," I said. "All that kiss has brought you is a world of trouble."

"That and a lot more good things, May. Don't ya worry about me, I'll make my way, I always have. And who knows, maybe we'll cut each other's trail again someday."

Two days later we parted company, but not before Chance gave it one last try. He was mounted and leading one of the pack horses Wind had given him in case he needed a spare.

"Ya know, you gals could sure use another hand drivin' all this stock you've collected," he said. "You're gonna have one hell of a time doin' that, just the two a' ya. Why don't I just ride with ya for a few more days, until ya get rid of some of 'em."

Wind shook her head and spoke to him in English: "If we ride into an Indian camp with a white man," she said, "especially a band that doesn't know us, the women and boys will drag you out of your saddle and beat you with sticks and rocks. They will torture you, cut your testicles off, kill you slowly, and scalp you . . . just because you are a white man, and they have suffered too much at your hands."

Chance smiled. "Yes, ma'am," he said, nodding, "that's just what the Comanches do with the white men they capture alive. Some of 'em, when they see they're gonna get taken, put the barrel of their gun in their mouth and pull the trigger." And then he said something in Comanche that Wind later translated for me as: "You take care of this girl."

"Good-bye, Chance," I said. "Head south on the main road. You'll be safe there."

He touched the brim of his hat with thumb and forefinger. "So long, May." He smiled a sweet, sad smile. "Been a real pleasure."

"For me as well, cowboy."

13 August 1876

Two days of travel after Chance left us, we came upon a small band of Lakota warriors and their families, and we spent several days in their camp. Wind speaks Sioux and knew some of these people. The men had fought in the Custer battle and told us about the great victory, and of the recent movements of the Army. We gave them a number of our horses, for which they were profoundly grateful, and they put on quite a feast and dance for us. They insisted, too, on giving us gifts in return for ours—beaded moccasins and jewelry; a new, ornately beaded hide dress to replace my old ragged, patched one; a warrior's knife in a beaded and fringed sheath for Wind. Except for a very few rudimentary words, I do not know the Sioux language, but I was happy to be back in the embrace of the native world.

Next, while traveling along Rosebud Creek, we came upon a mixed band of Cheyenne and Arapaho and divested more of our string, receiving additional gifts, although these people were considerably less affluent than the Lakota we had encountered. We camped with them for two nights. The first thing we asked was if they knew where Little Wolf and his people were, but of this they had no knowledge. Yet, intriguingly, one of their elders told us of another similarly mixed band they had crossed recently, one with white women among them—not as captives, but as full members of the tribe, and some of them warriors. I asked many questions of the old man, with Wind translating, but I was unable to garner any information about where this band might be either.

"We are all traveling," he said, fanning his hands apart, fingers spread to suggest the many directions the various bands have taken, "trying to find the few herds of buffalo the whites have not yet slaughtered, and trying to avoid the soldiers. Unless we come upon them, we do not know where the others are. These people I tell you about, with the white women, are following the medicine woman Ma'heona'e, Holy Woman, who had a vision and is leading them to the real world behind this one."

Wind tells me she knows Ma'heona'e, who is blind, and that she has great respect for her medicine. Of course, I have heard of this other world the Cheyenne believe exists, said to be a kind of paradise, with all the faults of this false one we inhabit corrected, which in these desperate times is a particularly seductive notion. Yet no one in the tribe has actually located such a haven, except in hallucinatory visions. Indeed, it seems to me that virtually all cultures have their supernatural myths of utopia, but none that I've heard of has ever succeeded in making them tangible. Still, I take this news as a hopeful sign that we may be able to find this band, and I don't expect they will suddenly disappear into that other world before we do.

18 August 1876

Good God, is there no end to it? . . . It was like any other day, but perhaps we were being less vigilante, for we had no warning of it . . .

we were riding down the trail, beneath a small overhanging bluff, leading what remained of our horses, now numbering eight, not counting those that Wind and I each rode or our two pack horses. Two men dropped from the overhang, one on Wind, who rode ahead of me, the other on me, knocking us from our horses, and as we hit the ground with the heavy weight of them upon us, they must have struck us on the head, for when we regained consciousness we were staked flat on our backs, naked and spread-eagled, bound at our wrists and ankles, our arms tied out to our sides, our legs open, our mouths gagged with filthy bandanas that tasted of sweat. My head ached and as my eyes focused, I looked into Jules Seminole's face leering above me.

"Ah, you see, *ma belle*," he said, "this is how Jules deals with murderers and horse thieves, and to lovers who have betrayed him. And this time those of us who did not enjoy the fruits of your favors on our last encounter will have our turn. As you can see, this time you have no hope of escape, no hidden knives and no place to hide them, you cannot move your arms, or close your legs, or bite with your teeth. Surely you remember Jules' distinguished colleagues, Curly Bill, Wild Man Charlie, and the Deacon. And there are two new members of our gang, to whom I must introduce you, Wee Willy James, ironically named, for as you are soon to discover he has a cock the size of a donkey's. Finally, there is Jules' old half-breed compatriot, Cuts Women, a true artisan and master knifeman who makes the most exquisite bracelets from the secret parts of women. And yours, my darling," he said, squatting and cupping his hand over my sex, "will make the finest decoration of all."

Now Seminole loosened the bandana that was gagging me. "If you have anything to say in your defense, *ma chère*," he said, "now is the time."

"I do have something to say, Jules," I answered, "though not necessarily in my defense. I want to say that you are the most repellent human being I have ever in my life encountered. Every time I look at you, I feel like vomiting. Wind believes you are a sorcerer, but I know what you really are—you are a pathetic, weak, cowardly lunatic."

"Ah, *mon amour,*" he said, shaking his head, "such hurtful things you say to Jules. But now I am afraid it is the time to shut your whore's mouth again"—he retied the bandana gag even tighter across my mouth—"so that Jules and his colleagues can enjoy you without the insults that issue from your tongue. Take solace, my darling, in knowing that when Cuts Women carves you up after all are finished with you, it will be Jules who will wear *ta petite chatte* upon his wrist in remembrance of our love."

I will not further record here what filth and depravity Seminole and the others spoke to us, what vile retribution we were to face as punishment for murdering their friends and stealing their horses, the monstrous acts described to us in such grotesque detail that I cannot speak of it . . . or of those things they did to us in prelude . . . The sun had set, dusk descending, and they built a fire while the Deacon squatted over us and read aloud violent passages from the Old Testament, so agitated in his recital that spittle sprayed from his mouth, showering us in mist.

They drank whiskey, and drew sticks to see in what order they would molest us. Wild Man Charlie won first turn. He approached us and knelt down beside Wind. "Do not think, you filthy squaw bitch, that I have forgotten what you did to me." He pulled his gun from the holster at his waist and ran the barrel along the inside of her thigh. "And then because I don't want to touch you," he said, "especially there . . . now you better pray that I don't accidentally pull the trigger."

At that moment, we heard galloping hoofbeats pounding the earth, and I managed to raise my head from the ground just high enough to see a silver dappled horse with a white lightning bolt painted on its chest, atop it a lone Indian warrior, his face completely covered by a pattern of red and black war paint that gave him the look of the devil incarnate. He let out a long, blood-chilling war cry and, as Wild Man regained his feet and leveled his gun, the Indian threw a knife.

As I lay there on my back, I could see each revolution of that knife twirling slowly in the air like a windmill turns languidly in a light breeze, until the blade buried itself up to the hilt in Wild Man's heart. Almost simultaneously, in that split second as it found its target, the savage's left arm came up holding a pistol. He fired twice as Wee Willy and Cuts Women were just scrambling to their feet from their place at the fire. Before they even managed to stand, they both collapsed. Curly Bill reached his horse, mounted, and spurred it desperately. But the animal, sensing its rider's terror, balked and reared with a shrill squeal, unseating the man and bolting. The savage reined up, his horse skidding to a halt. He slipped from its back, pulled what looked like an Army saber from a scabbard at his waist, approached Curly Bill, who crabbed clumsily backward on the ground, and ran him through the heart. From my poor vantage point, I did not see Seminole or have any idea where he was. Only the Deacon remained in view, on his knees beside us now, weeping and blubbering, appearing to have lost not only his faith but control of his bladder, as the savage approached him lightly on moccasined feet. The Deacon raised his arms toward this vision from hell, begging to be spared, but the merciless executioner spun in a full circle as graceful as a ballet dancer, his sword gaining momentum in its arc, before lopping off the Deacon's head. It rolled now on the ground, coming to rest next to mine, looking me in the eye as if still alive. The savage picked the head up by the hair and tossed it aside, and I assumed that my time had come. But I was in a strange state of detachment, oddly calm for whatever was to befall me. Instead, with the end of his sword blade, he cut the ties from my hands and feet and removed my gag, then did the same to Wind, who spoke to him in a low voice and a native tongue I could not make out. Did she know the man? I sat up and assumed a kind of fetal position, my legs tucked beneath me, trying to cover myself with my arms. He turned again and knelt beside me. I kept my gaze averted but finally raised my head and looked directly into his eyes, confronting him without fear, for I was in that moment fearless. But when our eyes locked, it was as if the painted face melted away, and I saw him clearly for who he was.

"Good God . . ." I murmured, "Chance?"

He smiled that sweet, gentle smile, so incongruous to the fierceness of his visage. "Yes, ma'am," he answered as he took me in his arms.

"Be careful," I whispered in his ear, "there's another one left, the most dangerous of all."

Chance stood then, drew the pistol from its holster, looked quickly around, and then carefully began to make the rounds of the camp.

"Jules Seminole is gone, Mesoke," Wind said. She, too, was sitting on the ground now, her hands gripping her shoulders, her arms covering her breasts, which are considerably fuller than mine and more difficult to conceal. Nothing renders a woman more vulnerable and defenseless than to be forcibly stripped naked, and for Cheyenne women, who are exceptionally modest by nature, this act alone is especially humiliating . . . not to mention, of course, that which followed. "He rode off as Chance was riding in. I told you, the man is a sorcerer. He cannot be captured or killed so easily. Don't you see how, when we are most alone, he reappears surrounded by other evil men who speak and act such filth in his name? And when they die, he disappears and later returns with more evil men. He is a devil, and can only be killed when a stake is driven into his black heart."

"Nonsense, Wind, he is man, a mortal, an evil one, to be sure, but a weak man and a coward who runs away." I saw then the blood on the inside of her thigh, where Wild Man was threatening her with the barrel of his gun, and with which I realized then that he must have penetrated her. And yet she had not uttered a sound of distress through her gag. Surely, she is the strongest, bravest woman I have ever known.

"Good God, he hurt you terribly, didn't he?"

"I have been hurt before, Mesoke" was all she said.

Chance returned carrying our clothes. "Ain't nobody left here, exceptin' the dead men," he said, keeping his eyes averted as he handed them to us. He spoke to Wind in Comanche with what seemed to me to be a particularly gentle tone, and she answered him. He turned his back to us as we dressed.

"Did you know it was Chance when he rode in?" I asked Wind.

"Yes, I recognized his war paint, the symbol on his horse, and his war cry as those of a Comanche warrior," she answered. "I did not think there could be another in this country besides him."

"And you, Chance, where in the world did you get your outfit?"

"I made it," he said simply. "I bought me some tanned deer hides at a tradin' post after I quit ya. I learned how to do such things from my grandpa. In case I was ever taken captive by them, he wanted me to know not just how to speak their tongue, but how to *be* Comanche. An' remember, May, ya told me that we was enterin' Indian country, so I figgered I'd do like you and be able to pass as a white man or an Indian, 'ceptin' that I got more a' the real blood than you do."

"And the sword? It's an Army saber, is it not?"

"That it is, bought it off a soldier I run into on the trail. He had deserted his company, and needed some cash.

"See, we got plenty a' soldiers in Texas, too," he continued, "an' in Grandpa's day down there, ya never knew if you was gonna be fightin' the Mexican army or the Comanches, or one after the other. Grandpa picked up swordsmanship hisself from some a' the Army soldiers. He was a tough ole cuss, my grandpa, and he knew how to do all kinds a' fightin'—with his fists, or Injun wrestlin', guns, rifles, knives, swords, or just an old stick, you name the weapon an' he pretty much knew how to use it, or learned real quick."

"He taught you well."

Chance smiled. "I picked up a few things on my own, too," he said, "like that fancy sword move I made on the man in black. I thought ya'd be mighty impressed with that one."

I laughed at his boasting. "You know, Chance, you really don't need to impress me any further than you already have. You saved our lives, and that is quite enough . . . but you're right, the sword move was *mighty* impressive . . ." I looked over at the Deacon's head lying where Chance had tossed it . . . "though you might have been a bit more considerate as to the direction the head rolled."

He grinned, exposing teeth that looked preternaturally white against the red face paint. "I'll sure work on that, May," he said, nodding, "but it's kinda tricky, 'cause they don't roll real straight when they land."

Wind and I had both dressed, and stood. If Chance and I defused the tension of the previous carnage with light banter, she did so with the practical native stoicism I have seen so often in my time among the Cheyenne. "We must see to our horses," she said.

We found our mounts at the picket line the bandits had set, as well as our two pack animals. Also picketed were their own four riding horses, still saddled, and six additional, probably stolen we guessed. Some of these were packed with their supplies, the others simply spare mounts. Of our eight horses remaining from the raid on the Army stock, we counted five untethered and spread out within sight, grazing placidly. They are, after all, social beings, and as long as there was grass available and others around them, they felt no need to wander. Of the three remaining, we expected them not to be too far away, and that they might rejoin us when we moved out.

The outlaws had not yet made the time to go through our affairs, as they clearly had more important business to attend to with our persons. What is it about the bodies of women that excites in gentlemen reverence, love, and passion, and in bad men the desire to pillage, defile, and mutilate? It occurred to me that between

Wind and me, and the timely arrival of Chance, we had now eliminated the entire Three Finger Jack gang, which seemed an unin-
tended but valuable service for those traveling in the plains, both
Indians and whites.

We gathered their guns and dumped on the ground the contents of all the packs we had removed from their horses. Chance
found a few other useful weapons and some ammunition and cash.
Now we left this camp of dead men, not giving them the dignity of
burial, but leaving the remains to the scavengers. I think it offered
some small comfort to Wind and me to imagine the turkey vultures squatting upon their corpses, pecking out their eyes, the coyotes and wolves coming in to flush the huge raptors, disembowel
the bodies, and feast upon the flesh, and all the other creatures
that consume carrion, down to the worms, cockroaches, and ants,
picking the last of it from the bones. It was a fitting end for these
wretches, who had no doubt robbed, terrorized, raped, and murdered others in their travels. Yet their guide, the "sorcerer" Jules
Seminole, was still at large, and that offered us no comfort.

We mounted and traveled a safe distance, far enough to be away
from the ghosts that Wind feared might follow us and take their
retribution. Chance, of course, came with us.

"I ain't leavin' ya again, May," he said. "You seen what happens
when I do. Plus you can always use an experienced wrangler to help
ya with your herd."

"I don't understand how you found us again."

"I been trailing ya for some time, takin' a couple a' detours
along the way to gather some supplies a' my own. Wind and you
was movin' a fair number of stock, an' I seen where you got rid of a
few head along the way, an' when I lost your trail, I didn't have no
trouble pickin' it up again. Travelin' alone, I could move faster than
you. I sewed my Comanche getup around the fire at night, made
myself some grease paint outta colored pigment, charcoal, and a jar

a' lard I picked up at the tradin' post. That's why it stinks so bad . . . I can hardly stand myself. Then, the day before yesterday, I seen that someone else was followin' you. I figured from their tracks how many they was, and how many horses they had, an' I could see that at least one of 'em was real capable at readin' sign. I didn't know who they was or their intentions, but I knew from how they was travelin' that they was after you, one way or another, so I kept as close as I could to 'em . . .

"So . . . where are we headed?" he asked.

"Wind and I are going to find our people. She believes that we are not far from them now. I'm not sure how exactly she knows such things, but she often does, and she is rarely wrong. But I already told you, Chance . . . you cannot come into our camp."

"Yeah, so you told me, May."

"And there are other reasons I haven't told you."

"Awright, May, so tell me then. You got nothin' to hide from me."

Perhaps, after all that had happened today, it wasn't the right time to unburden myself and tell the truth, but I felt I owed it to him . . . and probably there would never be a right time.

"Well . . . Chance . . . for one thing . . . because I'm married to a prominent Cheyenne chief named Little Wolf."

At this, Chance turned toward me in his saddle, with a dumbfounded expression on his face. "You're . . . *married*?"

"Well . . . yes and no," I equivocated.

"There ain't no yes and no about it, May. You're either married or ya ain't."

"Well . . . you see, in the Cheyenne way of such matters, I'm married. But Little Wolf has two other wives, as well."

"OK, I know how that works, the Comanche men do the same. So ya ain't married in the church by a preacher, in the eyes of God, then?"

"Well . . . not in a church exactly, and I don't know about the eyes of God, but it's true that we were married by an Episcopalian preacher . . . in a . . . uh . . . an outdoor ceremony, I suppose you could say . . . But when the time came, many of us did not speak the 'I do' part, so it wouldn't really count."

"Oh, now ain't that a relief . . ." he said, his voice thick with sarcasm.

"I told you there was a lot we didn't know about each other, Chance."

"Ya told me a whole pile of horseshit, is what ya told me, May."

"I've never heard you cuss before."

"A man has his limits. What else didn't ya tell me?"

"That I have a baby daughter who is with the tribe."

"You bring her along with you or have her by your chief?"

"Well . . . that's a little complicated, too, Chance. You see . . . I became with child by an Army captain at Fort Robinson, before we went to the Cheyenne. But Little Wolf and the rest of the tribe believe that he is the father."

Chance just stared at me now in utter disbelief. "A *little* complicated?" he said. "What else?"

"I was married back in Chicago to another man . . . well, not really married, what they call a common-law marriage. We had two children together."

He was silent now for a long time, staring straight ahead as we rode.

Finally, he turned to me again, his face hard, his voice different than I'd ever heard it before, angry and as venomous as a coiled viper striking. "No wonder ya go around kissin' strange cowboys ya don't even know. You're a bit of whore, ain't ya, May?"

"That's an ugly word, Chance. I am not a whore."

"How about a loosey goosey, then, or a hussy?"

"If it makes you feel better, you can call me whatever you want . . . except a whore . . . you have every right to do so. And this is exactly why I didn't tell you these things from the beginning. Yes, I've made mistakes in my life, I have regrets. But these are just the details out of the context of a much larger story that you can't possibly understand. I guess I hoped maybe a time might come between us when I would be able to tell you that story. And maybe you wouldn't detest me for it. But now, I see the revulsion on your face, and I don't blame you for that, either."

"See, the thing is, May, I don't need to hear the rest of your story, them details ya just give me are plenty enough for me."

He reined his horse around and spoke to Wind in Comanche, and she answered him. He put his heels to its flanks and hollered "Heeeawww git on now," and broke into a gallop, fleeing from me as fast as he could.

"What did he say to you, Wind?" I asked, my stomach queasy, tears of shame and anger coming to my eyes as I watched him go.

"He asked me if I knew where we were going, and I said yes."

"Didn't I tell you that all my loves end badly?"

The Real World Behind This One

They told the People they could dance a new world into being. There would be landslides, earthquakes, and big winds. Hills would pile up on each other. The earth would roll up like a carpet with all the white man's ugly things—the stinking new animals, sheep and pigs, the fences, the telegraph poles, the mines and factories. Underneath would be the wonderful old-new world as it had been before the white fat-takers came . . . The

white men will be rolled up, disappear, go
back to their own continent.

— *from* Lame Deer, Seeker of Visions
by John (Fire) Lame Deer
and Richard Erdoes

5 September 1876

"Gertie, if you think for one minute," said Lady Ann Hall, stepping forward, "that we intend to turn around and go back from whence we came, after all these weeks, these months of travel, let me assure you, that is quite out of the question. First of all, the notion of ghost camps, though excellent fodder for a tale by which schoolgirls might scare each other on sleepovers, is utterly preposterous. And I must say, I am surprised that a grown woman of your vast experience in these plains would even entertain the veracity of such apocryphal nonsense. And quite frankly, even if this did happen to be a ghost camp, I smell the marvelous odors of game roasting over open fires, and I, for one, would be honored to accept an invitation to sit down with these charming poltergeists and share in the feast."

"Aye, I ain't one to pass up a good scran, meself," said Hannah. "I didn't know that ghosts can cook. I'm puttin' me bum down right here."

"As you ladies can see, I have not yet succeeded in purging the vulgar Scouse language from my maidservant's mouth."

"Yeah, OK, you're right, Ann, and Hannah," Gertie admitted. "I just got a bit of a chill when I seen May and Molly standin' there together. Honey," she said to May, "we had it on the best authority that you died in a cave after the Mackenzie attack. Brother Anthony hisself gave you last rites, and I know him to be a man who don't tell lies. And you, Molly, I seen you with my own eyes jump from that cliff. Lady Hall here has been tellin' me some cockamamie story that maybe Phemie and Pretty Nose rescued you, but that ain't what I seen. We been arguin' about it on the trail ever since we left. But goddammit, here you two are, together. I don't know how the hell that happened, but I figger I'm gonna soon find out. In the meantime, honey," she said, approaching May, "I don't expect ole Dirty Gertie smells any sweeter than usual, but you asked for a bear hug, an' here it comes. An' I'm warnin' ya, you're next, Molly." She opened her arms and she and May embraced. "Goddammit to hell, it really is you, girl, and all flesh and blood. Welcome back to life."

"Thank you, Gertie, it is fine to be here," May said.

"You know, Cap'n Bourke told me he caught sight of a woman in the mercantile back at Tent City a while back who he thought might be you. That shook him up real bad. An' ya know what I told him? I says, Cap'n, you either seen a ghost, or you seen a woman who looked a little like May Dodd, an' you didn't get a real good look at her either. An' he tells me the stablemaster said her name was Abigail Ames, she was married and she an' her husband were horse traders from Grand Island, Nebraska. An' I says, Cap'n, you don't go from being dead in a cave above the Powder River with a bullet hole in your back to being a married horse trader from Nebraska in three months. An' he says, I guess you're right, Gertie . . . But I wasn't right, was I? That was you, wasn't it, honey?"

"It was, Gertie, yes."

"Damn . . ."

And then Gertie gave me a big bear hug. "By the way, Molly," she said, holding on tight, "me and my ole mule, Badger, been cartin' your goddamned ledger books around long enough now. I know I said I wasn't goin' to, but I read 'em, too, thinkin', you bein' dead a' course, you wouldn't mind too much. But now me an' Badger is both gettin' old an' tired and we're real ready to give 'em back to ya." After Gertie finally let go of me, she looked back and forth between May and me, tears pooling up in her eyes, and she began to weep, great sobs, which, in my experience, is not an event one often . . . or possibly even ever . . . witnesses from Gertie. "The hell," she said when she finally collected herself, wiping the back of her hand across her runny nose. "Not only am I gettin' old, I'm gettin' soft . . . look what you gals has done, you've turned ole' Gertie into a damn crybaby."

After all had greeted each other or been introduced, we got settled again for a time on our robes and blankets around the fire circle, making space for our new arrivals. When the food was ready, we all went up and carved hunks of meat off the various carcasses, a true pagan feast.

"Where have you ladies been all this time?" I asked of Ann and Hannah as we sat back in our places to eat. "And why in the world have you come back?"

"Me, I came back to find me darlin' husband, Hóma'ke," said Hannah. "Tell me, is he in this camp?"

"Yes, he is, and if he's not around here already, he is sure to be coming to the feast and dance." At this news, Hannah leapt up from her place, not even finishing her meal, and said she was not going to wait, she would find her Little Beaver herself.

"Yes, the child is truly smitten by that boy," said Ann as we watched Hannah walk away. "It *is* one of the reasons we came back, but surely not my principal one, personally. Although, I must say, it did become extremely irritating listening to Hannah's endless whining and crying over her lost husband. Truly, there are few things more tiresome, or useless, than a maidservant pining away for love. And, of course, she put the blame for their separation squarely upon me . . . not unjustly, I admit. To answer your question, we took the train east at Medicine Bow station, and, after some lengthy travel delays here and there en route, we finally made our way back to New York. There I booked passage for us on a ship bound to England. However, the only berth available was on a vessel that was still on its way to the city, and we had to wait for it to make port. Unfortunately, the bloody thing sank somewhere in the middle of the Atlantic, which, of course, involved another long delay. During that period . . . and before . . . I had rather too much time to reconsider my decision to leave here. I could not get over that final image I had of you, Molly, and the confusion and disorientation it caused my essentially rational mind . . . which I believe I expressed in the letter I wrote to you. I had been greatly missing my home at Sunderland, but the more time I had to think about reentering the rather stultifying world of the British aristocracy, the less keen I became about returning there . . . Frankly, I began to miss my provincial friends here on the plains."

At this we all laughed, and Christian Goodman, who had now joined us with his wife, Astrid, said: "Yes, Lady Hall, it is true, we are peasants, one and all! And we missed you, too, reminding us of that."

"I realized that without my dear Helen," she continued, "I really didn't have a great deal to go home to. She and I kept largely to ourselves . . . due, of course, to the special nature of our relationship. And many of my old friends had made themselves scarce after that scandal became public, and I left Lord Hall. And so with all this damnable time on my hands, I spoke to a banker in New York and set in motion the long process of transferring funds from my accounts. Another ship finally arrived . . . but we let it leave for England without us. Instead we made again the long overland journey back here, and this time, the entire way, I had to endure little Hannah's insufferably bubbly excitement about the prospect of being reunited with her little husband, Little Beaver. Upon arrival at Medicine Bow station, I had no difficultly locating Gertie via the Army. She, too, as it happened, was considering a change of life, which I'm sure she will describe to you herself.

"And therefore, after what has seemed a long bit of aimless wandering, not to mention constant doubt and worry at the distinct possibility that we would make it all the way back and not find any trace of you . . . here we are . . ."

"There will be dancing tonight, Lady Hall!" said Lulu. "To celebrate your and Hannah's return, and May's. *Et aussi, la victoire,* and also the warriors' victory today on the battlefield."

"Splendid!" said Ann. "And I may just join in the festivities myself. You know that I'm mad about dancing, Lulu . . . for a girl with two left feet, that is. Truly, ladies, I feel already as if I've come home."

May and Gertie were in close conference together, two old friends reunited and catching up on what had happened to them both in these past months.

For my part, I had begun to have a strange . . . even an uneasy feeling about all of us coming together at this particular time . . . the living and the presumed dead. I don't know exactly how to say it, but it felt to me almost as if something was happening beyond us, out of our own control, for it seemed almost too much of a co-incidence that we would all converge at this moment and in this place. I had the sense that we were puppet figures being manipulated by some master force . . . a silly notion, I know, but one I couldn't shake.

I left the light of the fire ring then, as everyone chattered gaily away, and I went to sit alone in the darkness beside the creek. I lay on my back in the grass to look up at the stars for some kind of answer to a question I did not even know how to pose. Without moonlight, and in this dry plains air, the stars were so dense against the black sky that it was almost impossible to even identify the constellations, the Milky Way a vast smear of whitewash. I have always taken comfort in this view, in the inevitable sense of self-recognition it forces regarding what a minuscule place we occupy in this vast unknowable universe; we are no more important than specks of dust blowing on the wind.

A shooting star blazed across my line of sight, and I began to feel at that same moment my child moving in my belly. I took that as a good omen, and it anchored me back to earth. We must find a safe place for our children; it is the one overarching concern and responsibility of mothers of all species. For all my cynicism about the promise of a real world behind this one, the stars made me re-alize that anything is possible, and nothing unimaginable. Perhaps Holy Woman has brought us all together here, and we are getting close to finding that place. The birds and animals breed in the spring with the faith that their offspring will survive, and even if they don't one year, even if they are destroyed by weather or predation or pestilence, they breed the following year with this same unextinguishable faith . . . and hope. And so the medicine woman leads us in ever-expanding circles, with the expectation, the hope, that this time she will find the opening, the entrance, the fissure, between this imperfect world and the better one beneath. Maybe I'm becoming a believer yet.

The music is starting up, and it is time to go back to the dance.

The first event of the festivities is that of the warriors, recounting in dance today's victory against the Crow. To our surprise, the very first to present is our own Martha. All those of us who know her well, white and Indian alike, are seated on the ground together. The orphan children we took in after their camp was raided by the soldiers and the Shoshone wolves have joined us, including my little friend Sehoso, Little Snowbird, who lost her baby to the soldier's bullet. My little Mouse, Hóhkééhe, has also been waiting for me. The stars are so far away . . . but these children are right here.

Now Martha enters the dance circle, wearing white face paint, her eyes rimmed in red, dressed in leggings and moccasins and a new warrior's shift decorated with totem designs of birds, bears, and wolves. In addition she wears full battle regalia—a buffalo bone choker to protect her neck; a similarly styled breastplate with long rawhide fringe adorning each side; a leather-handled knife at her waist in a beaded and fringed sheath. On the other side of her waist, attached with a loop to the rawhide strap that serves as a belt, she carries a small beaded-handle stone tomahawk for close-in combat. She is stunning and terrifying at once, and I steal a glance at May, who stares in utter wonder at her friend.

Accompanied by two overlapping steady drumbeats, one of a deeper tone than the other, three gourd shakers, and two flutists—all of whom Lulu has been working with to broaden the range of our music and to personalize it for the Strongheart society—Martha begins with a simple, prancing two-step, waving her hands forward in a kind of dogpaddle motion, mimicking the gait of a galloping horse, and clearly meant to bring to mind a warrior riding into battle. Now bending down, she picks up a lance and a leather shield that have been placed for her in the circle. She wraps the thongs on the back of the shield around her left arm, and holds the lance in her right hand, the shaft tucked under her arm. She raises the shield, around the edges of which dangle eagle feathers, the center painted with three concentric red circles, in the middle of them a red hand in the universal sign meant to stop arrows and bullets. She faces the spectators, pointing lance and shield toward them, lowers her head and shoulders, bends her knees, and bounces slightly up and down to the beat of the music as if she is in the saddle and charging the enemy, her expression so fierce and focused that we have the uncanny sensation that she is charging us. As she rides, she moves the shield back and forth, up and down, ducking behind it as she deflects incoming arrows.

Suddenly, she thrusts the lance forward, knocking her enemy off his horse, and the audience lets out a collective exhalation of breath that sounded something like *aohhhhh*, as if we have all been thusly unseated. Now Martha drops her lance and executes a kind of twirling motion with her body to suggest dismounting. She slips the tomahawk from her belt, takes several quick steps forward, drops to her knees, raises it high, and clubs the enemy with a single deadly blow. Slipping the handle of the tomahawk back into its loop, she draws her knife from the sheath, reaches down and grabs her victim's head by the hair, and with a glint of firelight shining off the blade and a single sweeping backhand motion, she takes his scalp. She wipes both sides of the bloody blade on her leggings and slips the knife back into its sheath. As she stands, she detaches the warrior's real scalp from the rawhide strap around her waist, raises it in the air, shaking it for a moment to the beat of the music, and then lets out a long, triumphant, ululating war cry that brings the spectators to our feet, joining her in ululation and spontaneously dancing in place, a kind of native version of applause in honor of Martha's first kill and her extraordinary rendition of this feat. We white women are filled with pride for our Strongheart warrior. It is true that thus unleashed, we share the savage nature of all mankind, and why pretend otherwise?

Settled again in our place by the fire ring, Martha joins us, and all offer our congratulations and praise.

"But Martha," says May, who is surely the most astonished of all by her old friend's performance, "not to overlook your remarkably athletic accomplishments on the battlefield, how in the world have you learned to dance like this, so graceful and expressive? I don't mean to be unkind, dear, but you were never the most physically coordinated among us."

"For that, May," she answers, "I must give full credit to my dance and theater instructor, Lulu LaRue—actress, dancer, singer, and choreographer. Perhaps you have already been introduced. Take a bow, Lulu."

"*Oui, c'est vrai,* it is true that we have a grand tradition of mime theater in France. I studied this art myself in Marseille when I was very young, under the tutelage of the son of the great Jean-Gaspard Deburau. I think the form will translate well into the native world, and I teach Martha how to do. *Bravo, ma chère amie! . . .* your interpretation and performance is brilliant."

"You see, May, I have come out of my shell," Martha says. "I lived through an experience so ghastly that I am still unable to speak of it . . . but one day, I must tell you. The formation of our warrior society, and the training provided by Phemie and Pretty Nose, has strengthened my heart and my body and given me new confidence. I am no longer weak, and I am willing fight to my death for myself, for my people, and especially for my child."

"Where is Little Tangle Hair, Martha?" May asked.

"He is in the camp of your husband, Little Wolf, with his father, Tangle Hair, and his second wife, Mo'ke a'e, Grass Girl, perhaps you remember her. He is loved and well cared for. I elected to stay with the Stronghearts when our band split off after the battle at Greasy Grass. I was not yet fully formed as a warrior, and I could not bear the idea of returning to life as a squaw. I have vengeance yet to take, and a man's heart to drive a stake into."

"From what I have seen, my dear friend," says May, "I would say that you are fully formed now."

"Yes, but truly only today did it come to fruition, May. Today, for the first time, I felt my true power. Soon I must go back and find my son."

"Yes, as I must find my daughter, Little Bird."

The dancing and feasting went on all night, and they kept the fires burning, so that some of us simply curled up to sleep on the buffalo robes and blankets we brought to sit upon during the festivities, my little Mouse curled against me. We are all by now well accustomed to the steady, though sometimes monotonous drumbeat, but it also serves as a hypnotic and a soporific. Some of us wake periodically during the night and have those quiet, otherworldly conversations that seem to have a quality quite different from those by the light of day.

May asked Gertie if she was still running her pack string for the Army, and Gertie answered that she has retired, though she's kept a few of her mules, those that she's most attached to.

"What are you doing to make a living, then, Gertie," May asked, "if you don't mind my asking?"

"Oh hell, honey, ya know as well as I do that you and me can ask anything we want of the other, an' get a straight answer. So, I'll tell ya what happened. You know that I been burnin' the candle at both ends for a long time now, workin' for the Army and informin' the

Indians of the soldiers' battle plans. I done it for you and your group a' white gals, and I done it for Molly and her gang, too. I was takin' Molly down to Medicine Bow station, after Cap'n Bourke took her prisoner . . ." Gertie half rolled over now to address me . . . "Maybe you already told her this part, eh, Mol?"

"No, we haven't talked about it."

"OK, then," she said, turning back to May, "let's just say then that somethin' strange happened that didn't really make no sense. Now, you know that I lived with the Southern Cheyenne a long time, had babies by 'em, traveled and lived some among the other tribes, too. So I got real used to strange things happenin' that don't have no explanation in the white world. And I finally got Injun enough over my years with 'em that these same things started to make sense to me, didn't even seem strange no longer, just part a' the deal, ya know? But this time, pretty much all the white folks who was there saw Molly fall off a cliff to certain death. Far as I can figger, maybe only Martha saw her rescued, and Lady Hall, she saw some version of both things happen, like she jumped *and* got rescued. She's still got her knickers twisted about that."

"I am listening to this conversation, Gertie," Ann said in a low voice, "and twisted knickers might be a slight misrepresentation. If you want confirmation, since they were the rescuers, why don't you speak with our two native ladies, Pretty Nose and Phemie, now that you have the chance."

"I already done that tonight, Ann," said Gertie, "and they say whatever we each saw is what happened. An' that's all they'll say about it."

"That is a very enigmatic answer, and one that makes no sense."

"Nothin' makes sense, Ann. But, see, May, I saw what all the white folks saw—the soldiers, Christian, Astrid, Hannah—I saw Molly . . . not so much jump, but fall off that damn cliff, saw it with my own eyes, plain as day, disappeared over the edge, end a' story. Only, a' course, it ain't the end a' the story, 'cause Molly is right here with us. An' like I said, that's why I thought you was both ghosts. Now, I may be a white gal but it made me realize that I been hangin' around with the soldiers so damn long now I lost my Injun way of seein' things. I realize I been workin' for the wrong side, 'course that I knew all along, but I needed the job. I figgered I could use what I learned from the soldiers to help the Injuns, an' a' course, you gals. But see, there ain't no more help to give, nothin' that can save anyone now, you or them. This life is over for these folks. So when I found out that Lady Ann and Hannah had came back, and wanted me to help 'em find you all, I thought what the hell, an' I quit my damn job muleskinnin' for the Army. I decided to throw in with the last of the hostiles . . . that includes you gals, by the way . . . fight an' die with ya, 'cause that looks like how it's gonna be. As to makin' a livin', I'll do it the same way these folks do."

"You're a good woman, Gertie," May answers. "You've done everything you could for us, and for the Indians; you warned us time and again that the Army was coming. But these people are proud, and they aren't ready to give up, and some of them won't ever be ready. I don't need to tell you that those of us still here stay mostly because we have no place else to go, and some of us have children, babies. I don't know you, Ann Hall, but I was dear friends with Helen, and she spoke often of you. I know you're a tenacious woman, as was Helen, and I admire you and Hannah for returning. At the same time, I think you've made a terrible mistake . . . probably all of us have made a terrible mistake. Gertie is right when she says there's nothing to be done that's going to save anyone, and we're probably all going to die."

It was one of those brutally frank, middle-of-the-night confessions, the articulation of the thoughts and fears that nag us all in our dreams, wake us, and keep us awake until dawn comes, after which everything usually seems better, more hopeful, our night terrors exaggerated, and we go about our day. Now those of us who were awake at this witching hour and heard Gertie and May speak fall silent, recognizing the terrible truth of their words that will linger even after the first light of day, for the notion of death is not an abstract concept in this place.

As day broke, we heard again a loud commotion issuing from the perimeter of the camp, the sentries hollering, then yipping the vocalization of triumph. A few minutes later, a gathering crowd pushed into our formerly peaceful camp center, herding a man in the middle of the throng, women and children beating him about the legs and buttocks with sticks, others throwing stones at him. They laughed and harangued him with insults. The captive was clearly an Indian, but from what tribe, I did not know. I heard him trying to speak to his tormenters, but, of course, as I am not even fluent in our own tribe's language, I had no idea what he was saying.

We were all up and about by now, and getting ready to return to our lodges, though many had already done so, including Martha and May, who were bunking together. Now, catching a phrase or two of the man speaking, Gertie said: "Well, I will be goddamned, I wonder what the hell a Comanche brave is doin' up in this country. From what I hear, they got enough trouble a' their own down south, without needin' to come lookin' for it here. It don't look to me like any of these folks speak that tongue."

"How do you know he's speaking Comanche, Gertie?" I asked.

"Learnt it while I was livin' with the Southern Cheyenne. We were real friendly with the Comanches, traded with 'em an' sometimes made war together against the Apaches. Which is kinda a funny thing, cause they speak the same language the Shoshone do, and the Cheyenne and Shoshone are bitter enemies . . . I think I'll mosey over there and see what the poor fella has to say."

I followed her to the edge of the crowd. Gertie, being Gertie, pushed her way through it, as if swimming the breaststroke, speaking Cheyenne, and extorting them all to quiet down a bit and to stop beating the man. When she reached the captive, they had a conversation, and he looked relieved. Now Gertie turned to the crowd, waved her arms outward in a dismissive way, and announced that this man was a friend from the Comanche tribe in Texas, he came in peace, and to leave him alone. For some reason unknown to me, they dispersed on the strength of her testimony. She took the Comanche by the arm and led him over to me. He was a fierce-looking fellow, with a painted face that made him look like the devil, and it is no wonder they considered him an enemy.

"Molly, let me introduce you to Chance Hadley. He says he's a friend a' May's."

"Real pleased to meet you, ma'am," he said with a polite smile, despite the fact that he was clearly hurting from having just been sticked and stoned repeatedly.

"A pleasure to meet you, Chance," I answered, not unaware of the bizarre nature of this introduction. "You've come looking for May, have you?"

"Yes, ma'am, I sure have. Trailed her all the way here."

"And on what business, may I ask?"

"We are friends, ma'am," he said, "maybe . . . maybe even a little more than friends, if you understand my meaning . . . at least we was, 'till I did somethin' stupid . . . real stupid." Even beneath his paint, I could see that he was blushing like a lovestruck schoolboy and that was enough for me to believe him. "I may not look like it right now, but I'm actually mostly a white man, a wrangler by trade."

I laughed. "Yes, Chance, I rather guessed that from the way you speak English, and your accent. I would be happy to lead you to May's lodge, if you'd like."

"That'd be mighty kind a' ya, ma'am, and I would sure be much obliged. And you, ma'am," he said, holding out his hand to Gertie, "from the looks of things you saved my life, and I sure do appreciate that. I never expected to run into anyone up here who speaks Comanche, but I figgered it was better to try that out on 'em than it was to talk American."

"You're right about that, son," Gertie said, as she took his hand and pumped it in a manly handshake. "They probly would a' killed ya right off if you'd done that. But see, the Comanche language is real similar to what the Shoshone speak, because a long time ago they used to live together. And the Cheyenne hate the Shoshone near as much as they hate the whites. So even though no one here likely speaks that language, exceptin' me, they've heard enough of it spoke to recognize it. That's probly why they was being so rough on ya, and they surely woulda kilt ya anyway, real slow like. I'll let Molly take you over to where May is bunkin'. An' then later when we get a chance, love to have a chat with ya."

"Likewise, ma'am. But one other thing . . . I rode in this mornin' on a dappled gray horse. I figger these folks will have already divvied up my belongings, but you think there's any chance I can get my mount back?"

"The boys will be lookin' after 'em," Gertie said, "so they'll be well cared for. As to gettin' 'em back, I'll see what I can do, son. That's a touchy subject, as you probly know. Usually whoever caught ya and counted coup first gets to keep your horse."

"Yes, ma'am, I do know how that works. When I rode in, the sentries surrounded me, one of 'em knocked me outta the saddle, an' they all counted coup. But if there's anything you can do, I'd be much obliged. I'm real attached to that animal."

As I was leading Chance to Martha's tipi, he suddenly stopped and touched his face. "I don't mean to cause ya any more trouble than I already have, ma'am," he said, "but would ya mind terrible if we went down to the creek first so I can wash off this grease paint, 'fore I see May?"

"Are you afraid you'll scare her, Chance?" I asked. "And by the way, you can call me Molly."

"No, ma'am . . . I mean, Molly . . . it ain't that. She's already seen me like this. But this time, I just want to look a little more, ya know a little more, ah . . ."

". . . handsome?" I offered.

"Yes, ma'am, somethin' like that." He laughed and I could tell he was blushing again. "Also, I think a few of the rocks those boys were throwing at me cut my face up a little, so that way I can wash off the blood, too."

I was impressed that he didn't say this last with any trace of anger, or self-pity, nor had he when he described his capture and treatment by the sentries. "No trouble at all, Chance; we'll go down to the creek first."

I knew from our experience with Martha during her Red Painted Woman days that it is not so easy to wash grease paint off with cold creek water, but Chance clearly knew what he was doing. I sat up on the bank as he took his hide war shirt off and laid it neatly on the grass, knelt down by the water and scooped two full handfuls of mixed mud, sand, and pebbles, vigorously scrubbed his face with it, rinsed with clear creek water, and then repeated the maneuver a second time. Finally, he took two more handfuls of water in hand and combed his hair back, then splashed some on his armpits as well. He stood and picked up his shirt, dried his face with it, and slipped it over his head.

After he climbed back up on the bank, he looked at me and said: "How'd I do, ma'am . . . Molly . . . did I get most of it off?"

He is a handsome fellow, no doubt of that, with strong angular features and sun-darkened skin, reddened by the scrubbing. It occurred to me that he could almost pass for an Indian. I assumed because he spoke Comanche that he must have some native blood.

"You did well, Chance, and, indeed, you do look much more presentable for a reunion with your . . . your lady friend, if I may be so bold as to make that characterization."

At this he smiled broadly, and proudly. "Yes, Molly, I believe ya can say that . . . at least, I sure hope so."

I could see that Chance was one of those people who virtually everyone likes instinctively. He had an easy, natural way about him, entirely without artifice. He was polite, and manly, and I could see why May would be attracted to him. I smiled to myself as I remembered Susie and Meggie's remark about her, as by my count, in her little over a year and a half on the plains, she's had already three lovers—Captain John Bourke, Chief Little Wolf, and now Chance Hadley.

As we are walking back into the camp, I asked Chance how he and May met.

"Well, that's kinda a strange story, Molly. See, I was workin' as a wrangler on a cattle drive up from Texas . . . I caught May stealin' a horse from me . . . that's how we met."

At this, I could not help but let out a burst of laughter. "My goodness, how romantic!"

Chance laughed, too. "That's the funny thing, Molly, 'cause it *was* romantic."

I liked this man more and more, and I couldn't wait to deliver him to May. When we reached Martha's lodge, I scratched on the opening, and Martha peeled it back, saw us, and stepped out. "Hello, Molly," she said, regarding Chance with something between suspicion and curiosity.

"Is May inside?" I asked.

"Yes, Molly, I'm here," she called from inside. "I'm coming out, I'm just covering myself, I just woke up . . . that was a long night, wasn't it?"

Now May stepped out, wrapped in a trade blanket, squinting into the morning sun. She stood for a long moment, looking at Chance. "Good God," she said at last, with a small, sly, and possibly even loving smile on her face, "how the hell do you keep finding me, cowboy?" Then she laughed and threw her arms around Chance, her blanket falling from her body as he took her in his arms. "I followed your sign, May," he said, "like I always do."

"Why don't you come over to my tent for a visit," I suggested to Martha, "we'll make coffee."

She nodded. "Lovely idea, Molly."

7 September 1876

To my relief, Hawk and Wind arrived early this morning, herding before them the horses that May and the medicine woman brought to us. After the scouts relayed the news that they were headed across the valley, many gathered to watch them ride in, happy to find their leader, Aénohe, again, fully recovered from his wounds. Most in our band know also Little Wolf's trusted seer, Woman Who Moves against the Wind, and our own ladies, with me at the head of this contingent, trilled enthusiastically at their entrance. Even we have become rather proficient at this charming manner of welcoming our returning people.

Wind has been invited to sleep in the lodge of Holy Woman and her granddaughter, whom they call Howls Along Woman, Amahtóohě'e, a name bestowed for what reason I have not ascertained as I have yet to hear her howl. I would say that she is roughly fifteen or sixteen years old and appears to be both assistant and apprentice to the old woman. She rides with her, sets up her lodge, and serves as her eyes.

Hawk and I have pitched our lodge just on the edge of the confines of the camp, but not outside it as I might have preferred. Due to Hawk's position in the band we are expected to camp among the rest and not to set ourselves apart. Thus, speaking of howling, there would surely be no more of that in the throes of our passion. Still, we enjoyed a quite pleasurable, if less vocally uninhibited, reunion under the buffalo robes.

9 September 1876

The weather is changing; the temperate autumnal climate we have been enjoying these past days giving way suddenly to a cold wind blowing down from the north, presaging the coming season. Some of the young warriors who joined us from the agencies have taken their leave ahead of the approaching storm to return to their families and the scant handouts there from the U.S. government that are supposed to see them through the winter. There has been much nervous discussion among the band about making our permanent village for these next frigid months ahead. Some feel that our present location, which has been the longest bivouac yet during these past weeks of travel, would suffice—there is ample water, and grass for the horses to graze, as well as good visibility in all directions to identify the approach of enemies.

As I suppose with every society, tribal political structures are complicated, sometimes even byzantine, especially given the fact that we have several extended Arapaho families with us, and they operate under a different system. Since all the Cheyenne elders went with Little Wolf, our band has a quite uncommon composition—younger, with more children and white women, especially since the addition of May, Gertie, Ann, and Hannah. Now, with the departure of those young warriors to the agencies, we women actually outnumber the men, and, as a consequence, after much deliberation around the fire and passing of the pipe, we have reached an agreement regarding a new tribal council that reflects this unusual situation. Pretty Nose, an Arapaho, having already been designated a war chief, technically holds the highest rank. However, Hawk, because he is Cheyenne and respected by both tribes as a leader and warrior, has also now been given equal status. Other council members include Gertie, because she was once married into the Southern Cheyenne tribe; Phemie, due to her achievements on the battlefield; May, because she is the wife of the Sweet Medicine Chief; and Woman Who Moves against the Wind, Little Wolf's trusted advisor. One of the most interesting choices, because some believed that at least one peacemaker should be represented, is our Mennonite chaplain, Christian Goodman. Finally, filling the remaining seats of power are two of our other Strongheart members, Warpath Woman and Kills in the Morning Woman. Red Fox, Hawk's friend, and a young Arapaho warrior named High Bear round out the council, making for a total of seven women and four men. In this way, we have formed a unique kind of government, in a sense a new tribe altogether, yet one without a name, and with new rules still to be written . . . figuratively, of course . . .

Both Hawk and Pretty Nose have spoken with Holy Woman, who, as a seer, holds a special place in the tribe, based on the faith of those who wish to follow her, in the same way as a priest or pastor does in our society, though without political authority. Hawk, perhaps due at least a little to my influence, has become a bit frustrated by the intransigence of the old blind woman and her insistence on guiding us in circles, while Pretty Nose wishes to continue following her.

It did not appear that any decision had been reached on this matter until this evening, when the camp crier made his rounds, announcing that all were to prepare to move out in the morning, headed where, we have not been advised.

10 September 1876

We wake this morning to a near blizzard, unusual though not unprecedented, I am told, this early in the season. Surely, we will not be traveling in weather such as this, says Hawk. Yet shortly thereafter, the camp crier arrives in our "neighborhood," calling out his instructions to break camp and prepare for departure, his words barely audible over the sound of the wind buffeting our tipi. But this cannot be possible! Yet I crack open the tent flap and see that those who have received the news before us are already struggling to dismantle their lodges and load pack dogs and travois with their goods. Reluctantly, we begin to do likewise, for a tribal order must be obeyed.

It continues to astonish me with what exceptional speed and economy these peoples are capable of disassembling an encampment, even in such inclement weather, and I, too, have been well initiated into the proper procedures by Hawk's departed grandmother. My little Mouse, who has moved in with us again, is already quite competent at her assigned deeds and watches me attentively for instructions, which, in this wind, can only be accomplished with the use of sign talk. Inside of an hour, the entire band is under way, against an ungodly headwind stinging our faces with blowing snow that feels like we are being pelted with beads of icy sand.

Fortunately, with the new stock Wind and May have given us, all in the band are now mounted, and none afoot, even the children, some doubled and even tripled up astride a single horse. In the face of the tempest, there is no possibility of conversation. We wrap what protection we can around us, and I have covered Mouse, riding behind me, with a trade blanket, her arms around my waist, so at least my body offers warmth and serves as a kind of windbreak. I try to keep my eyes half shut, my face averted so as not to be looking directly into the maelstrom.

And thus we ride, hour after hour it seems, though we have no way of judging the passage of time or the direction we are taking, for the sun is obscured and we are enveloped in a cocoon of whiteness. The horses move slowly, putting their hooves down tentatively, taking each careful step as if seeking purchase, uncertain that there will be solid ground beneath. I begin to wonder, and not for the first time, if Holy Woman still has full command of her mental faculties, and, by extension, do we, for following her? And I begin to fear that if the storm continues and we do not seek shelter, we might all perish. As if reading my mind, Hawk signs me to say that he is riding ahead again to consult our guide, which he has done twice already since our departure. He is reluctant to leave us. Because the visibility is so poor, we all travel together in as compact a formation as possible, for if one were to become separated from the main group it would be virtually impossible to find them again. I nod, answering him to go ahead.

He is gone too long, and I begin to worry, yet I do not dare go in search of him. Time passes, the blizzard continues, even intensifies. I feel as though we are trapped in a nightmare, not moving through a storm, rather captives of it, being carried along to some terrifying destination. I long to break free, to see sunlight again, space, landscape, however barren, anything at all familiar. I feel Mouse gripping me harder around the waist, and I sense that she is afraid, or perhaps with her little head against my back, she simply feels my quickening heartbeat.

Now from the head of our expedition, carried on the wind, comes the most mournful wailing sound, a kind of brokenhearted animal

howl such as I have never before in my life heard . . . no, never. It is
not the cry of a coyote or a wolf, or even a whole pack of wolves, but
an expression of full-throated human grief so profoundly unsettling
that the horses all stop in their tracks, raise their heads to the wind,
nickering and neighing nervously. My mare, Spring, throws her head
and paws the ground, and I tighten up on her reins for fear that she
might bolt. I wonder what tragedy has occurred to elicit such a cry
and I am immediately afraid for Hawk, wherever he may be.

As our band rests frozen thus in place by the recalcitrant horses,
the tempest begins to lift, the wind to abate, the driving snow reduced to lightly falling flakes that barely touch the ground before
melting. It appears that we have ridden out of the storm at last, the
clouds that have imprisoned us parting to reveal patches of deep
blue sky above. A collective sigh of relief issues from the band,
most of whom, with the exception of those riding directly beside
us, have been invisible to me for hours. I see now that we have remained in a remarkably tight unit.

Our mounts, equally relieved, begin moving again, and from
our women now arises a sweet trilling. Mouse extricates herself
from her blanket and laughs lightly, and we both join the others in
thus welcoming the sunlight. At the same time, as I look ahead for
Hawk, I see several horsemen dismounted just off the trail, kneeling beside a figure prone on the ground. I break ranks with the
others, press my heels to Spring's flanks, and ride toward them. As
we approach, I understand suddenly the wail of grief, and from
whom it arose. Holy Woman is lying on the ground, young Howls
Along Woman kneeling beside her, keening in a low voice of despair. I quickly dismount, Mouse slipping in unison off Spring's
back, and go to Hawk, resisting my natural impulse to embrace
him, an act that became so commonplace when we were camping alone but is considered impolite behavior between couples in
public. In any case, despite my enormous release from anxiety at
finding him safe again, this is clearly not the proper occasion.

"What has happened?" I ask in a whisper.

"As we broke out of the storm and into the sunlight, Holy Woman fell dead from her horse."

"My God . . . we have been following her in circles all these weeks, and now she is gone?" I am ashamed as soon as this leaves my mouth, at how utterly insensitive it is to the poor dead woman at our feet, a respected seer, and her grieving granddaughter. I did not know Holy Woman, other than by sight, but I owe her some modicum of respect at this time, even though, in my more rational moments, which admittedly seem to come and go these days, I believed her to be a charlatan, leading us on the ultimate wild-goose chase.

"Do you see where we are?" Hawk asks. "Have you looked around?"

"No, I have only been worried and looking for you." But at his suggestion, I scan the surrounding countryside, taking in the broad valley in the same autumn season we enjoyed before the tempest, the mixed prairie grasses tall and yellowing as in our last encampment, the river bottom below lined by a wide forest of mature cottonwood trees, and, in the distance, across gently rolling hills, a herd of buffalo grazing.

"Amahtóohě'e tells me that her grandmother knew from her vision that she would die when we arrived here," Hawk says. "And so she has."

"Here?"

Hawk looks at me with the slightest wry smile.

Recognition of the death has now traveled among the band, which has stopped moving again, the women's trilling having faded away to join Howls Along Woman in a rising keening of grief for their fallen medicine woman.

"We make camp here," says Hawk.

This is the real world we live in, constantly moving between keening and trilling, heartbreak and joy, war and peace, blizzard and sunshine. Yet, I have to say, this does appear to be an agreeable valley in which to pitch our winter village.

THE LOST JOURNALS OF MAY DODD

Love and War Games

Then I saw two mounted women with baby boards strapped to their chests cantering toward us, the one in the lead raising her arm and waving, smiling. As she came closer, I recognized her; good God, how is it possible? We both slipped from our saddles at the same time and approached each other. I stared at the infant in the baby board and shook my head in denial. "No, it is not possible," I whispered to myself, "but of course, I'm having a dream—the storm, the clearing, the valley, the dead woman, the trilling, the keening, the horses running, everyone safe.

Wake me, Chance," I said, moving my arm out to touch him beside me at our sleeping place, "please, wake me."

—*from the lost journals of May Dodd*

12 September 1876

I do not know exactly how Wind knew that the destination fate intended for us was not too far down the trail, but after the cowboy Chance left us so abruptly, and angrily, she said it was a good thing he was gone, and we spoke no further of it. We rode largely in silence for the next few days. I was stung, I admit, humiliated, and angry myself at his vicious renunciation of me. So much for the grand words of love he had whispered in our intimate moments together. I was angry, as well, at myself, for having let my guard down, for having come to believe in someone for just a moment. God knows, my experience should have taught me better by now.

Eight days ago, we rode into the camp of the Cheyenne warrior Hawk and his unlikely wife, a fair-haired white woman by the name of Molly McGill, one of the second group of women sent mistakenly by the government as members of the already defunct Brides for Indians program. She is a tall, strong, large-boned girl, who looks like she would be quite at home on a farm somewhere, milking cows. No, that is a bit unfair; perhaps I'm jealous of her, for she's a pretty girl as well, who exudes a certain competence and self-confidence, and she and Hawk are clearly very much in love . . . Did I also experience a twinge of envy of the happy couple? . . . Yes, of course.

However, as it happens, Molly and I get on quite well together. She has a good grasp of the desperation of our respective situations, tied so inexorably to that of the natives, but she seems rather accepting and unafraid of it. She is going to have Hawk's child. That same afternoon of our arrival, she led me across a broad valley on the far side of which was camped the larger band formed after the battle of Greasy Grass, a battle she said she had missed, for reasons she did not disclose. With the acceleration of events here, there is much we have not yet had the chance to discuss, though she told me briefly a chilling story of her own reasons for joining the brides program. She is a girl who has known more than her share of tribulation and heartbreak.

On our way across the valley, we were briefly chased by a war party of Crow, but Molly rides as well as I do, and the chase ended as quickly as it had begun, due to the intervention of our own warriors who poured from the camp as we were approaching, to engage the Crow in battle.

Shortly thereafter, I was reunited with my dear friends Martha, Phemie, and my little Horse Boy, whom I have believed to be dead all this time, shot by Captain John Bourke at the beginning of the Army's attack on our village. What joy, astonishment, and incredulity I experienced in these reunions, the latter emotion especially, when I first laid eyes upon the formerly meek, unathletic . . . I must say, even uncoordinated, Martha Atwood. Such a personal transformation I have never before witnessed . . . Martha, a warrior woman? Good God! But, yes, that is exactly what she has become, returning upon her warhorse from the engagement with the Crow, bloodied and bearing a scalp belonging to an enemy she had vanquished in battle. It is a scenario I could not have invented in my wildest imaginings.

Later, at the feast and dance to celebrate the victory, Martha recreated her victory in battle, in a dance so profoundly evocative that she had the crowd on the edge of their seats (if I may be forgiven the metaphoric use of that phrase, for, of course, we were all seated on the ground).

I have gotten slightly ahead of myself here, because before the feast had even begun, as the game animals were still roasting and the People still gathering at the circle, who should arrive in the camp but my dear old friend Gertie, in the company of an Englishwoman by the name of Lady Ann Hall—yes, the one and same paramour of my dear, departed Helen Elizabeth Flight—accompanied by her maid-servant, a spunky little Liverpudlian girl named Hannah Alford.

It had not yet occurred to me that this coming together of us all, here and now, must have been . . . I cannot say divinely arranged, for I do not believe in such nonsense . . . but perhaps it did have some indefinable purpose we are yet to learn. I was so overwhelmed to find again my old friends, and in the case of Phemie and Horse Boy, those whom I even believed to be dead, that I had no time to consider anything, only to react and gratefully accept this grand gift . . . which is the way of life with the Indians . . . one lives in the moment and asks no questions.

A sobering time for us followed the festivities, for after the dancers had largely dispersed, our group remained on the buffalo robes to chat and catch up. In this frank middle-of-the-night conversation, we confronted head-on the dark reality of our future among these people, and their own future. Exhausted, and emotionally drained from it all, Martha and I bid the others good night, and retired to her lodge where she had offered to take me in.

I was awakened the next morning by Molly McGill, who scratched on the cover of the tent opening. Martha, already up and dressed, stepped outside as I tried to bury myself again in the warmth of the robes. But when I heard Molly ask for me, I rose quickly and covered myself with a trade blanket before going out to greet her.

When I came through the opening, I was confronted by yet another sight I could not have imagined. In that half-awake state, my vision blurred by the morning sun, I squinted and looked at him for a long time, just to be certain . . . I spoke to him . . . I do not remember exactly what I said . . . and he spoke back to me, and in that moment, my anger and humiliation fell away, and, almost against my will but unable to stop myself, I leapt into the arms of

the Comanche cowboy, Chance Hadley, and as I did so my blanket
fell away from my body.

Molly diplomatically suggested that Martha come to her lodge
for a visit, and the two of them made off with dispatch. I broke free
of Chance, grabbed my blanket, and covered myself again, grateful
as I looked around that no one from other tipis in the vicinity was
about. I ducked back in through the opening and held the skin flap
up for him to enter.

"Sit here," I said, indicating my sleeping place. He did so. "Before we go any further, we must talk." He nodded. "I want to tell
you that if ever again you call me a whore, or anything like it, I will
kill you, Chance."

"'Kill'? That's a real strong word, May," he answered.

"So is 'whore.'"

He hung his head then, unable to look me in the eye. "I never
spoke to a woman like that before," he said. "My mama would
be so ashamed a' me, and I'm ashamed a' myself. I am so sorry,
May. I came here to beg ya to forgive me. I know I don't deserve it,
and I got no excuse for what I said. I guess . . . I guess . . . maybe I
thought I was the first . . ." he said, sheepishly. "I know I shoulda
known better . . . but I ain't had much acquaintance with women,
at least not the kind you and me had. I ain't never been in love . . .
and when I heard what you had to say, I went a little crazy . . . I
went a lot crazy."

"Listen, Chance," I said, more gently, putting my hand upon his.
"I should have told you more about my past. But everything happened so fast between us, and I wasn't ready for that. I wasn't ready
to tell you the truth, because I knew it would disgust you."

"You don't have to tell me a damn thing, May," he said, "and I
won't never ask ya, neither."

"But I have to tell you . . . and I want you to know that in a way
you were the first . . . in the sense of the feelings I had for you.
You see, my common-law husband, Harry Ames, was the foreman
in my father's business. I was so young and impressionable, and I

believe now that I got involved with him in rebellion against my father's controlling nature. I had two babies, a son and a daughter, by Harry, and so I can never regret that.

"One night my father came to our house with others. They took my children away, and he put me in a lunatic asylum. The only possible way I could get out of there was to join a secret government program to go out West to marry an Indian warrior and have children by him. It was a means by which the government thought they could convince . . . *we* could convince . . . the Cheyenne to surrender, and bring them into the so-called civilized world. But you know how that turned out . . . I told you about the attack, and that was the truth . . .

"And, yes, right before the Cheyenne warriors were coming to Camp Robinson to take us away, I had relations with an Army captain who had befriended me at Fort Laramie, and who brought us to Camp Robinson for what was called the 'exchange' with the Indians—a trade of horses for white women. I make no excuse for what happened with the captain, either. He was a good man, I was afraid, and I clung desperately to him . . . I am, after all, a city girl, and I was terrified of what was to come . . . all of us were . . . terrified to go into the wilderness among savages . . . to marry them and have children by them, for God's sake . . . it scares me now when I think about how it was for us at the beginning. . . . But at the time, I put on a good front of courage for the benefit of the others.

"The Cheyenne chief Little Wolf chose me to be his bride . . . It is not as if we had any choice in the matter, but I was lucky for he is a great man, a great leader and warrior, and he was good to me. When I gave birth, it was obvious to all that my daughter was not Little Wolf's but John Bourke's. However, Little Wolf accepted the child as his own, and I have to this day never known if he knew or even suspected the truth.

"That is my story, Chance, and I should have told you before, but to be honest, I didn't think we'd ever see each other again after the first time we parted. When you rescued us from the bandits,

I thought I owed it to you . . . but it came out all wrong, and that wasn't the right time, either. Still, though I may decide to forgive you, I do not excuse what you called me."

"I ask for your forgiveness, May," he said. "I don't ask to be excused. I told ya there ain't no excuse for what I said. But now I want to tell ya somethin' else. If you do decide to forgive me, an' we get outta this mess somehow, together, I'll take ya to Chicago, an' we'll get your little ones back. I always wanted to see a big city in the east."

"Thank you, Chance, if only that could happen. And by the way, I wouldn't really kill you . . . but considering what I would do to you if ever you call me that word again, you might wish that I had."

Two days ago, for some reason I did not fully understand, we broke camp and traveled all night through a ghastly blizzard, a kind of whirling tunnel of wind and snow, in which I was certain the entire band would die, and if any did survive, our precious herd of horses would surely be lost. When first we set out into it, which seemed utter folly to begin with, I insisted that my dear Horse Boy stay close to me, for one could barely see beyond the head of one's own mount. Surely, without such attention, many would scatter in the maelstrom, and those lost left wandering with no visibility and no sense of direction would be forever lost. But the little scamp disobeyed my command, peeling off on his prairie pony to tend to the herd. I screamed futilely at him against the wind, weeping tears that froze instantly on my face, certain that I would never see the boy again.

Now the snow, driven by wind, was beginning to accumulate in drifts where we rode, through which the horses struggled valiantly. I expected that in the spring, when these began to melt, someone would find us all beneath the snow, the frozen corpses of men, women, children, dogs, and stock, spread out across the full length of our path.

It was within the dark depths of these imaginings that the wind began to abate, and the snow to fall straight in identifiable flakes, instead of horizontally like tiny pellets of stinging ice, and the unseen sky lighten incrementally. As we rode out of the mist, we saw the sky again, the dark storm clouds parting and drifting behind us, revealing the sun. The women began to trill. But suddenly we heard the most ghastly howl of grief, followed by a terrible keening, the shrieks of which were taken up by our women, a sound that always raises gooseflesh on my skin. We had regained the autumn, ridden into a valley, and I saw ahead Hawk and Molly, dismounted, bending over the body of the medicine woman I had so cursed, who lay dead at the feet of her horse.

I looked around and behind me, and saw with relief that the band seemed largely intact, and in the valley below, our horse herd was running free, joyously spreading out, some kicking up their back legs in exuberance, Horse Boy and the others riding beside them, an incongruous scene to the death sounds of keening.

I looked at Chance, who smiled back, and at Wind on the other side of me, and Martha, next to Chance, all alive. Turning, I saw the Strongheart women, native and white alike, Phemie and Pretty Nose included, who had all somehow managed to stay together, as they were meant to be.

Then I saw two mounted women with baby boards strapped to their chests cantering toward us, the one in the lead raising her arm and waving, smiling. As she came closer, I recognized her; good God, how is it possible? We both slipped from our saddles at the same time and approached each other. I stared at the infant in the baby board and shook my head in denial. "No, it is not possible," I whispered to myself, "but of course, I'm having a dream—the storm, the clearing, the valley, the dead woman, the trilling, the keening, the horses running, everyone safe. Wake me, Chance," I said, moving my arm out to touch him beside me at our sleeping place, "please, wake me."

"Do you not recognize your daughter, Mesoke?" said Feather on Head, looking at me strangely. "Do you not recognize me?"

I tried to answer, but I couldn't, my voice frozen as is sometimes the way of dreams. I put my hands on my forehead and managed to nod, and then I began to bawl, my body trembling uncontrollably.

The second horsewoman with the baby board had reached us now and dismounted, as Martha came up behind me. "Pull yourself together, May, it's just Feather on Head, and Grass Girl, my husband Tangle Hair's second wife," Martha said, as if this were the most normal thing that could possibly happen. "But perhaps you never knew Grass Girl. After all, she's barely more than a child. But really, dear, why in the world are you crying so, don't you see, they've brought our babies back to us? You know, I've always had this idea that perhaps when our children grow up, they will fall in love and get married. Wouldn't that be such fun to be grandmothers together, you and I?" Now I knew from Martha's nonsensical talk that this was not a dream. "But *what is* the matter with you?" she said. "I do not remember the *old* May Dodd behaving like such a baby."

I stopped crying and trembling, and I lowered my hands. "Shut up now, Martha," I said. "What in the hell are you talking about? Yes, I see who it is. I was just a little confused and overwhelmed when first they appeared. And I'm trying to understand how they can possibly be here."

"Now that's the old May I know and love!" she said.

"Our husbands Little Wolf and Tangle Hair sent us," said Feather on Head. "Woman Who Moves against the Wind had a vision. She saw our village attacked again by the Army, the babies killed in the lodges by the soldiers' bullets. They said we would be safe with Holy Woman."

"But where is your son, Little Egg, Feather on Head?"

She shook her head and looked away from me, grief stricken. "After we left you in the cave and found Little Wolf, we had to walk in the cold for ten days to reach the village of Crazy Horse. Pretty Nose and Quiet One looked after Little Bird, and I carried my Little Egg. You remember, Mesoke, that he was not a strong boy. We called him Vòvotse because he was fragile as an egg. I carried him against my skin for two days, but in the middle of the night on the third day he became sick . . . I could feel his little body burning up against me . . . and then it grew cold . . ."

"I am so sorry, dear. You saved my daughter, but lost your son."

"Pretty Walker and Quiet One saved Little Bird. She was stronger than my poor Little Egg."

"But how did you get here?"

"We arrived in your camp last night, as the storm was blowing in," Feather on Head explained. "The Arapaho family of Tall Bull took us in. We left with them this morning and traveled through the storm. We were very worried for the babies, but we kept them well covered. Do you not wish to hold your daughter now, Mesoke?"

"Yes . . . yes, of course I do," I answered, the tears beginning to flow again as I looked into Wren's eyes, and she looked back at me. "But she won't even remember that I am her mother. I have always wondered whose milk has nourished her all this time?"

"Do you remember in the cave when you were dying and you told Quiet One, Pretty Walker, and me to leave you and to take Little Bird with us?" she asked. "The last thing you did before we left was to put Little Bird on your breast to feed."

"Yes, of course, I remember like it was yesterday, and not a day has gone by since when I have not thought of it." I reached out now and touched my little Wren's face with my fingers. She smiled at me.

"Eleven mothers lost their babies on the first night of that terrible walk. And they all still had milk in their breasts. After Little Egg died, I fed Little Bird. And so did your friends, the red-haired twin girls, who also lost their infants. After we finally reached the camp of Crazy Horse, we had a whole camp full of wet nurses."

"I am so sorry for you, Feather on Head," I said, "and so grateful to you for keeping my daughter alive. You are her mother now."

"No, Mesoke, you just put your finger in her mouth again," she said, "as you did when she was born, and she will remember who you are. You are her mother, but I will stay here with you. I still have much milk to give." She turned now to Martha. "I nurse your son, too, except that he bites me, the little devil."

Martha and I unstrapped our infants from the baby boards and took them in our arms. Wind and Chance were both beside me now.

"Do you remember my Little Bird?" I asked Wind, turning to show her my baby.

She laughed. "Mesoke, it is you who do not remember," she said, "because when you gave birth, you were so weak from the storm in which you almost died. It was I who pulled Little Bird from you and into this world."

Somehow, my little Wren and I seem to have come full circle, through tempests, blizzards, bone-chilling cold, and back into each other's arms.

23 September 1876

Today I believe is the September equinox, auguring the official beginning of autumn. Since the tempest deposited us in this valley, we have enjoyed the most beautiful weather, cool in the morning and evening, and perfectly temperate during the day. The leaves on the cottonwoods along the river and the aspen in the foothills are assuming their medley of fall colors, turning from green to red, to yellow, to orange.

I have had no time for journal entries these past days, for we have all been occupied in setting up our village, no easy task, but one of the utmost importance. Lacking lodgepole pine trees to make proper tipis in the band's last camp, and, due to the storm, unable to transport those they did have, the men, women, and older children have ridden into the mountains to cut saplings and drag them back to the site of the village, which is beginning to take shape.

Chance and I are making our lodge in the circle of the Strongheart society, who have made me an honorary member, until such time that I can prove myself on the battlefield as a horsewoman, archer, gunwoman, and wielder of knife, lance, and tomahawk. The current members are all well ahead of me in some of these skills, even Martha, I am loath to admit, and I find it rather humiliating that I must be put to the test before being initiated. Wind, due to her status in the tribe, has already been granted full membership as a Strongheart. Fortunately she has given me a good deal of preparation as a warrior, and I do consider myself the equal of any of the others on horseback—with the notable exception of Wind, herself, Pretty Nose, and Phemie. All three of these accomplished equestrians have learned the ultimate skill of riding without holding the reins, having trained their horses to react to subtle pressure from their knees, thighs, calves, and feet, and even to respond to voice commands. Chance, too, owns this skill, having learned it from his half-Comanche grandfather, a tribe widely considered to be the finest horsemen on the southern plains. Of course, this ability offers an invaluable advantage to the warrior, who then has both hands free to wield his or her sundry weapons. I have been working with Wind to master it, but this will clearly take some time.

A word about the Strongheart chief, Pretty Nose. She is an Arapaho girl, with some Cheyenne blood, as I understand it, younger, I would guess, than I, and an absolutely magnificent specimen of a warrior woman—beautiful, strong, stately, and fearsome. She appears, as well, to be a single-minded soul, and despite all the work to be done in making winter camp, she still finds time to lead her soldiers in practicing for war.

To see her mounted on her painted war mustang, armed and dressed for battle, brings to my mind the Amazons of Greek mythology, whom I read about in my youth, and found so thrilling that I dreamed of becoming one . . . an odd ambition for a young girl growing up as a member of Chicago "society." However, it was exactly due to the stifling nature of that world that I was so attracted to these tales, and yet another reason, perhaps, that I rebelled against my family, ended up in a lunatic asylum, and find myself here among these people.

Now I actually have the opportunity to realize my childhood dreams, to become a pagan Amazon, and I have as my models Pretty Nose and, of course, my dear Phemie, who has always been equally imposing as an African warrior woman. The two of them make for quite a sight mounted together for battle, and the farm girl, Molly McGill, too, when she joins their practice sessions, against the wishes of her husband, Hawk, cuts an impressive figure. Not one to shirk a challenge or play second fiddle to anyone, I intend to join this pantheon of warriors as their full equal.

Assuming the fine weather holds, war games in which men and women alike compete are scheduled to begin as soon as the village is fully in place, stocked for the winter with game, tanned hides, firewood, and buffalo chips for the fires. When all is done is the traditional time for games and recreation, before winter descends and all are tipi-bound.

In the meantime, in what little spare time we have, I have been practicing with Phemie those other skills I must master to qualify as a full member of the Strongheart society. It is true that I have always been a competitive sort, perhaps to a fault, and I have no intention of being left behind any of the others in any contest. I have to admit, but only to myself, that I particularly look forward to matching my skills against Molly, who, in my long absence, I can't help but feel, has usurped my position as a leader among the women. Good God, adversity has not humbled me, rather only increased my vanity . . .

The broad valley in which we have settled and the mountains that surround it on all sides are well stocked with game animals of all sorts, buffalo and antelope in the flats, mule deer and elk in the high country, all fattened up for the coming winter. The Englishwoman, Lady Ann, with whom I have had a chance to visit, returned from New York with a new scattergun and delights in hunting the prairie chickens and sharp-tailed grouse that inhabit the hilly plains and the blue grouse in the mountains. Her presence here so reminds me of Helen; in fact, she has moved into a lodge with the young lover they have shared, Bridge Girl, assistant to my friend, the old scoundrel Dog Woman . . . who, much as I have tormented her in the past, I admit to adoring as the most unique of individuals. Rounding out the ample supply of nourishment provided by this rich country, the band's Mennonite chaplain, Christian Goodman, is particularly adept at fishing the river that flows near our village and the smaller feeder creeks that enter it from the mountains, all filled with fat trout, which he distributes to any in the band who desire them.

To be sure, I have had very little time for such pursuits, but I did sneak out with the chaplain early one morning for a couple of hours, leaving Wren with Feather on Head, and taking with me the fishing pole and gear I had acquired at the trading post in Tent City. I found Christian not only to be a fine angler but also excellent company, and we came away with a sack full of fish.

During our short time together, we spoke at length about his denomination, which seems to be a rather reasonable one, except for the typically patriarchal structure it shares with virtually every such religious and political institution of mankind. They all, savage and civilized alike, if you can even differentiate between the two, are fully designed by the male sex, relegating women to giving birth, raising children, and doing the chores, effectively removing them from any share of the power. In addition, as I frankly pointed out to the chaplain, as admirable and Christlike as I find the strict tenets of nonviolence in his faith, it does seem to be particularly ill-suited to the reality of life on the plains.

"Believe me, May," he answered, "that is an argument frequently expressed by your warrior friends, whom my wife, Astrid, I'm sorry to say, has joined . . . this I attribute to her Viking blood. But I ask you this: What has been the benefit to humanity of mankind's constant wars? What have they ever brought us besides chaos, death, and suffering? Isn't peace and harmony among peoples what all ultimately seek?"

"Well, that appears to be the problem, Christian, doesn't it? For not all humanity seeks those goals. Some, possibly even most, seek dominance over others. And to resist being dominated, and, in the case of these people, to resist being eradicated or imprisoned, one must fight back."

"Even if fighting back is futile?"

"Yes, this is their land, the earth upon which they have lived for ten thousand years. Isn't it worth dying to protect?"

"Yes, perhaps it is," the chaplain said after some reflection. "But if, as I think you know in your heart, May, there is no possibility of victory against the far more numerous and powerful foe you face, are you really willing to sacrifice the life of your child for a hopeless cause?"

I quickly realized that this was not an argument I could win. "No," I admitted, "that I am not willing to do, Christian."

For the sake of practicality, Chance and I, with, of course, my daughter, Wren . . . how wonderful this is to write! . . . and her wet nurse, Feather on Head, as well as my little Horse Boy will be sharing the same lodge. However, the humble wikiup we transported from our previous camp is far too small to comfortably accommodate us all for the coming winter. And so we are in the process of building a new one.

Chance has joined the buffalo hunters, along with several of our Strongheart women, including Phemie and Pretty Nose, to harvest sufficient beasts for hides and meat to dry to see us through the long cold season. He has acquitted himself well in this pursuit, having hunted the animals in Texas when he was still a boy, and from his running horse, he knows exactly the spot in which to thrust a lance or shoot an arrow to bring them down. I know from my time among the People that it can be a dangerous pursuit, one in which injuries are not uncommon, and are sometimes even fatal.

Feather on Head and I, old friends and tent mates, and accustomed to the work of squaws, join the other women in the field after a successful hunt to skin the buffalo, quarter them, load the sections on travois, and drag them back to the village with the help of horses and/or dogs. Indeed, we have recently acquired a canine, or, I should say, he has acquired us, having wandered one day up to our lodge under construction, while Feather on Head and I were busy butchering the meat and laying it out to dry, fleshing and tanning the hides, and attaching them to stretching racks Chance has built for us. He has also cut and peeled the lodge poles, and with them erected the frame to our new, luxuriously large tipi. Now we will simply wait for the tanning process to be completed so that we can stitch the hides together and attach them to the poles. The rest of the band is at work on similar projects, all keeping in mind that we race against the approaching season, and hoping for what we whites call an "Indian" summer of mild autumn weather.

Back to the subject of our new dog, he is an enormous, long-legged, shaggy beast, of a race common among the Indians. I have no idea from whence he came, nor do I recall having seen him about the village before we arrived here. He simply walked in, lay down, and watched us work, hoping, no doubt, that a piece of flesh or fat might find its way to him, which, indeed, some occasionally do. We had Little Bird propped up as usual beside us on her baby board, so that she could watch us work, thereby absorbing the daily rhythms of this nomadic life. She was absolutely fascinated by the dog, staring at him, smiling, cooing, gurgling, as if trying to engage him in conversation, and finally, he, too, appearing curious, came to his feet, stretched languidly, and began to move toward her. Not knowing what his intentions were, I instinctively stood and snatched her up on the board, and the dog simply lay down again, perhaps sensing my apprehension. I set her board back in its position, leaning against one of the tipi poles, and stood next to her for a while while he reclined beside it, seemingly quite comfortable and nonthreatening, she expressing baby-talk delight to have a new friend at her side. And thus did this dog, whom I have named Falstaff, after the Shakespearean knight Sir John Falstaff, insinuate himself into our family, becoming especially attached to Wren, and she to him. He's a fine fellow, always available for a meal, but always waiting politely until one is offered him.

A few more words about my Comanche cowboy, who has been quite readily accepted by the band, thanks largely to the recommendation of Gertie and Wind, and simply because he is such an essentially likable and helpful fellow. All of his possessions have been returned to him, including his cowboy attire, boots, and hat—much to the dismay of one of the younger sentries, Bad Horse, Hátavesévé'háme, who, being the third to count coup upon him, had claimed these items. He has also regained possession of his six-shooter, knives, and sword, and, most importantly, the beloved dappled stallion he calls King, a distinctly nonnative name, for kings do not exist in the Indian world.

Because he is a wrangler, and so knowledgeable on the subject of equines, Chance has proposed to the People a quite practical idea to supplement the scanty feed available for the herd in wintertime. Traditionally, the animals are left to forage what they can, digging down through the snow when not too deep, to reach grass that retains few nutrients, or eating bark off the trees, a similarly poor source of food. As a result, during severe winters, many die of malnutrition and exposure due to their severe loss of weight. Thus, Chance, when not hunting or building our tipi, is working tirelessly in the field with his sword as a scythe, cutting the tall fall grasses before they have completely dried, and stacking them in round formations about the village, for use as winter feed for the horses. As helpers in this labor, he has enlisted the aid of the camp's boys and girls, who use the longest knives they have been able to acquire from their families—some of the warrior knives having blades as long as sixteen inches.

All admire Chance's industriousness. However, there is some resentment among the Cheyenne regarding my having taken up with another man, especially a white man, when I am still considered to be one of Little Wolf's three wives. This is a censure I fully expected to face, for it is one thing for a man to "throw away" a wife, as they put it, yet quite another for a woman to do so to a husband, especially when that man is the Sweet Medicine Chief. However, I remember well a conversation I had with Little Wolf, after finally convincing him to surrender his band, and only a short time before the Mackenzie attack. I told him that once at the agency, he would be required by the whites to give up two of us—Feather on Head and me—and retain Quiet One as his sole wife. She was the first bride, the elder, the ruler of the lodge, and his favorite, and he agreed to do so, albeit a bit reluctantly. And so, having previously notified Little Wolf of this fact, and now being separated from him, at least until the spring thaw, I can rationalize having taken a second husband . . . and will just have to endure the disapprobation of the tribe. It is not the first time I've broken tribal precedent. Personally, I do not feel the need to make excuses for my behavior . . . After all, what's good for the goose is good for the gander!

1 October 1876

I should mention now something that has clearly been in the back of everyone's mind since our propitious arrival in this splendid valley several weeks ago. Yet we have all been so occupied with our individual families' heretofore described preparations, as well as those shared collectively by all in the tribe, that no one of my acquaintance has even verbally broached the subject . . . and that is: Where in the world are we?

A strange occurrence today brought that unasked question very much to the forefront. We watched at a distance what appeared to be a small war party composed of no more than half a dozen men riding toward our camp. Some of our Strongheart women assumed arms and mounted, as did a number of the men. I should mention that our men have not yet formed an official warrior society, as they represent both different tribes and at least half a dozen different societies of which each is only represented by one or two in our band. And so, although they have held numerous councils trying to come up with a formal structure, because of the Indians' renowned difficulty in reaching consensus, they remain disunited in a society, without a name or a founding principle. Further confusing the issue is the fact that Chance, a white man with one-eighth Comanche blood, is riding with them, and no one really knows what to do with him, for no white man has ever joined them in making war.

I was pleased that while I am still only an honorary member, Pretty Nose allowed me to ride with the Stronghearts today, and as we set out to confront the approaching interlopers, it was noticed that the brave at their head bore a white flag of peace attached to the end of his lance. As they came closer, Pretty Nose identified the war party as Shoshone, based on the style of their attire and the elaborate headdress worn by their leader. Unlike whites, Indians don't play tricks with the peace flag, such as pretending to be on a friendly mission when they actually have warlike intentions, and so we all relaxed and rode toward them with an attitude of simple curiosity.

As we came abreast and our parties reined up facing each other, their leader planted his lance in the soil and spoke in the sign talk at which I am rather fluent by now. He said: "We come in peace. I wish to powwow with your chief." Being the only one with that title, Pretty Nose rode forward toward him, as he did toward her, with a perplexed look on his face to be thus greeted by a woman chief. They spoke sign together, but I had difficulty reading it as Pretty Nose had her back to me and was partially blocking him. She turned and spoke to me in Cheyenne, asking that Chance approach them. Surprised myself, I passed this request on to him. An ingenuous and unflappable fellow is my . . . I suppose I can call him now, my husband . . . and he didn't seem at all astonished to be thus summoned, riding forward confidently. He was, of course, not wearing his war paint, but dressed in his buckskins, just dark enough of skin, strong-featured, and sufficiently longhaired now that he can almost pass for a mixed-blood. The Shoshone chief addressed him in his tongue, and Chance answered in Comanche in what sounded to my ears like a quite amicable tone. I have learned that the languages are quite similar, for some generations ago the two tribes were one, until the Comanche split off and headed to the southern plains. Now the two men had a rather lengthy conversation that Pretty Nose interrupted periodically with sign talk. Some laughter even ensued, the rest of us now dying to know what was going on. They finished with nods, and what sounded like grunts of *hou* all around, and at a command from their chief, the Shoshone reined their horses about and made a dramatic display of galloping off.

Chance came to me where I sat my horse next to Phemie, Ann, Maria, and Astrid. He was smiling strangely, as if working something out in his own mind, and said nothing for a moment. Pretty Nose reassumed her position at the head of our party and signaled to the others, and all turned to head back to the village.

"Are you going to tell us what that was all about, or not?" I asked impatiently.

"Well . . . yeah, sure I am . . . it seems like we been challenged . . . or maybe I oughta say *you* been challenged."

"Challenged to what? They're going to make war against us? We're mortal enemies . . . so what was all the laughing about?"

"Not war, exactly, more like war games . . . chasin' each other on horseback, wrestlin', countin' coup, hand-to-hand fightin', foot races, tests of strength, horsemanship, shootin' arrows, throwin' knives and tomahawks, wieldin' lances. Damn curious thing . . . it's kinda like makin' war, an' folks can get hurt for sure, 'cept no one gets kilt unless they accidentally do somethin' stupid. Real nice fella, named Chief Young Wolf . . . far as I could make out. He was laughin' cause Pretty Nose said it was you Strongheart women who would go up against his warriors, an' he thought that was real funny to be fightin' against girls, said he didn't want to do it at first, said he was afraid his warriors might hurt you. But then Pretty Nose says to him, and I translated for her . . . she says, 'You must be afraid you're going to lose to the girls, aren't you?' An' that made him laugh some more, see, an' her and me, we laughed along with him just to be polite."

2 October 1876

The arrival of the Shoshone war party with their challenge necessitated first a meeting of the Strongheart society, and then the tribal council. The former was held today, under the cottonwood trees down by the river, as no tipi had yet been completed that was large enough to accommodate the full group. As an honorary member, I was allowed to attend.

Chief Pretty Nose begins the meeting with an account of the Shoshones' visit, further explaining that the war games are to take place in eleven days, that many members of their band will be coming, not just as competitors but also as spectators, and that a number of the events proposed by Chief Young Wolf will be one-on-one contests, their best man against our best woman. Thus intersociety trials to choose the strongest, most capable among us in each discipline will begin immediately. She then opens our powwow to questions and general discussion.

Lady Ann Hall, who I have learned is a forthright woman and not one to beat around the bush, speaks first, asking the question on everyone's mind mentioned in my last journal entry.

"I am most curious to know," she says, "if anyone present here has the vaguest idea of where exactly we are? . . . and I am requesting a strictly geographic explanation, not being in the least bit interested in a supernatural one."

Gertie is the first to answer. "Well, *goddammit*," says she, "I been wonderin' myself when in the hell we was goin' to get around to that . . . been so damn busy . . . An' what with this fine country, good weather, plenty a' game, buffalo herds the size a' which I ain't seen now for many moons, at least not since the government put the word out to eradicate 'em, it is hard to complain too much about where we are. Or even to think about it. So maybe we oughta just consider ourselves real lucky, enjoy it while it lasts, and not try to figure it out."

"To make myself clear," Lady Ann answered, "I am not complaining; far from it, this is a spiffing landscape in which we find ourselves, I am simply asking where it is on the map."

"Well, Lady Hall," says Gertie, "I been knockin' around these mountains and plains for goin' on thirty years now, from north to south, east to west, so I know the lay a' the land pretty damn well, if I do say so. I ain't sure there's anywhere I ain't been before. But then again, that ole Holy Woman, 'fore she started climbin' the hangin' road to Seano, been here a hell of a lot longer than me, an' maybe she knew some secret places I don't . . . like this valley . . . that's what I'm thinkin'. Now, if I had to guess, I'd say maybe we was on the other side a' the Bighorns. I admit that's country I don't maybe know quite as good as I do some other. An' I'm thinkin' that way, too, on account of it bein' a party of Shoshone warriors showed up here, an' that's their home country over that way, them bein' more mountain folk than us."

Well, this seems a reasonable explanation, coming as it does from Gertie, and I think it puts everyone a little at ease, even if does leave certain questions unanswered. For instance, no one remembers climbing to the other side of the Bighorns to get here, and, furthermore, since the Shoshone are our enemies, scouting for and fighting with the Army against us, why is it that one of their chiefs came here with some of his warriors asking to play war games where no one gets killed? I am quite certain that I am not the only one to have these same thoughts, but thankfully, no one, not even Lady Ann, who brought it up in the first place, expresses them out loud. It is quite true that this is such a splendidly rich valley surrounded by lushly beautiful mountains, and we have everything in the world we need for the winter, why look a gift horse in the mouth? Why ask unanswerable questions? Why not, for a change, simply enjoy the good fortune we so seldom have?

Now I take the opportunity to speak up, respectfully requesting to be granted official, rather than honorary, membership in the Strongheart society, so that I might compete in the trials with the others for a chance to represent the tribe in the war games . . . and prove myself worthy. Pretty Nose privately consults Phemie, Woman Who Moves against the Wind, Warpath Woman, and Kills in the Morning Woman, and, after a short discussion among them, announces with a collective nodding and expressions of approbation that my request has been granted. Then all the Stronghearts welcome me into the society with the loveliest trilling that makes me proud and brings tears of pleasure and gratitude to my eyes. It seems to me that it has been a rather long journey back from being dead to being a member of both the tribal council and the Stronghearts, fully embraced by our new band, reunited with my daughter, and settled for winter in this resplendent valley, wherever it is.

7 October 1876

Only five days left before our contest with the Shoshone. We have met in tribal council, and all are in agreement about the event, though some expressed apprehension about a large contingent of historical enemies coming among us, in the event that their intentions are not so honorable after all. Yet the various tribes of the mountains and plains, enemies and friends alike, do observe a quite strict code of honor in such matters, and in this case most of the council feel secure, and are looking keenly forward to the arrival of the Shoshone band and the war games—both unprecedented events in their lives.

Of course, Dog Woman has been pressed into service to organize a feast and a dance to welcome our unlikely visitors and to celebrate the beginning of the games. Although we do not know exactly how many Shoshone are likely to come, she has instructed the hunters regarding her requirements for the species and number of game animals to be harvested. Certainly, nothing goes to waste among these people, and every part of the animal is utilized— whether consumed or made into attire, water vessels, and other practical items for the lodge: tools, medicine, jewelry, toys, or totems. It is clearly for this reason that the natives have been able to live off this land for countless generations without marking it, scarring it, or otherwise altering or destroying it. As Wind and I witnessed in our travels this past summer, since the gold and land rush of the colonizers began, with the destruction of the great buffalo herds and the introduction of non-native bovines, the gutting of the earth for what the whites consider to be its hidden treasures below, the construction of railroads, settlements, ranches, and Army forts—the earth, as these people have always known it, is disappearing before their very eyes.

9 October 1867

With the help of Chance, rather than Phemie, against whom I may be competing in certain events, I have been secretly practicing my warrior skills, so that the others do not have the opportunity to identify my strengths and weaknesses. I may not be as tall and lanky as Molly, but, thanks to Wind, I am well-muscled and strong for my size, quick and supple, and I believe I can compete with any of my contemporaries in arm wrestling and Indian leg wrestling. Plus, my cowboy, who himself learned this sport from the Comanches as a boy, has given me invaluable instruction, showing me its specific moves and tricks. I'm embarrassed to commit this to paper, but while practicing with him near the river, and far from any prying eyes of spies, as he was demonstrating one particularly effective hold, I became aroused, by the close contact and grappling, as did he, and we ended up wrestling nude, making exceptionally athletic love.

"It sure might be dangerous for me to put this in your head,

May," he said afterward as we lay exhausted together in the grass, "bein' as you're . . . a . . . don't know how to say it exactly . . . an' I don't mean no offense neither . . . bein' as you're an excitable sort . . ."

I laughed. "I think you mean 'passionate,' Chance, and I take no offense; it's not a dirty word, and I *am* passionate, exclusively with you, of course."

"Well, what I'm thinkin' is this . . . let's say you beat out your gals in the trials, and yer the one goin' to be wrestlin' a Shoshone warrior . . ."

"Ah, yes, I think perhaps I know where this is going . . ."

"Yeah, let's say you're in a close hold like we just was . . . Now, I'm hopin' ya ain't goin' to get excitable—"

I laughed again, interrupting him because, due to his lack of formal education, I have been trying, as gently as possible, to correct some of his most egregious grammatical errors and expand his vocabulary. "I don't mean to confuse you, Chance," I said, "but in this case, the correct word would be 'excited,' and as passionate as I may be, I can assure you that is not going to happen."

"OK . . . but it *can* happen, May," he said, "An' I wouldn't hold it against ya, neither. But if it does, it ain't goin' to do you no good 'cause you'll lose your focus . . . like we both just did. But . . . if you can just work *him* up to feelin' passionate . . . I mean to say excited . . . an' you know better than me, that ain't so hard to do with men—it might help you pin him and win the match, 'cause he's sure to lose his focus. So I'm gonna teach ya a few words of Comanche, somethin' you can whisper to him, quiet like, while you're wrestlin'. He'll understand, an' that'll take his mind real quick off the wrestlin' match. That's when ya make yer big move, and he won't be ready for it. Game over."

I laughed again. "God, I adore you, Chance! I can't wait to learn those words, so I can whisper them to you."

"You don't even need to do that with me, May."

In addition to our wrestling practice, Chance has broadened

and refined my equestrian talents, so that I, too, can now ride my mare Lucky reins free. And he taught me how to slide out of the saddle, onto her side, holding on with one hand to her mane and, with the other, shooting my pistol under her neck. Of course, because these will be games and not real warfare, we won't be shooting at each other, but one of the other main events of the competition will be displays of horsemanship so critical in actual battle. Chance says if I go up against the Shoshone in this, I may also have an advantage because I'm lighter than the men. However, I know quite well that there is no possibility of me besting Pretty Nose in horsemanship, and I don't believe anyone else can either, her closest competitor being Phemie. In fact, I think Pretty Nose will be able to beat all of us in every skill, but, to be sure, she can't take on the Shoshone warriors in every one of them. Thus, her being the chief, it is she who will choose who among us will compete in each of the challenges.

I must mention that in our last Strongheart meeting, held yesterday, Molly announced that because she is nearly five months pregnant, by estimation, and beginning to show, as we've all noticed, she has decided not to compete in the trials or in the competition. We are sorry to lose her, but all understand the decision. At the same time, my perhaps overly competitive nature feels also some small sense of relief that this is one less competitor, and a formidable one at that, against whom I will have to match my own talents.

The trials begin tomorrow . . .

19 October 1876

I have had no time whatsoever for journal entries these past days, and there is much to report. The trials and the war games have come and gone. The Shoshone arrived four days later than they had originally proposed, which was no great matter and one not unexpected. The Indians have a very different manner than whites of observing the passage of time, perhaps simply because they don't have clocks and calendars, but rather measure it by the seasons, the phases and subtle colors of the moon, the shifting position of the sun in the sky, and the changing length of daylight and darkness. Indeed, my group and I came to refer to this as "Indian time," in which four days is not even considered lateness. Plus it gave us all more time for our own preparations.

They made a most imposing entrance, coming across the hills at least sixty or seventy in number—men, women, and children— about two dozen of them in the lead, dressed in full warrior regalia, headed by several chiefs wearing magnificent headdresses, the feathers of which trailed nearly to the ground, mounted on prancing, elaborately painted mustangs. As we had not been expecting them until our scouts rode into the village to notify us, at which time they were already in sight, we were still dressed in our "work" clothes—that is to say, entirely without finery—so that when we got a good look at them as they approached, we felt rather shabby in comparison. To make their entrance even more impressive, they were singing, a rather melodic tune that carried over the rolling plains as if it were following the contour of the land.

Pretty Nose and a handful of us other Stronghearts, including Wind and Gertie, our two additional Shoshone speakers, as well as Chance, who seemed to have established a rapport with their head man, Chief Young Wolf, the last time they came here, mounted and rode out to greet our challengers. As we came near, the younger children in their band, chattering and giggling, boys and girls alike, ran out to touch our feet in the stirrups, the child's game of counting coup, a display of pure joy, mixed with nervous daring on their part, that I have always adored.

This time Wind spoke for our band, welcoming the visitors and suggesting a place near the river for them to pitch camp. It was midafternoon, and there would be no competition that day, but the invitation to the welcome feast and dance was extended.

By the time our little contingent returned to the village, our social director, Dog Woman, seemed in a state of near panic regarding the number of the Shoshone visitors, worried that there would be insufficient food, although she had already planned for more people than had been expected to arrive. Yet she is, after all, a true professional at her task, and was already giving orders to Bridge Girl and her other subordinates, regarding the laying and starting of fires and the beginning of cooking. Days before, she had laid out the contours of the dance circle and had more than enough firewood stocked for the various blazes. She soon had everything well under control.

As far as anyone in our band knew, and there was much discussion about this matter, there has never in the history of the tribe been a feast and a dance, let alone war games, at which the Shoshone, Cheyenne, and Arapaho came together in a social and peaceful recreational setting. Previously, our meetings were on the battlefield, attacking each other's camps, killing each other, and stealing horses. The dark, poisonous cloud left hanging over us by that horrifying sack of Shoshone baby hands still haunts the memories of all of us white women who witnessed it, an unspeakable act of barbarity for which there can be no absolution. And yet, we whites, our Army and government . . . all armies and governments throughout the course of history . . . have committed and will continue to commit equal atrocities, the vast majority of which the public remains blissfully ignorant of, until, like us, they find themselves in the midst of them.

I mention this only by way of highlighting the spirit of fellowship and cordiality we enjoyed with our unprecedented company that evening of the welcome feast and dance, in such stark contrast to the decades . . . the centuries of warfare and slaughter these tribes have suffered at each other's hands.

The Shoshone are a handsome race, and arrived dressed in their finest party clothes, the women wearing elaborately beaded hide dresses and moccasins, trade earrings, rings on their fingers, bracelets and necklaces, their braids wrapped with thin chains of small silver or brass trade beads of French manufacture; the men similarly attired in fringed hide shirts, breechclouts, and moccasins, all embossed with the exquisite beadwork of their wives, mothers, and sisters, some wearing feather headpieces or headbands, and some with painted faces. Truly, as in our tribes, and I speak of both the Arapaho and Cheyenne, the men are the parading peacocks, far more ornately outfitted and ornamented than the more sensibly modest women.

As had the contingent of Shoshone warriors who first rode in to challenge us to these games, the splendor of the tribe's apparel and accoutrements made us all aware of the rather threadbare nature of our own clothing. Our band, having been involved in two major battles, after which they had traveled for weeks, as had Wind and I, had upon our recent arrival in the valley concentrated our efforts on all the preparations required to set up our winter village. It is during the relatively idle season when the women are more free to pursue the activity of beading and other such sartorial efforts. But now we have had neither the time nor the requisite supplies for such handiwork.

Thus it is that we were especially grateful when our guests arrived at the dance circle that evening bearing gifts of all sorts: practical trade items such as tin plates and cups, pots, pans, utensils, and cured buffalo robes; tanned elk, deer, and antelope hides; and knives, jewelry, beads, trinkets, and articles of clothing for men, women, and children. They were clearly a wealthy band . . . and an exceptionally generous one.

Dog Woman was quite beside herself with the wealth of gifts bestowed upon us, at the same time more anxious than ever to ensure that the evening's festivities were a success. She herself was, as always, resplendently dressed for the occasion, not one to be outdone by the invitees, and regal in her authority and bearing as she organized the musicians and dancers. Of course, all tribes have their own specific dances to celebrate various events, and with our aforementioned lack of contact with the Shoshone, we, of course, had no knowledge of theirs. But after our own dancers performed a welcome dance, our guests, having watched the steps, and perhaps themselves having had such interactions with other bands of our tribe that might be living here, seemed to pick up our style and joined in enthusiastically.

Chance and I, as well as others in our group, were seated around the circle with Chief Young Bear, his wife, Elk Road Woman, and their three children—two boys, roughly six and eight years old, and a little girl of only about three years. Chance and Young Bear again got on quite well together, indulging in a lively conversation throughout the evening in their common language of Shoshone-Comanche, some of which Chance translated for us, and the rest of which he would describe to me later in the privacy of our lodge. Our other speakers of that tongue, Gertie and Wind, had been artfully placed by Dog Woman in different positions around the circle to facilitate communications between our tribes. Still, we all managed with the use of sign talk to make ourselves understood, and the evening passed most agreeably. All enjoyed the dancing, the music, and the food, much to Dog Woman's satisfaction. Because the games were to begin officially in the morning, and our guests had made a long trip here, the event wound down at an early hour, the Shoshone retiring to their own camp and we to our lodges.

The war games themselves lasted a total of three days, and were splendidly executed by both tribes. We Strongheart women . . . and I am even prouder now to include myself in that company . . . acquitted ourselves rather well, if I may say so. Most of the day's first events were held on the ground. Running short and long distances, arm and leg wrestling, archery and shooting . . . there was even a competition in rock throwing, for particularly in the old days, which reside in the historical memory of the natives, these primitive objects of the earth were frequently used as weapons, and even today, when no other implement of war presents itself. I will confess that in this contest, we women were roundly defeated by the Shoshone men. It was something we had neither anticipated nor practiced, and an activity in which girls growing up, both Indian and white, do not often have occasion to indulge.

The very first event was the long-distance race. This was greatly to our advantage, as had we started with the rock throwing, which came later, we would have been humiliated to begin the competition so poorly. Furthermore, no one in our tribe had ever beaten Phemie in a running contest, although for reasons politic, or simply sympathetic, now and then she did let others win. We were most confident that she would prevail.

In this race, Phemie was matched against a young man by the name of Little Antelope, who appeared to have no more than fourteen or fifteen years. He was quite tall for both his age and race, had long, sleekly muscular legs, and as he approached the starting line he displayed a confidence, even a cockiness, that seemed impressive to those of us spectating. Phemie was as unflappable as ever, barefooted and regally nude, but for a breechclout that barely covered her sex, which lack of attire seemed to be a source of some consternation among our guests. She smiled pleasantly at the young brave, who was so nonplussed he could hardly bring himself to look at her.

They took their positions, the starter armed with a French flag, presumably obtained from the traders who come down out of Canada. He held the flag aloft on its stick and spoke something none of us except Chance, Gertie, and Wind understood, being the only three familiar with the language. However, he said it in a cadence that suggested a countdown, at the end of which he slashed the flag from high to low, and the race was on.

The young warrior made a beautiful start, fast off the line and assuming a graceful, long-legged stride that easily matched, even outmatched Phemie's. We all instantly recognized that he was a force to be reckoned with. Nor did he make the usual mistake that did others going against her, of running too fast early in the race, thus tiring themselves out before the end. Indeed, he kept even with her, now and then, as if showing off to the yipping and trilling of his tribe, pulling effortlessly ahead, all the while running with the easy certitude of a winner.

It was a long race, the course set out across the rolling prairie, with spotters from both tribes posted along the full route. We lost sight of the runners after only a few minutes, when they crested a hill and dropped down on the other side, but they reappeared again for a moment on another crest, and this time it was clear that Little Antelope was well in the lead.

I should mention that Pretty Nose had appointed Phemie our official runner without requiring her to participate in the trials, based simply on her reputation, past performance in the sport, and distinguished position in our warrior society. But now it occurred to me that none of us knew what long-term ill affects her body may have suffered from her severe wounding during the Mackenzie massacre last winter, for it was not something she ever spoke about, wearing silently the prominent scars on her body.

When we got one more brief look at the runners, on a more distant hilltop, the boy's lead had lengthened even farther. In this young Little Antelope, whose naming animal is the fastest runner on the plains, Phemie had clearly met her match.

There was no way of knowing the exact length of the course, though Christian had ridden it earlier and judged it to be between seven to eight miles, roughly circular, of course, so that the runners finished where they began. It was an endurance test, albeit not an especially long distance for the Indians; an entire tribe able to run all night if necessary.

After about thirty minutes had passed, we saw the runners again, having made the loop and heading back toward us, again appearing and disappearing in the hills and swales, the boy farther ahead each time we caught sight of them. When finally they reached more level ground, still perhaps three hundred yards away, it was clear that Phemie could not possibly make up the Shoshone's lead. She was laboring while he still appeared fresh, and I believe we all experienced the same heart-sinking sensation that in our very first event, our master woman runner, from whom we had expected certain victory, was going down to ignominious defeat. We felt at the same time a tremendous sympathy for Phemie, one of our strongest, bravest, and finest warriors. It was clear that her loss was going to taint the rest of our competition.

The Shoshone women were already trilling for their young prodigy, when Phemie, as if reinvigorated, suddenly lengthened her stride. Even from this distance one could see the sweat glistening off her dark brown skin in the morning sunlight. Now from a lope, she was running instantly at full speed, her long coltish legs stretching out, with such astonishing power and grace; it was the old Phemie I remembered from her very first competition in Little Wolf's village, when the Southern Cheyenne came to visit us. How long ago that now seems . . .

Still, I feared that she had waited too long and that there was too much distance yet to make up, for the boy, glancing over his shoulder at her, also increased his speed. However, the steady stride he had kept up suddenly seemed less effortless; now with well over a hundred yards to go, he was paying the price for the long lead he had consistently increased with such easy confidence throughout the race. The trilling of the Shoshone women had gradually changed from a tone of celebration to one of encouragement, tinted even with a bit of desperation as they watched Phemie gaining on their boy with now less than a hundred yards to go. At fifty yards she was only several strides behind him and seemed to be flying through the air, as if her feet were not even touching the ground, her arms pumping, shiny muscles rippling, God, what a magnificent woman! At twenty yards she had pulled ahead of the boy, whose legs seemed now to have become rubbery and uncooperative, nearly uncoordinated in his exhaustion. As Phemie crossed the finish line, we could see the beads of sweat spraying like mist from her body. Our men erupted in yipping, our women in trilling. As the Shoshone boy crossed behind her, he collapsed. She turned and went to him, lifted him to his feet, called for water, and, with her arm around him holding him upright, walked him slowly until he regained the use of his wobbly legs. One of our Arapaho boys brought a water vessel, and Phemie poured some over Little Antelope's head to cool him off a bit before giving it to him to drink. He was crying, the poor thing, presumably both from sheer exhaustion and because he lost the race he was so certain he would win. Phemie was talking to him as they walked, in what language I do not know, but even if he didn't understand her, he must have taken some solace in her reassuring tone, for he stopped weeping. It was a fine sight to witness—our African queen, consoling the young Shoshone warrior—and an appropriate manner in which to begin these games.

I hesitate to boast in describing my own participation in the competition, but as I am the only person who will ever read this journal, I may take the liberty of singing my own praises . . . just a little. It is true that Chance prepared me wonderfully for the wrestling competition, and in the trials, I had beaten both Warpath Woman and Kills in the Morning Woman, not necessarily because of greater strength or skill, but simply because they are both considerably older and a bit less supple than I. Astrid and our little Mexican Indian girl, Maria, had also qualified as wrestlers, for the Shoshone had announced that many of the events would be held with a number of different competitors, so as to give all a chance to participate in the games. Pretty Nose, Wind, and Martha all elected not to try out for the wrestling, as did Phemie, preferring to compete in their favored skills. I don't believe any of us could have beaten three out of the four of the aforementioned women in this particular event, and who knows any longer about Martha's capabilities? She told me privately that, due to her experience with Seminole, she was unable to grapple with any man, under any circumstances, and could not even bear to be touched by them. So perhaps we were not necessarily fielding our best team in this event, but, again, this gave all a chance to play.

I was matched in the wrestling against a Shoshone fellow by the name of Short Bull. Truly, the Indians have an uncanny way of aptly naming each other. He was only about my own height, but stocky, with a slightly humped back, short, thick arms, and had the look of a buffalo . . . or a bulldog . . . I admit to being greatly intimidated when first I laid eyes upon him.

After all of us had been introduced to our Shoshone adversaries, we huddled with Chance, who had also helped to train the others, although the tactic he had imparted to me remained a secret between us, as it was certainly not something he could share with the other women.

I have not spoken enough of them, but little Maria, being of Indian blood herself, seems to me the most well adapted to this life of all the women in Molly's group. Indeed, the Cheyenne have accepted her as one of their own, bestowing upon her the very flattering name of Tsehéseméʼeskóʼe, an impossible mouthful in Cheyenne, even to me, but that translates roughly to Mexican Cheyenne. I found that she was a feisty handful in a wrestling match, an activity she tells us she had practiced since childhood among her own people in the Sierra Madre. She is considerably smaller than I but strong and ferocious. The two of us wrestled twice against each other in the trials. I felt like I was tangling with a wild bobcat, could not gain any purchase upon her, and she beat me quickly the first time. I bested her in our second contest, but only due to sheer luck on my part.

Similarly, the Norwegian girl, Astrid, is a force to be reckoned with, powerful as an ox, and not in the least bit shy about using tactics that might not be considered fair in wrestling, such as quick almost imperceptible jabs with her fingers, fists, or knees, usually mistaken by judges as being simply aggressive grappling. She doesn't mind hurting people, and in our first match in the trials, she kneed me in the crotch, and I forfeited in protest. In the second, she poked me there with her fingers, and again it hurt like hell. I lost my temper and grabbed and squeezed her hard in the same place. Pretty Nose, laughing, called off the match. "I think it will be best if you save those moves for use against the Shoshone men," she suggested.

"I'm sorry, May," Astrid said. "Pretty Nose is right. I was just practicing it first on you, to get ready for the men."

I couldn't stay too mad at our Viking warrior. I am just glad that we are on the same team, for if this is how she treats her friends, I would not want to meet her in battle as an enemy.

"No hard feelings, Astrid," I said. "I can give as well as I can take."

She laughed. "So I see."

I was to go first against Short Bull. "How can I possibly beat him, Chance?" I asked in desperation. "Look at his arms!"

"Just remember what I told ya, May. Try to fend him off as best ya can; fight like Maria, move real fast and wild, make a lotta noise, slip his holds, don't give him a chance to get those arms tight around you, but if he does, and you find yourself against him . . . like we was . . . relax, move your hips a little, like ya did to me, an' if your head's next to his, take a little lick on his ear, and whisper the nasty in Comanche that I taught ya. An' even if your head ain't next to his, you do that . . . But damn, May . . . I sure don't need to explain to you how to get a man excitable . . . I mean, excited . . . I can't believe I'm tellin' ya this . . ."

I couldn't help but laugh, which helped to briefly relieve my nervousness. "I can't either, Chance . . . Good God, you're telling me to seduce a Shoshone man in a wrestling match?"

"Only if it's a last resort, May," he said. "I got one more piece of advice for ya. What's most important, right now . . . you under-stand me? . . . right now . . . is for you to pretend that this is for real . . . pretend you've come upon Jules Seminole again, and he's grabbed hold a' you, and now it's a matter a' life and death."

That last piece of advice penetrated to my deepest core, triggered the substance that fuels us in times of danger, flooding my blood, carrying with it a river of terror, rage, desperation, and pure hatred. I turned immediately toward Short Bull, and, before giving him a chance to take hold of me, I charged him with an unearthly scream that seemed to come from somewhere primeval in my soul. Shoving him hard in the chest with both hands, I knocked the unwary warrior off his feet; he fell on his back and I atop him, straddling him, still howling like a mad woman. With an inhuman strength I do not own, I struck his shoulders again with my palms, pinning him to the ground. Later, I would be glad that I was not wearing my knife, for in my blind rage I might have killed him. So astonished was Short Bull that he barely had time to resist. The match was over that quickly, and I had won.

I stood to accept the praise of yipping and trilling from my compatriots, raised my fists in the air, and shook them in triumph as the flood of hot blood began to recede. I looked at Chance and he at me, shaking his head in wonderment. I went to him. "Thank you for that," I said, still breathless from my exertions, "and, see, I didn't even have to get him excitable!"

Other events over those three days in which we prevailed, and in some failed, included horse racing. In the long-distance horse race, which is a question of both stamina and speed, as on foot, no one can beat Phemie on her tall white stallion, a wild beast who loves nothing more than to run and, as the alpha horse in his herd, insists on being in the lead. The field was a large one in this race, with at least thirty-five competitors between the two teams, but Phemie crossed the finish line at least ten lengths ahead of the second-fastest horse.

In the short race, a matter of a quick start off the line, and a burst of speed, the smaller mustangs, ridden by the majority of the Indian warriors, usually prevail. I was proud to come in second, mounted on Lucky.

Given my brief career as a horse thief, as well as having learned from Wind how to capture the wild equines of the prairie, I should mention a word here about these extraordinary creatures that play such an enormous role in the lives of the Plains tribes. Although the Cheyenne have no written history, they maintain a lively oral one, and within these stories of their ancestors, they tell of the olden days, before the People had horses and went everywhere on foot.

According to Lady Ann, who seems to know about such matters . . . and many others, sometimes to distraction, if I may say so . . . it was the explorer Coronado who first introduced the famed "Barb" horse from the deserts of North Africa to the Americas. These were a mix of Arab and Spanish stock, a small, stocky, athletic breed that adapted well to the dry grasslands of the Southwest. After an uprising of the Pueblo Indians, the Spaniards finally abandoned New Mexico toward the end of the seventeenth century, leaving vast numbers of their livestock behind. They became a valuable commodity of trade between the Pueblos and the other native inhabitants of the region—the Kiowa, Apache, Comanche, Southern Arapaho, and Southern Cheyenne. Many others simply became feral and spread out across the southern plains.

I was impressed that my Chance, who, despite little formal education, and the fact that he expresses himself considerably less eloquently than our grand lady, knew a great deal about this subject on a purely practical, hands-on level. As a boy, he had learned to ride from his grandfather's Comanche people, who were widely reputed to be among the greatest horsemen on earth and had amassed vast herds of these animals in west Texas. He says that most cow horses in that part of the world came from this original stock and, due to their strong build and quick-footedness, were particularly well suited to work cattle, my own Lucky clearly a descendant. Eventually, the mustangs made their way to the northern Plains tribes as well, but due to the frequently severe winters, their numbers were never as prolific as in the south.

Over the centuries, of course, there was a good deal of inter-breeding of the Spanish horses with those escaped or stolen by the Indians from white settlers, ranches, cattle drives, and wagon trains passing through. Thus, the mustangs of the western Ameri-can plains came in all sizes, shapes, and colors, from Phemie's big, spirited white stallion to small, nimble paints that, when captured in the wild, frequently became the first mount of a favored child.

Molly, who also rode in the race, because it was a relatively safe event for a woman with child, finished a nose behind me on her mare, Spring, perhaps simply because of our difference in weight. A Shoshone warrior named Falling Star won first place.

In riding with loose reins, both hands free to shoot arrows at targets from a running horse, Pretty Nose won a spectacular vic-tory against a number of extremely talented Shoshone horsemen. It was a closely contested competition, and a wonderful event to watch. For my part, although I managed the no-reins part well enough, the accuracy of my shooting was abysmal, and I was very quickly eliminated.

Nor had I been sufficiently talented even to qualify in our inter-society trials for the competition in which one hangs on to the side of the horse while shooting a pistol under its neck. Again, I had managed the first part but never hit a single target in the second. In the real games, Pretty Nose won that event as well. Truly she is a phenomenally gifted warrior, the equal of any man on the field during those days.

Which is not to say that the Shoshone warriors did not win their fair share of competitions. I mark here the highlights of our Strongheart society, but our visitors, too, had great successes, both on land and on horseback. Indeed, in the shorter-distance footrace, in which a large number of contestants competed, young Little An-telope prevailed, this time beating Phemie. I do not wish to detract from his victory, but I know her well enough to suspect that she graciously allowed the boy to win in order to restore his confidence.

Not to forget Lady Ann Hall, who, due to her long absence from the tribe, did not feel fit enough to compete in the more strenuous events and instead put on a splendid display of shooting with her double-barreled scattergun. She stationed half a dozen boys spread out in front of her, to each of whom she has given a number. They have small piles of different-size rocks at their feet, some merely small stones, and when she calls out their number, the boy hurls one in the air, as hard and far as he can. Some of the softer rocks turn to a cloud of dust when she hits them, the harder ones cut into pieces or deflected whole onto tangents. Starting with one shot at a time, she is soon calling out two numbers, in different locations, for instance: "One! Six!" and the two boys on opposite ends of the line simultaneously each throw a rock. She swings and powders one after the other, never missing. Our guests were most impressed with her skill, and also appreciative that she supplied our cooks with a supply of prairie grouse to add to the feast on the Shoshone's last night with us.

Finally, I must also mention that there was a coup stick game arranged for the children of the two tribes in which the respective teams scattered out down in the trees by the river, some of the younger simply trying to find a place to secrete themselves from members of the other team, hoping that one of the "enemies" would come by, at which point they could leap out from their hiding place and touch them with the stick before being touched. The older and bolder among them sneaked through the trees and bushes, trying to find an "enemy" upon whom to count coup, and if two from opposite teams came face to face, they executed an athletic dance to touch first and avoid being touched. Those upon whom coup had been counted had to lie down and pretend to be dead. This the children played tirelessly for three days, making up and changing the teams and the rules as they wished, at one point even emulating the adults with all girls against all boys, so that in this case children of the different tribes were together on the same team. All day long we heard arising from the river bottom the laughter, giggles, shouts, and squeals of surprise as they counted coup upon each other. Are there any sounds sweeter and more beautiful on earth than those of children playing? There would be no carnage here . . .

And that, perhaps, is the finest thing about these war games, as exemplified by the children—the general spirit of conviviality and good sportsmanship . . . well, except in my case, as I was certainly the worst offender of that bonhomie when I knocked poor Short Bull off his feet, winning my wrestling match unfairly, to be quite honest. Yet, belying the warrior's rather brutish appearance, he turned out to be a charming fellow who was not only amused by my tactic but actually congratulated me for it, saying that it was just the kind of thing a smart, overmatched warrior would do in such a situation. He surprised me by addressing me in English, and he explained that he had learned it from a British explorer who had come down from Canada and married into the tribe.

"You caught me off guard," he said, "and you were as strong as any man I have wrestled, and I do not often lose. But just remember, I will be ready for your tricks the next time we meet."

"Ah, yes, but I have yet another trick," I answered, with a sly smile, "that I did not have the opportunity to show you."

"I look forward to it."

"Well . . . I think perhaps you should."

The children's joyful exuberance reminded us, too, of the other wonderful quality of these games: they were just that—games—challenging and great fun, and no one was killed or even seriously injured. Nor did either tribe keep count of the total wins and losses, for some events were repeated more than once, with different contestants competing, and with different results, so that there was no final winner or loser proclaimed, no prizes or trophies given out to the prevailing team. All of us just admired the skill and prowess of the others.

I will only tell of one notable incident that occurred at our last feast and dance, celebrating the end of the war games. I have no idea how they managed to talk Dog Woman into it, and it came as a complete surprise to all of us . . . except for the participants. This . . . performance . . . I must call it, was evidently organized by the French girl in Molly's group, who goes by the stage name of Lulu LaRue, a charming little thing, with whom I enjoy chatting in my limited command of her language. Lulu, like Christian Goodman, eschews all violence, even in game form, and is not, obviously, a member of the Stronghearts. She seems to have been an aspiring actress, songstress, and dancer in France, who came to America, fell on hard times, and got involved with the wrong man . . . such a familiar tale that is, and one that might apply to most of us in both groups of brides.

Well after all had finished eating, and midway into the dance portion of the evening, Dog Woman cleared all dancers from the circle, and in a sonorous voice announced a special performance for our new friends, the Shoshone. She then clapped her hands briskly, and Lulu led Astrid, Warpath Woman, Lady Ann, Pretty Nose, Hannah, Kills in the Morning Woman, Phemie, Little Snowbird (Molly's protégée, Sehoso, who is training to become a Strongheart, Molly herself sitting out the dance, being with child and having exerted herself sufficiently in the horse race), Maria, and Martha, into the circle. Each of the women in the troop wore over their hide dresses a kind of short skirt made from bouquets of yellow autumn prairie grass tied together. Except for Lulu, who was beaming proudly, the others wore expressions somewhere between mild embarrassment and amusement. Lulu signaled to a number of our band's musicians who were strategically stationed outside the dance circle. These included two flute players, two drummers, and two gourd shakers. They struck up a tune—not the most refined of melodies, I have to say, but a rather original effort nevertheless—an Indian beat with a certain undeniably French flavor. As the music began, the dancers, arms hooked together at the elbows, executed a little prancing step in unison, turning to the right, making a slight kick with the right foot, turning to the left, slight kick with the left, repeated back and forth. As the music increased in tempo . . . albeit rather off-key, the kicks grew incrementally higher. Those who wore hide shifts (all of them except for Lady Ann, who wore her knickers, with the grass skirt atop) had untied or at least loosened the leather lacing to free their legs, and as they kicked one saw the briefest flashes of bare flesh, their little tutus flying up and down. Of course, I realized then that this was a version of the French cancan, about which I had once read in the *Chicago Tribune*—an entirely scandalous affair, as that newspaper reported.

Now, at the direction of Lulu, the girls all unlinked their arms, placed their hands on their hips, elbows pointing out, and facing straight ahead in a line, with broad, bold, unabashed smiles on their faces, began kicking, higher and higher . . . well, some of them kicked higher than others . . . "*Remember, my girls,*" Lulu called out, "*kick the stars from the sky!*" This she repeated in French, Cheyenne, and Arapaho, and that was the first I knew that she was such a natural linguist.

The spectators were enthralled, whether shocked by or enjoying the spectacle, I could not say, though some were laughing uproariously, the children wide-eyed and giggling. I myself was laughing, both in appreciation and amusement. Poor Lady Ann, while apparently enjoying herself more than any of them, did not display the same dexterity on the dance floor as she did in the field with her scattergun, her kicks hilariously clumsy and poorly timed . . . though that is unkind of me to say, for she was so utterly enthusiastic. Lulu herself danced like a true professional, able to kick well over her head. Pretty Nose, Warpath Woman, and Kills in the Morning Woman each seemed to possess a certain natural grace of movement, dancing with the same light-footed, supple facility with which they rode horses; Phemie, too, her dance step as regal and elegant as everything she does; little Hannah, wonderfully lithe; Astrid, her kick especially athletic; young Sehoso slender and coltish, matching Lulu's kick for kick; and Martha, whom I had already seen dancing, performing with her new nimble confidence.

"I ain't never seen nothin' like this before!" said my Comanche cowboy, Chance, seated beside me and speaking in a voice of pure wonderment.

The dancers, too, had started laughing at their own efforts, clearly having great fun. Although this was a gross breach of social dance etiquette, Dog Woman, to my astonishment, was simply watching the performance with an expression of great satisfaction, even pride, on her face, as if she had organized the entire thing . . . and perhaps she had, for permission must have been requested and given for her to be so sanguine.

The spectacle was contagious, and all present, regardless of whether they approved or not, were well caught up in it, especially the children, who began rushing into the circle, trying to mimic the kicks of the troupe, some quite well, others giggling so hard they fell down, rolling on the ground in hilarity.

I thought this a fine way to end these games between men and women warriors of enemy tribes, although I do not believe that any of us here felt like enemies. I looked around now at this gathering, at the dancers, the guests, and the members of our own band—Cheyenne, Arapaho, Shoshone, French, Mexican, Norwegian, American, British, African, and those of mixed blood like Hawk, part white, part Cheyenne, part Sioux. To this list, I wish I could add Irish and Swiss . . . my other friends . . . Meggie, Susie, Gretchen, Daisy, and their half-breed babies . . . and my dear little Sara, who was the very first of us to die in the savagery of mankind's wars.

I began to weep, remembering them each so vividly, so acutely, wishing that they were here now to share in the camaraderie, the joy, and the peace.

THE DISAPPEARED

by Molly Standing Bear

In 2016, **5,712** indigenous women and girls were reported missing, but only **116** were logged by the U.S. Department of Justice's federal missing persons database, according to the National Crime Information Center.

506: The number of indigenous women and girls who have disappeared or been killed in seventy-one urban American cities in 2016, according to a November report by Urban Indian Health Institute.

1 in 3: That's how many Native American women have been raped or experienced an attempted rape, according to the Justice Department, more than twice the national average.

84 percent: That's how many indigenous women have experienced physical, sexual, or psychological violence in their lifetime, according to the National Institute of Justice.

—The New York Times *(April 12, 2019)*

"Do you know why I keep coming back here every now and then?" I asked JW Dodd one night during a visit to his trailer. I had been coming to check on him periodically, and on this night, I rode my horse over.

"Because I'm your sex slave?"

"That's not funny. No, because I'm like that little bitch dog I told you about. I come back to have a safe place to sleep."

"You're homeless?"

"You could say that. I don't have a permanent home. I move around a lot."

"And the rest of the time, where do you sleep? Where do you keep your horse?"

"Here and there. I have friends. I keep my horse at a friend's ranch. In good weather I sleep outside, make a little nest of insulation behind the trading post . . . only kidding about that last part."

"This is not really my business, Molly," he said, serious now, "except that it is, in a way . . . I have to ask you, do you sleep with other men? And I'm not asking out of any kind of jealousy or possessiveness, only for reasons of hygiene . . . protection, you understand?"

"Yeah, of course, I understand, JW," I answered. "I'm surprised you haven't asked me sooner."

"Well, it's been on my mind, but for some reason, I've had the feeling you were smarter than that, and you wouldn't take unnecessary risks."

"But I have with you. So why wouldn't I with others?" I asked.

"Well, because I was thinking you probably trusted that I don't take unnecessary risks, either. You may have noticed that I'm a rather tidy, borderline germaphobe."

"Yeah, I got that part. OK, so that makes two of us . . . except for being a germaphobe, which I am not . . . so we're both smart about protected sex, except with each other."

"Yeah, something like that." He shrugged.

"I don't sleep with anyone else, JW," I said, "just so you know. I used to be stupid, but not anymore."

"OK, so thanks for telling me that, Molly." Then he got pensive: "It's funny, we really don't know much about each other, do we?" he asked. "You don't tell me anything about yourself, and I don't ask you questions any longer because every time I do, you're either evasive or flat-out won't answer them. And you never ask me any personal questions, either."

"Trust me, JW, it's best that way . . . for now. By the way, I brought part of the journals you've been pestering me about with me this time."

I picked up my leather saddlebags that I had left inside the door of the trailer when I arrived, those that had belonged to the soldier boy Miller, who died with Custer and his 7th cavalry at the Little Bighorn. I pulled out a bundle of several ledger books and part of my manuscript, all bound together with a leather thong. "I want you to read the original of these, then what I've done with them, JW, and tell me what you think about my editing job. You will learn things you don't know, that your father didn't know. His research was incomplete, through no fault of his own. You will be surprised."

"Thank you, Molly," he said, taking the bundle reverently in hand. "What made you change your mind about showing them to me?"

"I got thinking about what you said, that we shared them in a way, due to our respective ancestors, and I realized that maybe you're right. So, to get back to our original conversation, what did you want me to ask you about yourself?"

He laughed then. "I don't know, Molly . . . it doesn't really matter, does it? . . . Anything . . . you know, just the basic things people ask to get to know each other better."

"OK, I can do that," I said. "So, why are you still here? On the res? You've been hanging around for what . . . six, seven weeks now? Did you quit your job? Sell the family magazine? Who's running the business? "

"I took a leave of absence. I left one of my editors in charge."

"Why?"

"That's a good question, Molly, but I'm not sure I have a good answer," he said. "I've been feeling all this time like I have unfinished business here . . . but I haven't quite figured out what that is." He held up the bundle. "Maybe this is the reason." He shrugged and smiled. "And I feel like you and I have unfinished business, too."

"Like what kind of business?"

He laughed again. "Like getting to know each other. You come by here at strange hours, spend the night with me, we share sexual intimacies . . . Then you disappear again, until the next time. And so I guess I've been waiting around for that next time, without ever knowing if it was going to come. But I never expected you'd bring these to me."

"When you read them, JW," I said, "the pieces will begin to fit, you'll understand more about why you're still here."

"That's good to know, Molly. Can you give me a hint before I start reading?"

"You remember when we were kids?" I asked. "You were the first white boy I ever met, and we liked each other right away, even though we're of different races and have completely different backgrounds. You were a little rich white kid from Chicago whose family owned a fancy magazine, of which your dad was the publisher. You went to a good school with other rich white kids, got a good education, played sports . . . like golf and tennis . . . all those things rich white kids do. If you had been someone else, I probably would have hated you, resented you like some of the res boys did . . . I may even have helped them beat you up. I was an angry girl, and I'm an angry woman. But I liked you right off, because you didn't come across as a privileged rich kid, you didn't act superior to us poor, alcoholic, uneducated savages who live in this third-world country most Americans know nothing about and don't want to know anything about, even though it's within the borders of your giant, rich country, and they should pay attention."

"I liked you right off, too, Molly," JW said, "and I didn't think of you as an inferior, poor, alcoholic, uneducated savage."

"Gee, JW, that's the nicest thing you've ever said to me."

"So what's the hint you were going to give me?"

"That's it, you'll know when you read the journals. That's when I realized the main reason we liked each other from the beginning, and were still attracted to each other after twenty years." I placed my hand on the bundle in his lap. "These are what brought us together here as kids, and now as adults. You see, despite the fact that we're of different races, and from different worlds, as you pointed out, we have a common ancestral link."

"I thought you told me we weren't related?"

"Not by blood, but we each have ancestors who knew each other . . . who were friends. And right here," I said, patting the bundle, "we have a historical record of that, written in their own hand." I could see the gooseflesh rising on JW's arms, and the blood to his face. "Read them."

"I'm going to do that right now . . . if it takes me all night."

"Good, I'm going to bed," I said . . . "Don't you want to come keep me company for a little while . . . you know, help me get to sleep?"

He looked at me with a smile. "Well, as long as you ask, Molly, and being the altruistic fellow that I am, I suppose I could help you out with that."

"Wow, yeah, what a guy . . ."

I woke up in the trailer the next morning to the scent of coffee brewing in the French press JW uses. He has a propane stove on which he heats the water, but no electricity out here. I think often of the fact that coffee was such a luxury to my ancestors, introduced to them by the first French traders who came down from Canada. Perhaps that was the beginning of our seduction by the worldly goods of the whites . . . but of course, there was also the tobacco they brought us, the beads and trinkets and blankets . . . the list goes on and on, and has resulted today in an epidemic of diabetes on the reservations . . . it's so much easier for the whites to kill us now, all they have to do is feed us their crappy junk food, which is killing them, too.

When he saw that I was awake, JW poured me a cup, brought it to me, and his own, and sat down on the edge of the bed. He has two couches in his rig, one in the front, just inside the door, and the other in the back, both of which fold out into beds. He keeps the one in the back folded down so he doesn't have to make the bed every day. He told me that when he was a kid his dad slept back here and he slept up front. I liked his trailer, it had the same kind of rounded coziness as a tipi lodge.

We sat in silence for a while, drinking our coffee and just looking at each other. I had the sense that something had changed between us overnight, and clearly as a result of the journals.

"Well?" I finally asked.

"That's our ancestral link, isn't it?" he said. "May Dodd didn't die in the cave, after all . . . she and Molly McGill knew each other, your ancestor and mine were friends . . . competitors, too, in a way, because they were both alpha women, but mostly friends. And that's why we liked each other as children, and again as soon as you came to my office, even though I didn't even recognize you at first."

"Yes, I believe that it's a kind of genetic memory, passed down through the generations. The same chemical, neurological qualities that made them like and respect each other were manifest in us."

He smiled at me in a gentle way. "I don't know about those things, Molly," he said, "but it's an interesting theory, and if it works for you, by all means, count me in. What I need to know now is what really happened to May. I see that you're right, my father had incomplete information. But Brother Anthony's testimony of her death seemed unquestionable, and he was the only person to have seen her at the end . . . except it wasn't the end, was it? One thing for certain, it is her handwriting in these journals. I've read the original batch, dozens of times since they came into my father's possession. He had them, and the letter she wrote to her children, professionally authenticated by a forensic handwriting expert. I would do the same with these if you allowed me to, but I'm familiar enough with her style by now to recognize that they're the real thing.

"So are you holding out on me, Molly? Why won't you show me the rest of the journals? Do you know what happened to May, when and where she really died?"

"I'll bring the rest the next time I come, JW, after I've finished my own work. They're in a safe place."

"You're not answering my question," he said.

"That's because it's not a question I'm capable of answering. You have to trust me about that. You'll have to come to your own conclusions after you've read them."

"So why didn't you just bring all of them this time, and let me do that?" he asked.

"I'll tell you why, JW . . . because you're a journalist and this is a story about your family. I was afraid that if I brought all the ledger books, and you read them, you would leave here, go back to Chicago, and write your own story."

He laughed. "You really think I would try to steal these from you, Molly, is that what you're saying?"

"Not steal exactly . . . I know you're too honorable to do that, and if you tried, you know how handy I am with a knife. But journalists are journalists, and a story is a story. It's like you said to me once, 'It's my job.'"

At this he smiled and nodded. "You're right about the knife part," he said. "I wouldn't dare try to take anything from you that wasn't offered."

"The other thing is . . ." I started to say . . . and then I got embarrassed. "Never mind . . ."

"Ah, no, that doesn't work, Molly. What were you going to say?"

"OK . . . I was going to say that for personal reasons, I was afraid you were going to leave here, and I didn't know when or if you would be back. I'm never coming to Chicago again. I loathe the white man's cities, and you would have no way to find me if you did come back. I do dangerous work, JW, and, like you said, we have unfinished business, you and I. As long as we're here together, we may as well try to finish it."

"That sounds good to me, Molly," he said, "but let's not talk about business for a while. Do you remember when we were kids, and we finally got away from the boys you were always hanging out with. You were a real tomboy, and the leader of the pack. Dad was off somewhere on the res, and you and I came here to the trailer together. I made sandwiches for us . . . bologna sandwiches on white bread for a picnic, you remember?"

I laughed. "Of course I remember. How could I forget those revolting white-man sandwiches? You put so much mayonnaise on them that when I took my first bite, the bologna squirted out the back of the bread."

"Yes, I remember that," he said, laughing. "It's true, they were a little slippery. But that was early in my culinary career. I'm a much better cook now. Why don't you stay here with me for a few days? I was thinking I could make us a little picnic today . . . I promise it won't be bologna. We'll go fishing like we did that one time, after we finally got away from your entourage of boys. We'll take our picnic and my fishing gear and walk up the river. We could even camp out for the night, I've got everything we need in the trailer. I could cook trout for our dinner."

"That sounds like a fine idea, JW," I answered. "But I can't leave my horse tied up here. I'd have to ride him. What are you going to do, walk along beside me?"

"I've been thinking about that . . . could you get another horse for me?" he asked. "I haven't ridden for a while, but I'd like to again, and I brought my old cowboy boots with me. Dad kept horses on our farm in Libertyville outside Chicago, but I sold them after he died."

"I stable my horse with a woman friend who raises them here on the res. Are you willing to pay to rent one for a few days? She needs the money, and we could put you on a nice gentle horse for greenhorns."

He laughed at this. "I'd be happy to rent one from her . . . but I've ridden most of my life, so I'm not that much of a greenhorn."

It was decided that we would drive JW's Suburban over to my friend Lily Redbird's ranch. She's a single mom with three children, having kicked her alcoholic, abusive husband out three years ago. Luckily the ranch belonged to her family and not his. She raises and trains mustangs there, which she sells to white ranchers in Montana and Wyoming. Her horses are much prized as cow ponies, and because they come from native stock, they are uniquely hearty and well adapted to the severe winters in this country. Still, it's not an easy way for a woman alone with three kids to make a living.

Lily was in her corral working horses when we arrived. She's a proud, handsome woman in her midthirties, dark-skinned and with the kind of strong distinctive features of the old-time Plains Indians you see in the photos of Edward Curtis and L. A. Huffman, before our blood was diluted by intermarriage with whites, poor diet, alcohol abuse, and historical trauma. She and I spoke together mostly in Cheyenne, and after I introduced her to JW, I explained that he was the son of the man J. Will Dodd, with whom most people on the reservation were familiar, at least by reputation. She nodded in recognition of the name, though she still eyed JW with some suspicion, partly I think because she was so surprised to see me with a man . . . and a white man at that. I asked her about renting one of her horses and tack for a few days.

Lily turned to JW and addressed him directly in English. "Why don't you just buy one of my horses, Mr. Dodd," she asked him, "rather than wasting your money on rent?"

"Because I live in Chicago, Ms. Redbird," he answered, "and it would be complicated for me to bring a horse back there."

"Well, you see, I really don't like to rent my horses . . . especially to people I don't know. This is a working ranch, not a dude ranch."

JW smiled at her directness. "I'm not really a dude, ma'am," he answered.

She narrowed her eyes appraisingly. Lily is a good business-woman and accustomed to dealing with white ranchers. "I'll tell you what I will do, Mr. Dodd," she said. "I will give you a good deal on a well-trained mustang, and I'll fix you up with used tack at a fair price. I have just the horse in mind for you. He's a barrel racer, has won a few competitions, knows how to work cattle—a good, steady gelding, and gentle as a kitten. I don't even have to use a bit on him, just a hackamore."

"I don't believe I'll be doing much barrel racing, Ms. Redbird," JW said, "or working of cattle. And I still have the issue of living in Chicago."

"I was just getting to that part, Mr. Dodd," Lily said. "See, you don't need to take him back to Chicago. I'd be willing to board him for you right here, and keep him in good shape. That way, whenever you come out, you'll have your own horse to ride. And you won't have to worry about finding one to rent, because no one on the res is going to rent you a horse and tack"—she smiled—"including me."

JW laughed at her attitude. "So I buy a horse from you, Ms. Redbird," he said, "and I pay you to board him all year, so I can ride him *if* I come out here for my two-week summer vacation."

"Exactly right, sir," she said.

"And what are we talking about in terms of price?"

"The mustang will cost you one thousand dollars," Lily answered, "which is a great bargain for a fully trained animal. The tack will cost you about five hundred, just to keep things rounded. And I'll make you a real good deal on the boarding . . . one hundred dollars a month. And you pay the first year in advance."

JW looked over at me with an amused, quizzical expression.

Having lost pretty much everything we ever had to the rapacious white man, people on the res tend to enjoy the opportunity to stick it to him when the rare occasion presents itself. To his credit, JW turned back to Lily. "Alright, Ms. Redbird," he said, "it's a deal, with one stipulation. I'll put a cash deposit down on the horse right now, after you show him to me, of course. And you fix me up with tack, so I can ride him today. On Monday, I'll drive to the bank in Billings and bring you the rest of the funds upon my return."

"In cash," Lily said, and not as a question, but as a statement of fact.

"Yes, ma'am," he said, smiling and shaking his head in amusement, "cash it will be."

"Let's go look at your mustang, Mr. Dodd, and if he pleases you, we'll shake on it."

"Please call me JW, Ms. Redbird. Mr. Dodd was my father."

"Very well, JW, and you call me Lily."

The gelding was a handsome little buckskin, solidly built and with a good head. JW looked him over and ran his hands on him, picked up his legs and looked at his hooves, like he actually knew what he was doing. "Yes, he'll do very nicely, Lily," he said, and they shook hands. "Does he have a name?"

"Indian," she said with a smile. "I'll go pick out some tack for you, JW. One of my sons and I will come back with it, saddle you up, and you'll be on your way."

As Lily walked back toward the barn, JW turned to me and said, "That's the most expensive rental horse I've ever heard of. Did you know this was going to happen, Molly?"

"Sure I did," I said with a smile. "Lily and I are old friends, we went to school together, got abused by the same priest in the basement. She's a Strongheart woman. We take care of each other. By the way, you behaved like a gentleman, JW. I was proud of you for accepting her terms. She works hard for her money. It's not easy making a living on the res."

"Well, now that I own a horse," he said, "it looks like I'll be spending more time out here."

"That's what I was hoping for. I'm glad you had the idea."

I suggested to JW that I ride his new horse back to the trailer, and that he drive the Suburban. I knew a shortcut through private property that was faster and safer than following the highway, and, most importantly, I had permission from the owners. Also, although by now virtually everyone on the res knew that the son of J. Will Dodd was camped in his trailer down by the creek, he could still run into the wrong men, who might take exception to a white man riding his horse across sovereign territory, which would be a largely unprecedented event.

Because he arrived back at the Airstream well before I did, JW had already prepared our picnic and organized his camping and fishing gear for our outing. I had arranged for Lily to include a small set of used canvas pack panniers in the tack she sold him, for which, always the businesswoman, she insisted he pay an additional $50.

"You're going to like Indian," I said as I rode in. "He's real easy and biddable."

"I already like him," JW said, cradling the horse's neck in his arm and scratching his forehead. "I think he's fair value for the money. And I liked your friend Lily. She's the real thing."

"All of us Strongheart women are the real thing, JW."

"Knowing you and reading the journals, I can see that, Molly."

I dismounted and looked at all the gear laid out on a tarp under the awning. "Damn, you're such a white guy, you buy all this on Amazon?"

He laughed. "No. Can't you tell? It's all my dad's old stuff. I had the sleeping bags and the tent cleaned before I left Chicago. They were a little dusty from the years in storage." He picked up an old leather fishing rod case. "He bought me the bamboo fly rod in here when I was twelve. We used to camp out and fish a lot, and we took some pack trips into the high country together . . . but we didn't have to buy our own horses back then."

"Did you pack something for our dinner, in case we don't catch any fish?" I asked. "You know, it's always bad luck to announce a trout dinner before you've actually caught any."

"You're quite right, Molly," he said, "and I have a backup, and also something for dinner tomorrow night. And I'm bringing some wine, if that's OK with you. You know, we haven't had time to talk about your edits yet, but we can discuss that later. I just wanted to say that I'm sorry for the troubles you've had in your life . . . all those you wrote about but haven't been able to tell me."

"Writing about them, and letting you read it," I said, "is just a different way of telling you, JW. And I don't need you to feel sorry for me, because I don't. Although I might wish that some of those things hadn't happened, they did, and all of them have made me who I am today, and for that I have no regrets. I am not a victim, and I don't want you thinking of me as one."

"I don't, Molly."

JW locked up his trailer, asking me if I thought it would be safe here, unoccupied.

"I can't make any promises about that," I answered, "but it looks to me like it would be no easy matter to get inside."

"It would if someone had the right tools and really wanted to," he said. "I'm taking my laptop with me just in case."

"I don't think anyone will mess with it. The crackheads are more likely to steal your vehicle."

"I put the hitch inside the trailer, so they couldn't take both of them."

"I don't think they'll come back here. You haven't seen them since I chased them off, have you?"

"No."

Now we were under way, riding side by side. It was a good feeling to do something together besides having heated sex in the Airstream, and I think JW felt the same way, because we kept looking at each other and smiling in acknowledgment. It was late summer now, with just a hint of fall in the air and on the foliage, the time of year when the temperature is perfect, warm but not hot during the day, cool at night. Because it was already midday, after a bit over an hour, we stopped for the picnic and to make our camp in a stand of cottonwood trees beside the creek.

JW served chicken he had grilled back at his trailer, salad, hard-boiled eggs, a baguette, and French wine and cheese, all purchased in Billings, where he drove once a week for supplies.

"Are you trying to impress me?" I asked.

"Maybe a little . . ."

"I have to admit, JW, this is a whole lot better than the bologna sandwich you served me twenty years ago." I don't drink much for obvious reasons, but I took a sip of the wine he had poured for me in a small glass mustard jar he told me his father had always used for camping and picnics. It occurred to me once again what different worlds we lived in. We were a tiny microcosm of the vast chasm between our people—a privileged white boy, and an Indian girl from the res—never to be breached. "Are you trying to seduce me with good food and fancy French wine and cheese?"

"I was just trying to make a nice lunch. Do I need to seduce you?"

"I like you in the same way I did as a kid, JW," I said. "But I'm the one who seduced you."

"That's true," he admitted. "Why did you, Molly?"

"Because you're different from what I know. That doesn't make you any better, just safer."

"I don't understand, safer in what way?"

"You and I can never really be together. You know that as well as I do. Our planets are so far apart they may as well be in different solar systems. But that doesn't mean we can't enjoy each other. After we get the tent set up, we're going to take a nap before we go fishing, right?"

"That's what I was thinking."

"So instead of 'sharing intimacies' as you put it so genteelly, or 'fucking' as I put it so vulgarly, we're going to make love for the first time. And then after we wake up, we're going to talk about things . . . like you said, JW . . . things that people talk about to get to know each other. But understand this, JW, we're living in the moment . . . and that's all."

"Understood," he said. "That's a splendid idea, Molly. You know, we're only a little farther upstream from where we went fishing that day when we were kids. I kissed you on the bank of the creek . . . do you remember that?"

"Sure I do."

"You were the first girl I ever kissed."

"And you were the first boy for me."

"You think our ancestors May and Molly are watching?"

I laughed. "God, I hope not!"

"Yeah, me, too."

"The day after that, you got beat up when you tried to take me to the movies on a real date, and we didn't see each other again until I showed up at your office. So much for young romance between different races . . ."

"I never came back here with my father again," JW said, "but for years, I wondered what had become of you. You were my first 'crush,' as we white kids used to say back then."

"Well, now you know what became of me. And you're soon to find out more."

"I look forward to that." JW held up his glass jar of wine in a toast, and I mine. We looked in each other's eyes. "To the moment," he said.

After lunch we went about setting up our camp. We had already watered the horses and hobbled them so that they could feed on the thick grasses of the creek bottom yet not wander so far away that we would lose sight of them. When we finished putting up the tent, we strung a rope between two trees and picketed them. I collected some pieces of dry deadwood under the trees for our campfire, while JW dug a small firepit with a collapsible shovel his father had among his camping gear. He put his fly rod together, mounted the reel, strung the line, and tied a dry fly on the leader.

As we went about these preparations, I think we were both

feeling a certain self-consciousness, a kind of shyness, in the face of this unfamiliar domesticity. Somehow, by having mentioned making love, I had suddenly changed the nature of our relationship. Despite our numerous and often wanton couplings in his trailer, I felt again like that little girl, about to be kissed for the first time, and all aflutter with nerves. I believe JW felt the same way, because he went about his campsite duties with a certain quiet formality.

"Well," he announced, finally, looking around our tidy camp, "I guess it's naptime."

"I guess it is," I said.

It was an old-style, two-man canvas pup tent, secured to the ground by metal stakes. We squatted down to enter. JW held the flap open. "After you," he said.

"Thank you," I answered . . . God, you'd think we had just met . . .

The sleeping bags were old-style, too, with a faded green-and-blue-plaid-flannel interior, and an Army green, box-stitched exterior. JW had zippered them together to make them one . . . which I found sort of sweet. I sat down, still fully dressed in my hide shift and moccasins. JW was wearing jeans, a light denim shirt, and his old cowboy boots. He sat down next to me and pulled his boots off.

"Since you slept in this tent with your dad," I asked, "doesn't it make you feel weird to be here with a woman, and about to make love?"

"Damn, I wish you hadn't said that, Molly . . ." he answered. "I feel weird enough as it is . . . I feel like a virgin, and I'm having performance anxiety . . . and now you've got me thinking about my dad?"

I laughed. "I'm sorry, JW. I'm feeling weird, too. But your performance has never been an issue so I don't think you need to be anxious."

"You know, maybe this lovemaking business is not such a good idea for either of us," he said. "Maybe you should just straddle me, put your knife at my throat, and sit on my face."

We both started laughing then, which seemed to break the ice between us.

"Look, JW, just because we're going to make love," I said, "doesn't mean we can't do all the other stuff, too. I mean, we don't have to be like an old married white couple, consigned to a lifetime of the obligatory missionary position."

"OK, that's good to know, Molly, but could you get my dad out of the tent, first?"

He makes me laugh, which is a good thing, too. "That's easy, JW," I said, wriggling my shift up over my hips and lifting it off my head.

He looked at me and took a deep breath. "Yeah," he said, nodding his head affirmatively, "he's gone . . . he got embarrassed."

I confess that our lovemaking that afternoon, and thereafter, was of a different nature than that described by the other euphemisms JW and I had previously used, including those genteel, impersonal, or vulgar. It was no longer simply a matter of taking our individual pleasure, but of giving it, of tenderness, exploration, and the raw, nearly overwhelming emotion of becoming one being together, experiencing both our own and the other's erotic euphoria. I have spent my life thus far protecting myself against such closeness to a man, against such a union, and now I was beginning to wonder how I would manage to live without it.

Afterward, we curled up together, and both fell asleep. When I opened my eyes, the light filtering through the canvas of the tent had turned to the softer golden shade of late afternoon. JW's eyes were open as well. "Have you been awake for a long time?" I asked.

"No, just a few minutes. I can hear fish rising in the creek."

"You made that up. But waking to the sound of the water running is lovely, isn't it?"

"That's one of the best things about camping out by a river or creek."

"I sleep outside a lot," I said, "but I have to admit your dad's gear makes it more comfortable . . . though not as comfortable as the tipis where I sometimes stay in the other world."

He propped himself up on an elbow and looked me in the eyes. "I look forward to hearing more about that," he said, "but right now we should go fishing while we still have the light. All we need is two fat trout for dinner tonight."

"What about breakfast?"

"OK, four, then. Let's get moving."

It is a beautiful high prairie creek that meanders a winding path, with deep pools against the bank where it turns, fed by riffles spilling over shallow rocks, and stretches of long, gliding runs. Willow bushes grow along the banks, in places sometimes so thick that they are almost impenetrable. Moving through one of these spots to reach open water, we came face-to-face with a female moose with twin calves. These creatures have notoriously poor eyesight, and in such a situation frequently charge intruders with a mother's protective instinct. She bellowed at us, pawed the ground, and readied herself to charge. I told her in the language of moose, which I speak fluently, that we meant no harm to her or her babies, and she turned and lumbered off into the willows, followed by her twins, all moving with the particular gangly yet graceful gait of the species.

"What did you just do?" JW asked.

"I became a moose," I answered. "Didn't you notice?"

There was a late-afternoon hatch of insects on the water, and we could see the trout rising beneath them, leaving delicate circles of wake as they sipped them from the surface.

At the first pool JW cast into, and on the first cast, I watched his fly land delicately on the surface, almost instantly disappearing in one of those circles, sucked down like a vortex by a trout. He was wearing a pair of old sneakers now, and, from the higher grassy bank from where he had made the cast on his knees, holding his rod high, he stepped onto the gravel beside the water. After a short struggle, he waded into the shallows to land the fish. It was a native cutthroat trout, nearly a foot long, and fat with the bounty of late summer, but this was to be his last ill-chosen meal. Holding him on his back, JW rapped the fish's head twice sharply on a rock. We admired its beauty for a moment, with the same bittersweet gratitude the hunter feels toward his game, before he slipped it into a canvas creel he wore on a strap around his neck across his shoulder.

We moved down to the next pool, and he handed me the rod. "Your turn, Molly, give it a try."

"No, that's OK, you go ahead, JW," I said. "Fly fishing is a sport for rich white guys and girls. They don't send the Orvis catalog here. But maybe tomorrow, if we decide to fish, I'll cut a willow branch, dig some worms, and borrow one of your leaders and a hook. I worked for a while as a bartender in Sheridan. In the summer, at the end of the day, a lot of out-of-town fly fishermen would come in for a drink. They were always congratulating themselves for releasing all the fish they caught. Sometimes they'd show me the grip-and-grin photos on their cell phones they had their guides take of them, smiling proudly and cradling their fish in their hands, before they put it back in the water. I only fish when I want to eat one, and I don't throw them back unless they're too small."

"I used to fish a lot with my dad," JW said, "but I don't do it much anymore, and I know just what you mean. The fly fishermen can be a little self-righteous. I'm a meat fisherman myself these days. It began to seem hypocritical to me to torture a fish for my own pleasure and then let him go, like it was an equally matched sporting event for both of us, testing our wits and brawn. Of course, the fish is fighting for his life, while we're just having fun. So like you, Molly, I catch-and-kill-and-eat, and not very often, because I have rare occasion to fish. I remember we fished with worms the last time we were here."

"Yeah, but we didn't catch anything because we were too busy making out."

In three more casts, in three successive pools, JW had our dinner and our breakfast (the latter he would serve with fried eggs).

It gets cool here at night this time of year, and we ate early just as the sun was setting and there was still light in the sky. JW rolled the trout in flour and fried it in butter in a cast-iron skillet over the fire. He had a bag of small new potatoes he had purchased at a farmer's market in Billings on his weekly trip there for supplies, and these he sliced thin and browned in the skillet with the fish. He had brought a plastic container of washed lettuce, with a jar of dressing he had made. And he had lemon.

I have to say, he is not entirely helpless . . . That's what I meant by different . . . white privilege rears its ugly head again. Here on the res, the vast majority of the jobs are held by women. The wives work all day, come home and have to do the housework, feed the kids and their deadbeat husbands, who have spent the whole day sitting on the couch watching television. It's not entirely the men's fault . . . as soon as we were put on the reservations, they were emasculated by the white man, a process that continues one hundred and fifty years later. They have no traditional male role to play. They can no longer train their sons to be warriors or hunters, for they are no longer warriors and hunters, and today many have largely given up. It is the women who do the work, who take care of the children, who keep the tribe alive. JW's dad had obviously trained him well to take care of himself, his mother having died when he was quite young, and his father never remarrying. And, of course, they are white men, and I say that without bitterness; I simply state the reality.

After we had finished dinner and cleaned the dishes, we put more wood on the fire and had a last glass of wine. Well over a three-quarter moon had risen just after the sun set. "Damn, JW, you brought a bottle of both red and white wine on a camping trip? You know, you are definitely a little too civilized for me."

"I know, Molly," he said, "I was worrying about that myself. I was thinking maybe you could make me a buckskin outfit like Chance had. Maybe you'd be more comfortable with me like that?"

"I'm pretty comfortable with you right now," I said. "But you might look cute in buckskins. I do like that cowboy, Chance, though. Your ancestor May Dodd was lucky to have found him."

"And he was lucky to find her. Are you going to tell me what became of them?"

"I told you, you'll know when I bring you the rest of the journals."

"Since we didn't have a chance to talk after our nap," he said, "it seems like now is a good time to begin getting to know each other better."

"I feel like we already know each other better."

"We do."

"So go ahead and ask me anything you want, JW, and I'll give you a straight answer . . . at least as straight as I know how. But I'm not going to tell you about the journals, because I want you to discover them for yourself. There is something about reading the originals, in their own handwriting, that gives you a completely different sense of what those people were going through, isn't there?"

"Yes, there is," he agreed. "OK, Molly, so I'll ask you an easy one for starters. You mention that you used to bartend in Sheridan. I'm curious to know how do you make a living now? You seem to have no home, no permanent residence . . . how do you support yourself?"

"I work . . . kind of undercover, you might say . . . for a group that searches for and tries to bring back the disappeared . . . and, when possible, we identify and find the perpetrators."

"The disappeared?"

"You must have read about them in your newspapers, JW, though shockingly little attention has been paid to them by your media, and much less by your government. Indigenous women and girls . . . of all ages . . . little girls . . . teenagers . . . have been disappearing, both off the reservations and in cities where they live. We don't even have accurate current information about how many of them there are . . . because the federal government and law enforcement don't give a shit about us and don't keep those records. The most recent statistics are from 2016. That year alone, 5,712 native women and girls were reported missing. Yet according to the National Crime Information Center, only 116 of them were listed on the federal missing persons database kept by the U.S. Department of Justice. Yeah . . . 116 out of 5,712 . . . that's some kind of justice, isn't it?

"Here's another statistic for you: murder rates for Indian women are ten times higher than the national average. And another: one in three Native American women have been raped or been victims of attempted rape, and eighty-four percent have experienced physical, sexual, or psychological violence in their lifetime . . . and that percentage includes me. And one last statistic: in that same year, 2016, 506 indigenous women and girls disappeared or were killed in seventy-one American cities.

"OK, now let us just imagine for a minute, JW," I continued, "that these disappearances, murders, and rapes were happening to white women and girls with the same frequency, in, say, Beverly Hills, Chicago, Manhattan, Palm Beach . . . you name it. How do you think law enforcement agencies, federal, state, and regional, and the media would respond to such an epidemic of crime? The president of your country . . . because it isn't ours, it isn't mine . . . would declare a national emergency . . . the National Guard would be mobilized, the murderers, rapists, kidnappers, and sex traffickers would be hunted down, or at least massive efforts would be made to hunt them down. But because it's happening to indigenous women and girls, the story gets a little article in your national newspapers every few years, and is then forgotten again.

"That's what I do for a living, JW, and that's where I go when I disappear from here. That's what we Stronghearts do . . . and it keeps us busy."

"Christ, Molly . . . yes, you're right, I've read about this from time to time, but haven't seen the statistics you quote. But, realistically, what can you do in the face of the enormity of the problem?"

"Very little, it's true . . . but we do have individual victories, and those mean a lot, too. We find women, and girls, bring them back, get help for them. We find perpetrators and punish them."

"You turn them in to law enforcement agencies?"

"God no . . . we don't go to all that trouble to track them down, just so they'll be back on the street in two hours, which is how the law deals with them. I told you, we punish them . . . Due to my ability as a shape-shifter, that's kind of my specialty."

"You kill them?"

"Sometimes . . . but often I just make them wish they were dead."

"That sounds like vigilantism."

"We call it justice. We think of ourselves as righteous avengers, seeing that evil people are brought to justice. Someone has to do it, and neither your government nor your law enforcement agencies are doing a damn thing."

"Who pays you to do this work?"

"The evil people we catch . . . you'd be surprised how much they're willing to pay just to keep their cocks and balls, not to mention their lives . . . but no matter how much they give us, it is never enough to spare them."

I took a deep breath now, and put my hand atop his. "Now listen to me, JW . . . we're on a little mini-vacation out here, aren't we? Riding our horses, picnicking, fishing, camping out . . . having fun . . . living in the moment . . . It's white people stuff, right? . . . Kind of like a honeymoon so far . . . without the marriage part. I'm having a fine time with you . . . maybe the best time I've ever had . . . does that sound sad for me to say about one day? I've been forthcoming with you, but let's not ruin it by talking about this anymore. That's all I have to say about my work. Now I just want to get in that tent and snuggle up with you again."

"Me, too, Molly," he said. "So OK, no more questions . . . You're right, it's growing cold out here, let's get in the tent and under the covers."

THE LOST JOURNALS
OF MOLLY McGILL

The Dead World
Behind this One

By now, everyone in our group was looking
at each other with expressions ranging from
confusion, to disbelief, to fear, to shock. I felt
a strange tingling sensation run up my spine,
that I believe was shared by the others . . .

—*from the lost journals of Molly McGill*

21 October 1876

I have not made a single entry on these pages in weeks. I watch May scribbling away in her spare time, which is no greater than mine, and I feel ashamed for being such a poor keeper of my own journal. Truly, the woman is indefatigable, and prolific; she seems to have the damn thing in hand nearly all the time, taking notes even at our Strongheart meetings and at the social, as well as competitive events during the visit of the Shoshone.

She and I have developed a fine relationship, able to speak frankly to each other, and close enough not to maintain any pretenses. Although we have quite different backgrounds, we seem also to have a similar sensibility, and sense of humor, without which one simply will not survive here.

For whatever fragility May occasionally displays beneath, she possesses atop it an indomitable fierceness of spirit, forged in fire by her own experience. She tells me that her overriding concern, above all others, is to be reunited with her children in Chicago and introduce them to their sister. Despite knowing this to be an impossible dream under the circumstances, she hangs on to it with tenacity. She has found a good man in Chance, an exceptionally competent, straight-ahead fellow, utterly without guile, who clearly adores her. He's a fine horseman and warrior, and is learning the Cheyenne language. He and Hawk have struck up a friendship and frequently ride and hunt together, and I often wonder what they have to say about their respective mates when alone.

———

Since the departure of the Shoshone after what we white women have come to refer to as the warless war games . . . and how refreshing to report that no one was killed on either side . . . there has been much distress expressed about our seemingly idyllic valley. While the fall weather holds, groups of scouts have made forays of several days into the surrounding mountains and plains, to get the lay of the land . . . and, not incidentally, to try to determine where exactly we are.

Throughout the course of the games, the Shoshone—men, women, and children alike—seemed to be inordinately fascinated by the white women among us, and our Black woman, Phemie. Thus at the feast and dance the last night, we gathered all our group and their husbands, when that was the case, in a large circle among our guests. Pretty Nose, who had so distinguished herself in the war games, appears to have struck up a flirtation with a handsome young Shoshone warrior by the name of Two Crows, against whom she had competed. Among that tribe surrounding us, Chief Young Wolf, a splendid fellow of roughly our age, and his lovely wife, whose intriguing name, according to Chance's translation, is Appears on the Water Woman, sat beside us. Although Young Wolf speaks a smattering of both Cheyenne and Arapaho, and we had the common hand talk by which to communicate, we were also fortunate to have Wind, Chance, and Gertie there to speak for us and translate our guests' language. The three of them engaged in lively conversation with the visitors in the Shoshone/Comanche tongue.

Both our translators asked a number of penetrating questions about our valley, and about where their own village lay. Young Wolf said that they lived on the other side of the mountains, a four- or five-day ride from here, and that he had been born and spent his life in that country. Like all the Plains tribes, their bands split up in summer to follow the buffalo herds, but they respect the boundaries of each other's hunting lands, and there is enough game for all.

They obtain certain practical goods from French traders who come south from Canada in the spring, summer, and fall, some of whom have married among them and have families but continue to ply their trade until too old to do so, at which time they usually take up permanent residence with their Indian wives and families.

Young Wolf told us that his people trade with the other northern Plains tribes—Arapaho, Blackfoot, Cheyenne, Sioux, Nez Perce, Pawnee—and even travel south from time to time to trade with the Comanche, Apache, Navajo, Puebloans, Hopi, and Zuni. They maintain large herds of horses and appear quite prosperous—particularly judging from the rather luxurious, one might even say exotic gifts they brought to us. Among these are articles of Navajo jewelry and Hopi pottery (how they transported the latter, given their fragility, I have no idea.) They, too, are in the process of making permanent winter camp now that the season is upon us.

We asked them if the other tribes also had villages here, a question that seemed to puzzle Young Wolf and Appears on the Water Woman. "Yes, they, too, have villages in this country. But they are very large. Sometimes we visit with them for war games or social gatherings, as we have with you."

"Do you not make real war against each other?" Gertie asked in Shoshone, with Chance translating for us.

"No, we only play at war and other contests of skill, as we have with you."

"Do the white soldiers come here?" Gertie asked.

"Our medicine men and women tell stories of the white soldiers, stories that come to them in visions," Young Wolf explained. "They say that the white soldiers live in a different world than we, 'the dead world behind this one' it is called. There, all the tribes make real war against each other, they kill each other, they kill each other's children and infants, as do the white soldiers who wear blue coats and make war against the tribes, slaughter the buffalo herds, steal the land, and drive the People from the earth. These stories the elders tell to the children to teach them the way not to live, for that is how the dead world came to an end and the new world came into being. We do not know for certain if this is so, for no one has ever seen the white soldiers. They live only in the stories told by our medicine men and women. But we believe them."

By now, everyone in our group was looking at each other with expressions ranging from confusion, to disbelief, to fear, to shock. I felt a strange tingling sensation run up my spine that I believe was shared by the others . . . except apparently Gertie, who seemed strangely unsurprised by this news.

She spoke then to Appears on the Water Woman. "Have people from the dead world ever come here?" she asked.

"The medicine men and women say that long ago our ancestors escaped from the dead world before it died," she answered, "and came here to make the new world."

"Do people from the dead world still come here?" Gertie asked.

Appears on the Water Woman again looked puzzled. "New bands, like yours, come here from time to time," she said. "But we do not ask where they are from."

"Are there white people here?"

She smiled shyly. "Yes, the French traders from the north and now and then an English person," she said. "When they marry among us, or the other tribes, some of their children are light-skinned, but we do not think of them as white people, just light-skinned Indian people."

I was seated beside Gertie, and in order to indicate me, for to the Indians it is impolite to point, she put her hand on my arm. "Do people who look like this woman"—she touched her chest— "or me"—then waved her arm to take in the rest of our group—"or any of the other light-skinned people you see among us live here?"

Appears on the Water Woman smiled again with downcast eyes and appeared to blush.

Now her husband, Young Wolf, spoke again. "Some of our people whose fathers are traders from the north," he said, "have hair and skin as light as some of you. Before my warriors and I came to see you, we heard from members of other tribes who live on this side of the mountains that a new band had arrived with men and women like you. It was to learn if this was true that we came, for all the People wanted to see you. No band like yours has ever been here before."

It was typical of the Plains Indians in general that despite all the questions we had asked them, they asked none of us, and thus we felt no obligation to explain our presence here, which, in any case, would have been difficult to do, as we didn't really understand it, either.

"Might you ask them," said Ann Hall to Gertie, "if any of their people have ever traveled from here to the dead world?"

This Gertie did, and we learned that, indeed, no one to their knowledge ever had done such a thing . . . "Why would we wish to?" they asked, "when our people fled from there long ago?"

"I believe, ladies," said Ann, in a nervous tone of voice, "that a council meeting must be called for tomorrow immediately upon the departure of our guests, and open to all band members who wish to attend. We have much to discuss . . . for instance . . . rotten to the core though it may be, I am suddenly beginning to miss the dead world . . . our world . . . After all, I have a lovely hunting estate there . . . a stable of horses . . . a kennel of sporting dogs. Upon my return here, I was not aware that it was meant to be forever. Therefore, the first thing we must explore tomorrow is . . . how in the bloody hell do we get out of here?"

"*Ah, oui*," said our ever sunny and optimistic Lulu, "but let us not permit a little news to distract us from the entertainment portion of the evening. I see that Dog Woman is signaling us, and our musicians are taking their places. We have a *spectacle* to put on for our guests. To the dance circle, *mes filles*, our public awaits us!"

I don't believe that any of us really felt like dancing just now, as we were each, in our own way, trying to make sense of something that made no sense. Although this subject had certainly resided in the back of everyone's mind since our arrival here, it was one we had largely avoided discussing, or even pondering at great length, preferring to allow ourselves to be seduced by the tranquility, security, and fecundity of our hidden valley. Yet now, as Ann suggested, a sinister element had been introduced into this seeming oasis . . . the possibility that we were not simply wintering here, as had been our short-term plan, but were quite possibly permanent residents in another world . . . as ludicrous as that seems to say.

I had trained young Sehoso to take my place in the dance, in deference to my growing belly, and took my place beside Hawk with the other spectators. Our dancers began tentatively, all still nonplussed by the news we had just received, and also mildly self-conscious about the distinct possibility of making fools of themselves . . . a feeling I knew all too well. But soon the discordant, yet oddly rhythmic music—flutes, drums, and rattles—while not to be confused with the New York Philharmonic Orchestra, had a kind of hypnotic effect upon them, and their steps became more certain, more lively. They were, of course, performing the one dance in which Lulu had instructed us, the French cancan, and as the tempo increased, they seemed to forget for a moment their worries. It is the nature and business of music and dance to provide an escape from the ordinary routines and activities of the day, whether these be in the house or the tipi, both for the spectators and the performers, a freedom of movement and expression . . . and joy. I wondered if the baby I carried heard the music and I stood to join my friends in the dance circle after all, though eschewing the high kicks and adopting a modest, rhythmic step, bouncing her gently I danced with my daughter.

The sounds of laughter and happy astonishment arose from the audience. Soon we were laughing ourselves . . . our troubles forgotten in the moment . . . When the children joined us in the dance, including my little Mouse, and some bold young women from both our band and the Shoshone, I couldn't help but feel that perhaps it would not be such a terrible fate to be trapped in this paradise, to explore this virgin country, hunting and fishing, and following the buffalo herds . . . I could grow a garden here—I am, after all, a farmer—raise a real family, and live out a life of peace, security, and happiness. It certainly offered a vastly more agreeable future than did a life sentence in Sing Sing prison, without being able to speak a word to anyone . . . or, for that matter, life on an Indian reservation in the dead world behind this one. Of course, I understood that May and some of the others had different concerns and responsibilities, but it occurred to me as we danced, that, indeed, I was not a prisoner here at all; I was married to a man I loved, I was going to bear his child, and perhaps others by him as well. This was no sinister nightmare but a dream I had unknowingly sought all my life.

After the performance, I went directly to Hawk, and when he stood from his seated position on the ground to greet me, quite to his surprise, and well outside the norm of proper Indian behavior for couples in public settings, I threw my arms around him and kissed him full on the lips. "I love you," I said.

22 October 1876

Our Shoshone guests left this morning, and as Lady Ann Hall had suggested, we held our council meeting this afternoon. In addition to the official members, with their spouses, all our Strongheart society women were in attendance, as well as noncombatants such as Feather on Head, Grass Girl, Lulu, and Hannah. We had invited, as well, Holy Woman's granddaughter and apprentice, Amahtóohé'e, Howls Along Woman.

A pipe was lit and passed first to our chief, Pretty Nose. Because it was Ann, a Strongheart but not an official council member, who had called for the meeting, Chief Pretty Nose asked her to begin it. Ann speaks Cheyenne tolerably well, but she asked Gertie, who is multilingual, to translate for her, took a puff of the pipe, and directed her first question, a direct one as might be expected, to Howls Along Woman.

"Young lady," said Ann, "did your grandmother tell you how one goes about leaving this real world to return to that from which we came?"

"No," the girl answered, shaking her head.

"In that case, having lived and worked with your grandmother, do you have any ideas of your own on the subject?"

"I believe that one must travel through the storm," Howls Along Woman answered, "to return as one arrived."

"Yes, but you see, there are storms all the time; can you be any more specific about which particular storm one must travel through, or at least what kind of storm?"

The girl considered this for some time before answering: "A big storm with snow and wind. Grandmother said that some people wander off the trail and die trying to get here through the storm, and so it must be to return."

"Which is not to say that all big storms with snow and wind will lead one back, is that correct?"

Again, Howls Along Woman thought this over for a moment before nodding. "Yes, not all big storms."

"Do you know how your grandmother chose the storm that brought us here?" Ann asked.

"My grandmother knew such things, she saw them in visions."

"And do you know these same things, do you see them in visions?"

"I do not know yet."

"Well, then," said Ann, addressing the rest of us, "this is not terribly helpful, is it?" She passed the pipe back to Pretty Nose, who handed it to Hawk as the other ranking member of the council. He took a puff on the pipe and, to my surprise, handed it to me. "I will let my wife speak," he said.

I was not prepared for this, and it took me a moment to compose my thoughts. I took a long, slow drag on the pipe to give me time to do so. That is the nature of Indian council meetings, which proceed in a traditionally leisurely fashion, and do not usually begin as directly as Ann had done.

"Of course, I cannot speak for all of us white women . . . or men," I finally said, Gertie also translating for me, "but I believe it is safe to say that as we followed Holy Woman none of us actually believed we were going to find the real world behind ours. Our highest hope was to find a good place to make winter camp, which we have surely done ... although I think we expected it to be in our own world. During the course of the games with the Shoshone, and particularly last night at the feast and dance, we seem to have received some confirmation of the fact that we now reside in a different ... and unfamiliar place."

"Molly," said Gertie, "I know it ain't correct for me to interrupt ya in council, but I need to say that even though you count me as a white woman, I been around these folks so long that I did kinda believed Holy Woman was goin' to get us here. You remember that I didn't think you'd been rescued by Phemie and Pretty Nose back on the cliff, because I didn't see it with my own eyes, I saw you jump. That's a white man way a' lookin' at the world. But now I got my Injun mind straight again, and I know that ya don't need to see everything to believe in it."

"Thank you, Gertie," I said with a smile. "I stand corrected.

"Perhaps it is too early to ask this," I continued, "but I'm wondering how many of you have already decided that you wish to return to where we came from? I am not going to ask for a show of hands, I would just like to hear the thoughts of each of you who choose to answer. Ann, I think we know your feelings, so why don't we start with our chief, Pretty Nose." I handed the pipe back to her.

She took a puff. "I, too, believe that we have found a good valley to make our winter camp," she answered. "But I was not made a war chief to play games. I have family where we came from that I must protect. The war is not over yet, and, win or lose, I must return to fight the soldiers."

She handed the pipe to May, who took a drag. "My husband and I have spoken at length about this," she answered, "and as lovely as it is here, we need to live in our own world. I have two children there with whom I hope one day to be reunited. We are going back if that can be managed. Feather on Head will accompany us, for it is her world, too, and my daughter is as attached to her as she is to her mother." May handed the pipe to Woman Who Moves against the Wind, who sat beside her.

"Yes," said Wind, nodding, "I come with you. Those many moons ago, Chief Little Wolf sent me to make you well, and bring you back, and now I will." She passed the pipe to Phemie.

"I am nothing in that world," Phemie said, "not even considered to be a human being. They say my people are free since the war, and to that I say, not even close. I am known now on the plains as a warrior, and I have killed soldiers. If I go back they will surely hang me. Black Man and I are going to have a child. We will stay here and are happy to do so." She passed the pipe to Maria, seated beside her.

"I have said before that Chucho el Roto will kill me if I go back to Mexico . . . or worse. Rock and I do not believe that we can win the war against the soldiers; we will either die fighting or be put on a reservation. We do not wish to live in such a place. We like it here and we stay." The pipe went to Martha.

"Most of you probably know my answer already. If May and her daughter Wren leave, so do I and my son Little Tangle Hair. I speak also for Grass Girl, who will come with me for the same reason that Feather on Head will go with May. They brought our babies here, and we shall all return together." She passed the pipe to Hannah.

The poor thing looked at Ann with a stricken expression, as if she were betraying her. "I am sorry, milady, but Little Beaver and I are happy here. If you leave, I must give my notice now."

Ann smiled at her. "That's quite alright, dear, I understand, and I should very much like for you to be happy. I shall find another suitable maidservant. However, you are not rid of me yet. We do not even know if we can leave this bloody place."

Hannah handed the pipe to Bridge Girl, who spoke up in her perfect English with a British accent learned from Helen Flight and further advanced by Ann. "Lady Ann, although you have not invited me, I am staying here with Dog Woman. I do not wish to cross the sea, for that is not my land on the other side."

"Of course it isn't, my dear girl," Ann said, "and I did not invite you simply because I knew you would not come. You are quite right, you will be much happier here. You would at best be an object of curiosity in Great Britain, like a zoo animal, and the two of us together would be scorned."

The pipe went to Warpath Woman now, who puffed and then drew her knife in response, holding it up for all to see. "I go home to fight the soldiers," she said. "That is why they call me Vé' otsé'e. I am a Strongheart."

And to Lulu. "*Mes chers amis, vous me connaissez, assez bien,*" she said, "you know Lulu well enough. I am not a warrior. *Mon petit écureuil,* my little Squirrel and I are in love, and we are going to stay here and have a family together. *Bien sûr,* I must give up my dreams of becoming an actress . . . but I have an idea to form a little traveling dance and theater company, and take my troupe to perform in front of the different tribes here. We will soon start auditions to entertain us through the winter."

To Méona'hané'e, Kills in the Morning Woman: "I stay with the Strongheart society, wherever they go," she said. "It is my duty to fight the soldiers."

Both Hawk's friend Red Fox and the Arapaho warrior High Bear expressed similar allegiance to rejoining the war.

The pipe now made its way to Astrid. "We have not yet decided," she said, handing it to Christian.

"While I was among the Shoshone these past days," he said, "I witnessed a very similar kind of society to my own, one that follows the nonviolent teachings of Jesus."

"Except that they know nothing about Jesus, Christian," said Astrid, "so don't spoil it for them." We all felt the friction between them.

"Astrid wants to go back with those who want to make war against the soldiers," Christian said, "while I personally would prefer to stay. At the same time, it has occurred to me that as the people who live here appear already to embrace the path of Jesus"—he looked now at his wife—"*even* if they know nothing about him, I can serve a higher purpose by returning to what the Shoshone so aptly refer to as the 'dead world' and try to spread his word there . . . where it is most needed. And by the way, just so that you all know, I am not unaware of the irony of a man who does not believe in raising his hand against another human being, even in self-defense, being married to a woman Viking."

He handed the pipe to Gertie. "Aw, goddammit to hell," she said, "I seen a lot a misery in that ole dead world . . . saw my own babies slaughtered by Chivington's soldiers at Sand Creek . . . ya think I can ever get that outta my head? I'm tired now and I'm too old to fight, and I don't want to kill those young fellas that the Army sends out to the plains . . . they're just kids, they don't know no bet-ter . . . I wouldn't mind killin' some a' the politicians and generals who send 'em, though . . . Phil Sheridan, for one . . . but I'll have to leave that job to someone else. I like this country, I don't give a damn if it's in another world . . . looks like a better place to me. Ole Gertie is goin' to live out the rest a' her days right here."

Now the pipe had made the full circle and been repacked with tobacco three times as it did. "So I think that's everyone, ain't it?" Gertie said, "'cept for you, Molly." She handed it to me. "You started this, so let's hear what do you and Hawk got in mind to do?"

I looked at Hawk beside me, who smiled and nodded. I took a deep drag of smoke and exhaled. "I believe I have the skills to be a warrior," I said, "but as all my Strongheart friends here know, my heart's never really been in it. I don't want to kill soldiers, I never did . . . I just want to have my baby in a safe place. I left my first little girl with her drunk, crazy father . . . and like you, Gertie, do you think I'll ever get that out of my head? I couldn't bear to lose another child, and I'm not going to have one in Sing Sing. That's why I jumped off the cliff. You saw it right, Gertie. I let myself fall off that cliff . . . we were both going to die there, my unborn baby and me . . . *and* I got rescued. Both those things happened, I don't know how, and don't expect I ever will, but they did. Hawk lost his whole family to the soldiers, and his grandmother is gone now. We've decided to stay in whatever this place is. We're happy together; we think we can make a good life and raise a family here. Why would we risk that by going back to where we were trying to escape from in the first place?"

"Well, goddammit, then, honey," said Gertie, slapping her knee, "you just remember, and you other gals, too, who are stayin' put, you remember that as long as she's still kickin', you got ole Auntie Gertie to babysit for ya when the time comes. Ain't nothin' I love better than little Injun babies, an' that's what they're all gonna be, no matter what color they come out."

It occurred to me then that the one person whose plans we hadn't asked yet was young Howls Along Woman. "You came here with your grandmother, Amahtóohě'e," I said. "Now do you wish to stay or to go home?" I tried to pass her the pipe but she waved it away. As the successor to her grandmother, and after hearing everyone speak, she seemed to feel a heavy burden of responsibility.

"Tomorrow I leave on a vision quest," she answered. "Perhaps when I return, I will know."

"Which would you prefer?" I pressed.

"Whichever my vision quest reveals. If I learn the path home, I will go, and I will lead those who choose to go with me there."

"And if it reveals nothing, and you do not learn the path home?" I asked.

"Then I will wait until I make another vision quest."

"Is there anything at all," asked Ann, "which might precipitate a successful quest . . . anything, for instance, that I might be able to do to help you, child?"

The girl shook her head. "One makes a vision quest alone."

28 October 1976

The fine autumn weather has held, though the nights have turned cooler. The skies are a clear deep blue, and the leaves in the mountains that surround us have changed colors but are now falling rapidly from the trees. The fall rutting season of the elk in the high country is coming to an end and the bulls have mostly stopped bugling, a lusty bellowing sound that travels all the way to our village. Hawk tells me that the adult bulls seduce the cows in this manner, gathering a harem that they guard jealously from other interloping bulls, with whom they frequently fight, their antlers clashing sometimes to the death of one of them, and occasionally both, especially if their horns become locked and they cannot separate, in which case they die slowly together. Which points up the fact that it is not only the men of our species who behave foolishly during women's estrus.

Ann Hall, still much agitated, has announced that she is planning to leave during the first serious winter storm, and if that doesn't lead her out, in every storm thereafter, assuming she survives those that don't. She seems terrified now of this vast virgin landscape, although it hardly seems different than that which we left, except for the fact that we rarely see anyone but those in our band, there are no railroad tracks, and we have no need to worry about running into soldiers or enemy bands, a fact that those of us who have elected to stay find of great comfort. But I think it is that which most disturbs her, finding herself in a place by all appearances untouched by civilization, a fear of open space, and the sense of being trapped here. We try to calm her anxiety, but to no avail; even her friend Bridge Girl is unsuccessful in these efforts.

Hawk and I have finished preparations of our winter camp— the spacious lodge erected and well supplied with buffalo robes for our sleeping places, backrests built, all the wood and buffalo chips we might need for the fire stacked outside, and a good stock of cut grass for our string of horses. We know it won't be long before we are tipi bound for the long cold season, and so we have decided to take advantage of the still-temperate weather and make a three-day tour of the surrounding countryside. We left Mouse in the care of Martha and Grass Girl and rode out on an invigoratingly crisp fall morning.

Hawk has an innate sense of direction and perfect recall of the touchstones of landscape to guide him as surely as a printed map, even in country with which he is unfamiliar. As we ride, I remember the story I had been told of him as a boy, running away from the hated Indian school to which he was sent in Minnesota, after he and his mother were captured by soldiers. Twelve years old and he walked alone all the way back to Chief Dull Knife's village over a thousand miles away, finding it with the unerring instinct of a homing pigeon . . . or rather a hawk soaring high, with a perfect view of the world beneath him—the path home.

He carries still as his own remembrance of his trials the scars on the backs of his hands, where he had been beaten repeatedly by the Jesuit schoolmaster for refusing to speak English. I sometimes take them in my own hands and kiss him there, as if this act of tenderness might heal them . . . and perhaps it has in a way, these small gestures of love. To me his quiet confidence in moving so gracefully through the natural world gives me a sense of security and completeness I have never before known.

I remember how lost I was in bitterness and despair when first we met, as I think was he. It was during those hours after the attack on our train, captured and riding behind him on his horse, my arms around his waist, my head against his back, breathing in the scent of his wildness I have always loved, that we found each other, and our hearts began to fill again. He has since taught me to defend myself, to read the signs of flora and fauna as a means of survival on this earth. He even taught me how to behave if ever confronted by a grizzly bear, a skill passed down to him by his grandmother, Bear Doctor Woman.

I believe he respects me for the constant questions I ask him, and my eagerness to know everything he knows, and he treats me as an equal, not as a possession. What do I bring to him? Perhaps some womanly skills that for a man are also worth knowing—tenderness, affection, the pleasure of erotic acts given, received, shared . . . although I am surely no expert in that field, and those things we learn together.

Now Hawk looks up in the air and smiles. I follow his eyes and see a pair of hawks soaring high, their wings set and catching the wind, so that they seem to tilt in unison from side to side. "Are they hunting or just flying for pleasure?"

"For pleasure."

"Tell me what it's like to fly."

"Have you ever dreamed about it?" he asks.

"Yes, many times."

He nods. "It's like that."

"After I returned from the cliff, I dreamed day and night of riding on the back of a giant raptor, my face buried in its feathers. I was naked and the feathers were soft, and smelled like you. I became aroused. I thought I was going crazy."

He looks at me, smiles, and nods again. "Yes."

"What does that mean, yes?" I ask. "Was it you in my dream?"

"Yes."

"Good, I thought so."

"Do you know how Phemie and Pretty Nose saved me? I can't remember."

"Yes."

"OK, my man of few words, that's enough yeses. How did they save me? . . . I remember falling."

"Yes, you fell, but I caught you and lifted you back up, and Phemie swept you away."

"Why have you never told me this before?" I ask.

"Because you've never asked me," he answers.

"Yes, that's true," I admit. "I think I was afraid to find out . . . because it's so bizarre . . . Sometimes, it seems to me that it's better just to let things like that happen, be grateful for them, and not ask questions. Gertie told me that a long time ago about living with Indians."

"Gertie is right."

"It's funny that Ann saw what happened, and she was the most skeptical of all about anything without rational explanation. Yet Gertie, who lived among your people, and had children by them, saw nothing."

"I did not wish for her to see," Hawk surprises me by saying, "because she was working for the soldiers and I did not fully trust her."

"So you get to decide what other people see, and what they don't?"

"Sometimes. You cannot be a shape-shifter without knowing how to do that."

This was the conversation we had not yet had . . . and I realized as we spoke that it was because I didn't want to have it, I didn't want to be a nonbeliever, in the same way that I resisted believing in the real world behind this one. I did not want to be forced to believe something unbelievable. And somehow Hawk had known this all along, learned surely from his own experience. Such things scare people, shake the foundations of our beliefs, make us think we must be insane.

"And you can really fly?" I ask, breaching the final frontier of my disbelief.

"Of course."

"Can you teach me how?"

He laughs. "It is not something that can be taught. But you know what it's like from your dreams . . . and from riding in the air on my back."

I start laughing then, too, both in relief and for the absurdity of it. "I'm glad we had this talk," I say, "for now we know everything about each other. Now that you mention riding on your back, I feel again the softness of your feathers against my skin, and the smell of you. We need to stop right now and take care of that."

"Yes."

Having worked as long and hard as we had preparing the village for winter, it seemed to be a kind of holiday on which we were now embarked. The small portion of country we were able to travel through in two and a half days was magnificent. In order to have a view across the valley and get a better sense of the range of the landscape, we climbed into the foothills to the west to spend the first night. Earlier in the day, Hawk had killed a young antelope in the flats. We had dressed it out, saved the skin for tanning, and packed the meat in the panniers of our pack horse. It would feed us for these few days, and with the cool weather it wouldn't spoil so that we'd have plenty to take back with us.

In the early afternoon of the third day, the wind suddenly came up, the temperature dropped precipitously, and dark clouds began to build over the mountains.

"We must start back now," Hawk said. "This is not the place to be caught in a winter storm."

We were only several hours' ride from the village, and had planned on staying out one more night and returning in the morning, but clearly our long "Indian summer"—a term our French girl, Lulu, had taught us to describe a stretch of unseasonably mild fall weather—was coming to a rapid end. And so we turned our horses toward home . . . such a strange concept . . . a place that was to be our home, perhaps for the rest of our lives.

The snow beat us there, but it was still only falling lightly, just enough so far to leave a skiff on the ground. The sun had just set, and darkness was descending. We unsaddled, curried and tethered our mounts at the lodge, and put out hay for them. I told Hawk that I needed to look in on Ann and the others and try to talk them out of doing something rash.

I found a number of them conferring in May and Chance's lodge, not far from ours. Some had tethered their horses and pack horses there, the former already saddled, the latter loaded. Including the hosts, seated around the fire sharing dinner were Ann, Martha cradling her child, Grass Girl, Wind, Feather on Head holding Wren, Astrid and Christian, Gertie, and Howls Along Woman.

Not in any mood for small talk and pleasantries, I came directly to the point. "I see that your pack horses are already loaded," I said. "Surely you're not planning to leave in the morning?"

"Indeed," said Ann, "Howls Along returned from her vision quest yesterday. In it she saw the storm coming and us traveling through it in the dark. We are leaving tonight."

"But that's utter madness, you'll all perish out there if the storm strengthens, which by all appearances it will. You must at least wait until dawn before leaving."

"Save your breath, honey," said Gertie, "I told 'em the same thing, but they ain't listenin' to reason."

"May, Martha, you're going to travel with your babies at night in what's likely to be a full-blown blizzard? Have you both gone mad?"

"It's alright, Molly," said May, "calm yourself, our horses will be tied together, as will the pack animals."

"So what?" I asked. "How will you even know in what direction you're heading? And you, Chance, you think this is a good idea?"

"Not the best, Molly, I gotta say, but I can't stop 'em, and I sure can't let 'em go alone."

"Red Fox and High Bear have agreed to leave, too?" I asked.

"That's right," Chance said. "Everyone who said they were leavin' is comin' with us."

"Astrid, Christian?" I asked. "You're going?"

"Yes," she answered. "I'm going to make war, and my husband is going to make peace."

"I have to keep trying, Molly," Christian said, "spreading the word of Jesus . . . even to my own wife."

"Why can't you all wait until just before dawn," I said, "when it's still dark, but will be daylight soon?"

"No," said Howls Along, "I saw my grandmother in my vision. She spoke to me, she said we must leave tonight. She said we must let the storm close around us and carry us there. If we wait too long, we won't be able to get inside."

"Nonsense!" I said angrily. "You're all going to die out there in the dark, and you're going to kill your infants. Wait for the next storm, for God's sake, I beg you."

"It is this storm or none," said Ann. "Holy Woman told Howls Along in her vision that it is our only chance to go back. If we miss it, we will be stuck here forever."

"That also is nonsense," I snapped, "and coming from you, Ann, of all people . . . and would it be such a terrible fate, to live our lives out together in a safe and beautiful land?"

"For you, perhaps not, dear, but for me, yes, it would be."

My anger dissipated then, replaced by an immense sadness. I nodded.

May came to me, knelt beside me, and put her arms around me, and we held each other. "It's alright, Molly, really, we'll be okay, we're going to make it. Howls Along saw that in her vision as well. She saw us come out of the storm on the other side at dawn . . . all of us."

"You really believe that, May? You believe in a girl's vision? Maybe she's just telling you this to save face, because she doesn't know how to get back."

"I do not think she would risk all our lives to save face," May said. "Her grandmother got us here despite the fact that we did not believe, and I believe this girl will lead us back."

"When do you leave?"

"In less than an hour. We must be on the trail before the tempest intensifies too much."

"You and Chance went to all the trouble of building this lodge," I said, "and now you're leaving it? I thought we would all stay together. I thought you would at least stay through the worst of the winter."

"So did I, but it came up so suddenly, and in this case, we all need to do what we need to do, when we need to do it. I think you and Hawk are quite right to stay here, and Phemie and the others, too. But you know as well as I that my goal from the day I left Chicago has been to return there to reclaim my children. And now, with Chance, I may have a way of doing that."

"I'm happy for you, May."

"Will you look after Falstaff for me, Molly?" she asked. "Let him sleep in your lodge on cold winter nights? He's very well behaved, and he will look after you and your baby when the time comes."

"Of course, I will, my dear friend."

All of our group who had elected to stay gathered to see them off. It was an emotional moment as the heretofore abstract notion that we would never see each again became an incontrovertible reality. Indeed, we would never even know for sure if they had made the passage safely . . . unless someone happened to come upon their remains in the spring . . . or some of the horses survived and found their way back. At the same time, they would never know what became of us.

"We won't even know what direction you've taken," I said, "so that when the storm clears we won't be able to come look for you if you need help."

"We will take the direction of the wind," said Ann. "That is what Howls Along saw in her vision. Don't bother looking for us. We'll be gone from here."

I laughed. "Just out of curiosity, Ann, when did you, the most rational among us, suddenly become a believer in visions?"

She smiled. "Well, I am not entirely a believer, I must confess, dear. But then again, Molly, the last time I said good-bye to you, you fell off a cliff and ended up on the back of a horse. Very difficult to determine these days what to believe in, isn't it?"

"Whatever happens," I said, "I'm going to imagine you back at your hunting estate in England, with your stable of horses and a kennel full of sporting dogs."

"That's the spirit, my girl. And I'm going to imagine you right here in this lovely valley, raising a brood of children as brown as nuts . . . although with Hawk's mixed blood, some are sure to be fair . . . Yes, brilliant!—you, Phemie, Maria, Lulu, and my dear Hannah will populate the land with skin and hair of all colors. One thing for certain, Molly, they will all be beautiful."

It was not easy for any of us to hold back our tears while saying our good-byes, and most did not succeed. But the wind had come up and the snow was blowing, and it was time for the travelers to be on their way. We all embraced before they mounted.

"We lost you once, May," Phemie said, hugging her. "Don't let it happen again, girl."

"Don't worry about me, Phemie, you said it yourself, I'm the cat with nine lives. You know it was my beloved Shakespeare who wrote that?"

Hannah fell completely apart in Ann's arms. "Will you go see me parents, milady?" she blubbered through her tears. "Tell 'em I'm happy, married to a good boy, and they're going to have a grandkid soon. And me brothers and sisters, too, tell 'em all that I love 'em."

"Of course, I will, dear," Ann said, tearing up herself, "and I'll see that your family is taken care of."

Pretty Nose, my war partner, with whom I had been through so much, was, as always, stoic, already mounted and waiting for the others. I knew it was difficult for her to display affection, but when our eyes met, I smiled at her and nodded, and when she did the same back in acknowledgment of our bond, I saw her tears glistening."

May and I embraced. "God, I'll miss you so, May," I said.

"And I you, Molly. Ours was a too short but beautiful friendship. You will always be in my heart."

"And you in mine. For the rest of my life, I will imagine you reunited with your children."

Gertie, overwhelmed, stood back a bit behind us, her head downcast, and scuffing the gathering snow with the toe of her boot. She could not bring herself to embrace or say good-bye to anyone, even May, who knew her well enough to leave her alone.

Only when all were mounted and their guide Howls Along Woman gave the signal to move out, the most perfect replica of the howl of a wolf I have ever heard did Gertie look up, raise her fist in the air, and holler into the wind: "*You gals, you ride this goddamn storm like a fuckin' buckin' bronc, don't let go, and don't fall off!*" And then she let out an Indian war yell, the warriors among the departing, men and women alike, answering her in kind as they rode into the dark night.

{ A LAST WORD }

by

Molly Standing Bear

"After your people exterminated the plains buffalo, and we had to eat our horses, and the often rotten beef the government sent us on the reservations, that's when we started getting sick, both in body and spirit. We had coexisted with those animals for thousands of years, our entire way of life depended upon them, we considered them our brothers. And I don't mean *like* our brothers, I mean we believe we are related to them. I'll bet you've never looked a buffalo directly in the face before, into his or her eyes, have you? They are not like your stupidly vacant bovines . . . it's difficult to explain but there is a certain sentience in their regard, a kind of ancient wisdom, and an almost human quality to the structure of their faces."

About ten days after JW's and my little camping trip, a couple of the tribal elders paid him a visit at his trailer and told him he was going to have to move on. He'd been parked at the pull-off down by the creek for almost two months, and they had turned a blind eye to him all this time, due mostly to their respect for his dad. But now that he had a horse tethered next to the Airstream, a few bales of hay stacked, and a bin of oats he bought at a feed store in Hardin, they got the not unreasonable idea that he was taking up permanent residence. Word had been out for some time now that he and I are involved, and that probably didn't help his case much, either. Not being a registered tribal member, I'm considered an outside agitator on the res, and the elders on the council are afraid of my power.

I was away briefly on missing women's business at the time this happened, but JW rode over to Lily Redbird's ranch and asked her to board his horse as she had offered, and also asked if he could pay her to park for a short while on her property. Lily isn't highly thought of herself on the res, for having thrown out her deadbeat husband, and for being a successful businesswoman on her own. There are few things that threaten the elders more than strong women who don't respect the authority of the patriarchal tribal government. Plus they know she and I are friends and do some kind of work together, though they don't know what, and that, too, doesn't help her reputation. She also knew the news that she had let the white man move in over there would spread like a prairie grass fire, and be about as well received. But she doesn't give a damn what people say or think about her. It's one of the many qualities I admire about Lily.

JW keeps to himself and doesn't know anything about this whole dynamic, and, if he did, he wouldn't have even asked her. But, of course, she told him he could camp there as long as he liked; she wasn't about to turn down another source of income.

I got back a few days later. I had spoken with Lily on the phone while I was away, and I knew all that had happened. The creek runs right through her ranch, and she'd made a spot for him where he could park his trailer beside it. Late on the night of my return, I took another batch of the journals and my manuscript in young Josh Miller's saddlebags, and I walked there from town. I slipped into the Airstream, which he still never locks . . . on purpose, I know now, because he's always hoping I'm going to show up. I hiked my shift up and straddled him on the bed. "I'm home, cowboy," I whispered. "Are you happy to see me?"

He opened his eyes. "Aren't you going to hold me at knifepoint, Indian?" That's what we call each other sometimes now, cowboy and Indian.

"Only if you want me to."

"No, that's OK. How was your trip?"

"It was alright."

"You want to talk about it?"

"Maybe a little; there are some things you should know."

"Tell me where you were."

"Denver."

"Did you find bad guys to punish?"

"Yeah, plenty of them, but they don't all get punished at the same time. Did you know that three quarters of American Indians and Alaska natives live in cities now, and not on the res? Many of the women and girls who disappear are kidnapped off the streets by sex traffickers. They prey on Indians because they know they can; they can take advantage of the institutional racism of your system, and the fact that there's no federal database tracking how many of us go missing every year. Still, FBI figures suggest that Indian women disappear at twice the per capita rate of white women, though we represent a much smaller population. I should tell you now that I'm going to have to go away again soon . . . maybe for a long time."

"How long?"

"I don't know yet. But I'm going to disappear for a while."

"What does that mean, Molly?"

"Look, JW, I'm tired and I don't want to talk about it anymore right now. But we will later, I promise. I brought you some more journals and my edits to look at. You can read them in the morning."

"Will you still be here?"

"Of course, I'll be here . . . You wanna have some fun now, cowboy?"

"What kind of fun, Indian?"

"What kind do you think?"

"Always."

"Good. Then we'll sleep. I'm so damned tired."

"Maybe you should find another line of work?"

"Yeah."

The world looked better the next morning. It's fall now, and getting cold at night. I slept late, buried under JW's comforter. He was already up and about by the time I woke. He'd found the saddlebags and was reading the journals and my edit of them. I raised myself on an elbow, peeled back the curtain to look out the window, and saw that the sun was at about the 10:00 A.M. position for this time of year. "Wow, 10:07 already, huh?" I said. This was a game we played.

He smiled and looked up at me, then at his watch. "Not bad, Indian. 10:11."

"Damn, four minutes is outside my margin of error. Are you going to bring me a cup of coffee?"

"Of course," he said, standing and taking the kettle off the stove. "Got the water hot, just need to pour it in the press."

"How's the reading coming?"

"Fascinating. I've been waiting for you to wake up, so we can talk about it."

I snuggled down under the covers again. "Bring me my coffee when it's ready, cowboy, and we'll do that. You know I don't like to talk much until I've had my first cup."

"Yeah, I know."

JW brought my coffee, and I propped myself up with pillows against the wall so I could drink it. "Damn, this is getting so domestic between us, isn't it?" I said.

He went back to his little foldup writing/dining table, returned with one of the ledger books and my notebook, and sat on the edge of the bed. "From what you said last night, Molly, it doesn't sound like our domesticity is going to last much longer. And I felt from you a certain urgency in our lovemaking . . . like . . . like something is coming to an end."

"Only temporarily, JW. I'll be back, and I'm not leaving just yet. I'm going to finish this project first. I have one last entry from May's journal to deal with."

"It kept me awake last night, thinking about you out there on the streets of the city."

"Yeah, keeps me awake sometimes, too. Funny, isn't it, how the things that torture us at night seem so much less important in the morning?"

"In this case, not to me," he said. "I don't know exactly what you've got planned, Molly, but whatever it is, I can't talk you out of it, can I?"

"No. But I'll be OK, JW . . . really, I can take care of myself, I think you know that. Let's talk about this later . . . let me drink my coffee. So what do you think about this last batch of journals?"

"I like what you wrote about our camping trip."

"Thank you. And . . . ?"

"I'm having issues with credibility."

"Issues? How so?"

"The other world behind this one."

"Hey, I told you . . . you didn't believe me, and now you have proof."

"Did you figure out some way to doctor these?"

"What?" Now I was getting angry . . . and I hadn't even finished my coffee. "Doctor them? Yeah, JW, I found a supply of antique pencils for sale on eBay, and I erased parts of May's and Molly's original text, and I perfectly reproduced their respective handwriting . . . No, wait, better yet—I found a couple *dozen* unused antique ledger books also on eBay, as well as the pencils, and I wrote the whole damn story, including the parts that your father and you published, so I also perfectly imitated Margaret's handwriting and that of Lady Ann Hall. In addition to being a shapeshifter, I'm a master forger. And you're an asshole."

JW started laughing then. "You're right, Molly, we're so settled in our domesticity that we're already treating each other like a squabbling married couple. In this short time together, we've covered the entire relationship spectrum. Divorce will be next."

I laughed, too. "I'm not quite ready yet for divorce . . . but you're still an asshole. And, by the way, cowboy, it's you who has admitted to fictionalizing journalism, not me."

"You're right, I'm sorry, I *am* an asshole, forgive me. But it is a wild notion, isn't it? I mean, virtually all cultures and societies have legends of alternate worlds, but as far as I know, there aren't any first-person accounts of those who claim to have been there . . . OK, so if you didn't forge the journals, my backup thought is that their band really did find an idyllic valley in which to winter, and May and the others who left did so out of a kind of hysteria."

"You know why you have issues of credibility, JW?" I asked.

"No, but I have a feeling I'm about to find out."

"Because you're a white man, and a journalist, and you think with a western mind-set. Presented with all evidence to the contrary, you can't let yourself out of your little box, because it would frighten you to do that. It's like Gertie suggested, you only believe the things that you can see. That is a very narrow way to live."

"She was a good woman, Gertie."

"They were all good women."

"So you want me to believe that you go to that other world, too?"

"Look, I don't care what you believe. That is entirely your business. Except when you accuse me of being a liar or a forger. There is such a thing as faith, you know."

"I'm not really a big believer in that, either."

"What do you believe in, JW?"

"Do you know the painting by the French artist Gustave Courbet, called *L'Origine du monde*? The Origin of the World?"

"Yes, I do. But of course, I've never been to France so I've only seen pictures of it in books."

"Dad took me there, the summer after the last time I was here. I saw that painting."

"Yeah, so?"

"That's what I believe in."

I smiled at him tenderly. He may be a white man, and an asshole, but, despite these shortcomings, I was kind of falling in love with him anyway.

"That's not a bad thing to believe in, cowboy. Maybe you'd like a bird's-eye view of the real thing again?"

"I thought you'd never ask, Indian."

Because I travel so much, I have entrusted all the journals to May Swallow Wild Plums, who is a direct descendant of May Dodd. It was she and her ninety-six-year-old grandfather, Harold Wild Plums—the son of May's daughter, Wren, Little Bird—who had given May's original journals to JW's father, J. Will Dodd. It was these that were first published in serial form in the family's city magazine, *Chitown*, under the title *One Thousand White Women*.

May lives alone in a prefab house in the country, several miles outside Lame Elk. She is a handsome woman in her late fifties now, who has known hard times herself—rape, spousal abuse, alcoholism—but has come through them to become a certified counselor on the reservation. I have a great deal of respect for her, and I knew she would take good care of our journals. We had made a secure hiding place for them outside the house, the location of which only she and I knew, so that I could come and go, to take a few at a time when I needed them.

I, too, stabled my horse at Lily's ranch, and two days after my return from Denver, during which we had read, cooked, made love, and slept, I suggested to JW that we ride over to May's place together, so that I could leave these journals I had brought for him to read, and bring the last one back to the trailer to work on.

It was a deeply autumnal day, which I have to say is not my favorite time of year. I much prefer the rebirth of spring, and even the long, silent winter, but fall is the dying season, and I'm always filled with a certain sense of trepidation, butterflies in my stomach . . . I don't know why exactly. And maybe this year, knowing where I was headed, I felt it even more. I think JW did as well, for we rode largely in silence, a light, cold breeze blowing the first leaves from the trees. I always try to avoid riding alongside the paved highways on the res, and although it's more circuitous and takes longer, I have a route to May's house that keeps to the trails and smaller dirt roads.

Now and then a pickup truck belonging to one of the ranchers or ranch hands came by, and when they did, we dropped down off the road to ride in the borrow pit. They all knew me, and I knew them. Most were polite enough to slow down as they passed, to avoid raising too much dust, but a couple of others intentionally accelerated.

"Is that for my benefit?" JW asked, the second time this happened.

"For both our benefits," I answered. "Things haven't changed that much here. You're still not supposed to take me to the movies, let alone cohabitate with me."

When we reached May's, we dismounted and looped our reins around a hitching rail in front of the house. She came out on the small porch to greet us, and we walked up the steps to her.

I introduced JW and started to explain who he was.

"You don't need to tell me that, Molly," she said with a wry smile. "Everyone on the res knows who he is, and pretty much his every move. And yours, too, of course." And to JW she said: "You probably don't remember me, but we met once a long time ago when you came to my grandpa's house in town with your dad. You were just a kid then."

"Of course, I remember you," he answered, "the famous May Swallow Wild Plums, named after my family's relative. My dad was so grateful to you and your grandfather."

"He was a good man, your father, we liked him very much. We were sorry to learn of his passing."

"May Swallow is a beautiful name," JW said.

"Thank you, I owe it all to your great-great-great . . ." She laughed. "I lose track of the number of greats, but you know who I mean."

May invited us in for a cup of tea. I took my moccasins off in the entranceway inside the door, and JW, taking the cue, pulled off his boots and entered the living room in his stocking feet. In addition to being a counselor, May is also a traditional medicine woman, and she told us, as I knew she would, that she must bless us upon entering her home. Having experienced this ritual many times before, I went first, so that JW could witness the procedure.

From her woodstove, she gathered a few coals of cedar wood in a small metal pan, and with the other hand took up her feathered, beaded prayer fan. She brushed me lightly with smoke, turning me to face each of the Four Directions, gently sweeping the smoke-infused feathers across my shoulders and breasts, down my arms and legs, and between my legs. Knowing the drill, I opened my hands at my sides, palms facing out, and she brushed them, then placed her right hand lightly upon my heart. I always find this blessing to be soothing, the smoke and her gentle touch wiping away my autumnal anxiety. She is a wise woman, May.

She repeated the blessing with JW, and he thanked her, telling her how good it felt. I could tell May liked him, for he displayed the same polite respect and gratitude with which his father always treated people here.

We sat in chairs around the woodstove and she served our tea. I told her we had come to return the journals I picked up the other night, and take the last one with me to work on.

"You know, having just read these journals," JW said, "it seems strange for me to be sitting here one hundred forty-three years later, talking with two women named May and Molly, who carry the blood of your ancestors . . . I wish my dad could be here to see it, and to know the rest of the story."

"Perhaps he does know it now," says May. "By the way, JW, I must tell you that your father made a mistake in his epilogue."

"Really? That surprises me. Dad was such a meticulous editor and a stickler for confirming source material. Tell me his mistake."

"He wrote that after Little Wolf surrendered at the agency, he got drunk and killed Jules Seminole. As you know, the greatest crime a Cheyenne can commit is to kill another tribal member, and the punishment is lifelong banishment."

"Yes, of course, I know that," JW said.

"But it wasn't Jules Seminole Little Wolf killed," May explained, "it was a man named Starving Elk, who for years had been coming by his lodge to flirt with the chief's wives. By the strict rules that governed the Sweet Medicine Chief, Little Wolf was never permitted to take his quirt to Starving Elk, or even object and send him away. He just had to endure this insult. But shortly after he had surrendered his band, Little Wolf got drunk, and he went to the agency store, where he found Starving Elk making lewd comments to his daughter, Pretty Walker. The chief went back to his lodge, got his gun, returned to the store, and shot Starving Elk dead."

I could see that this news disturbed JW. "Even though it's been twenty years now since Dad published those journals," he said after a moment of consideration, "I'll issue a correction in the magazine. I can't imagine how it happened, but I suspect someone must have told that to my father, and he neglected to confirm it with a second source. It's unlike him, but those things do happen in our business now and then. Thank you for telling me, May."

"Just so you know, JW, it does not diminish at all our respect for your dad."

"That's good of you to say."

"There's something else I must tell you," May said to him. "I'm hearing of some discontent among the Crazy Dog Society regarding your presence on the reservation. That society can be a bit . . . how should I say . . . rash. I think it might be a good idea if you didn't stay here too much longer."

JW nodded. "OK, thanks for letting me know that, too. It seems that Molly will be leaving soon," he said, looking at me, "and there's no reason for me to stay after she goes."

"May, I know we made a pact," I said, "not to tell anyone else where we keep the journals, but I want to ask your permission to show JW. I *am* going away soon, and I don't know for how long. Just in case anything were to happen to me, I'd like him to have access to them. I think you know I wouldn't ask if I didn't trust him completely."

"Listen to me, Molly," May said, "I don't have any problem with that." She looked at JW and smiled. "I trust him, too. But I do have a problem with something happening to you. I felt your anxiety while I was blessing you. Please, don't do anything stupid."

"I'm many things, May, but I think you know that stupid is not one of them. I'll be careful."

JW and I rode our horses a short distance down valley from May's house to a rock formation, where it is said that Sitting Bull had his famous vision after the battle of the Rosebud and before the Battle of the Little Bighorn. In the vision, the great Sioux medicine man saw the soldiers falling upside down from the sky like grasshoppers, which was taken as a sign that the Indians would win the battle. And so they did.

We dismounted, and I led JW to a large, flat stone amid a number of others at the base of the formation. "You need to move this one aside," I said, toeing it with my moccasin. "I'd do it myself, but it's heavy, and as long as you're here . . ."

"Sure."

He did so, and buried beneath it was the hermetically sealed steel case in which we store the journals. JW lifted it out, and I showed him the combination to the lock. I opened it and replaced those ledgers I was returning, took out another, and looked inside the cover to make sure it was the correct one.

"Yeah, this is it." I relocked the case. He placed it back in the hole and wrestled the stone back into place. Then I smoothed out the disturbed dirt with my hand. "Look around, now," I said to him, "and get your bearings. There are a lot of rocks here and you need to remember which it is."

He smiled. "I got it, Molly."

"And never tell another soul about this place."

He laughed. "I'm going to print a detailed map of it in the magazine so that tourists can come visit."

"Ha-ha."

Back at the horses, I slipped the ledger book into soldier Miller's saddlebags, and we remounted for the ride back to Lily's ranch.

"May knows what you do, doesn't she, Molly?" JW asked.

"Yes, May is my friend, she knows everything . . . almost everything."

"Whatever you're planning, it was clear that she didn't have a good feeling about it. And neither do I. Please, tell me more."

"I'm going back to Denver, JW. I'm meeting another Strongheart woman there, an Arapaho girl I work with, but I'm not going to tell you her name. We both know the city, and we know the area where a lot of the Indian women are disappearing. We believe there's a well-organized international sex trafficking operation in place, but we don't know where they're being taken. We think maybe first to Canada, because, of course, it's the closest border crossing. But there is only one way for me to find out."

"I was afraid you were going to say that . . . to get kidnapped yourself, right?"

"I need to get inside."

"Both of you?"

"Just me. My Arapaho colleague needs to stay outside so I can contact her when the time is right."

"Jesus Christ, Molly, that's crazy! They'll drug you and you'll end up like all the other women. And, like them, no one will know where you are. You likely won't even know where you are. You'll get raped by a few hundred men, until it kills you, or you're so beat up none of them want you anymore, and then they'll kill you."

"Look, JW, with all due respect, I know a good deal more about these people than you do, and I am well aware of the risks. You may still not choose to believe it, but I have big medicine . . . power . . . I can deal with this, and it's the only way. That's all I'm going to say on this subject now. We're not talking about it anymore, OK?"

We rode in silence the rest of the way back to Lily's. It was mid-afternoon by the time we returned, and I went to work in the trailer with my notebook, transcribing and editing May's last ledger book. JW went about making preparations for our dinner. He's a better cook than I am, but he was running low on supplies, and as we were both planning to leave soon, he didn't want to make another trip to the market in Billings. Lily kept a kitchen garden, it was harvest season, and she had told us to help ourselves to the vegetables.

"I know Lily's going to charge me dearly for that privilege," JW said, "but it's well worth it." He had more or less gotten over his little snit by now, and while I worked, he picked some ripe toma-toes, zucchini, yellow squash, eggplant, and lettuce, and unearthed an onion and a head of garlic. He made a salad and a wonderful ratatouille for our dinner, and served it with his last buffalo steak, seared on the grill, and his last bottle of red wine. I had told him about the rancher couple in South Dakota, who raise the animals on thousands of acres of restored native prairie, harvest and butcher them in the field one at a time, and sell the meat through their company, Wild Idea in Rapid City. It's too pricey for us Indians, that's for sure, but, of course, JW got online and ordered some of their steaks . . . I think he was trying to impress me . . . you know, sensitive, liberal white guy embracing native ways . . . that kind of thing.

"After your people exterminated the plains buffalo," I told him, "and we had to eat our horses, and the often rotten beef the government sent us on the reservations, that's when we started getting sick, both in body and spirit. We had coexisted with those animals for thousands of years, our entire way of life depended upon them, we considered them our brothers. And I don't mean *like* our brothers, I mean we believe we are related to them. I'll bet you've never looked a buffalo directly in the face before, into his or her eyes, have you? They are not like your stupidly vacant bovines . . . it's difficult to explain but there is a certain sentience in their regard, a kind of ancient wisdom, and an almost human quality to the structure of their faces."

"Maybe I'll take that route on the way back to Chicago, stop and visit with those ranchers, and have a good look at one. Maybe I could write a piece about their operation for the magazine . . . I know what you're going to say, Indian, you're going to say, yeah, so that rich white city folks can buy the meat of animals your people hunted wild for a thousand years, and we nearly wiped off the face of the earth."

I laughed. "Yeah, something like that. You're getting to know me a little too well, cowboy. It's probably good that we're going to part company soon."

"No, it isn't," he said, in a serious voice. "When you get back, Molly, will you get in touch with me right away?"

"Hey, I'm not going anywhere just yet, let's save the good-byes for later."

But I *was* going somewhere. I was planning to stay up all night if I had to, and finish my edit of the last journal, and then I was going to slip out early in the morning before JW woke up. That's why I showed him where May and I kept the journals, so he could put it back himself. I didn't want to say good-bye to him, because I figured we'd both fall apart, and I needed to stay strong . . . and so did he.

THE LOST JOURNALS
OF MAY DODD

Still Alive

At this shocking request, so matter-of-factly stated, my relief and gratitude were breached by waves of anguish flushing through my body, gooseflesh rippling over my skin, a terrible tingling sensation, my head reeling as if from a physical blow so that I feared I would faint. "Leave my daughter?" I managed to say. "You ask me to give up my child?"

—from the lost journals of May Dodd

1 November 1876

I don't know what Howls Along Woman had in mind by having us travel in a blizzard at night, except it seemed an essential part of her vision that needed to be respected for us to reach our destination . . . which, in retrospect, I suppose was sufficient reason. But I have to say that it was one of the most terrifying experiences of any of our lives, and I think we all nearly immediately regretted having left . . . and, given the choice, would have turned back to the safety of our band's winter village . . . that is, if we knew where *back* was.

The blackness of the night was complete, even the blowing snow that stung our faces. It was like being blind, and I wondered how our horses could possibly see; I saw not even the head of my horse, let alone Chance's mount directly in front of me . . . if he was still there . . . no possibility of shouting to each other, for the roar of the wind drowned out all other sound, our senses completely disordered; no concept of direction, up, down, or sideways; no sense even of forward motion but for the flexing of Lucky's flanks as she walked. It seemed that we were not moving, perhaps even being pushed backward; no sense of time, has it been five minutes, one hour, five hours, the entire night? When we left the village, Feather on Head rode to my left, with Wren's baby board hanging on her breast, the straps of it tied securely to her back; Martha to my right with Little Tangle Hair similarly fixed upon his board, but I had no idea if they were still there, either, and I was terrified for them. My little Horse Boy, fulfilling his duties, rode with the herd and the pack animals. He is a slightly built child, and I remembered Gertie's parting words, the cold wind swirling so hard around us, that I feared he would be blown off his mount, and I would never

see him again . . . We were all of us locked in our own private maelstrom, each attached to a stationary horse, walking in place in the
middle of an ungodly blackness that would never end; wherever we
were going, if we were going anywhere, we would never arrive, that
was the only thought certain in my mind. Molly was right, this was
insane, we were all fools for listening to the girl's vision. I thought
I knew what dying felt like and maybe this was it, a whirlwind of
darkness.

And then it was over . . . I can't say that the storm gradually
lifted, or that we rode out of it, rather it simply, suddenly, released
us from its grip and was gone. Chance turned around in his saddle.
"I guess we made it, Mesoke," he said with a smile. "But I was star-
tin' to have my doubts. Don't think we're goin' to be travelin' that
way again real soon."

It was true that the friends we left behind just last night suddenly seemed impossibly far away. "I don't think so either, cowboy."

Martha and Feather on Head, each with our babies, were safely
on either side of me again, and both began to weep with relief, as
did a number of the others. It looked to be just the first light of
dawn wherever we were, the sun not yet risen, cold but windless,
the winter further advanced here, it appeared, than in the other
world behind this one.

Pretty Nose now rode back through our line, to make certain
all were still with us. "We need to sleep now, right here," she announced in English, Arapaho, and Cheyenne, as she made the
rounds.

We were in a rolling semiarid landscape, cut with a series of
deep coulees, and canyons that looked a little like some of the country around the Tongue River. She posted three sentries, and we led
the horses into one of the coulees, at the bottom of which a small
spring ran. We watered and hobbled them but left them saddled,
took out blankets or buffalo robes from the pack panniers, and collapsed on the ground, I with Wren wrapped in my arms, after she
had fed contentedly at Feather on Head's breast, Chance at my side.

Horse Boy slept with his horses, who appeared to be as exhausted as we were. I felt sorry for the sentries. I knew they would be relieved in an hour or so and would be allowed to sleep then, but I didn't know how they could possibly keep their eyes open. We slept.

We did not wake until midafternoon, except for Pretty Nose, who had wisely sent out Red Fox and Warpath Woman to scout the surrounding area to be certain that we were in a secure place. They returned with news that there was an Army detachment encamped roughly four miles from us, although the Indians do not observe distance, or time for that matter, in the same way as we, so we translate the number of miles based on how long it took them to ride there and back. Pretty Nose says that the soldiers have no Indian scouts with them, which means they are probably returning to their base camp having already fought, and their wolves have all gone home, which is what they do after being released from duty. The soldiers must have been still asleep in their tents when Red Fox and Warpath Woman came upon their camp, and did not appear to be moving today, for there was no activity and no fires burning. Even the sentries they had posted on two sides of the encampment were asleep. She believes this is further evidence that they have been engaged in battle, and are now resting . . . which means their guard is down. Pretty Nose surprised us then by saying that we are going to attack them tonight.

"We are going to ride part of the way there, leave the horses with the boy, and go in on foot, to kill as many of the soldiers as we can in their tents."

"How many tents are there?" I asked her.

With her hands she counted to thirty, which would suggest that that there might be roughly sixty soldiers altogether, assuming two to a tent.

"And how many horses?

She indicated about seventy-five.

I looked at our tiny band and did the head count again. We had four Indian Strongheart women—Pretty Nose, Warpath Woman,

Kills in the Morning Woman, and Woman Who Moves against the Wind; two Indian men warriors—Red Fox and High Bear. We had four white Strongheart women—Martha, Astrid, Ann, and me. We had two noncombatant white men—Christian and Chance; Red Fox's wife, Singing Woman, and their two young sons of about eight and ten years; High Bear's wife, the Arapaho girl, Coyote Woman, and their son of four or five years, and daughter of about six or seven. We had Horse Boy, about eleven; and two babies—Wren, and Little Tangle Hair, and their nannies, Feather on Head and Grass Girl. Twenty-three altogether, with only ten warriors. Against the soldiers, we were at least at a six-to-one disadvantage, except that they would presumably be asleep in their tents, not expecting attack. But then there was the likelihood of a fellow who wasn't asleep, or one who had gone outside to take a pee, and those would surely cry out to warn the others . . . and then what would become of us? Still, Pretty Nose was our war chief, and I did not question her judgment . . . at least not aloud to the others. To Chance, I whispered, "What will you do?"

"You know damn well, May, that I can't take up arms against my own Army, my own people. Is this really what we came back here for? I thought we were goin' to Chicago and get your kids back."

"I know you can't, Chance. But I can. They killed my friends and their babies. I have a score to settle. If the soldiers came upon us now, they'd do the same thing again. After this we'll go back to Chicago."

"I guess that's why them Shoshone folks call this the dead world, because that's what we all do here, ain't it, we just kill each other."

"I asked what you will do, Chance, meaning will you ride with us there, or stay here and wait for our return?"

"I'll stay here," he answered. "Someone will need to look after the other women and children, and your babies, in case you don't come back."

"You don't sound that upset about the possibility. You just sound mad at me."

"Hmmm," he muttered, gazing away at the landscape—the plains, the undulating hills, the buttes and rock formations that seem to stretch out forever in this country, and he nodded. "That's what you think, is it, May, that I ain't upset about losin' you? That I'm just mad at you? Maybe I'm upset about losin' you, and mad, OK?"

"OK, Chance," I said, placing my hand on his.

That afternoon and evening were spent arranging our weapons and warrior outfits. The killing was to be done with knives, but if the camp were to be alerted to our presence, and we were forced to fight our way out, those of us with guns were told to take them. Thus I would be wearing my gun belt and Remington single action Army revolver in a holster at my hip.

Lady Ann came to me to say that she had decided not to go on this mission. "I'm going home, May, and this time for good. I might be willing to make war against the soldiers if we were attacked or were attacking them on the battlefield. I hate them for killing my Helen and your other friends, but I'm not going to sneak into their tents like a common criminal and murder them in their sleep."

"Tell me, Ann, what is the difference," I asked, "between that, and them attacking our camp at dawn on a frigid winter morning, shooting low into the tipis to kill us in our beds? Killing old women, men, and children, as well as our warriors?"

"I'm sorry, May, but this is not my fight any longer. Helen is gone, and I don't have the heart for it."

For that I had no further argument. I nodded. "Alright, I understand."

"I should also tell you, though she will herself, that Astrid, too, has decided not to participate. Christian's pleas have apparently won out."

Now we were down to eight warriors instead of ten.

Feather on Head, Grass Girl, Singing Woman, and Coyote Woman went to work mixing grease paints of bear fat and various colored pigments. They would paint our faces after we ate;

there would be no sleep tonight. We knew that each of us was to be paired with a partner, and having learned now of the defectors, Pretty Nose told us who our teammates would be—she and Wind, Warpath Woman and Kills in the Morning Woman, Red Fox and High Bear, Martha and me. I was a little surprised that she had not paired me with Wind, with whom I had experience, and taken Martha for herself. But then I realized that as chief and our most experienced warrior, Pretty Nose was simply trying to create the strongest teams, and to do so she was keeping the Indian women together. I was untested in battle, and Martha, despite having taken her first scalp, was hardly a veteran warrior. With Ann and Astrid both deferring, and our strongest warriors, Phemie and Molly, no longer among us, we were the last of the white Strong-hearts and clearly the weakest of those going out tonight.

We ate lightly of dried buffalo and hardtack biscuits—a sort of tasteless, thick cracker—that the Shoshone had obtained from traders and given us as one of their numerous gifts when they came for the war games. Martha and I did not have much appetite, both of us nervous about the coming encounter. Especially after hearing Ann's description, I did not feel that we were going to war but on an assassin's mission. Other than the bandit Three Finger Jack, who deserved it, I had never killed another man, and though well trained by Wind on the subject, I wasn't even certain I would be able to ... At the same time, I knew that if either Martha or I hesitated, and one of our victims woke up, we would risk giving the others away.

We finished dressing in our warrior outfits—I in my hide shift, leggings, and moccasins, my hair braided, an eagle feather affixed to one of them, a bone choker around my neck, and knotted around my waist the strap of buffalo hide that served as a belt and held my knife in a beaded sheath. A loop on the strap served to hold the stone-headed tomahawk Wind had made for me back at the cave. I donned my gun belt.

Finally, the four noncombatant women applied our grease paint. I possessed the small mirror I had purchased back in Tent City, and after Feather on Head had finished her work on me, I looked at myself in it. I did not recognize the savage woman looking back at me, her face painted red, large black circles like the mask of a raccoon around her eyes. Martha was similarly colored, but the pigments reversed—her face black, eyes rimmed in red; the painted faces of our Indian women were equally fierce, Pretty Nose simply with lightning bolts on both cheeks. As I regarded the others, I could only imagine how terrified those young soldiers would be, awakened by a slit throat, these hellishly painted faces the last sight they would see on this earth.

Chance came to my side as I mounted. "Look, I know I ain't goin' to talk ya outta this now," he said. "So you just take care a' yourself, May. Don't do anything stupid . . . although I guess it's too late for that, too . . . Do what you need to do, but then you come back to your daughter and me."

"I promise, Chance. But just in case . . . something happens . . . I want to say, thank you. I want you to know how grateful I am to you."

"For what?"

"For being who you are, for being my husband, for loving me. You are the finest, sweetest, most loving man I've ever known . . . I'll see you back here when this is over . . . and then we're going to Chicago."

There were no tears, we were too scared for tears.

We rode out, Martha and I side by side. Horse Boy, too, among us. He was needed to guard the horses while we went about our gruesome business in the camp. It was a cold night, with a full moon in the sky that in this dry plains air lighted the land like a beacon, boldly casting our shadows moving across the ground.

"May?" Martha whispered.

"Yes?"

She turned to me. "Look at us . . . Did you ever imagine this? . . . did you ever imagine when we left Chicago only a year and a half ago, that we would be dressed and painted like this? . . . Riding off with an Indian war party to attack a U.S. Army encampment of soldiers?"

"That's all the time it's been, is it?" I said. "Good God, it seems like an entire lifetime has passed. No, Martha, I could never have imagined this, nor anything else that's happened to us, and to you, since we've been here."

"Do you think you can do it? Do you think you can kill a soldier in his bed?"

"I don't know . . . and you?"

"I killed that Crow warrior . . . I took his scalp . . . I've become a savage . . . but I don't know, either . . ."

"I killed a man in his bed, Martha, I slit his throat. I haven't told you. I was glad I did it. But this is different. Still, we must remember that the soldiers would kill us if they had a chance. They've already killed our friends and their babies."

"It would be easier if we were fighting them in a battle, they would be our enemies then."

"That's what Ann said to me. But they're our enemies now."

"Did you read Meggie and Susie's journals, May?"

"Yes, and I have them. Molly gave them to me, all of them, hers, too."

"They thought that taking vengeance against the soldiers would give them some release from the pain of losing their infants. But it didn't, it just made them feel worse."

"I'm not looking for release from pain," I said, "which, in any case, seems an impossible goal. At this point, I just want to survive."

"So do I," said Martha. "And yet we're leaving our babies back there, and risking our lives to kill a few soldiers? How does that help us to survive?"

"We're Strongheart women, Martha, we took a blood oath to

support each other. We're going because Pretty Nose asked us to. These people are fighting for their way of life, and for their lives."

"Yes . . . ," she said, "and you and I don't even know if we can do it."

We arrived at the spot Red Fox and High Bear had scouted to leave our horses, and dismounted. We were still some distance away from the Army encampment, but close enough that we could smell the smoke and see the dying glow of their fires.

Pretty Nose came to Martha and me. "You two will stay back here."

"Why?" I asked.

"To help Horse Boy look after the horses. And if you hear a signal from us, to ride in with them . . . in case we need to escape. I've already told the boy, he knows what to do."

I was certain now that Pretty Nose must have sensed Martha's and my hesitation. "You don't trust us to go in with you, do you?" I asked.

"It is not that, Mesoke. I do trust you. But you are white women, and you do not move as we do, like ghosts. The soldiers will not know we are there . . . unless something happens. That's why I need you here, in case the camp wakes, and you must come for us."

It is true, what she said, and Martha and I watched as the warriors began to run toward the soldiers' encampment, spreading out across the plain, their gait light, lithe, and silent, as if their moccasined feet barely grazed the ground, running with the same balletic grace of a herd of antelope. It was only Phemie among us who could match, and even exceed, the elegance of their stride. Truly, they did move like ghosts, like another species of human being altogether, one perfectly adapted to this landscape in which they have evolved, and where they belong far more than do we.

"What kind of signal do you think Pretty Nose will send," Martha asked, "if she needs us to come with the horses?"

"I don't know, but whatever it is, I'm sure we'll recognize it."

"How many soldiers do you think they will kill?"

"I have no idea, Martha . . . I'm just glad now that we don't have to do it."

She nodded. "As am I."

"Now all we can do is wait . . . and hope to see them running back toward us."

Horse Boy kept the mounts gentled. We seemed far enough away that if they became nervous and whinnied, it would not carry to the Army camp, but then again, sound, like light, travels great distances in the plains, and horses can communicate farther apart than we can. He sat in their midst now. He had been identified at age five as having an affinity with the animals. They were so accustomed to and comfortable with him that he was like a member of the herd, which is why Pretty Nose had wanted him along with us tonight.

We waited . . . an hour or so passed. Martha announced that she had to relieve herself. There was not much cover here, and we have little need to be modest with each other in such situations, but she rose and went into a shallow depression just behind us. Her movement seemed to make the horses suddenly restless. Horse Boy stood to calm them. Martha, I have to say, is one of those people who has never had a strong relationship with equines; she makes them nervous, with the exception of her little donkey, upon whom she dotes.

But it was not Martha who had caused the restlessness among the stock, for when I heard her behind me and turned in my seated position to look, I saw that Jules Seminole walked beside her. He wore a brown cavalry hat with the top cut out, a feather protruding from it, and the brim turned up in front, a tattered navy blue Army coat, with sergeant's insignia, and filthy light blue cavalry pants. A holstered pistol hung at his right hip, and a sheathed sword on his left.

Seminole had his arm around Martha's shoulders, his head bent toward her, speaking to her softly, intimately, like a lover. "That terrible woman took you away from Jules, *ma chérie*," he said, "but Jules never lost faith that you would escape and return to him."

I had come quickly to my feet. Martha's face was fixed in a kind of blank stare, as if she was in shock, or, God forbid, had returned to the state Molly had described to me after her rescue from Seminole. Now Seminole, as if he had just noticed me, turned his regard in my direction. "Ah . . . mais . . . but . . . but who is this lovely vision that stands before Jules? Is it possible? Have the two great loves of Jules' life returned to him together? Is it not his uncle Chief Little Wolf's lovely bride, May Dodd, upon whom Jules is gazing?" I saw that in his other hand he held Martha's knife. I drew my revolver from the holster, cocked the hammer with my thumb, and pointed it at him. He gathered Martha closer against him so that he was standing half behind her, and raised the knife to her throat.

"Let go of her, Seminole."

"*Ah, non . . . non, non, non,*" he said, shaking his head. "It is you, *ma chérie,* my darling girl, who must very slowly and very gently release the hammer and lay the gun down at your feet."

"Don't," Martha said. "Don't do it, May. Take your shot. I know you can. Or let him kill me, I don't care, and then shoot the bastard dead."

"Now that would not be wise," Seminole said, and then he called out, "*Mes amis, viennent,* come out now." From the tall grass in the depression behind him, seven Crow scouts stood, all armed with Army-issue gun belts.

I wouldn't have fired, even if I could have made the shot, for I knew that would wake the entire Army camp and jeopardize our warriors. I did as Seminole told me and laid the gun down.

Our horses now were increasingly unsettled . . . I believe that they can smell evil . . . Horse Boy was trying to calm them.

"But what in the world are you doing here, my loves?" Seminole asked. "Did you just come in search of Jules? And who do these horses belong to?"

"None of your business," I said.

Now he threw Martha aside and she fell to the ground. Three of the scouts quickly surrounded her as Seminole approached me, drawing his sword and placing the tip of the blade beneath my chin. "That is where you are quite mistaken, *ma petite*. For Jules is now an honorary sergeant and chief scout for Colonel Ranald Mackenzie's force of eleven companies of the Second, Third, Fourth, and Fifth United States Cavalry regiments. The sooner you answer Jules' questions, my pet, the sooner we shall enjoy our *petit ménage à trois* . . . *bien sûr*, of course, Jules will be forced to bind you both, and he knows from our previous erotic adventures how that excites you."

"So if I don't answer you sooner," I asked, "but rather later, does that mean we would have to postpone our *ménage à trois*?"

He pressed the blade tip harder under my chin, piercing the skin, and, as I raised my head, I could feel the blood trickling down my neck. "Are you making fun of Jules?" he said. "Do you not know how much Jules detests that? No, it does not mean postponement, it means that one member of our *ménage à trois* will participate as a corpse. Now Jules would find that *very, very* exciting . . . but perhaps less so for you, whose role that would be."

"Martha and I no longer live with the Cheyenne," I said, making this up as I went along . . . "Could you please lower your sword?" He did so. "We are traveling with a group of Shoshone," I continued, "and they left their horses here to approach the Army encampment. They went on foot and unarmed so as not to be mistaken as hostiles. The Shoshone are allies of your Army, and many of them scout for you, do they not?"

"What are their names, these Shoshone?" he asked.

"Neither of us speak their language, so we have not learned their names. We've only been with them for a short time."

"*Très bien*," he said, sliding his sword back into its sheath, "very well, that is excellent information. Jules and his scouts are headed to the bivouac ourselves. Of course, Jules will have to hide you, for if the Army discovers that he has taken two white women captive, they will take you away from him, as they did with the big fair-haired white girl I captured, the one who stole Jules' bride. Do you know her?"

"No, I don't."

"She mocked Jules, too. She is dangerous, that girl. Jules was going to have to kill her first so that he could make love to her, but your old lover, Captain Bourke, took her away before he could."

We heard then our warriors' unmistakable distress call coming from the camp, in the form of the ululations of a pack of coyotes.

At the same instant, we heard behind us pounding hoofbeats and the rustle of dry grass, and a moment later, Ann, Astrid, Chance, and Christian appeared in the faint moonlight, their horses in a line, galloping down upon Seminole's scouts. All but Christian rode without holding their reins. Chance, face painted and wearing his Comanche attire, carried his sheathed sword at his side, and was raising his knife to throw; Ann held her double-barreled scattergun to her shoulder; Astrid drew an arrow back in her bow, releasing it at the same time as Ann fired her first barrel, and, immediately after, the second; Chance threw his knife. Astrid's arrow struck one of the Crow in the chest. He went down, as did the two men Ann shot. The blade of Chance's knife buried itself up to the hilt in the neck of the fourth scout, who tried to pull it out but collapsed before he managed to. Astrid pulled another arrow from the quiver on her back, set it in her bow, drew, and released, as Ann opened her scattergun, loaded two fresh cartridges, and fired one after the next, taking three more of the scouts down. The last Crow scout standing had drawn his revolver, cocked it, and raised it, aiming at Chance, who now rode down upon him, and with a mighty slash of his sword severed the man's arm at the elbow, the revolver still in his hand firing when it hit the ground. Chance reined up, turning his horse in a tight circle and in the same motion, sword spinning over his head as if he were twirling a lasso, he lopped off the Crow's head. So perfectly choreographed, the whole bloody attack had taken no more than fifteen seconds.

Seminole, cowardly as always, was running to his horse. He had one foot in the stirrup and was about to swing into the saddle when Martha, chasing behind him, leapt onto his back, her arm around his neck, and with a war cry of vengeance and the superhuman strength of rage, pulled him off, the two of them tumbling to the ground. I was running right behind her, my knife already drawn from the sheath. I reached them as they were wrestling fiercely on the ground. Aiming for Seminole's throat as I stabbed, I missed my mark, my knife blade glancing off his jawbone. It was not a killing thrust, but blood sprayed from the wound, and Seminole stopped struggling. I put the blade firmly against his throat. "*Ah, non, non, mes chéries,* do not hurt Jules. You know that no one has ever loved you as much as Jules."

From the rawhide belt at her waist, Martha pulled out her stone tomahawk, one end of which was tapered to split skin and skulls, the other blunt for bludgeoning. "I counted first coup, May," she said sternly, warning me off the kill.

"Of course you did, Martha, I wouldn't presume to take that away from you."

"*Ah oui, mes filles, c'est ça!* . . . you have both counted coup upon Jules, first and second coup. I felicitate you both for your skill and bravery as warriors, and for the magnanimity of your hearts in letting Jules go free. Such admirable sportsmanship! Now we shall be able to amuse ourselves like this another time."

"Good God," I said, "you really are out of your mind, aren't you, Seminole?"

"My coup *and* my kill," Martha said. From the beaver hide pouch she wears at her waist, Martha pulled a sharpened wooden stake. "Wind told me that the only way to kill a sorcerer is to drive a stake through his black heart. I have carried this ever since, knowing that one day I would have this chance to use it."

With one hand, she held the sharpened end against Seminole's left breast, and as she did so, to prevent him from struggling, I pressed the knife even more firmly against his throat, until I pierced the skin and a thin line of blood appeared.

I heard the others ride up behind us, but I raised my other hand to stop them. This was Martha's moment.

Seminole began to weep. "*Ah, non, je t'en supplie, ma chérie,*" he said, "I beg you, please don't kill Jules."

Martha raised her tomahawk, and, using the blunt side of the stone, she struck the stake a terrific blow, driving it into his chest, her second stroke of the club piercing his heart, the wood splintering. Seminole's back arced up, the blood spewing from the wound as black as oil, his eyes opening wide as if they would leap from their sockets, and then he fell back, dead.

It was done. We ran to our horses and mounted, Horse Boy already in the saddle, with the six saddled but riderless mounts under his control. Chance conferred with the boy and would help drive them. We set out.

Halfway to the soldiers' camp, we saw Pretty Nose and the others running toward us. A dozen or so soldiers were riding out behind them; they had obviously been alerted to trouble when they heard the reports of Ann's shotgun. We reached our warriors, who swung onto their horses' backs as they were still moving, and we turned and galloped back, taking the same path we had ridden out, following Chance in the lead. He knew that the soldiers would be slowed when they came upon the bodies of Seminole and the scouts. We rode right through the dead men and kept going. Plans had been made for us to meet the rest of our band on the trail and travel through the night, putting as much distance between us and the soldiers as possible. This had been arranged as a wise precaution, but Pretty Nose and Chance, who now rode together, agreed that it was unlikely the soldiers would try to follow us. They had no scouts to read our sign at night, and not only did they have Seminole and the dead Crow to deal with, they had their own dead in the encampment. Not knowing how many of us there might be, or where we were, it would be folly for them to pursue.

And so after a short time, we slowed from a gallop, not wanting to exhaust our horses by pushing them too hard. I was riding beside Ann. "What made you decide to follow us?" I asked her.

"Well, dear, it was a rather simple decision for us to reach," she answered. "We may not have been enthusiastic about killing soldiers ourselves, but we bloody well didn't want you to be killed by them, either. Chance employed his considerable tracking skills to follow you. We weren't planning to interfere in your mission, just to back you up, in case you needed help . . . which you clearly did."

We rejoined the band in less than two hours, all of us traveling together for another hour or so before making camp for what little was left of the night. I learned from Wind that between them they had killed seventeen of the soldiers. Although Martha and I had peripherally participated in it, I was more than ever relieved that Pretty Nose had not called upon us to go into the camp with the others. Nor was I comforted by the news of the dead soldiers, which I realized could only lead to more reprisals from the Army. Whether Jules Seminole was a sorcerer, as Martha believed, or simply an evil lunatic, as Molly and I considered him to have been, I felt we had accomplished something far more important by killing him, rather than soldiers in their beds.

At dawn we move out again.

12 November 1876

Today, due to a communication between Wind and her sister . . . and by communication, I mean the sort that happens between twins but cannot be explained by natural laws . . . we found Little Wolf's winter village on the upper Tongue River. It was a moving homecoming for me, to be so well received by old friends and acquaintances.

Upon our arrival, the sentries escorted us into the village, the full length of which we rode. I had been so long believed dead that people came out of their tipis, simply to confirm that I was really alive, and not a ghost. Some touched my legs just to be certain. Satisfied upon that score, the women took up the joyous trilling sound of welcome. Quiet One and Pretty Walker stood in front of Little Wolf's lodge as we approached, and they, too, were trilling. We reined up our horses and Feather on Head, with Wren on her baby board, dismounted and went to them. The sisters, fellow wives, embraced tenderly, and then Feather on Head and Pretty Walker made a similarly warm greeting. I was riding beside Chance, who wore his Comanche outfit, for it would hardly do for him to ride into an Indian village as a white man. He had let his hair grow long these past months; his skin, which had a little original native pigmentation inherited from his great-grandmother, darkened from constant exposure to the sun and elements, and the fact that he rarely wore his cowboy hat any longer; his features strong and angular enough that he could reasonably pass for a mixed breed.

I let Quiet One, Feather on Head, and Pretty Walker have their moment, and to give Quiet One and Pretty Walker time to fuss over Little Bird, before I dismounted and went to greet them. I hugged Pretty Walker, to whom I had always displayed more white-woman affection than I allowed myself with her mother, who was both more reserved and as "first wife" accorded a more formal respect. But now Quiet One took both my hands in hers. "I am happy you are home, Mesoke," she said to me in Cheyenne, which touched me deeply.

"I, too, my old friend," I answered, "but I will not be able to stay here long. Is your husband, Little Wolf, well?"

She looked at me curiously, due to the fact that I had not said "our" husband, as we had always referred to him together. "Yes, he is well . . . but for the worries he carries for the People. Would you like to speak with him, Mesoke?"

"I will return later, after we have made our camp," I said. "And I will leave your sister and our baby with you while we are here."

We made camp on the outskirts of the village. Of course, when I told Chance that I needed to walk back to Little Wolf's lodge to speak with the chief alone, he understood the delicacy of the situation.

"What will you tell him?" he asked.

"The truth. What else is there?"

"This would not sit well with a Comanche chief. He may want to challenge me."

"I don't believe so," I said. "As I've told you, I came to think of Little Wolf more as a father figure than a husband, and I think he came to think of me more as a daughter than a wife."

I returned to the chief's lodge just before the sun set behind the hills and scratched on the flap. To my enormous surprise, Crooked Nose, the crone, opened it. It was she, when first I arrived here, who so tormented me with her stick while trying to teach me correct tipi etiquette. Yet we had finally made our peace and become quite fond of each other. The last time I had seen her was on the morning of the attack, when instead of fleeing with the rest of us out the back of the lodge she had stood her ground, armed with her club and stepping out the front of the tipi to face the invaders.

"Vohkeesa'e!" I said in my surprise. "I thought the soldiers killed you."

She smiled her toothless grin. "The soldiers can't kill me, Mesoke. I kill them. I thought they killed you."

"They can't kill me, either, my old friend."

She invited me in, and I saw that Horse Boy had already taken up residence again. He played with Little Bird, who was out of her baby board and crawling on the buffalo robes. Little Wolf was in his regular position, reclined against his backrest like an emperor on his throne. He nodded and smiled at me. I sat down to the left of the opening as is expected of arriving guests—one of the first things I was taught by Crooked Nose's stick. Quiet One tended the fire and prepared dinner; Feather on Head and Pretty Nose were chatting, clearly catching up on each other's news. How strange it felt to be back here after all these months, inhaling the familiar scents of the tipi and its residents . . . but comforting, as well. The only thing that was missing, to remind me that I no longer lived here, was my old sleeping place.

Little Wolf signaled me to come to him. When I did, he spoke to me in a low voice. There is little privacy in an Indian lodge, but they manage to create as much as possible with their soft manner of speech. "Woman Who Moves against the Wind has been to see me," she said.

"Which one?" I asked, as a small attempt at humor.

He smiled. "She who was with you."

"Thank you for sending her to me, my husband," I said, addressing him thus out of habit and respect. "She saved my life."

He nodded. "She tells me you have taken another husband, a mixed-blood Comanche warrior."

"I have."

Again, he nodded. "It is a good thing that you have done, Mesoke," he said. "I am growing old, and two wives are enough for me." He smiled. "Sometimes they are too many."

I was so relieved at his reaction, and grateful, that tears came to my eyes. "Thank you, my husband," I said. "I came here to also tell you that I must leave the People soon, for I am going back to my old home, and to my children there."

"Yes, Woman Who Moves against the Wind told me. I have only one last request to make of you."

"Tell me."

"We must soon go into the agency again," Little Wolf said. "Our old life we have lived here is over. Our ancient prophet Sweet Medicine told us long ago of the coming of the white man. He told us that this person was going to destroy for us everything we depend upon; he was going to take over all the land throughout the world. And so it is. You know this is why I went to Washington and asked your president for the gift of one thousand white women as wives for our warriors, to teach us and our children the new life that must be lived when the buffalo are gone. Now our brothers, the buffalo, are almost gone, and we, the People, are almost gone.

"Thus I ask that you leave our daughter, Little Bird, with us. You understand, Mesoke, that the People all believe, as do I, that

Maheo gave to me, the Sweet Medicine Chief, a white baby to teach us this new life. If you take her away now, the People will lose all hope . . . and of that we have little left. For your release as my wife, I ask only this of you, that you allow us our faith in the miracle of our daughter's birth."

At this shocking request, so matter-of-factly stated, my relief and gratitude were breached by waves of anguish flushing through my body, gooseflesh running over my skin, a terrible tingling sensation, my head reeling as if from a physical blow so that I feared I would faint. "Leave my daughter?" I managed to say. "You ask me to give up my child?"

I looked at Wren, my happy baby, smiling and gurgling, as Horse Boy played with her, and then at Feather on Head, who regarded me directly now. I could tell from her face that she knew what Little Wolf had asked, as she could clearly tell, as well, from my reaction. In her expression, I saw the clash of one mother's agonized sympathy for another against her desperate hope that she might be allowed to raise Little Bird as her own daughter. We sat for a long time, just looking at each other, both well aware that there was no solution to this impossible decision that was not going to break one of our hearts. Finally, I went to Wren in a kind of proprietary fashion, as if to claim her. I picked her up off the buffalo robe and cradled her in my arms, I touched her sweet, soft little face, I put my finger in her tiny hand and she gripped it . . . *oh, God . . . this is hard . . . this will kill me* . . . but I moved over to Feather on Head on my knees. I kissed my baby's face, her lips, I whispered to her, and I let a little drop of spittle fall into her mouth, so that she might always carry the taste of her mother.

I handed Little Bird to Feather on Head. "It must be time for your daughter's feeding."

I left the lodge of Little Wolf for the last time, without saying good-bye to anyone. I walked through the village until I came to the end of it. Then I started running across the plains; I ran as fast and far as I could, the tears streaming like sweat off my face, until I collapsed in the grass and wailed out my grief.

I went back to where Chance and I had pitched our modest camp. He could clearly see that I was in a bad state. "We must pack up and leave first thing in the morning for Laramie," I said. "We'll go to the courthouse there to be married, but as I have no identification, we will first have to find someone in the town willing to make papers for me, with a different maiden name. I still have enough money for that from the sale of horses, and for train tickets to Chicago."

"I got some money stashed away, too," Chance said.

"I'm going to finish writing in my journal tonight, and then I'm leaving all of them with Wind, including those of Meggie and Susie, and those that Molly gave me of hers before we parted. I don't know what will become of any of them, except perhaps one day my daughter, Wren, might be able to read them, and learn of her real mother, who loved her with all her heart."

"You're leaving Little Bird here?" he asked.

"I cannot bear to talk about that right now, Chance . . . but yes. I'm going now to speak with Martha and Ann. I think they will both wish to travel with us—in Ann's case, at least as far as Medicine Bow station, and Martha will surely want to accompany me to Chicago with her son . . . And you, Chance?" I asked. "Are you sure this is what you want? I know you said you were going to take me there, but I won't hold you to that. You don't have to marry me if you don't want to. I can manage without you. You're a cowboy . . . and an Indian . . . you're not a city boy. I'm afraid you'll be terribly unhappy there."

"May, I'm in love with you . . . I want to marry you . . . have ever since the first time you kissed me . . . when you were stealin' my horse. I promised I was goin' to take you back to Chicago. I'm a pretty resourceful fella, you know that, I can do plenty a' things. And it ain't like we have to spend the rest of our lives in the city, either. If it don't suit us, we'll make a new plan."

"Thank you for that, Chance," I said with a sense of relief. "I'm in love with you, too."

"Of course y'are, May, I know that."

And that's about it for my western adventure. There is not much here left to say. I've lost another child, and I don't know how . . . or if . . . I'll manage to get my other two back. That part, I haven't worked out yet. We still have a long way to go, with challenges to face before we get there. But as Chance said of himself, I, too, am a pretty resourceful girl.

May Dodd, still alive, 12 November 1876,
somewhere on the Tongue River,
Montana Territory

{ EPILOGUE }

by JW Dodd, III
Editor in Chief, *Chitown* Magazine

Chicago, Illinois
June 2019

It has been nearly eight months since I last saw or had any word from Molly Standing Bear. She left her notebooks in my trailer on the morning of her departure, which contained therein her full edit and organization of May Dodd's and Molly McGill's journals. She left, as well, May's last journal that we had taken the day before from its hiding place on May Swallow Wild Plum's property. I put it back where it belonged that afternoon. She must have stayed up most of the night transcribing and editing it in her notebook, all by hand, I should mention, as she doesn't have a computer.

I don't know what time she left that morning because I was still asleep when she did. But I had a strange dream that woke me up, at least I think it was a dream. Like everything about Molly, as the reader of these pages may have ascertained, there was something a bit "off" about her. Being an editor by trade, you'd think I might be able to come up with a better word than that to describe her . . . but I can't. Not to get too mystical about it, but she has a certain indefinable quality, as if she inhabits a different space than the rest of us. I never really even found out where she lived, though she did say that she was "mostly homeless," whatever that means, because it seems to me that you either are or you aren't. There were many other things I've never really been able to pin down about Molly.

Regarding the dream that woke me up that morning . . . and I hesitate to write this as there are few things more boring and banal than hearing about other people's dreams. Plus, when I describe it, the reader may well think that I, too, am a bit "off" and quite likely,

I am. I dreamed that Molly was preparing to leave and came to sit on the edge of the bed to say good-bye. She was caressing my face, kissing it, and whispering to me. I was trying to wake up so that I could send her on her way, but I couldn't. Speaking of banality, everyone is familiar with those dreams in which one knows one is dreaming and tries to wake up but can't.

Of course, time passes differently in dreams, and I finally did wake up. I had been sleeping on my side with my head on the pillow, and when I opened my eyes I was looking directly into the eyes of a mountain lion sitting beside the bed watching me. He, or she, had the same blue-green eyes as Molly that seem to change color in different light. I didn't dare move, as I had no idea what the animal's intentions were, but I saw out of the corner of my eye that the door to the Airstream was wide open, the morning light spilling in across the floor. I assumed that Molly must have left it that way, which, though unlike her, was obviously how the lion got inside. Only later did it occur to me that I was less afraid of it than I should have been. We looked into each other's eyes for at least a minute, while I considered my limited options. We could continue our staring contest until one of us acted. Or I could very slowly raise myself on the bed. Quick movements did not seem a good idea. Or I could speak to it . . . although I was fairly certain it wouldn't respond to voice commands.

Then, as if it had lost interest in me, it turned, trotted the length of the trailer to the open door, and leapt to the ground. I got up quickly then to go to the door, and watched it lope away down the bank of the creek, muscles rippling and moving with that powerful, elegant feline grace. It stopped once to turn and look back at me. And then was gone. I felt lucky to have had this experience and I knew I had a good story to tell back at the office, and in bars, where no one would believe it.

I saw that Molly had also left a letter for me on top of her notebooks and May's last journal, which were stacked on the foldout dining/writing table. I reproduce it here:

Dear JW,

You know, I have never actually written a letter to anyone where I have used the salutation "Dear." It has always seemed odd to me to address perfect strangers that way. Then again we still find a lot of white man ways odd. But I'm making this exception in your case because we're not strangers, are we?

As you can see, I'm leaving my notebooks with you, and I give you permission to publish them in serial form in your magazine. But let me be clear about one thing: I DO NOT give you permission to make any changes, edits, etc. Whether or not you approve of the way I arranged and edited them, I want them to appear in your magazine exactly as they are. And if I find that you messed with them in any way at all, I'll be wearing your scalp on my belt . . . and I'm not kidding about that . . . well, maybe a little. And by the way, this edict applies to my own little commentaries scattered throughout the journals. I know these are likely to cause you some embarrassment due to the sexual content of some of them, but that's just tough shit, white boy. Instead of hiding behind your desk for the rest of your life in your Editor in Chief disguise, it's time you had a little skin in the game . . . so to speak.

We had some fun, didn't we, cowboy? And I don't mean just in bed . . . although that was not so bad, either. I like you, JW, I always have, I could say that I love you if I let myself. But, as I explained to you, I have more important business to attend to right now. I have no idea how long I'll be gone, as I don't even know yet where I'm going. So please, don't waste your time trying to find me, and don't bother trying to find other Strongheart women, either. We have an oath of secrecy, and you never will. I realize I broke that oath when I told you about Lily being one of us. It just kind of slipped out, I guess because I felt so comfortable and secure with you. I had to tell her I did that . . . it was a serious violation on my part. She forgave me, because she could see what was going on between you and me. And she likes you, she thinks that for a white boy you can be trusted, which is high praise coming from Lily.

OK . . . so long, cowboy. I hope we cut each other's trail again one day. In the meantime, take care of yourself. And if you come across a good woman, I won't hold it against you. Of course, you'll never find another like me . . . but then I don't need to tell you that, do I?

Love,
MSB

P.S. Sorry about leaving the trailer door open, but I had to let the lioness out.

I left the Tongue River Indian Reservation the next morning, settling up first with Lily Redbird. I send her a check every month for $100, the boarding fee for my horse, Indian, and I always ask her if she's had any news from Molly. But she never writes me back. I phone her every now and then to check in and ask the same question. She always tells me that she's had no news at all, and I sense from her voice that she's worried about her friend, too, though she will never say that to me. As regular readers know, the first serialization of *The Lost Journals of May Dodd and Molly McGill* came out in *Chitown* in the April issue. Now I enclose a copy of the magazine with my rent check to Lily every month.

I haven't changed a word, not even a comma, or any other punctuation, grammatical, or spelling error that Molly made in her notebooks, and I instructed my copy editors not to do so, either. Of course, that is totally against all magazine policy, and caused much debate in the office. But I'd rather receive a few critical letters to the editor from nitpicking readers who live to point out typos than risk my scalp for cleaning one up.

I, too, hope Molly and I cut each other's trail again one day. I miss that woman. The last sentence of her letter was the truest thing she ever said to me.

Acknowledgments

As this is the third and final book of the One Thousand White Women Trilogy, I would like to take this opportunity to thank my loyal readers, who have been with me from beginning to end. I have always maintained that the process of writing and reading a novel is a collaborative one, and I am so grateful to all the individuals, among them the many members of book clubs across the country, who have fueled the word-of-mouth support of my work. You, the reader, have allowed me to write these three novels, and you have brought them to life for me. Thank you.

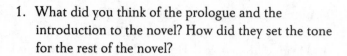

1. What did you think of the prologue and the introduction to the novel? How did they set the tone for the rest of the novel?

2. How did the narrative structure of the novel affect your reading experience? Did the firsthand accounts make the women's experiences seem more relatable?

3. On page 135, Molly says, "Yes, she had a dream, and she found herself in that perfect world, and in her dream I'll bet she could see again. And now we're all traveling to find her dream." What is the role and significance of dreams throughout the novel?

4. Compare and contrast all of the powerful women in this novel, especially May, Molly, and Molly Standing Bear. How does each of their experiences move the narrative forward? What do they accomplish with what life has handed to them?

5. How does the addition of Molly Standing Bear, a contemporary Native American woman, as one of the narrators succeed in bringing the novel into the present era? Did you learn anything of which you were previously unaware about the challenges and dangers faced by modern Native American women? Do you feel that it is act of cultural appropriation for a white male author to write in the first-person voice of a young Native American woman?

6. Consider this statement on page 116, made by May: "I realized in that moment that I am, and always will be, two different people, and that I need to reacquaint myself with this stranger staring back in the mirror, who did not appear to recognize me either." How have May's circumstances changed her into two different women? Were you surprised by the manner in which all these women embraced the culture of the Cheyenne people?

7. Examine this statement on page 141: "Yet, there is much to be afraid of in both worlds, isn't there? . . . And from both peoples." How truthful is this statement, and how does its truth manifest throughout the novel?

8. How did the undercurrent of Native American mysticism that runs through the novel (e.g., "the real world behind this one," shape-shifting, Molly's "escape" from the cliff) alter your perceptions of Native American beliefs? In what ways does this mysticism affect the decisions made by the women characters in the novel? Do you feel that the author did a realistic job of presenting this aspect of Native American life?

9. "I am still sometimes amazed that having been city born and raised, I have adapted so thoroughly to life in the wilderness." When you learned the truth of May's backstory, how did it affect how you viewed her character in the present? What do you think about the evolution of May as an individual?

10. Compare and contrast the different types of love and relationships—both romantic and not—that are present throughout the novel. Was there one in particular that stood out as the most authentic to you?

11. As the narrative alternated between May's and Molly's journals, was there one perspective that you connected with or enjoyed reading more than the other? Why or why not?

12. How did the end of the novel make you feel? What do you imagine happens next for the characters?

13. If you read the other two installments of the One Thousand White Women Trilogy, what did you think of this final installment? Is this what you imagined for these characters? Were you pleased with how the story ended?

About the Author

Stephen Collector

JIM FERGUS is the author of six novels and two books of nonfiction. He divides his time between southern Arizona, the northern Rocky Mountains, France, and French Polynesia.